THE JANE LOOP

A NOVEL

GRAHAM JACKSON

Cormorant Books

Canada Council **Conseil des Arts**
for the Arts **du Canada**

ONTARIO ARTS COUNCIL
CONSEIL DES ARTS DE L'ONTARIO
an Ontario government agency
un organisme du gouvernement de l'Ontario

Canadian Patrimoine
Heritage canadien

Canada

The publisher gratefully acknowledges the support of the Canada Council for the
Arts and the Ontario Arts Council for its publishing program. We acknowledge
the financial support of the Government of Canada through the Canada Book
Fund (CBF) for our publishing activities, and the Government of Ontario through
the Ontario Media Development Corporation, an agency of the Ontario Ministry
of Culture, and the Ontario Book Publishing Tax Credit Program.

LIBRARY AND ARCHIVES CANADA CATALOGUING IN PUBLICATION

Jackson, Graham, author
The Jane loop / Graham Jackson.

Issued in print and electronic formats.
ISBN 978-1-77086-480-1 (paperback). — ISBN 978-1-77086-485-6 (html)

1. Title.

PS8569.A254J36 2016   C813'.54   C2016-904416-5
                                            C2016-904417-3

MIX
Paper from
responsible sources
FSC® C016245
www.fsc.org

The interior of this book is printed on 100% post-consumer waste recycled paper.

CORMORANT BOOKS INC.
10 ST. MARY STREET, SUITE 615, TORONTO, ONTARIO, M4Y 1P9
www.cormorantbooks.com

For
Gareth Bate
and
Janet Stickney

1

THE NEW SUBURBS OF SIXTIES Toronto lived up to their reputations. They were safe, comfortable and convenient. They didn't ask too much of their residents. On the perfect lawns, around the pristine pools, by the deliciously smoking barbecues, a plain language of favoured words was spoken: nice, new, neat, clean, young, sweet, marry, child, order, mine, God, bargain, among a few dozen more. For the majority, the distant city, known as "downtown," was smelly and old, dirty and mean, riddled with crime. Husbands went there daily to earn a living, sons and daughters to attend the university; there was really no need for permanent departure. A network of freeways guaranteed a quick return to the good and godly life among the hydrangeas and spiraea.

But none of this was true for Neil Bennett, almost seventeen, who resided with his parents and older sister in a smart, newish red brick storey-and-a-half in the western suburb of Islington. Though he could see and smell the benefits of rich green lawns, leafy green hedges, and the paler, more delicate green of the weeping willows that had survived suburban expansion, he couldn't wait to board the bus at the top of the street for his next foray "into town." He didn't mind the packed buses, the noise, the crowded streets; as far as he was concerned, journeys into town were exciting and pleasurable.

His sister Valerie, who worked part-time at the Eaton's store downtown at Queen and Yonge, had asked him one day what was so attractive about the city. He'd answered, "The city never lies." At this she'd rolled her eyes, called him a weirdo, and left the room. But it was true for him: the city kept its promises, promises of adventure and excitement, promises of novelty. The city was upfront. Nothing seemed hidden or dark or uncertain there. Everything glowed in the never extinguished light of street lamps and store windows. There was the constant movement, too: clanging streetcars coming and going along seemingly endless thoroughfares, movie theatres drawing in and spilling out their avid customers at all hours and lunch counter ladies in pale blue or tan or maroon uniforms clearing space every few minutes for another hungry customer or two. All this movement was strangely reassuring — the way a river often is, ever changing, but always the same.

And, of course, there was the library, specifically the Runnymede Library, where Neil shelved books. Here, all movement, all noise, all the usual city bustle changed complexion and became hushed and wonder-filled. There were promises here, too, of course, promises galore, but of a very different order. In his mind, the Runnymede Library contained all the knowledge he could ever want.

Heading back home was quite another issue. To Neil, suburbia was the furthest thing from paradise. It was an arid grid of streets lined with lookalike houses — either of the bungalow sort or the rather more impressive, but still complacent, storey-and-a-half. In the city, the presence of dwellings always promised a vibrant life, one that flowed out onto porches, or into gardens crammed with brilliant flowers, or over the busy streets themselves, full of kids and gossiping neighbours and boys on bikes. But that wasn't true "back home." Suburban houses were mute. They occupied tidy green lots on avenues empty of all life except cars. Their residents appeared to be mostly absent, or, at least, invisible. Porches sat untenanted. Front yards offered only faint hints of flowers. A sphinx-like mystery hung about them, even in the middle of the day. And if there was anything Neil hated, it was self-satisfied mystery.

On top of this, he found the ditches, the hedges, the big garages shut off from the world by blankly staring doors, to be anything but reassuring. The opposite, in fact: as potential hiding places, they spelled danger to him. If asked why, he would have given his broad shoulders a slight shrug and said, *I don't know*, but that wasn't true. The danger, whatever form it took, was related to his father, who had a penchant for playing nasty tricks. If he wasn't very vigilant, he would end up caught or, worse, immobilized.

It was the four-block walk from the bus stop to his parental home that posed the biggest challenge. Since he worked at the Runnymede Library at least two weeknights and all day Saturday during the school year, and even more in the summer, it was a challenge frequently met. He could make out the crimson maple that dominated his parents' yard from the moment he stepped off the bus, but there was still a gauntlet of hedges and bushes to negotiate before he reached that safety. Dread frequently overtook him. Sometimes, he would respond to it by walking brazenly down the middle of the road, moving to the shoulders only when traffic demanded; sometimes, when he had been to a late movie with Tony and Rick, he would get one of his friends to stand watch at the top of the street as he made his descent; and sometimes, hardly breathing, he would run the distance, hoping against hope that whatever threat was lurking in the foliage was not faster than he. If it was still light out when he got back, the journey was an easier one, of course. But for most of the year he was coming home in darkness. And the darkness ... well, as his father was wont to say, *Anything can happen in the dark.*

ON ONE VERY WARM FRIDAY night, in late June of '62, his seventeenth birthday less than three months off, the usual dread decided to keep its distance.

Neil had watched the rich blue twilight giving over to night from the bus window and had felt no apprehension, no anticipation of ambush awaiting him upon arrival. With his new bundle of books in their plastic library covers jittering on the seat beside him, he was looking forward to the moment when he could pull the stop indicator and feel the bus edging into its familiar niche beside the red and white pole.

No one could've guessed that he hadn't got a wink of sleep the night before. Though his father's dinner-time description of masked prowlers lurking in the neighbourhood had kept him wide awake till dawn, there was no trace of fear in his large grey eyes or around his wide-lipped mouth, no cowering or tension in his lanky, awkward frame, nothing worrisome at all except perhaps a spot of acne. One might have expected a little twist of nervousness at least, a slight faltering in his step as the brightly lit bus pulled away, but there was none of that. He looked up into a sky splattered with stars, and smiled. He was happy and the sky was a perfect mirror.

There were good reasons for his happiness. Hours before, just three blocks from the library, he'd run into Tony Colero outside the Coleros' fruit and vegetable shop. Tony, his best friend since the very first day of Junior High, was, as usual, kibitzing with the clientele. Neil watched him for a while, undetected, with a deep, vibrating pleasure. When finally Tony caught sight of his buddy, he'd opened his eyes wide in mock-astonishment and, wiping his hands on his strawberry-stained apron, called out, "Slumming again, are we?" Then, squeezing Neil's shoulder, he'd invited him to spend Saturday evening with him above the shop, babysitting a nephew named Gio.

On the surface, it wasn't much of an offer, but Neil knew from past visits that they would play cards and eat Italian sweets and, when the little kid dozed off at eight thirty or so, they'd have two or three hours to themselves alone. He'd accepted Tony's invite promptly and been rewarded with a goofy grin and an admonition, "Jacket and tie required, and not one of your cheap Eaton's store ties either!"

After, he'd been overtaken by a sudden urge to visit his Aunt Violet and Uncle Herb, who owned the shoe store next to the Polish church on the other side of the street. Although they were far too busy to chat, Aunt Vi, flashing with big jewellery and a gold tooth, had whispered dramatically, "Go past the Runnymede." She meant the cinema, of course, and when he got there he saw instantly what she was referring to: in the display case next to the box office, a hand-painted sign in sweeping blue letters announced a very special double bill — "Opening Soon" — of Audrey Hepburn in *Breakfast at Tiffany's* and Elvis Presley in *Blue Hawaii*.

He couldn't care less about Elvis or *Blue Hawaii*. However, the chance of having Audrey so close would surely change his mother's mind about the movie's suitability for a not-yet seventeen-year-old boy. Why proximity should sway her he couldn't say.

As he pulled himself away from the cinema's bill of fare he was almost dancing with pleasure. The mood stayed with him long after he walked through the heavy oak doors of the public library.

Normally Friday evenings at the library were a bit dull. Fewer customers meant less chance for chatting about books and more chance for shelving and, even worse, shelf-reading. Miss Boughton, the myopic second-in-command who was always in charge Fridays, seemed to have a thing for perfectly read shelves. But that evening, Miss Boughton was away for undisclosed reasons. The branch head, Elizabeth Fairfield, was filling in. The thought of regal, white-haired Miss Fairfield, with her quiet demeanour and fluttering smile, playing such a menial role was almost shocking.

She came up to him soon after his arrival and said, "We seem to be very busy tonight, so there won't be a lot of time for shelf-reading. Please stay close to the counter." And she was, as usual, right. There was a constant flow of people demanding his attention at the circulation desk, with the result that he spent most of the evening checking out books and chatting with the borrowers.

At break time, Miss Fairfield produced cupcakes topped with his favourite, caramel icing. The contrast with Miss Boughton's usual spread of Peek Freans was remarkable. Later, just before closing, as they waited for stragglers to bring up their books for checking out, Miss Fairfield suggested to the library assistant, a Mrs. Nina Negulescu, that she teach Neil some Romanian phrases. Mrs. Negulescu — who, with her plentiful hair held up by gleaming amber combs, always looked so glamorous — chose *Thank you very much* and *Good evening*. She rehearsed him until, she claimed, he could say *Mulţumesc foarte mult* and *Bună seara* without accent.

At the very last minute, a bony, angular, wild-haired young man of twenty-two or so, whom Neil knew from his library card to be Rob Neville, rushed in. Fixing Neil with his intense eyes, he thrust the anthology of *Best American Plays, 4th Series* towards him with the words, "Have you read *Cat on a Hot Tin Roof*?" Neil's obvious ignorance pushed Neville to insist, "You have to, you have to. It's all about the truth, telling the truth. You must read it." And with that, he was gone.

Mrs. Negulescu rolled her big brown eyes and Miss Fairfield said, "Not the best Williams. By a long shot." But *Best American Plays, 4th Series* was among the books Neil checked out at the end of his shift.

On the way home, the bus ride — usually a fairly tame experience — produced a couple of noteworthy sightings. A young man in short-shorts, who had boarded the bus with him at the Loop, made a great point of eyeing the tall, handsome Mediterranean who got on at the Riverside stop. When no return glance was offered, the young man appeared so disconsolate Neil felt sorry for him. Then, at Royal York, another good-looking man in a navy business suit took the seat in front of Neil, and without a second's notice of his fellow travellers, lifted a rumpled newspaper to read. That gave Neil the opportunity to learn that the Netherlands had just banned thalidomide and that the Toronto police had arrested three men for indecent behaviour in an alleyway off Bay Street Tuesday night. Neil had some knowledge of the thalidomide story, but what was meant by indecent behaviour he hadn't a clue; it sounded both awful and vaguely exciting.

Full of such magical moments, Neil made his way down the long, dark street towards home. That night, the bushes and hedges were only bushes and hedges. All the houses were brightly lit from the inside, all alive with mysterious comings and goings and TVs flickering — all of them, that is, except the Doyles'. Poor Davy Doyle with his shirts always buttoned up tight to the neck. He was probably performing at some awful piano recital organized by his mother, Corinne. But Mrs. Doyle's sour, cantankerous face wasn't spoiling things for Neil. He felt sorry for her dark little bungalow crouching silently alongside its showier neighbours, like something that had been disowned.

As he passed the Doyle house, a voice accosted him. "Hey."

Neil turned.

Ghostly white, Davy Doyle stood in the darkness of the driveway, with a schoolbag in hand.

"Sorry. I didn't see you."

"I wish I was invisible right now," Davy answered in a plaintive voice.

"Where you going?"

"Nowhere you want to know about." He looked away as the taillights of his mother's reversing Dodge splashed the pavement red at his feet.

Neil moved off.

"Don't say goodnight or anything."

"Okay, I won't."

At the edge of his parents' lawn, Neil stopped to breathe.

The Doyle car passed him heading south. No farewell honking greeted him. No wave from the open window.

He checked the sky again. It was still glittering.

His gaze fell onto the perfectly mowed lawn. As usual, he took note of its formidable expansiveness.

You won't find many lawns like this in Toronto, his father always said, by which he meant not only its size but also its impeccable verdure. *People thought we were crazy buying a corner lot, but you see how they all stop and admire. We have lawn on three sides!*

The lawn was impressive — and, in its relentless demand for care, tyrannical, too. For a brief second or two, a feeling close to anxiety stirred in him. It resembled nothing more than the breeze rustling in the branches of the red maple. It was there and gone, but in that interval, he had an image of prowlers patrolling the darkness.

He scanned the neighbourhood for a reassuring sign. It came in the form of the Gordons' car, lying contentedly somnolent on its gravel driveway. This driveway, in which Neil had frequently played as a younger boy, marked the fourth, grassless side of the Bennett property. Neil smiled to himself as he thought of his father's many rants on having a car squatting at his back door.

He crossed the lawn to the slightly tilted verandah — another of his father's pet beefs. The front door was open. Through the screen he could hear the reassuring purr of Ellington on the hi-fi, and over that a pleasant jumble of voices. Mom's, Dad's, Mrs. Gordon's, Mr. Knight's. They were at their poker. Probably just beginning. He checked his watch: nine thirty, early yet.

Neil absolutely loved poker nights. He loved the laughter, the gossip. He loved the cards, the poker chips, the kitty. He loved the food his mother prepared, the special sandwich spread of egg and cheese and green olives, and, of course, the refrigerator cake, a sarcophagus-shaped dessert of chocolate wafers and whipped cream, which she served with coffee as the grand finale. He loved, too, how well his father played the game. Frank Bennett was such a bluffer. Even when he didn't have a great hand, he could make other players think he did. He often won just by bluffing.

Most of all, though, Neil loved the way the Gordons and the Knights changed the atmosphere in the house: how they turned his father's drinking into a friendly sociable thing, how they made his mother's reserve seem less sad or disappointed somehow, how they helped to restore a sense of contentment to rooms that were often tense and edgy.

As he opened the door, Mona Gordon, his favourite player, was saying, "And Lana thinks he's a real dreamboat. I told her, there's no accounting for taste."

"Which went a long way to improving mother-daughter relations," Mr. Gordon commented.

"You know, I don't think I've even seen him up close." That was his mother's unassuming, unhurried voice.

"I have," Mrs. Knight added. "He looks quite refined actually, though I wouldn't call him a dreamboat."

"I'm her dreamboat," was Mr. Knight's comment. "Right, Duchess? I'm your dreamboat."

"You're a big oaf!"

"Now look who's here!" Mona Gordon's gesture towards Neil was, as always, roomy in its affection. "Give us a kiss."

He did as he was commanded.

"Here's the real thing!" Mona held up his hand as if she had just proclaimed him the winner of a prizefight.

He blushed and said his hellos to the others. His pale, pretty mother offered her cheek to be kissed. His father merely raised his dark, bushy eyebrows at him.

"Who's the dreamboat you're talking about?" Neil asked.

"Don't you worry, you have no rival as far as we're concerned," Mona said. "No rival at all. He's the new bread-man."

"What happened to Mr. Ralph?"

"Dropped dead. Two months ago." Mona snapped her fingers. "Fifty-two years old. Ten years he's been delivering for us, hasn't he, Nora?"

"I think so. He was always reliable, always polite." Neil's mother liked reliability and good manners better than anything.

"He was here when Phil and I moved in, and that was seven years ago," Mrs. Knight offered. "He was a Maritimer, you know."

"Oh, well, we're talking about a god then, eh, Duchess?"

"Hardly a god, but he was a good soul — like Nora says, a very fine bread-man. It means a lot when you're a housewife, having people you can rely on like that. And then he dies. Just like that. It's very sad."

Mrs. Knight always seemed to have just stepped out of a show window. Everything about her was polished, poised, immaculate, even her expressions. When she spoke her voice seemed to come from somewhere else, so little impact did speaking have on her face. Her little pearl earrings were more animated. By contrast, Mona Gordon was a great ruffled mess of white hair and lipstick and shapeless blouses. She seemed to spill out everywhere. But then, next to Mrs. Knight, even his own neat-and-tidy mother looked a little unkempt, uncared for. As for Phil Knight, whose arms now encircled his wife warmly — well, big oaf was probably a compliment, going by appearance, but there wasn't a kinder variety and Mrs. Knight knew it.

"I've got a confession to make," Gus Gordon said solemnly. "I wouldn't know the bread-man if I fell over him. I hope that doesn't disqualify me from playing with you folks, though."

Everyone laughed. Mr. Gordon's laconic way was one of the neighbourhood treasures. It went with his wire-framed glasses and his big cigars. People liked to call him the quiet type, but Neil knew from their cribbage games on the Gordons' porch that he could be fiercely competitive.

"He seems pretty young for a bread-man," Neil said.

"A summer job, he told me. He's a university student," Mrs. Knight supplied.

"He loves to chat, I'll say that for him," Mona added. "Asks a million questions."

"And do you think the new man's a dreamboat, son?" His father gave Neil a crooked smile.

Mona Gordon laughed. "Aren't you a card!"

Neil stepped back from the table.

"There's some ginger ale in the fridge, dear," his mother said.

"Wait!" said his father. "Don't you want to see what I found outside?"

Everyone looked at him expectantly as he opened the top drawer of the buffet behind him and extracted a nylon stocking. He fluttered it in front of his neighbours.

Mona glanced at Nora. "Where'd you find that?"

With uncanny speed, Frank pulled the stocking down over his head and face. Then, slowly, he surveyed each player at the table, his features grotesquely disfigured.

"Frank! What are you doing that for?" Mrs. Knight looked away.

"Visitors," he said in a croaking voice, peering through the nylon at Neil. "Last night. Outside on the lawn." He jerked his head towards his son.

"Good heavens!" Mrs. Knight looked to her husband for help.

"The stocking improves you. Quite a bit, I'd say. What do you think, Nora?"

Neil's mother stood, pushing in her chair. "He's too advanced for me. Would you like your sandwich now, Neil?"

He followed her into the kitchen as Mona demanded, "What visitors are you talking about?"

"Prowlers. Outside the house, checking out the windows. I chased them away."

"Oh, Frank, you're the limit! Prowlers indeed!"

"If only I'd known, I'd have called the police!" Mr. Gordon's low laugh was not entirely comfortable.

In the kitchen, Neil grimaced at his mother as she laid two slices of bread on a plate and pointed to the toaster with a question in her eyes.

"Nora! Did you see these prowlers?" Mona's voice was demanding. "Take off that damn stocking, you crazy man!"

Suddenly his father was at the kitchen door, unmasked, face flushed, staring at his wife and son. To Neil he said, "There's something for you in your room. Your end of school present." Then, with a wink, he added, "I told you there were prowlers, didn't I?"

Neil looked down at the sandwich spread as his father, smiling, returned to the game.

Nora said, "Just ignore him, darling. It's better that way."

"Hard to ignore, don't you think?"

"Nora, are you coming? We want to play poker! Neil can finish in there."

Neil sat down at the kitchen table with his sandwich and listened to the game recommence in the adjoining room. Neal Hefti was playing on the stereo now. *Rare But Well Done.* It was a favourite of his father's. Mona Gordon was laughing at some stupid joke of Phil Knight's and his mother was handing around the chips and pretzels. Mr. Gordon was a great pretzel-eater. Soon after, a review of upcoming summer vacations got underway. Mrs. Knight announced a visit from the one sister who still resided in Prince Edward Island, to which his mother responded with a lively, "I've got a sister visiting, too! Sylvia's coming, from LA."

The prospect of Aunt Sylvia's visit was more than pleasing. Neil would have been happy to imagine taking her around to all his favourite places, but for the moment he was too busy replaying the earlier discussion about the dreamboat bread-man.

He had seen the bread-man once, two weeks earlier, heading up the Gordons' driveway around noon with bread for both the

Gordon and Bennett households in hand. His features hadn't been very clear because, unlike Mr. Ralph, the new bread-man wore a cap, a peaked cap with the bakery's name sewn on it in red. The cap cast dark shadows. His physique, however, had certainly been visible. With no difficulty, Neil could recapture the compact build, the springy step that somehow managed not to be boyish, and, thanks to the three undone buttons of his uniform, the hard and hairy chest. He remembered his surprise and excitement at the sight of the exposed chest, and his sense that the bread-man was playing with fire. What if the neighbours reported him, Neil had wondered?

And then he had seen him again, a couple of deliveries later, from the back this time, as he walked in the other direction, down the Gordons' driveway back towards his truck. His springy step was even more apparent from behind, and there was something provocative in the movement of his hips. Neil didn't know men could move like that. It both embarrassed and excited him. Since the second sighting, the bread-man had been much on his mind, and he was really pleased to find that he wasn't the only one who had noticed how special he was.

Neil stood and rinsed his plate in the sink. From the window, the Gordons' smooth driveway was visible under the streetlamp. He imagined watching the bread truck pull up and the bread-man, shirtless, jumping down with an armload of freshly baked loaves and an inviting smile on his face. *Want a taste?* the smile seemed to say.

He was ready to answer, *Sure,* when the reverie was suddenly broken by his father's voice calling him. Neil poked his head into the dining room, where his father sat smugly fanning himself with his five-card hand.

"Did you say hello to Miss Fairfield for me?" his father asked, as he always did. He claimed close ties with the library system.

"Yes, Dad. And to Mrs. Negulescu, too." He had done no such

thing, but he wanted an opportunity to mention her.

"Oh, such a fine Scottish name," said Mr. Gordon.

"She taught me how to say good evening in Romanian. *Bună seara*. Romanian's a Latin language, like Italian and French."

"Romanian! Frank, Nora, this one's looking for trouble!" Mr. Knight guffawed and slapped the table. The poker chips danced a little fandango.

As if on cue, Neil's sister Val came beaming into the archway between the living and dining rooms, clutching a big bouquet of long-stemmed red roses. Beaming was one of Val's talents, and her canary-yellow dress and shoes lent it an extra electricity. "Hello, hello, everybody!"

Slightly behind her, one arm around her waist in what Neil considered an unnecessarily possessive way stood Mike Dennison, beaming equally brightly. By his side on the floor sat several shopping bags.

"Look at those flowers! You're a lucky girl!" said Mrs. Gordon.

"They're not from Mike. They're from the people I work with at Eaton's."

"For being the prettiest girl in the store, I'll bet," Mr. Knight suggested.

"I don't think so, sir," Mike said. "Not that she isn't — but most of them wouldn't have time for a pretty girl."

"Not have time for a pretty girl! What's the matter with them?"

"They're 'fairy' nice men, sir." Mike's smile couldn't have been more self-satisfied.

Mona roared. "You're the limit. Really the limit."

"He is the limit," Val said. She left Mike's side and moved next to Mrs. Knight, who sniffed the roses gingerly. "They've been really good to me and I'll miss them."

She scowled at Mike, who shrugged like a boy caught with his hand in the cookie jar.

Such a jerk, Neil thought. *The crew cut suits him.*

"I forgot this was your last day!" Mona Gordon smacked her forehead. "You're headed for Windermere, aren't you?"

"Mike's Uncle Pete has a guest home there, and he's taken me on. I thought it might be nice, a couple of months in the air and all before nursing school."

"Gus was born near Windermere, weren't you, Gus?"

Gus admitted that was so. "Nice place. Nicer people."

"Oh, do come and visit me," Val said. "It would be such fun. But, I'd better put these in water now. I don't want them to droop."

"I'll help you," Mike said.

"No you won't. You're not wanted. Neil will help. Come on, Neil."

In the kitchen, at the sink again, Neil rinsed out the long fluted white vase his mother had received as a wedding present twenty-two years ago. Val delicately pulled the lower leaves off the rose stems and, in her quietest voice, which somehow managed to also sound exasperated, she commiserated with her younger brother over their father's prowler story. This was a voice Val had perfected over the years for talking to Neil. It had become a kind of habit, and Neil knew enough not to get upset by it. She told him to ignore their father in two or three different ways, but as this was the usual advice offered by people who weren't the butt of Frank Bennett's humour, he ignored it, preferring to watch her feed the roses into the long throat of the vase. The roses were simply luscious.

"You know, he's just jealous of you."

Neil was shocked by the suggestion.

"You're smarter than he is, that's all. Mother agrees with me." She stood back to admire her floral arranging. The roses looked brilliantly red in their white container. "They're pretty, eh?"

"Gorgeous," Neil said. He planted his face in their heavily scented midst.

"You don't need to eat them, for heaven's sake!"

He spun away, heading for the staircase to his basement den.

"Say goodnight first," Val said, rearranging a couple of the stems.

Neil looked back at her, wondering as he always did if the fact that she was three years older made her commands worthier of consideration. He could hear his father offering Mike Dennison a drink amid protests by his mother. He could hear Phil Knight bellowing encouragement and Mona Gordon agreeing.

But goodnights could wait.

He wanted to get back to the image of the bread-man doing his hippy walk up the driveway.

"Later," he said. "There's refrigerator cake."

2

TWO GIFTS SAT ON HIS pillow. One was in the blue and white paper bag of Eaton's candy department. It had to be either hard caramels, his favourite, or humbugs, his second favourite. The other was rectangular, flat, and wrapped in brown paper. Probably a book. Paperback. Second hand.

Neil didn't go near them. He turned on a lamp, sat down on his couch and stared.

The sounds of the poker game above rose and fell in waves. Mrs. Gordon's laugh was very high, very loud. For a second it annoyed him, distracting him from the bread-man, but he quickly relented. Summer nights, as a small boy, lying alone in the house, straining to catch some reassuring sound of his parents' nearness, it was most often Mrs. Gordon's laugh that told him everything was all right. Over the lonely whistling from the train yards at the end of the street, it would sound like a bright fanfare, and afterwards he would be able to sleep.

Staring now at the gifts perched on his pillow, he was reminded of a particular night many years before. A starless, humid summer's night promising storms. He might have been four. Ignoring his pleading, his parents had gone to have drinks with the McDonalds across the street. *Your sister's not a scaredy cat!* they'd said. The Gordons must have been invited, too, because strain as he might, he couldn't catch even a sliver of Mrs. Gordon's voice. He tried to make soothing music out of the train whistles and the passing cars; when that failed, he turned onto his stomach and, clutching his pillow to his chest, began to drum the mattress with his feet. As he was drumming and drumming, hoping that the effort would somehow protect him from whatever dangerous powers lurked in the lonely night, he suddenly felt the room turn cold and he couldn't move his feet anymore; they were frozen to the sheet. Something was in the room with him. He could almost smell the danger. He turned his head in the direction of the doorway, where, to his horror, he saw a man whose face was tilted in just such a way that the hall light turned his eyes into glittering marbles of bronze. The rest of the man was a pillar of pure darkness. Neil dropped his face back into the pillow — it was the smallest of movements — and, lying perfectly still, trying not to breathe, said to himself over and over, "If he thinks I'm dead, he won't hurt me, if he thinks I'm dead, he won't hurt me," until he finally heard the hall light click off and silence sweep through the house again.

For years afterwards, Neil wondered who his midnight visitor had been. He had never really suspected his father, always reasoning that Frank would have spoken to him, but Neil now knew for certain it had been him. He couldn't say how he knew. It had something to do with the presents, which were a kind of compensation for all the prowler stuff from the night before.

He thought about getting up and throwing them into the wastebasket unopened, but Audrey Hepburn stopped him. She, as Holly from *Breakfast at Tiffany's*, smiled down at him from the centre of his pin-up board. Elegant in rhinestones and evening gloves, Cat draped around her neck like a scruffy boa, she seemed to say, *Don't do anything drastic, darling. It's not worth it.*

With an accepting nod, he reached into his record cabinet, drew out the original cast recording of *Camelot*, and plopped it on the turntable. King Arthur and his beloved Guinevere — just right.

He turned up the volume so that the game upstairs almost disappeared. Then he fluffed up the cushion behind him, leaned back and closed his eyes.

For a long while he remained with his eyes closed, as still as if he were sleeping. But behind his eyes he was wide awake, achingly awake to a shifting romantic landscape of greens and golds, peopled with lords and ladies, knights and magicians, and a king whose heart was broken and a queen whose passion led her at last to the convent door and the mercy of Sisters. This was the part of the story that always got to him most, the queen's withdrawal from the world. Every time it came, he would wish with all his heart that some other way might be found. Sometimes, he would even imagine that the story *was* going to end differently, that the queen would be reunited with her Arthur and the glory of Camelot would be restored. His disappointment that it didn't do so was so sharp that he'd sometimes vow never to listen to *Camelot* again.

His eyelids fluttered slightly. He took a deep breath and Guinevere began to sing one of his favourite songs, "I Loved You Once in Silence."

A knocking at the door, soft but insistent, broke in on him.

His eyes blinked open, full of surprise and annoyance. He sat up.

"It's Val."

He turned down the music, ran a hand through his sandy hair.

She was carrying an Eaton's shopping bag. "I got you something."

It was a sweater, a sweater of unbelievable hues: bronze, gold, red, orange, green, brown and even purple. But better even than the blend of colours was its softness. He rubbed it against his face, held it out in front of him, rubbed it against his face again. Then he stood and tried the sweater on. It fit him perfectly. "It's so beautiful. Where'd you get it?"

"Mr. Fraser told me I could take a few things from the sale

table. I took a couple of shirts for Mike and a couple for Daddy and then I saw that and I thought you would like it."

"Oh, I love it, I love it."

Val's smile showed some embarrassment at her brother's enthusiasm. She moved to go, but caught sight of the bulletin board that hung above her brother's couch and made a face. "She's so skinny."

"You sound like Mother."

"Well, I could have said, 'She's just a clothes horse.'" They both knew this was their father's opinion of Miss Hepburn. "But I think her clothes are gorgeous. She's the problem." She moved closer to the bulletin board. "Bernardo." She pointed to the photograph of a dark-haired young man with sideburns. "He's dreamy. I'll have to go see that movie again. He's — Who are *they*?" Val was pointing at his images of bare-shouldered young men, thick-lipped young men, curly blond young men, brooding dark young men, staring intently at the camera, at one another, and out at unseen vistas beyond — all ads for movies with titles like *Long Beach*, *Cherry Ripe*, *Boys of the Sun*, *Night Games*.

Neil shrugged unconvincingly. "I don't know who they are. They're from Hollywood."

"They don't look nice."

They both stared, Val frowning. "You like them?" she demanded.

"They're all right. They're from Aunt Sylvia. From Hollywood."

Neil was lying. The ads captivated him. And worried him, too. He knew the men they depicted weren't nice young men, that they didn't go to school or live at home or eat three meals a day or maybe even obey the law, but knowing that didn't stop him from wanting to be there among them on their sandy beaches, sprawled nearly naked on their blankets or towels, transfixed by the sound of the undulating surf. "They just fit with the rest," he said, and made a gesture to the board as a whole.

"Fit with Audrey Hepburn? How so? And your flag cards?"
She pointed to a bright trio of trading cards pinned one above the
other, showing the flags of Colombia, Sweden and Turkey. "I don't
get it!"

They lapsed into a sullen silence. Val turned again to go.

"Val, what's the matter? What have I done wrong?"

"You're just strange. Everybody in this house is strange." She
looked at him. Her eyes were wet.

"Are you sad about leaving Eaton's?"

"Yes!" she said, and her voice was almost angry.

"So why did you?"

"Because it seemed like a good chance to try something different. But I don't really want to go to Windermere. I won't see anyone
all summer but bloody strangers."

"You'll have Mike every weekend."

Her eyes scanned his face as if searching there for some gauge
of his capacity to understand. Finally, she blurted out, "He's trying
to own me."

Neil couldn't find anything to say except, "Don't let him."

Val turned and left without another word.

He stood for a moment in his soft, soft sweater, feeling puzzled.
He didn't know why, but Val's words, with their frisson of desper-
ation, brought tears to his eyes again.

Camelot had finished.

Slowly, he walked to his bed. Hesitating only briefly, he opened
the presents.

Humbugs.

And a book. *Cat on a Hot Tin Roof* with a picture of Paul
Newman and Elizabeth Taylor on the cover. Elizabeth Taylor was
wearing only a slip that barely contained her big breasts and Paul
Newman's pyjama top was partly open showing his chest, smooth
and strong. Inside the cover, his father had written, *Goodbye
Grade 11* and signed his distinctively ornate initials, *FJB*.

He walked the book over to his nest on the sofa and slowly sank into excited contemplation of the cover. It took him a moment to realize that inside were more photos from the movie: photos of Liz and, especially, Paul — Paul as Brick, Paul the hero. As Neil was gobbling the photos up, a second knock interrupted him. His father entered, carrying a generous slice of the refrigerator cake on one of the transparent glass plates his mother brought out only for guests. "Your mother sent this down." He handed Neil the plate. "I see you opened the presents."

"Thank you very much."

"They were pouring the humbugs into the tray when I got there." Frank Bennett examined his son like a man searching for a flaw in a perfect gem. "I'm proud of you, you know." He frowned then, a showy frown. "But why you want to read Williams when you could read Bernard Shaw, I'm sure I don't know."

They had had this discussion before, when Neil was reading *The Glass Menagerie*, so he only said, "It's funny. Some guy at the library tonight told me I should read *Cat on a Hot Tin Roof* and here you've gone and bought it."

"Well, don't tell your mother. Keep it in your cupboard." He was referring to the secret compartment under the floor.

Neil nodded, waited, as his father surveyed the room with obvious pride. It was his father and Uncle Herb — but principally his father — who had finished the basement. And most of the furnishings, except the Danish teak sofa, were from his father's workshop next door. Many years before, Frank Bennett had attended a modern furnishings exhibit where, in the guise of a potential buyer, he had enquired about the measurements of certain Scandinavian submissions: a pair of end tables, a coffee table, two armchairs and a buffet. On the sly he made precise drawings of these pieces, which he later constructed for his new suburban house. They represented the first furniture Neil had ever known. Now they were his.

"You take good care of things. I like that," Frank said. He picked up the record jacket for *Camelot* and said "Richard Burton. Now there's an actor. You wouldn't find him doing Williams."

Neil said, "Lots of great actors have been in his plays."

"You call those great actors?" He pointed to Newman and Taylor.

"They got Oscar nominations for those parts!"

"Oscar, Oscar — I wonder about you sometimes!" His father's gaze landed for a second on the bulletin board. He sniffed. "And that Hepburn woman!"

"I really, really want to see *Breakfast at Tiffany's*. It's coming to the Runnymede."

Frank glanced again at Hepburn as he left. "She's no Loren, that's for sure. But, I'll speak to your mother about it. There's another piece for you upstairs. Come up when you're done with that. They enjoy your company."

Alone again, Neil reveled in his dessert. Once done, he gazed up at the bulletin board. To Audrey, gleaming down from the sheet music for "Moon River," he whispered, "I love you." At the three flag cards, he shook his head. His sister had completely missed the point. Each flag was accompanied by the image of a man: the Colombian man, dark-skinned, barebacked, hard at work on his knees; the Swedish man skiing down a snowy slope; and the Turkish man doing some kind of martial dance with a sword. Of course they fit! Nothing was accidental. Bernardo fit, even Audrey fit — she was the inspiration for all these men. Including the young men in those disturbing ads he had accidentally discovered among the articles Aunt Syl had sent him.

Neil scanned them now, closely, as he had done hundreds of times already. Satisfied they were all where they should be, he selected one to concentrate on: a curly-headed blond with puffy lips and a look in his eyes of Neil-wasn't-sure-what, something really bad. The inevitable happened.

He looked away.

Now? Or later? That was the question.

Upstairs the game had resumed. He could make out Val's voice. She and Mr. Knight were goading each other. Then he heard Mr. Knight say, "You better watch out for that Mike, I tell you! There's a light in his eye!"

Now? Or later?

Later, it would be different, dark. He'd be in bed.

The puffy-lipped blond was right here, right now.

He went for the box of tissues on his night table and took four, five.

Returning to the couch, he stopped and listened again.

His father was saying something about outboard motors. Evinrude versus Johnson, a favourite debate topic.

He opened his pants.

3

THEY LEANED OUT THE WINDOW over the street and inhaled the city.

It was nine o'clock. Saturday night. The last night of June. Twilight had finally arrived, just in time for Ray Charles to moan for the third or fourth time that day, "I Can't Stop Lovin' You." Neil searched the street below for the car radio responsible.

Two streetcars rumbled past, one headed east towards downtown, the other west to the bus and streetcar terminus at Jane Street, known by everyone as the Jane Loop. It wasn't an elaborate structure, nothing more than a brick wall with a porch-like roof on either side. The suburban and trolley bus path took up the south side, the streetcar tracks the north. Openings in the wall allowed the bus riders quick access to the streetcars and vice versa. Neil knew that as a site it had nothing beautiful or interesting to recommend it, but the vision of trams constantly coming and going from the Loop always gave him goosebumps of pleasure. Movement was certainly part of its appeal to him, but so was the promise of distant destinations.

Tony liked the Loop, too. Because of all the crazy, magical things they'd witnessed there, he called it Disneyland. Or sometimes "Inferno," after Dante.

Neil glanced at him. Tony stood on his left, laughing at

nothing, laughing at everything. He realized they'd stood in exactly the same position countless times since their first meeting five years earlier. Even though the apartment itself belonged to Angie, one of Tony's many sisters, they called the window "our place," and their Saturday night surveys of Toronto's major artery, Bloor Street, "our routine." Both place and routine were part of what made them such fast friends. They gave the boys free rein to express their huge curiosity about the world — and to openly acknowledge how similar they really were "deep down," to use Tony's words.

"I wish I lived here," Neil said.

"You want to live with Angie and Bruno?"

"No! But I mean, if this were just my place ..."

Tony gave him one of his lopsided grins. "Yeah. That'd be all right. I like the sound of the streetcars. The going-away sound." His grin took on a slightly self-satisfied quality. "I did a bunch of drawings of your favourite place."

"The Jane Loop?"

"You got it. Drawings of streetcars. And a couple of buses. But mostly streetcars. Oh, and a plate of fruit. A still life. Angie wants me to give her the still life. I told her it's worth a lot of money. An' you know what? Bruno offered me twenty-five bucks for it. I was only kidding."

"You should've taken it. You'd have had movie money for a whole year."

Tony laughed. "I did say I'd trade him, though."

"For what?" Neil couldn't help admiring the shine in Tony's dark, dark hair and the brightness of his even darker eyes.

"A coupla silk shirts."

"From his store?" Bruno Zamboni's men's store was very classy. "What'd he say?"

"Asked me what colours. I told him deep blue and red. Deep blue for me, red for you."

"Me!" Neil was astonished.

"Sure. Share the wealth. That's what my ma says."

"I can't see myself in a silk shirt."

"How come?"

"You've seen where I come from. And a red one, too."

"Red'll look good on you. Deep blue'd make you look too serious. You're already too serious." Tony laughed, and then added, "Those shirts aren't cheap either. They're worth way more than twenty-five bucks!"

"And Bruno was okay with that?"

"More than okay." Tony winked. "Sometimes I think he likes me better than my sister."

Neil looked down into the street, swallowing the excitement stirred by Tony's comment. A couple paused under a streetlamp nearby and lit cigarettes from a silver lighter shaped like a cruise liner before moving on, arms around waists.

"But then everyone finds me irresistible." Tony's laugh burst into the cooling night air like a firecracker.

It was answered by a shout from the other side of the street. "Fruits! Look at the Parma fruits!" followed by loud guffaws.

The store sign below their window, which Tony had designed, was a medley of fruits and vegetables arranged in a crescent moon shape and suspended to the right of the large black letters, *Parma Fruits and Vegetables*. He and Tony were probably standing just above the word *Parma*.

"Takes one to know one," Tony said, not quite loud enough to be heard.

The two boys opposite swung away, hurling taunts like litter into the pathway of others.

"It's a great sign, though, isn't it?" Tony leaned out into the night with a sham boldness. "Your boss was in the store today — Miss Fairfield. She talked Ma's ear off about Parma. She was there last summer. That little pin she wears, the little violets, she bought it in Parma."

"Parma violets." Neil tried to picture the pin.

Silence fell between them, gently. Even more gently, a breeze wafted by. The night was beginning to smell slightly of storm. More streetcars rumbled past. The eastbound one was packed with people. Where are they all going? Neil asked himself. Dancing probably, like Angie and Bruno, dancing and drinking, or maybe the late show. Or maybe the Bohemian Embassy. Neil loved the sound of the Bohemian Embassy. A den of poets and actors and musicians.

As a smile of delight broke across his face, he spied a figure on the sidewalk below. Two figures, both young men, one talking animatedly, hands fluttering, the other still and sure. He recognized the latter, his springy walk, the subtle sway of his hips. Bread-man. Neil felt a catch in his chest, a slight breathlessness.

The two men had stopped. The talkative one was turning his pants pocket inside out, obviously looking for something. Bread-man's voice was very clear: "It's probably on the hall table, where you always throw it." Those words, spoken with an affectionate exasperation, inspired a boyish laugh in the other, which in turn seemed to trigger the sudden lighting of the street lamps. Bread-man was a special man indeed.

Neil wanted Tony to see, but before he could point the bread-man out, Tony's voice broke into his wondering. "She travels a lot, eh, your boss?"

Neil watched the backs of the two young men disappear into the indigo twilight.

Tony poked him in the ribs. "Neil? You there?"

"Yeah, yeah. I just recognized someone." He hesitated. "Someone from church."

"Okay, so what was I saying?"

"Miss Fairfield goes everywhere," Neil answered smugly. "Every summer. She's even been to Africa."

"I'd like to travel like that, you know," Tony said, with a sigh.

"Remember, you're coming to Italy with me when I go to study art."

"But what would I do there?"

Tony looked at him, cocking his head to one side and grinning. "You're an artist, too."

Neil made a scoffing face.

"You are! I dunno anybody who looks at things the way you do. You notice colours and smells and the things people eat and what they wear, and people's faces and bodies." Tony wiggled his eyebrows. "You see things ..."

"But that's not being an artist!"

"It's a big part of being one. You're so smart, you'd figure something out and then you'd learn Italian pretty quick, like you learned French and German. You could write! I paint, you write. Perfect."

The two of them traipsing around Italy while Tony studied art — the picture *was* too perfect for words. He looked at Tony drumming his fine, bony hands on the window ledge. He knew, beyond a shadow of any doubt, that Tony was way more than a "best friend."

Tony looked back, a softness in his angular face that said, "I'm with you." Then, he stuck out his tongue.

Neil laughed again, "Clown."

Tony shook his finger. "No, no, that isn't what you're thinking."

"What am I thinking, smart ass?"

"*Pensi che sono un bello ragazzo!* "

"I think you're a beautiful something ...?"

"Boy. Beautiful boy!"

"I think you're the most conceited boy I know."

"I've got a lot to be conceited about. Come an' look at my drawings, if you don't believe me!" Tony did a little dance backwards into the living room, almost falling over a footstool in the process. His save stopped just a little short of graceful.

"Clumsy as well as conceited!"

"Huh, just you wait. I'm going to go check on Gio!"

Neil picked his way through the obstacle course of heavy, dark Old World furniture that made up the room to the large, plump pink sofa, which, sitting boldly amidst the rest, seemed almost immodest, naked in its velveteen fleshiness. He kicked off his shoes and turned on the ornate Venetian glass fairy tale of a lamp that occupied the adjoining table. He was so happy that even the lamp, which usually struck him as unbelievably gaudy and tasteless, seemed like a thing of wonder. He lost himself in the tinkling golden light and the frilly girandoles of purple and yellow and orange — and pink, more pink. He started to hum "Johnny Angel."

Eventually, Tony returned, his large sketchpad in hand. His face was a bit damp and he now only wore his undershirt, a sleeveless white undershirt that hung loosely about his very thin torso. Against the whiteness of the undershirt and the pallor of his skin — for Tony was as white as a saint — the dark hair that coursed up his arms and sprouted on his chest seemed very black.

Tony turned on the TV, tuning in to what looked like an old movie.

"That's Henry Fonda," Neil said. "I've seen that movie, it's about the Great Depression."

Tony gave no response. He adjusted the TV volume so that it was just audible and took his place on the sofa next to Neil. Too casually to be really casual, he said, "Rick has it so lucky. Every summer he gets to go with his folks to Europe or somewhere."

"I wouldn't want Rick's dad, though. He's like an army captain."

"Yeah, but think of the places Rick sees."

"I still wouldn't want his dad."

As they chatted, Tony laid out his sketchpad so that half of it rested in his lap, half of it in Neil's. "You ready?" he asked in the pause. With a mock flourish, he then peeled back the paper cover. "Ta-da!"

The first drawing, in pen, was of a young woman in an apron standing next to a bin of oranges. In the background were other bins and shelves of produce.

"Who's that? I thought you were drawing streetcars."

"You know who that is, it's Vicki."

Neil frowned. "Vicki's not that pretty!"

"Well, she's not ugly." Tony seemed put out.

"I didn't say she was, but she's not that pretty."

Tony scrutinized the drawing for a minute through hooded eyes. Then he tore it from the pad. "You're right, it's not a good likeness." He pressed his leg closer to Neil's, ostensibly to keep the sketchpad flatter. He nodded his head towards another drawing. It was a streetcar, a pair of streetcars hitched together as they often were during rush hour, captured in charcoal.

"They look so mysterious."

Tony grinned.

"The charcoal makes them look like ... I don't know — like European trains from the war!"

"How do you come up with that stuff?" Tony laughed. He let his hand fall onto Neil's thigh.

Looking at the white hand with its long, slender fingers, Neil scarcely dared to breathe.

"Does it look like a streetcar, though?"

Neil tapped his temple. "No, it looks like an airplane!"

"I love it!" Tony said, turning the page with his left hand. His right remained on Neil.

"That one's great, too. It looks like it's about to go out on a dangerous mission."

Another page flew by.

Tony's hand, which had been semi-clenched, slowly unfolded on its resting place. Neil turned his head just enough to catch Tony's profile, just enough to note that his cheeks were red and that there was sweat on his neck and shoulder.

"Well …?" Tony asked, catching his eye and directing it down towards their laps.

A bus this time. The number 50 bus according to its sign.

"My bus," Tony said. Then he flipped quickly to the next page. "Your bus." The second bus bore the number 50-A.

Neil's voice was soft. "I really, really like these."

Tony's hand began to stroke his thigh. Neil knew this was the cue to slip his own hand under Tony's caressing arm and begin a similar gently rhythmic fondling.

More pages turned, more streetcars came into view. Some had people clambering in or out; some were perfectly still, silent, waiting. A couple were military looking, promising aggressive combat if provoked, others were as playful as fairground rides. Most were charcoal, two or three were pen, and one was coloured pencil, showing crimson and tan cars against the reddish brick walls of the Jane Loop.

Neil saw the drawings were all remarkably accomplished, but as one streetcar after another passed, he lost sight of their special properties and surrendered more and more to the sensations of exploring hands, which soon left the thigh for nearby regions.

The still life appeared eventually, the one Angie wanted, the one Bruno offered to pay for. A bowl of fruit — tangerines, pears, a pomegranate, a banana — and beside it a glass, half full, and a knife and egg shells on a blue plate. Neil had enough presence of mind to identify the plate as one of Mrs. Colero's.

The pad suddenly slid from their knees. Tony, turning abruptly towards him, said, "Let's," in a voice not quite his own.

In unison then, using the back of the pink sofa as a brace, both boys lifted up and wrestled their trousers down over thighs, past knees, to ankles, where they pooled darkly in the flickering light of *The Grapes of Wrath*.

"That's more like it," Tony whispered.

WHEN THE TIME came, Tony insisted on taking the 50-A back to the suburbs with Neil.

Neil said, "It's really all right. I'm not scared or anything tonight."

Tony wouldn't hear of it. "I want to. I don't mind a few extra blocks."

They sat in silence almost the whole way, shoulders and legs pressed together, Neil feeling that he finally understood what people meant when they said, "over the moon." It had been a hackneyed phrase until tonight.

At the bus stop, Neil wanted badly to hug Tony, but he settled for a smile and a squeeze of the hand.

Tony took up his post by the letterbox. "I'll watch you down Avery Street."

Neil managed to wave at Tony three or four times during his descent. When he reached Dominion, the cross street on one corner of which sat his parents' house, he stopped, turned around and waved again, watching for Tony to begin his hike northwards.

As he did, a long, low red and white car pulled into Dominion from Howard Street, and, headlights suddenly extinguished, moved slowly, almost stealthily towards him. He didn't see it until it was almost on top of him, blocking his passage across the street. Neil frowned, then glanced at the car's driver. It was an unfamiliar face, angular, with high cheekbones, prominent nose and dark stubble. Good-looking in a careless, sneering sort of way. He was not alone in the car.

"Hey," the driver said, smiling. It seemed to be a nice smile. "Are you a 'mo?"

Neil's frown turned into alarm.

"My friend here says you're a little 'mo."

Neil recognized the passenger then. Archie Ross. He lived at the other end of Dominion Street. For as long as Neil could remember, Archie had picked on him.

Archie said something to his chauffeur, followed by a high, mean laugh.

"You haven't answered my question, kid," the driver said again, his smile disappearing. "I want to know, are you a 'mo?'" He enunciated his words very clearly.

"No!" Neil said and started to make his way around behind the car. But the driver was expecting this and immediately put the car into reverse.

Stopped in his tracks, Neil headed in the other direction, but the car lurched forward to meet his moves.

"Now, now, that's not nice," said the driver.

Archie continued to laugh.

"We know you're a little 'mo, and we just need to hear you say it. Say it!"

Neil could feel his heart pounding in his chest. He didn't trust himself to do anything and so he just stared at them.

Archie's laugh grew falsetto. It was almost comically high.

"Say it!"

Neil twisted his body first one way, then another.

"I guess we'll have to see for ourselves, eh?" the driver said, putting the car into neutral.

Neil's eyes widened.

"Maybe you need a little corn-holing. Archie!" The voice was commanding. "This fairy is begging for it!"

Archie's expression wavered for an instant between malice and uncertainty, as the driver slowly opened his door and got out. He was tall, very tall, like a basketball player, and his shoulders and arms were powerful.

"So, is the boy a fairy or not?" asked the driver.

Archie was outside the car now, his moon face shining with spite, but he made no move to join his pal. He hovered in the background, chanting, like some demented chorus, "He's a fairy! He's a fairy!"

The driver took a step towards Neil.

"Stop," was all Neil could muster.

Archie's laugh cut through the silence of the night like breaking glass. The driver laughed, too, and called back to Archie, "This is way too easy! He's dying to give it up."

Neil understood none of this. The words were not registering. He desperately scanned his parents' house across the street for some sign of light or life, but everything there was in darkness.

The driver advanced another step, then another, forcing Neil to keep backing up, until the shoulder of the road gave way to lawn and his feet deserted him on the uneven ground. He fell with a thud onto his back. His library book skittered across the grass to lie sparkling in the light of the street lamp. The driver advanced quickly then and, straddling Neil's body, loomed over him, a Colossus in khaki pants and shiny pointy-toed boots. Archie was there, too, still hovering behind his friend, a nervous shadow.

Neil began begging them to leave him alone, to take his money or his books, or his shoes, or anything they wanted, just to leave him alone. The only answer this babbling got was a mock-sorry shaking of the head from the towering driver and another shriek of laughter from Archie.

Suddenly, the driver leaned down and deftly pulled Neil's belt open. "Let's see what we've got here now."

Neil found his voice at last. He began to shout. Immediately the driver was on his knees, sitting on Neil's torso and gripping his jaw shut with a powerful hand. Neil struggled to free his head, but his assailant only tightened his hold. Neil could taste blood in his mouth. All resistance gone, he looked up with pleading in his eyes, only to find the eyes staring back at his full of their own sort of pleading. Later, waking frightened in the small hours, Neil would try to interpret his opponent's pleading look, but without much success.

Lights flashed on in the Knights' house behind them, illuminating his red and frightened face and his torn shirt and now belt-less trousers. The belt lay like a coil of black snake in the grass beside him.

Archie squealed, "We're caught. We're caught."

"Shut the fuck up!" his comrade commanded, jumping to his feet.

They bolted for the car. It turned the corner and headed north up Avery at top speed before Neil even managed to sit up.

Before he knew it, a pyjama-clad Mr. Knight was beside him, helping him stand and cursing Archie. Mrs. Knight was on the porch in her housecoat saying, "Bring him in, Phil. Don't let him sit there on the grass. He'll catch his death!"

Mr. Knight was, of course, quick to obey, but suddenly there was another figure to contend with. On the front porch of 31 Dominion, Neil's father was watching grimly, hands on his hips. Neil could tell then he was going to get it for being so late, and he wanted nothing more than to ask Mr. Knight if he could stay with him and his wife for the night.

By the time they reached the porch, his father had propped open the door and turned on the hall light. Neil could tell he had been sleeping, probably on the living room sofa. A light alcoholic fog clung to him.

"You should have been home long before now," his father said, his eyes boring into him. "You're asking for trouble."

Mr. Knight stood back, shaking his head. "It was the Ross boy."

His father grimaced. "He'll come to a bad end, that one." For a second Neil wasn't sure whom his father meant. "The older one's in the pen."

"Here's his belt, Frank," said Mr. Knight. "Neil, your book. Take good care of yourself, boy."

Neil looked at him gratefully, and waved at Mrs. Knight who still anxiously occupied her doorway across the road.

In the brightly lit kitchen, his father questioned him about his second attacker with a curiosity that reminded Neil of Tony's face the Saturday evening he discovered Bruno's hidden *Playboy* magazines. This was always his father's way with people he identified as "from the wrong side of the tracks," and Neil found it intensely disturbing. Having no answers to give regarding the giant in the pointy-toed shoes, Neil opened the door to the basement.

"They tore your shirt." Frank scowled. "Your mother won't be pleased."

Neil stared into the darkness of the stairwell. Yes, his mother would be annoyed, but right now it didn't matter. All that mattered was Tony. He prayed Archie and his buddy wouldn't catch up with him. Tony was a fast walker. He walked so fast sometimes it was almost like running to keep up with him. Tony'd probably be in bed by now.

"I can give you a bit o' brandy." His father's arm reached for the liquor cupboard.

Neil declined and headed down the stairs.

Frank Bennett scowled again. "Next time get home at a decent hour."

4

NEIL WOKE THE NEXT MORNING with the terrible knowledge that after more than a year, Archie Ross was back on the prowl for him. And now he was armed with a friend, a very scary friend, scarier by far than Archie himself. What would have happened if the Knights hadn't woken? Neil turned onto his side. He didn't really want to know the answer to that question. It was enough, the mocking faces, the large hands grabbing at his belt, the impassive stare of the streetlamp.

He lay for a while very still, eyes closed, taking in the silence of the house. Birds rustled in the bushes outside his window, but he could detect no human sound. His sinking feeling turned into mild alarm. Maybe they had left him.

The clock read ten thirty. He had slept late.

It was Sunday. His mother would be at church, his sister would be with Mike at Mike's church, the Anglican church next to the bus stop. Frank would be outside, puttering, maybe fooling around with paints. He had been working on a painting for the back patio. It was a big noisy piece, huge spills of automobile lacquer — black, blue, pink, rust-coloured. Abstract Expressionism, his father called it with a deadpan face. But like all his other paintings, it was more joke than anything else, something to shock the neighbours with, something his mother could shake her head over, and Val could laugh at. Something else Neil could feel overwhelmed by. If only the painting had some power to protect him, some magic property that would send the Archies of the world running, but the painting seemed to him to be made of the same stuff as Archie. It was pushy, threatening, mean. It wasn't finished yet, and Neil already hated it.

How he wished he could confess everything to Tony. He wanted to tell him about last night, about the attack, the torn shirt and the bleeding mouth, but he was too embarrassed by the nature of the taunts he'd received. Nor could he tell him about his father, about the scare campaigns and the terror they provoked. In Tony's mind, Neil's dad was "lots of fun," and, not only that, an older guy who knew about making art and things. It would be impossible to make him understand what he had to go through. Tony had no experience to compare it to. Neil felt ashamed for wanting more of his friend, but he did, especially that morning in the eerie quiet of the house.

His sinking feeling was back. With it came the thought that he would have to be even more careful now, more watchful, if Archie was out there looking for trouble. And that thought made him furious. He kicked off the sheet, jumped out of bed.

FOR A FEW seconds, Neil stood at the back screen door, staring into the Gordons' empty driveway. Mrs. G. and Lana were at church, too, of course, and Mr. G. was no doubt snoozing in a lawn chair on his front porch till "the ladies" returned.

His mother would have laid out breakfast for him. The half grapefruit would be in its magenta bowl covered with Saran wrap. There would be strawberries for his bran cereal and raspberry jam for his toast. Neil was hungry, but he couldn't give in to the hunger yet. The terrace beckoned.

There he found his father in his painting clothes.

"At last." His father stepped back from the canvas. "What do you think?"

Neil turned to look at the huge painting on a board propped against the terrace wall. His father had obviously been busy spraying it with white lacquer. The white was new and strong and it pushed almost all the other colours back, as if they'd been caught in a hailstorm of icing sugar and gone running for cover. The black, however, hadn't budged. It looked like an oil slick.

As if to demonstrate a point, Frank Bennett picked up the old industrial paintbrush, and dipped it in the pot of paint at his feet. With a dramatic pause or two, which assured him of Neil's attention, he flicked the brush violently at the canvas. More hail, more icing sugar, more runaway colour.

Neil looked away. They would soon have this painting hanging from the terrace wall. Another neighbourhood sensation.

"Very Pollock, eh?"

Neil made no answer.

"You should know your artists, son."

Neil stepped off the terrace onto the soft lawn, the lawn they called "backyard." It was so green. His father had spent a fortune on new sod that year. And the flourishing elm hedge that surrounded it, not to mention the flowerbed, now blooming with roses, and the handcrafted goldfish pond. It was, as his father repeatedly pointed out, "Elysium."

The only flaw in the picture was a gaping hole in the hedge between the terrace and the Gordons' backyard, a hole the size of a garbage bin lid. Years ago Gus Gordon had tripped on the way to his tool shed, spilling a tin of some kind of acid or chemical into the hedge. His father still referred to it with an angry frown. This morning, however, Neil liked it better than the perfection of the rest. He silently thanked it for being there.

"This is yours!" His father tossed something at him, but as usual with any game of catch, Neil missed. He bent down to retrieve a small plastic tomahawk-wielding Indian chief in head-dress and blue loincloth, one of his beloved Indians from wars gone by.

"I found it on a branch of the sumach."

Neil glanced at the tree in the back corner of the yard. He had played under it with his cowboys and Indians for years, and continued to find refuge under it on hot summer days with a book and a soda.

"How'd it get there?" he asked, more to himself than his father.

"I'm sure I don't know." His father stood back, squinting at his work. "You'll see. The Guggenheim will come calling."

Neil knew the Guggenheim was a famous gallery, but he wasn't going to comment.

"You survive the night?" his father asked.

Neil shrugged.

"Knight's been down there this morning. Helen Ross says she'll have a word with the boy. We all know what that means."

Neil sighed. Mrs. Ross's sweet, watery smile and faded blue eyes could maybe manage a spilled cup of tea or a stale biscuit. They were no match for hoods like her son.

"Don't worry. I'm thinking of investing in a gun. Or maybe a stiletto. You can cut his throat. Go for the jugular." His father brandished his paintbrush stiletto-style against his own throat. "Zip. And it's done." He made lurching-to-his-death moves.

Neil turned away.

"Your mother will be home soon," his father called after him, for what reason Neil couldn't say.

She was home before he finished his breakfast, in fact. He had just made himself a cup of tea, a new habit, and was wondering how long to leave the teabag in, when the front door opened. His mother removed her small pale blue hat, an arc of feathers on a ribbed frame, and deposited it on the dining table along with her pale blue purse and gloves. She was wearing his favourite pieces of jewellery, the bluebell necklace and bracelet his father had bought her one Christmas when he was a little boy.

She smiled but her face was lined with worry. "Were you hurt last night?"

He sighed. "Sort of. I had blood in my mouth."

Uncertainly, she joined him at the kitchen table. She was often uncertain, even shy, with him. "What about your teeth?"

He offered her an exaggerated smile to show her how intact they were.

"Silly. You have the shirt?"

"I'll get it."

"Finish your tea."

He could tell she was really upset, but like so much else with his mother, she couldn't talk about it. She swallowed it down, whole, unrefined. He wondered where she put it all. He imagined it might someday just spew out of her like a geyser and then everyone would see just how much she had felt about things.

"Please call us the next time you're traveling home late. We'll pick you up at the bus stop."

This offer made him smile. "He hasn't bothered me in a while, but he had somebody with him last night."

"June Barry's son."

"Who's June —?"

"A church lady. Vera Knight recognized him. He's been in trouble with the law."

"What kind of trouble?"

"Oh, dear, we don't need to know that."

She rose and made herself a cup of tea, the bluebells at her wrist tinkling lightly. All her gestures were precise and neat. Neil loved watching her take care of things, inanimate things like cups and ironing and bread. She was like one of those Japanese women he'd seen at the Exhibition, exquisitely arranging flowers, folding paper, pouring tea. She seemed to have such a clear sense of how things needed to be handled if they were going to function well. He wished he had that gift. Things fell out of his hands so easily, or refused to do what they should, sometimes with calamitous consequences.

She asked after his father, but made no comment about the painting.

Suddenly, Val's voice was filling the vestibule. "Mother! Mother!" She appeared instantly in the dining room, followed by Mike, both of them very flushed and agitated in their Sunday best. "Did you hear about Mrs. Doyle? She's been broken into!"

"That's putting it mildly," Mike suggested.

Nora's face registered disbelief. "Someone's robbed the Doyles?"

"No, no, not robbed! Someone broke in and wrecked the place."

"Stuff smashed to smithereens," Mike added in a tone suggesting much experience of such things. Neil groaned silently.

"Dishes, vases, glass in the picture frames. And then they emptied flour and honey and all the contents of the fridge all over the place."

"And slashed the sofa with a knife or something and the mattresses, and even her piano, they dumped molasses all over the keys and water into the body of the thing. It's ruined, absolutely ruined. Quite the spectacle."

"And they took tins of house paint and splashed the walls all over with it! I guess the Doyles had it around, in the basement or something. It happened Friday night they think."

Neil had a sudden vision of the Doyle Dodge heading south on Avery Friday night. It must have happened just after.

"Have they caught the burglars?" Nora asked.

"They weren't burglars, Mother. Nothing was taken, not a penny. They just wrecked the place."

"Maybe it was Archie and Mrs. Barry's son," Neil said.

"Archie? Archie Ross?" Mike asked with a sneer. "Nah, Archie's a goon. He wouldn't have the brains for something like that!"

Neil stared at Mike. Some guys feel they know everything.

"It was someone who knew them, I bet," Mike added. He put his Bible down on the dining table next to the feathered hat and blue purse. "It's going to cost them a pretty penny to clean up that mess."

Neil tried a shrug on to up his coolness. "She probably has a lot of people who hate her."

"How can you say that!" Val cried. "You should see the house. All her possessions, all the family pictures and keepsakes and everything — wrecked. I almost cried for her and I'm not one of her fans. It was terrible." Her eyes were wet. "She was standing on her lawn, sort of wringing her hands when we came by, talking to Mrs. West. She looked really frightened."

"What about Davy's stuff?" Neil asked.

"They just emptied everything of his onto the floor and soaked his bed in shaving lotion. He got off light."

Nora sat down at the table with her tea, but she didn't drink. She stared helplessly into her cup.

"I can't believe it, it's so awful!" Val took a chair opposite her mother. With a slump of her pretty shoulders and a weary droop of her strawberry blond head, she managed to look a little pathetic, too.

Rolling his eyes, Neil headed for the basement door. "I'm going to get my shirt, Mom."

He paused in the landing. The always dramatic, grey-bobbed Lydia West was on the Gordons' front lawn, hands flapping, probably telling the same lurid story to Mr. and Mrs. G. Their daughter Lana was there too, with bright pink curlers in her hair.

I would love to see the inside of that house, he thought.

5

THE REST OF THAT SUNDAY, Dominion Day, was taken up with conferences about the Doyle family's bad fortune.

Val, as the only person in the neighbourhood known to have witnessed the carnage, was much in demand. Vera Knight and Mona Gordon consulted her separately for details. So too did Mrs. Hamilton, who with her husband might have modeled for *American Gothic*. And so would have the portly Mr. and Mrs. Chard, if Nora Bennett hadn't put her foot down — "Val! You're going to Windermere tomorrow, aren't you?" — leaving Mike, who ended up staying for both lunch and supper, to fill in the Chards while Val packed.

Neil's father showed little interest in the affair — at least, not until after supper, at which point he, in a sly, *sotto voce* kind of way, started implying that maybe he was the housebreaker and vandal. He did so as everyone, including the Knights, the Gordons, and the Hamiltons, collected on the back terrace for a farewell drink to Val.

The suggestion was greeted with stupefaction, then a burst of raw laughter from Mona Gordon.

"It's not funny, Daddy," Val said.

His wife didn't think so either. She twisted in her lawn chair to face away from him.

He countered by shaking his head. "Nobody believed me about the prowlers either."

"What prowlers?" Mr. Hamilton asked, in his brisk commanding officer voice.

"Oh, Mr. H., don't get him going, it's just another of Daddy's jokes," Val said.

"Not a joke, Val. Ask them." He nodded towards the Knights and then the Gordons. "They saw the stocking." As the group considered how best to protest, Frank leaned forward and said, "I told those boys not to damage any of the personal stuff, especially not the piano, but they never listen!"

Neil wanted to excuse himself. He squirmed in his chair a few feet from the others at the edge of the patio, hating where the evening was going, hating it with an anger that had him gnawing on his nails for release and muttering under his breath, "It never stops. Never stops."

"Look!" Frank suddenly pointed out into the garden. Whizzing through the blue twilight was a pair of bats. "Carmilla," he whispered, "and Oswald."

Mrs. Hamilton looked as if someone had just told her the earth was flat. "Names for the bats — well, I never heard anything like it."

"My assistants," Frank said.

Another laugh from Mona, and Mike, too, who slapped his thigh for punctuation.

"I think Frank missed his calling," said Mr. Knight.

Neil sank even deeper into his chair as the group tried to come up with his father's true "calling." Comedian, clown, actor, magician were all suggested, with Gus Gordon favouring the magician role because, as he said, "You'd look good in a top hat and cape!" This picture only made Neil think of vampires and he cringed.

When his father announced that he had something to show everyone, Neil almost bolted. The painting was going to have its first airing, and it would provoke more of the usual ridiculous reactions. It had been painted to do just that, after all. In his mind he cursed the painting, cursed his father, and cursed the neighbours whose responses egged him on. He could almost predict what they'd say.

The wrought iron lamps hanging from the slatted roof of the terrace blazed to life. The canvas, which had been facing the wall all evening, was turned around, and there was a collective gasp. His father bowed, once, twice, three times, like some kind of circus monkey, but the comments he was expecting didn't materialize.

A great silence ensued, disturbed only by the crickets and cicada.

Obviously discomfited by the lack of outrage, Frank filled the void with hurried explanations. The work was called *Windermere '62*, in honour of Val's trip, and he hoped it gave the viewer a reasonably accurate portrait of summer resort life in Muskoka. This provoked a laugh from Gus Gordon. Carmilla, the bat, was then credited with being the principal inspiration for the work because of her "boundless sensitivity." Frank also claimed she was adamantly opposed to letting the canvas leave Islington until it was really and truly finished. "She thinks it's a major opus. Might take years to complete."

Mike Dennison applauded when he'd finished. "I'm sorry it's not coming with us, sir."

"I'm not," Val muttered.

Nora Bennett looked stern.

The only response to the painting itself came from Vera Knight. "I rather like the little coloured ribbons-y things in the background, but what does all that white mean?"

"A new epoch in human civilization!" Frank crowed.

Another silence descended.

Mona Gordon turned to Neil. "What do you think of it, darling?"

"Neil doesn't get my art, Mona," his father said.

"I don't believe that! Neil's the smartest one here."

Frank's brow wrinkled with pretend concern. "Just a bit dull, though."

"Dull? Neil? Nonsense!"

"I think it's ridiculous — and ugly as sin," Neil said loudly. Hurtling out of his chair, he almost ran from the terrace. The last word he heard from his father was *envy*. He went into the kitchen and began rifling the refrigerator for a snack.

Neil was soon joined by Mike, who had come in search of beer and lime rickey. Mike stepped up to him. "Ever heard of the commandment, 'Thou shalt honour thy father and mother?'"

"Thanks for the lesson, Reverend."

Mike grabbed him by the arm and squeezed hard. "Honour them!"

They heard the back door open. In the background, fireworks were exploding.

"Mike! What are you doing?" Val stood in the kitchen doorway, hands on hips.

Immediately retreating, Mike grabbed the bottles he'd set aside. "Your father's worth a hundred of you, you little fairy!" he grunted.

6

THEY ALL WENT TO WINDERMERE the next day — all except the painting, and Neil.

He slept till well past noon. In the afternoon, he cut the grass and watered the flower beds. Then, feeling he needed to see what, if anything, was happening at the Doyle house, he ambled up the street.

The place looked sad as usual. It also looked vacant, as if both its occupants had fled. Something was missing, but Neil couldn't place it until, just as he reached the corner of Stanton, he recalled the blue flower boxes full of pansies and petunias that used to hang from the porch railing.

He walked back then and paused once more to survey the house, imagining Davy Doyle in the living room window staring bleakly out at the street in search of solace. He was about to offer help to this vision when the real Davy barged into his fantasy.

"Entertained?"

Neil spluttered, "I'm sorry. I heard about the break-in."

Davy, who had been watching him narrow-eyed from the edge of the lawn, headed for the porch. "That doesn't make you special, you know."

"Can I do anything?"

"Why do you care?" His face, very white, almost pasty in the bright sun, seemed to be wrestling to contain something, which Neil translated as pain and sadness.

"It's horrible."

"So? It doesn't change a fucking thing. Except that now I get my piano lessons," he nodded towards the large bound volume under his arm, "from some dirty old man over by the fucking mall. You satisfied, Mr. Snoop?" His face was no longer trying to contain anything. It was a bleached, thin-lipped picture of anger and bitterness. "Now get lost, Bennett. This isn't a sideshow." Davy disappeared into the house, slamming the door behind him.

Caught off guard, Neil looked around to see if anyone had witnessed the exchange. The street was silent, the kind of silent that comes with muggy days. Nobody was about, not even kids. He went home, embarrassed and more than a little hurt. His had been a friendly gesture, after all, an expression of sympathy. Neil couldn't believe Davy had tossed it back in his face — well, not even that, had refused to receive it and then insulted him.

For the rest of the evening, all through supper at the Gordons' and the two cribbage games he played with Gus on their porch afterwards, and even later, trying to read *Cat on a Hot Tin Roof* from *Best American Plays, 4th Series*, Davy's pale face, both sullen and sad, was there. And it was still there, in the darkness, when he finally took himself to bed in the too-quiet house, now with an accusing look that frightened him. He couldn't make any sense of it and tried to push it away, but it wouldn't leave him alone. He tossed and turned in the still night like someone possessed, wondering how he would ever face Davy again.

Eventually he slept. He dreamed that he was looking for something in a huge room, a room in which the walls and doors and windows were mostly invisible, though every now and again he would catch a glimpse of white mouldings. Hanging from the very high ceiling were curtains, similar to stage curtains, but made of a billowy, silky material that floated away at his touch. These curtains or veils or whatever they were, were deep, mostly dark colours, greens and blues, reddish browns and greys, and there were more and more of them. As Neil tried unsuccessfully to get his bearings and find a way out, it began to dawn on him that what he was looking for was actually not an exit but the solid shape of the room. The curtains multiplied, the silky fabric fluttered elusively, mysteriously drawing him on, until his anxiety finally breached the barrier of sleep.

Neil sat up with a jolt.

From upstairs he could hear his mother's voice, angry.

His alarm clock said 12:41.

"I don't know why you have to go on and on."

A muffled reply from his father.

"The first time was funny. It was embarrassing after that. I'm sure Mike's uncle wondered what kind of craziness he's gotten mixed up with. It's always the same."

Another reply, even fainter, eluded his straining ears. He hated these disputes, but he had to listen.

Eventually his mother said, "I'm not your momma. Now goodnight."

Silence crashed down. Neil lay back, his dream forgotten, and listened to his father making his way to the liquor cupboard. He fell asleep again soon after.

At well past two, Neil was awakened again, this time by the sensation that something or someone was in the room with him. Immediately on high alert, he turned to his other side to squint into the darkness between bed and door. With a sharp intake of breath, he spied a figure hovering next to his clothes cupboard.

"Who's there?" His voice broke.

The someone made no answer. Only the sound of a car honking angrily in the distance disturbed the silence.

His voice even more strained, Neil asked again.

This time the figure answered with a noise somewhere between a grunt and a bleat.

Neil flicked on his lamp and sat up.

In what was left of the shadows, the intruder pointed helplessly towards his own face. It was covered by a nylon stocking that mashed the countenance grotesquely, making it seem more demented than criminal, but dangerously demented. It could have been the face of an escapee from a psychiatric prison.

The figure advanced slowly, almost robotically. Wide-eyed, Neil retreated towards his headboard. With the part of his brain that discriminated between true and false, he knew it was his father, but the sheer outrageousness of the figure's presence in his bedroom during the small hours of the night seemed to make that an impossibility. His father was a decent man, after all.

A foot from the bed, the figure paused and raised his other hand. A substantial carving knife came into view. Stunned, Neil couldn't recall ever having seen it before. It glinted sullenly in the light of the bedside lamp. For one terrifying moment, he had a very real fear that his father had actually lost his mind and was going to do him serious harm, but then, once more making his strange sound, the intruder pressed the knife point menacingly against his own neck and made as if a throat-slitting were imminent. In the moment of contact, the face beneath the stocking turned from crazy to demonic.

"Stop!" Neil's voice was not only sharp but also very loud. Its resonance in the dim room scared him. It also seemed to deflate the man in front of him.

Frank Bennett shook his head. "She got me. You know, she got me." With these words he turned and wobbled hopelessly towards the door, the knife dangling from his hand like a child's toy.

THE NEXT MORNING, when Neil emerged for breakfast, he found his mother folding freshly ironed linen napkins at the dining table. He enquired how she'd liked Val's summer place, and she gave him a sad smile.

"The people are nice, dear. Very nice."

"That's all?" he asked, gulping down his orange juice.

She turned tired eyes on him. "Nice is good enough."

Surprised by her terseness, Neil blinked a few times. He'd made up his mind to tell her about his midnight visitor, in part to test her willingness to intervene, but he could see she had no spirit for it, so instead he said, "Windy Pines. Sounds like Anne of Green Gables, doesn't it?"

A smile barely surfaced. "Do you want a Waldorf salad for your supper break today?"

"Are you kidding?" Neil moved to embrace her.

"There, there," his mother said, freeing herself, "no need to get mushy."

At noon, just after his mother left to go shopping for the salad ingredients, the bread truck rolled up to the foot of the Gordons' driveway. Neil was at that very moment making his way from the terrace to the back door. He slowed down so that he would still be outside when the bread-man came with his loaves.

Today, for some reason, the bread-man was not wearing his red cap. Neil could see his face clearly as he approached. It was a very alert face with high cheekbones and a defined jaw. The bright eyes weren't quite laughing, and the full, red mouth wasn't quite lush. But it was a gorgeous face, Neil thought, better than anything he had imagined. And the hair — thick, wavy, golden brown — how he wished he had hair like that.

The bread-man smiled at him as he passed, a big generous smile that showed remarkably even, white teeth.

Neil blushed. That smile was so pointedly meant for him. He steadied himself by opening the screen door, then hovered.

Bread-man went to the breadbox at the back of the Gordon's house, then returned carrying the Bennett household's loaf of brown. "Do you want to take this in yourself, or shall I perform my little bim-bam ritual?" He mimed opening and closing the breadbox.

"No, I'll take it." As the loaf passed hands, Neil couldn't help admiring the hairy chest left exposed by the unbuttoned shirt.

"You know," Bread-man said, "you're the only folks on the street that take brown bread. That's very unusual. Even a bit — well, freakish."

Neil knew he was just having fun with him. "Well, it's supposed to be better for you."

"No doubt, no doubt. But sometimes you need things that aren't good for you — just to keep a balance." Bread-man smiled. "Though I bet you're a pretty balanced guy."

"Me? Oh, I don't think so. I mean, living out here."

"In suburbia." Bread-man created a comic gap between the first and second syllables.

Neil flushed, then grinned. "It's very sub!"

"Compared to?"

"Urbia!"

Another smile lit up the bread-man's handsome face. "You know the city?"

"A bit. My dad works at City Hall."

Bread-man said, "City Hall does not a city make."

"I know Sam's, the record store."

"Sam's is good. And?"

"Eaton's and Simpson's,"

"Simpson's is good," the bread-man said. "Eaton's is a bit dowdy, though, don't you think?"

Neil wasn't sure what *dowdy* meant.

"Worn out. Frumpy."

Neil gulped. "Our family shops there."

The bread-man laughed. "Pay no attention to me. I'm just a snob. What else do you know?"

"I know about the Bohemian Embassy," Neil said, "and I've been to the O'Keefe Centre and the Royal Alexandra a couple of times for plays."

"What plays?"

"Oh, a couple of musicals, that's all." Neil felt suddenly like a little kid. "I want to live downtown."

"Well, the city's not going anywhere."

Neil could see it now: a collection of grand old buildings waiting patiently for him to show up. "Do you know the Jane Loop?"

"Sure do. The doorway to real life." With a wink, he turned to go.

Not wanting to lose him, Neil said, "Where do you live?"

"Just up the road from the Loop. In Not-Quite-Suburbia," Bread-man replied, "but close enough to feel the pull, the terrible pull. On Baby Point." He pronounced it "Babby Point."

"I know where that is. My Aunt Marian lives on the next street down. Raymond Avenue."

"Lucky Aunt Marian of Raymond."

"I saw you over there the other night," Neil shot out. "Saturday, on Bloor Street. With someone who was talking a lot." *Like me*, he thought immediately, with shame.

"That was probably my younger brother. He loves to gab. About guitars especially. And where were you?"

"I was up above you," Neil said. "Leaning out a window."

"Spying, eh? Well, I'd love to stay and explore that one, but I'm afraid I have to get about my business or they'll be after me with tar and feathers." Bread-man's laugh was not amused. "SOBs, you know."

Neil didn't know, but he didn't let on.

Bread-man started down the drive with a "See you Friday," thrown breezily over his shoulder and a slightly cheerier laugh.

Neil watched him walk as he had done a week or so ago, once again mesmerized. Bread-man could have been an acrobat or a dancer. At the foot of the drive, never pausing, never once breaking his flow, he turned and waved at Neil. Then he jumped into the truck and shouted, "Whistle, if you want to."

Neil turned a deep scarlet.

7

BY THE TIME NEIL SET out for the library at three o'clock, the bread-man had become his principal reason for existing. He desperately wanted to tell someone about their conversation, but the only person he would even consider telling was Tony, and he wasn't sure whether he wanted Tony to know the effect the bread-man had had on him. He couldn't think of anyone else, however, so the moment he got off the 50-A bus at the Jane Loop, he made a beeline for Parma Fruits and Vegetables.

Mrs. Colero was at the till as usual, her gold hoop earrings dancing. When she saw Neil, she immediately, without fuss, nodded her head towards the back of the store. "Break," she said. "Outside."

Neil wended his way through the closely packed bins and counters. Gingerly stepping into the dark, crate-filled stock room, he went towards a wide doorway opening onto a small concrete yard. At this time of the day, the yard was typically littered with stray lettuce leaves, plum pits and cigarette butts, but Neil didn't see any of that. The hot and glaring sun blinded him for an instant. He had to pause. As his eyes adjusted, he realized there was a figure sitting on the third stair of the fire escape.

Tony. And he wasn't alone. Standing in front of him, almost at his knees, with one hand on the railing and the other brandishing a cigarette, was the shop girl Tony had drawn last week, the one called Vittoria — Vicki. Her black hair gleamed in the sunlight, and as she flirted, her pink lipstick seemed to pop like bubblegum.

Instinctively Neil stepped back into the shadows to watch. Their laughter struck him as the private kind, possibly secret. Their gestures seemed even more so. Tony was staring unabashedly at her breasts and legs, and Vicki was altering her pose every few seconds to enable him to get a better view. In these games, she came off so much older than his friend, punctuating every shift with another puff of her blue Russian cigarette or another slow smoothing of her lime-coloured uniform. It was, for Neil, uncomfortably intimate, uncomfortably revealing.

It was certainly no place to talk about the bread-man.

He made his way back into the shop, fearful of Mrs. Colero's curiosity. Without being told, he knew that the picture of Tony and Vittoria chatting intimately on the back stairs would not be a welcome one. Fortunately, she was busy cashing out a demanding customer as he passed, leaving room for a wave and a smile, no more.

Outside in the bright sunlight, he stood very still for many minutes wondering if some important tie to Tony had just been broken. But there were no answers to be had from the signs and awnings, nor from the sight of his Aunt Violet sweeping the entry way to her shoe shop across the street.

A streetcar was coming from the Jane Loop, heading for what the bread-man called real life. Was that what Tony was doing with Vicki? Would Neil miss out because he was unlikely to ever have a Vicki? But as the streetcar passed, he looked at the wildly different profiles in the windows, and remembered how bread-man had assured him his time would come. And for a minute, his confidence resurfaced.

IT WAS QUIET in the library. With just a small trickle of borrowers searching for mystery and romance, Miss Fairfield asked Neil if he wouldn't mind putting some order into the Polish and Ukrainian language books, which were inclined to be wild and unruly.

Only too happy to be of service to Miss Fairfield, he spent almost two hours at the task, thinking there was no better job in the world than being a page at the Runnymede Library. It was way better than bagging groceries at Loblaws or pumping gas at the Esso station, way better even than selling fruit and vegetables at Parma's, wonderful though Parma's was. He could live in the library. That thought made him shiver. To reside in a world where the answers were always there, just at your fingertips, would be a luxury above all luxuries. He would never feel uncertain or frightened again.

When he finished straightening and ordering, Miss Fairfield said, "They've never looked tidier. You take an extra five or ten minutes for your break."

Neil's lunch was interrupted when Mrs. Negulescu appeared at the lunchroom door and announced to him, in a voice the equivalent of warmly glowing embers, "There is someone to see you."

It was the disheveled, dark-eyed young man who had pressed him to read *Cat on a Hot Tin Roof*. Mr. Rob Neville of 255 Durie Street, wearing black running shorts, sneakers, and a long, loose white shirt that almost hid the shorts. Under his arm were library copies of *Sexus* and *Plexus*. "Did you read it?" was his greeting.

"I finished it last night," Neil said, thinking that for all his messiness, Rob Neville had a romantic quality, like a gypsy maybe, or a highwayman.

"What did you think?"

"I liked it. You know there's a movie —"

Neville brushed away the suggestion. "The movie's nothing, worse than nothing. I told you it was about lies, didn't I?"

"I like that word Big Daddy keeps using — mendacity," Neil said with a touch of self-satisfaction.

"'*Mendacity*'s one of them five dollar words cheap politicians throw back and forth at each other,'" Neville replied in a loud Southern accent.

Neil glanced quickly at the patrons nearby, a couple of older women and a teenage girl, all browsing the light reading shelves. They didn't seem the least bit put out by Neville's showiness. He, however, felt uneasy, disturbed. How had he ended up talking to this person as if they were old acquaintances?

"Well, I've found out the play itself's a lie. Can you believe it?" He glared at Neil, almost as if Neil had had a hand in this deception.

"I don't understand," Neil said.

"Bowdlerized."

Neil wasn't familiar with the term.

Rob shook his head and sighed, "Censored. It's been censored. The play's not the one he wrote. It's the one *they* wanted him to write. They cut it to ribbons."

Neil didn't know who "they" were but he didn't dare to ask. "Oh," he said, "It's still a good play, though."

"You don't understand. You don't understand. In the original, the homosexual thing is explicit. Brick's a queer. I thought you would understand. But there's no one home here, is there?" Rob Neville tapped Neil's chest above his heart. "No one home. I'm disappointed in you." And with those words, he turned and rushed from the library, tossing *Sexus* and *Plexus* onto the circulation desk as he passed.

Neil stood very still, stunned almost. Something about Neville's energy scared him.

Mrs. Negulescu touched him on the arm. "*Este nebun.*"

Neil stared at her wide-eyed.

"He's crazy. *Este nebun.* A useful phrase, you should learn it. Come, finish your salad. I've put on the kettle."

8

WHEN HE LEFT THE LIBRARY that night, he knew he might not make it home without a soaking. The heavy sky rumbled. The wind blew in gusts.

He hurried along the street briskly. His aunt and uncle's shop was dark. So was Parma Fruits and Vegetables. Tony would be long gone. That made him feel really lonely. And somehow fearful.

That creep Rob Neville — who did he think he was? *No one home.* Where did he get off saying something like that? Neil may not have known much, but one thing he did know was that he was anything but heartless.

Striding along the windswept street, streetcars scurrying past, Neil tried to puff up his indignation, fuel his anger, by inventing put-downs he could use on Neville when he saw him next, but they made no dint in his anxiety. The memory of "snooping" outside the Doyle bungalow suddenly rose up, as if to accuse him and say, *Neville's right. You've got no heart.*

A few large drops of rain fell, then stopped, as if waiting for a better moment.

Neil began to run.

As he neared the Loop, he found himself praying that he might meet someone special on the bus platform, someone open and friendly, someone who would take an interest in him, talk to him, invite him for a walk or a movie or even a couple of hours listening to records — it didn't matter what kind of records either. He needed someone close to help him shut out the feelings Rob Neville of Durie Street had stirred up.

The bus arrived just as he did. All seven people waiting to embark turned and looked at him, almost in unison. None of them was the someone special. For a brief moment, he felt terribly self-conscious, convinced that he had dribbled mayonnaise on his chin or chocolate torte on his shirt.

The bus slowly disgorged its city-bound passengers, and Neil climbed aboard. There was a splatter of raindrops against his window. Then, again, nothing. He looked out. Night would be falling soon, but the storm-laden sky was already a deep charcoal.

His worries clung to him as the bus rolled along. People got on, clutching unopened umbrellas. People got off. The wind was kicking up a fuss, turning pieces of newspaper into dervishes, lifting skirts waist high, evicting squawking birds from their perches. Neil shivered in spite of the closeness of the bus. As if in answer to his shiver, the rain began to fall. Gently at first, gingerly testing the ground, almost delicate and well-mannered. Then the sky shattered and the gentle rain became a deluge. The world outside vanished and the bus slowed to a crawl.

The storm was so impressive, so unabashed and unapologetic, that Neil's dread lifted. He had never been scared of storms. He very nearly laughed.

The woman opposite him said, "My poor roses."

"Roses love the rain," said a big-boned blond man in a shiny blue suit with shiny buttons and shiny shoes.

"This isn't rain. It's a waterfall."

For the remainder of the journey to Avery Street, the rain kept up its attack. As Neil stepped off the bus, he took a deep breath, telling himself that nobody, troubling or otherwise, would be out in such a storm. He let the rain have its way with his hair and clothes. He even considered taking off his sandals to finish his trek barefoot, but recalled just in time the possibility of glass or gum or, much worse, worms, underfoot — in fact, he told himself, there were sure to be worms.

He hadn't gone a block when he became aware of a car following him. It had slowed down after turning the corner at Greenland Road. He looked back nervously. It was the car from the other night, the old red and white Edsel. This time there was only one person in it, and it wasn't Archie.

Neil refused to walk more quickly, certain it would show fear to the man at the wheel.

The car pulled up beside him.

"Hey," the man said, "hey, you wanna ride?"

He glanced quickly at the driver.

"I mean it." There was no obvious menace there, but Neil was not reassured.

"No thanks, I don't have far."

"I know how far you've got. Look, I'm sorry about the other night. It wasn't my idea, I swear."

"You're a lot bigger than Archie."

"I wouldn'a done anything."

Neil looked at him incredulously.

"I'm not shitting you."

"Yeah … right." Recalling the pleading eyes, Neil peered at him again. His expression looked almost kind. "I've got to get home."

"Too bad. You're missing out on a great experience."

Neil stole another glance. The driver was now smiling, a soft, sexy smile. He felt a tiny rush of excitement.

"If you ever want to try her out, you won't be disappointed. The Edsel's the best car ever made. We could have a lot of fun. Name's Jim. Later." With that, he put his foot to the accelerator and squealed away down Dominion Street.

Still excited, Neil ran across the sopping lawn. As he reached the top step of the porch, he realized that though there were no lights on in the house, the front door was ajar and even the screen was partially open.

Neil pulled on the screen, nudging the other door with his shoulder. It banged into something.

The door to the closet behind must be open, he thought.

He stepped into the vestibule, reached around the front door, and gave the closet door a shove. It didn't close. Something was blocking it. Neil looked down. There were things all over the floor: a few coats, hats, a pair of gloves, two or three of his father's pipes, the contents of his father's briefcase. On the vestibule floor, and into the living room as well. Something had happened. The storm, perhaps the storm, the lightning. But nothing seemed burned, nothing singed. He didn't know, he couldn't make it out.

He kicked the debris out of the way and shut the closet door. Then, like someone in a trance, he moved into the living room. Sofa cushions were all over the floor, one of the armchairs was overturned, and magazines were scattered everywhere. One of the lamps had fallen, too, crushing its shade. On the hearth lay the mint-green ashtray his father had only a week ago glued back together. It was broken again. A shredded newspaper littered the stairs to the second floor. The dining room chairs, lying sprawled on the carpet, looked like victims of a shoot-out.

We've been broken into. It hit him like a hammer: broken into. He stood staring in disbelief. Then terror.

What should I do? What should I do? Like a needle sticking on a record, the question repeated itself. His brain refused to work. He had an image of his father. Where was his father? His father must be around somewhere.

He turned on the spot for several seconds, then faced the staircase. He should at least make sure his father was not up there, injured, unconscious. But he couldn't move. Someone other than his father could be up there. He might have interrupted a break-in. He would go get Mr. Gordon or Mr. Knight.

A bang jolted him out of indecision. From the vestibule, the sound of doors colliding. His first impulse was to back away, but stepping on a sofa cushion and nearly falling changed his mind. He moved cautiously back into the front hall.

The closet door had popped open, that was all. It must have been the wind playing tricks. It blew around the house, angrier than before, as if it wanted in. The rain hit the screen door with a steady, relentless rat-a-tat-tat sound.

He stared into the darkness of the closet, into the bank of coats that still hung there, sensing danger. He had to get Mr. Knight. Neil reached for the front door knob, and at that very moment, the bank of coats separated.

His father, body slumped, eyes shut, shirt splattered in blood, fell face forward onto the floor.

Neil screamed, at first unable to move. When words returned, they were a high-pitched "I'll get help, I'll get help!" He stepped clumsily over his father, pushing at the screen.

Something gripped his ankle.

He looked down.

His father's hand, cool and sticky, held him.

Neil screamed again.

His father's head lifted. He made choking sounds. "Burglars, burglars." His head crashed to the floor again.

"I'll get Mr. Knight. I'll get Mr. Knight."

"They got me. They got me. Slashed me."

"Let me go! I'll get Mr. Knight." His father continued to hold his ankle like a ball and chain. "Dad, please let me get Mr. Knight. Please."

His father's choking sounds grew in intensity as his hand turned into claws, tearing into his ankle. Neil's only thought was, *He's dying. He's dying.* And then it stopped. The hand went soft and the choking subsided. An eerie silence took over the vestibule.

Neil hovered a minute. Then he slowly bent down. He touched his father's shoulder, shook it slightly. "Dad? Dad?"

Only stillness.

Neil straightened. Strangely, he thought of the man in the Edsel, of his height, his power, his smile: there was a man who could handle this. He needed someone like that right now. Hardly knowing what he was doing, he backed up towards the door.

A voice stopped him. "I don't think we need Mr. Knight. We can clean it up ourselves before your mother gets back."

Neil knew it was his father's voice, but he looked around for the speaker just the same.

The corpse sat up slowly, smiling, bright and curious, if somewhat creased. It peered at him, waiting.

Neil shook his head, feeling that at any second he might fly apart into thousands of pieces. His eyes burned.

"You were awfully late coming back. I was getting worried. And then I saw you, from the bathroom window, you and your friend in the Edsel."

Neil said nothing, his eyes glued to the bloodstained shirt.

Slowly smiling again, his father pinched the shirt at its most gruesome point. "Food colouring. Silly boy." He held up his sticky hand. "Honey. I got some on your pants."

Neil stared down at him. Then around at the wreckage. "You did all this," he whispered. "All this."

"Just for you."

"I can't believe you ..."

"I'm very resourceful. I thought you knew that."

9

THE MOCK BREAK-IN WAS SO elaborate and such an unqual-
ified success that Neil fully expected to hear it talked about for
weeks, even months. Instead, a puzzling silence reigned on the
subject. Frank did not allow even his wife in on the joke; when she
had queried them about the dent in the lampshade, he'd said only,
"Knocked it, by accident."

The silence was no comfort to Neil. His father's tricks usually
came in clusters. He knew that there would be another before too
long and that he couldn't afford to relax his guard or breathe
too freely. He tried telling himself that the next trick wouldn't
be nearly as big or as convincing as the break-in, but he wasn't
fooled. The silence was just too much. It pointed to deep and
devious plotting.

On the surface, however, his father was more pleasant than
normal to him. The night after the "break-in," Frank brought
home Licorice Allsorts from Eaton's candy department, and, later,
even offered to frame a pair of prints Neil had purchased at the
Exhibition the summer before. They were prints from the Chinese
pavilion: one a moody grey landscape with birds, the other a
sensitive portrait of plum blossoms. At the time, his father had
merely complimented him on his good taste. On their return home
from the fair, though, he invited the neighbours to ooooh and

aaaah over the purchases, and made sure to repeat his compliments in front of them. That night, working on the frames in his workshop, he again praised Neil for his aesthetic sophistication, offering only one small cavil: "Someone with such a good eye should be able to see the beauty of my work. But then you're not a modernist, I guess."

On Friday, Neil rose early. He put on a white shirt and nice slacks, impeccably pressed by his mother, and joined his father and Mr. Hamilton as they climbed into Gus Gordon's car for the commute downtown.

It was a commute the three men had been making for the last ten years, one usually conducted without much in the way of small talk. However, on special occasions, for instance when a guest was along for the ride, the men would be more voluble.

"What are you up to today, Master Neil?" Gus Gordon began. "Off to eye the city girls?"

Neil just laughed. "At ten I go to get my eyes checked."

"Ah, so I was close."

"You don't need perfect eyesight to appreciate city girls, young man." Mr. Hamilton, who sat beside Neil, tapped him on the thigh as he spoke.

"Neil has a crush on Miss Jordan."

Miss Jordan was his father's secretary, a pretty young woman with a gently embracing smile. Neil had been enchanted with her when he was younger.

"Oh, Miss Jordan, is it?" Gus said. "A bit young to have settled on one girl."

"Play the field, play the field," Mr. Hamilton said. "You'll be sorry later."

"What happened to that sweet little redhead we used to see you with?" Gus Gordon asked.

Neil squirmed. Linda King. They had kissed and petted a couple of times, but then Linda, who was a year older, told him she wanted more and promptly unzipped his pants. Neil's response was a loud and nervous *No*, which offended the enterprising girl and caused a permanent rift.

"Oh, she has someone else now, someone older than me."

"They're fickle, that's for sure, very fickle." Mr. Hamilton tapped his thigh again with his thick finger.

"Neil's more interested in Audrey Hepburn than real girls."

"Well, I'm with Neil." Gus said, chuckling at the wheel. "Audrey's a looker."

Neil turned to look out the window. On one side of the expressway was the lake, calm and glistening in the morning sun, on the other, factory buildings and billboards that carried the promise of a wider world. Ahead was the bank tower — the tallest building in the Commonwealth — and his favourite, the Royal York Hotel. He couldn't imagine a more beautiful building than this hotel, which his father once told him was Art Deco style. *Looks like a wedding cake, if you ask me*, his father would say. To Neil it was glamorous and mysterious, the good kind of mysterious. He could easily see Audrey Hepburn staying there. For a few seconds, he pictured himself at the reception desk, formally attired, receiving her in her black evening gown and rhinestone necklace. He would pass her the registration book for her sure-to-be flowing signature, while she removed her dark glasses and one, just one, evening glove. Then, in a low, sweet voice, she would say, *Thank you, Mr. Bennett.*

"Yes sir," Gus Gordon said, "a real looker."

MR. GORDON, WHO worked at the Motor League at Yonge and Adelaide, typically let his passengers off at Bay and Adelaide to make their own way north: Mr. Hamilton to the household appliance department at Eaton's, where he'd been manager for years, and Neil's father to City Hall's real estate division. It was a walk the two men could do in their sleep, but for Neil every step offered something wonderful to consider. The smell of coffee and cigars, the restless clatter of traffic, the sometimes deafening rumble of street repairs, the elegant, polished shape that a street number made on the façade of a building or the ornately lacy way in which grillwork protected a glass doorway.

But it was mostly people that caught his attention. People in their going-to-work wear, moving self-importantly at a great clip or sauntering, tea and bun in hand, as if they had hours to spare. Women in pastel summer dresses and stiletto heels clicking along the already steamy pavement, men in white shirts and dull-coloured suits, looking constrained and often glum. Now and again a man with a bright tie passed, or one wearing a suit the colour of mocha or ivory, and Neil would light up with excitement. There were a few men Neil felt required no extra colour, no special grooming, no finer clothes — they were just so handsome. One of them, a dark-haired man of maybe thirty, wearing a light grey pin-striped suit, actually smiled at Neil as their paths crossed in the middle of Queen Street. When Neil quickly turned his head to catch another glimpse, he found the man turning back to look at him, too. Neil blushed, grateful that his father and Mr. Hamilton were several steps ahead.

When they arrived at City Hall, a sooty pile of late-Victorian confidence, Mr. Hamilton bid them farewell and marched off to Eaton's, tall and very upright. Neil and his father continued their way up Bay, turning right at Albert Street to enter the old building from the north side.

In the damp-stained, blackened archway, his father held a muffled conversation with a couple of uniformed men who apparently knew him well. One of them, the older, never smiled but there was in his face a certain wryness that could have passed for humour. This man checked his watch. His father did, too. Then the younger man, who had stepped out into the street, said, "It's coming."

His father beckoned Neil into the shadows of the archway as a large van pulled in and stopped. Policemen got out. After a very brief conversation of their own with the two men at the entrance, which Neil strained to catch, they unlocked doors at the back and proceeded to unload the van of its human cargo.

"Paddy wagon," his father said in a very low voice.

Neil looked at him, a trace of alarm on his face.

"Watch!"

Neil turned and saw a man step down from the wagon onto the pavement, a loose-limbed, almost clownish-looking man in dirty clothes. He seemed to know what he was doing, though, and without any hesitation moved towards an open door Neil hadn't seen before.

"Court," his father said.

One after another, a sad lineup of men, ten in all, descended and filed dutifully, without fuss, into the building. The men weren't young. They weren't old. Like the first, most were thin, scrawny even, with weather-beaten or maybe drunken-brawl-bashed faces. The eyes were wary, tired, anxious, but not exactly frightened. One of them had a limp. One of them was missing fingers. One of them was very, very well-dressed in evening clothes, tall and almost refined, but without any of Mr. Hamilton's uprightness. A loose, sensual quality to his face, especially his thick-lipped crimson mouth, gave Neil the feeling he was the cruelest one of the bunch.

Only one of them noticed Neil or at least let on he noticed him. He was a painfully thin man with the haunted look of a trapped animal, perhaps a fox. He appeared unwell, maybe feverish. His pale blue eyes were red-rimmed and seemed on the verge of tears. Neil couldn't bear his gaze, which said nothing more than *Who are you and what are you doing here?*

His father stared at the men with a familiar fixity. It was a stare that might seem hard, practical, assessing to others, but

Neil knew it wasn't any of those things. It was a stare of almost ravenous curiosity that transformed the jailbirds into throat-slicing pirates, outlandish plume-hatted highwaymen or maybe Prohibition-era gangsters.

What was almost worse was the smile. On his father's lips quivered a little smile that didn't know quite whether to burst into a maniacal cackling sort of laughter, or to dissolve into inconsolable sadness. It scared Neil, almost as much as his father's mashed face under the nylon stocking had.

The last of the men passed through the doorway into the custody of the city's justice system, and the policemen followed. The archway suddenly felt abandoned. Neil stared at the pavement, almost hopelessly, until he followed his father into the Hall through another doorway and began to climb the marble stairs.

"Why did you want me to see that?" he asked.

"You should see it. You need to understand the world's not Hollywood."

"I know that already."

His father turned a sulky face towards him. "Well, in that case, I won't let you in on things. You can find them out for yourself."

"I felt sorry for them."

It was only as they reached the second-floor landing that his father answered him, muttering, loud enough for Neil to hear clearly, "Poor sons of bitches."

On their arrival at the real estate office, his father immediately set about his tasks for the day. Neil took up his usual post in the corner armchair. Before he could lay his hands on the morning paper lying folded on the capacious oak desk, his father pulled a book from his briefcase and handed it to him. George Bernard Shaw. *Five Plays.*

"You like *My Fair Lady*," he said. "Start with *Pygmalion*."

Neil rolled his eyes at his father's retreating back, but his irritation was short-lived.

The office was coming alive. More and more people were arriving. Phones were ringing, typewriters clicking. He heard a woman say, "He can't meet you today, Mr. Brown. He's had a family emergency. You're to let him know if Thursday at eleven works. He's very sorry." It was Miss Fitzpatrick. Geraldine Fitzpatrick, or Gerry as the senior staff referred to her. Her voice was strong, self-assured. He liked it. He more than liked it. The sounds of his father's office were possibly even more thrilling than the sounds of the city street. The intensity was different, but not any less interesting. Urgency had its place there, too, urgency mixed with intimacy. Everyone who worked in the office seemed to be engaged in the same great mission, a mission to house and protect the city's residents. The sheer effort of this engagement bound them in a relationship of mutual respect and caring, or so Neil imagined.

At one point, his father's boss, Mr. Brown, stuck his head around the corner of the door to wish him good morning and congratulate him on his 88.8 per cent school average. Neil, as always surprised that his father spoke about him to others, thanked him. Miss Jordan appeared, too, with a cup of tea, saying, "I hear you're drinking the grown-up stuff now." As her trim little figure bustled out the door, Neil found himself baffled by his earlier attraction. His father was in and out of the office many times, often in company with a sycophantic junior named David, who Neil thought was more puppy dog than man.

For the most part, though, he was left alone. He followed instructions and read *Pygmalion*, which, as it turned out, he really liked. But he didn't get very far before his father was pushing him to smooth his trousers, tuck in his shirt and follow him to Eaton's.

Making their way through the division and then down the stairs again to the grand foyer of City Hall, they were stopped several times by people who knew or worked with his father. All of them greeted his father warmly, even, in some cases, affectionately. More than once, after his father had introduced him, the acquaintance or colleague would shake Neil's hand and say, "Lucky boy." Neil basked in the good feeling generated by these encounters, but he also felt strangely uneasy, as if he had been caught in a kind of charade.

More than once, he found himself thinking of Tuesday's staged break-in and wondered what his father's fans would think of such a display. Each time, he quickly reminded himself that no one else ever thought these tricks were anything but funny. He pushed the memory of his father splattered in blood-hued food colouring out of his mind and kept up his smile.

By the end of their processional through the Hall — for it seemed as if his dad was royalty — he was more than slightly put out that several of the people they ran into seemed not to recognize him, though they had met him before, more than once even. His father brushed away his irritation. "You can't expect them to remember you from year to year. You've changed quite a bit. Besides they've got a lot more on their minds than you."

Once they got to the department store, Neil felt his father's arm loosely encircle his shoulders. The gesture didn't feel especially protective or comforting, or even, for that matter, proprietary. He didn't understand it. He wasn't a child any longer. He wasn't going to wander off and get lost as he once did. There was no necessity for the gesture, unless his father simply wanted to demonstrate affection. But that consideration only made Neil wrinkle his nose and try to pull away.

His father would have none of it. Keeping Neil close to his side, he smiled at the shop girls as they passed, even spoke to one or two who beamed under his attention. An elegant man with a cane greeted them warmly from one of the side aisles as they neared a bank of elevators, and his father told him, "That's a war wound Mr. Webster has. Got it in France, in '44. The government decorated him for his bravery, you know. He saved half a dozen men in the process of getting wounded. The Bulge was a bloody scene."

Neil had heard all this about Marty Webster before, many times, but he couldn't be annoyed. Mr. Webster's manner was always so kind and friendly. He was fascinating, too, especially the way he carried his injury as if it complemented rather than detracted from the expensive suits and ties he wore. Indeed, his injury always had the aspect of a rather rare and precious accessory that only the most refined of men would dare put on.

"He worked at Eaton's before the war," Neil's father continued, "and they took him back after, injury and all. That's what makes this store great."

The elevator chimed its arrival. The grilled doors, which rattled when the liveried elevator man opened them, struck Neil as very posh. The elevator man, a dark-haired man of probably Mediterranean origins, also seemed to possess a special knowledge of the world which Neil longed to share.

At the sixth floor, Frank released Neil at last, like a dog from a leash. He walked briskly ahead to the reception desk of the optical department, well in advance of his son. "For ten, with Dr. Spiegelman," he was saying as Neil caught up.

The receptionist, an older woman with bright red hair and even brighter red lipstick, said in a very matter-of-fact way, "Have a seat, sir. He'll be with you soon."

"It's for my son."

"Ah, well the same thing applies, sir." The receptionist pointed to the blue leather-clad seats.

"I'll leave you in their care. Spiegelman's the best," he mumbled to Neil. "Twelve o'clock in the book department. You'll have time to look around. Records are on the fifth."

"I know, Dad."

"Good day to you," his father said grimly to the receptionist.

"Good day, sir." Her voice was quite cheerful. She looked at Neil, who smiled, and beckoned him closer with a crooked finger. "You're probably not going to get Dr. Spiegelman today," she said confidentially. "He has to fill in for Dr. Farrow whose wife just passed away, as well as do his own work. You'll be getting the new man, Dr. Brazier. You'll like him."

And when Dr. Brazier, who was a not very tall, yet well-built young man with thinning brown hair and a soft, soft smile, did come, Neil thought he was very likeable.

The exam itself took about forty minutes. When they were done, Dr. Brazier led Neil into another room where he had racks of eyeglasses waiting to be reviewed. Two other optometrists were there, fitting clients with eyewear at small tables dominated by round mirrors that swivelled.

"You're going to need glasses for distance. Not very strong glasses, but they'll help. You sit opposite me and we'll try on a few for size — and style, of course." He smiled.

The table they sat at was very shallow. As the fitting proceeded, Neil could feel Dr. Brazier's knees gently touching his own. He wondered briefly if he should move back in his chair, but thought it might look rude to do so or, even worse, compromising. If Dr. Brazier didn't think it was weird or unusual, why should he?

Neil was also aware, even more acutely than he had been in the examining room, of the lemony scent that the doctor gave off. It was very light, almost not there, like a piece of distant music floating in the wind. Neil thought he had never smelled anything so delicious.

The doctor selected a half dozen glasses for Neil to try on. Instead of handing them to Neil, he placed them on the boy's face himself, his hands brushing Neil's temples. The glasses sat too low on Neil's nose so the doctor frequently removed, readjusted, and reset them, his fingers making contact with Neil's cheeks and brow in the process. Neil made no move to retreat from these little intimacies, and the doctor didn't hesitate at times to let his hands linger at the sides of the boy's head.

Mesmerized by the almost silent process, Neil sat more forward on his chair, and their knees, which had been merely touching, now had to adjust to the greater proximity.

"These tables are very cramped, I'm afraid," Dr. Brazier said.

"It's okay," Neil answered. He was sure he was smiling stupidly.

"Why don't I spread my legs and you put yours between mine."

Holding his breath, Neil did as he was instructed. Dr. Brazier, smiling sweetly, said, "That's better, isn't it?"

Neil nodded.

The doctor smiled again, playfully squeezing Neil's knees between his own. Neil was excited by the amount of heat coming through the man's clothes. The doctor then continued with his fitting experiments for another few minutes, during which he squeezed Neil's knees several times. It might have been accidental, but Neil hoped otherwise.

"I think these tortoise shells look very good on you." The doctor turned the round mirror on the table so that Neil could inspect himself.

Neil was shocked to see his cheeks so red; he hardly took in the glasses.

"They suit you. Classically handsome glasses for a classically handsome boy."

Neil was sure he flushed several shades darker, but couldn't turn his head away. He couldn't stop staring at the doctor, at his pink lips, at his tanned skin with its trace of dark beard-line, at his straight nose, and at the grey eyes, which he suddenly realized weren't grey, but almost violet.

The doctor removed the glasses from the boy's face.

"You have nice eyes," Neil said.

"Do I?" It was Dr. Brazier's turn to colour.

"They're purple."

The doctor quickly scanned the other people in the room trying on glasses. Nobody was listening; they were all too intent on themselves. "You have nice eyes, too, Neil," he said very softly, "nice everything." Smiling, he pressed Neil's knees between his own again very deliberately before pushing his chair back.

Neil fumbled as he stood. He had an erection. The doctor took note and said, "Why don't you stay here a sec? I'll give in the order and be right back."

By the time Brazier returned, Neil was standing and composed. The doctor smiled, scanning his torso. "Everything under control?"

Neil was still too embarrassed to say anything.

Dr. Brazier squeezed Neil's shoulder shoulder and walked him slowly to the reception area. The heat the man gave off was not only confined to his thighs, Neil realized. "We'll see you in a couple of weeks, okay? Here's your appointment card. Just so you don't forget."

"Yes, Doctor. I won't forget."

The soft smile suffused his face again. Leaning into Neil he said, "I look forward to fitting you again."

"Yes, sir." Neil drew back, a fluttery feeling in his chest.

AFTER LUNCH AT Hushy's, the fast and furious corned beef palace on Shuter, his father took him to Diana Sweets, next to Loew's movie theatre opposite Eaton's, for dessert. It was probably Neil's favourite restaurant. They sat on barstools at the counter. His father ordered him an ice-cream sundae topped with warm caramel sauce, which came in an almond-shaped silver bowl. Neil felt strangely shy when the swarthily handsome young waiter placed it in front of him.

"What's the matter?" his father asked. "Something wrong?"

"No, it's wonderful," Neil said. "I love it." He picked up the long silver spoon.

His father didn't seem ready to accept this response. "You seem a bit off."

He denied being "off," but his father wasn't convinced, and over the next half hour, periodically probed his son for clarification. Neil had to dig for answers. He was tired, he was hot, he was overwhelmed by all the treasures the city held out, he was uncertain about the next school year.

Looking at himself and his son in the long mirror behind the counter, Frank Bennett remained suspicious. "Are you sure that's all?"

The problem, of course, was something Neil had no words for. He couldn't stop thinking about his hour with the eye doctor. He'd never experienced anything to compare it with. It wasn't like being with Tony. It wasn't even like any of his fantasies, which nearly always involved long-running love stories. This was something completely different, something immediately physical, where his body made all the decisions, created all the moods. Love and romance didn't have a place there. This longing, so exciting and at the same time so unsettling, had made Hushy's feel like a place he'd known once a long time ago, and even altered Diana Sweets enough to look out-of-focus, as if he were seeing it through a misty window. The doctor's body, warm and lemony under his clothes, was so much more vivid. Growing aroused again, Neil tried to think of something else, anything else.

He stared into the mirror at his father's frowning face.

"Nothing's wrong, Dad."

"Eat your sundae then, before it's soup."

"It was just funny in the eye place, that's all."

"What's funny about it? Spiegelman's one of the best."

"I didn't have Spiegelman. I had a new guy."

"You were supposed to have Spiegelman."

Neil did his best to explain why the good doctor had been unavailable.

"This new guy didn't treat you well?"

"Yes," Neil said. "He was great."

"You're being funny with me."

"I guess I don't want to wear glasses."

"Oh, for heaven's sake! No one wants to wear glasses!"

"I know. Sometimes I think I'm really weird or something."

"Well, you come by that naturally."

Neil laughed, momentarily relieved.

His father pulled a ten-dollar bill from his trouser pocket and passed it to him under the counter, as if it were illicit money. "Get yourself something you want at Sam's."

Neil thanked him and took the bill, but intense feelings of guilt came with it. He wondered what his father would say if he ever found out what had happened in the optical department. Try as he might, he couldn't come up with anything that sounded remotely plausible. If it were his mother, he could come up with lots of words and expressions of shock and horror, but his father's possible reaction eluded him completely.

"You done?" Frank Bennett wiped something from the side of his son's mouth with a finger dabbed in spit. "Caramel," he smiled. "You really love your caramel." He slid off the barstool. "It's been good having you with me today."

Neil rose, too, a bit light-headed, even dizzy. Gripping the counter for support, he glanced in the mirror only to find his father watching him closely. The scrutiny was all too familiar. He was surprised, too, by how similar he and his father suddenly looked.

"Make sure you call me tonight," Frank said. "I'll come get you at the bus stop."

10

IT WAS THE BLAZING EMPTINESS of the streets that decided him. He would walk the fourteen blocks from Sam's to the street-car terminal at Bloor and Yonge. Tucking his new album under his arm, he set off. It was a walk he and Tony had done many times since they'd first met. He felt an urgent need to have Tony with him then, a need that increased with every side street he passed. After his unsettling time with the optometrist, he was sure that Tony would restore balance.

Neil dropped by several stores they both loved. The first, Half-Beat Harold's, was a chaotic bargain record store where he and Tony had both struck gold on the same day in January: a sale copy of the musical *First Impressions* for him and, for Tony, an album of Italian songs containing Mr. Colero's favourite, "Al di Là." Next he paused for a melon drink at the Honeydew Restaurant on Carlton Street, where he and Tony had once been confronted by a scarred and threatening man who demanded their money, insisting he needed morphine. The cramped little curio shop opposite the bank at Wellesley was his final destination. It was always the last place they went after a day of exploring, and it could usually be counted on to produce unexpected things, like the furry little toy monkey for Gio, or the long-sought replacement for one of his flag cards — No. 40, France — which his mother had inadvertently vacuumed up one day.

As Neil neared the terminal at Bloor and Yonge, he remembered the fracas they'd witnessed the past fall, when a heavyset man shouting obscenities roughly escorted a very drunk woman in a tiny black skirt and ropes of fat red beads out of what he kept calling, *My reestorontay*. He could still hear Tony saying in disgust, "Who the hell does he think he's kidding? He's not Italian!!" This memory carried Neil onto the waiting streetcar, and as he took his seat, he told himself that his world was right side up again. Or almost. A whiff of lemon still teased his nostrils.

He arrived at Runnymede a half hour early and checked in immediately at Parma Fruits and Vegetables. Tony was nowhere to be seen. Mrs. Colero, fanning herself with a newspaper at the cash desk but otherwise unfazed by the heat, said, "He's gone on deliveries. Mr. Colero sick." She shook her head as if her husband's illness had been sent to try her. "Nothing we can do. I tell Tony. You come stay with him next weekend?"

"I'm looking forward to it."

"Good, good." She frowned at something over his shoulder.

Neil turned. It was Vicki, arranging Boston lettuces. "Hi, Vicki." She looked up, smiling a knowing smile.

"*La tua roba!*" Mrs. Colero hissed at her.

Vicki inspected the front of her lime-coloured uniform. The top button was undone, revealing a V of tanned skin. She gave a sour little smile. "It won't stay closed. The buttonhole's too big."

Mrs. Colero's smile was only a little less sour. "Try."

Neil said, "See you, Mrs. Colero."

She nodded, but she wasn't looking at him. Vicki was in the process of demonstrating how doing up a button could be as futile a task as anything Sisyphus ever faced.

Very disappointed at not seeing Tony, Neil crossed the street and peered in the window of his aunt and uncle's shoe shop. His uncle was sitting at the back of the store reading *The Globe and Mail*. He appeared to be alone. "To what do we owe this pleasant surprise?" he cried as Neil entered.

"I'm a bit early for work."

His uncle made him sit and hurried into the back room to get them both "ice cold" ginger ales. In his absence, Neil scanned the racks of shoes, neatly arrayed and patiently waiting for the right owners to appear and claim them. *It's so pleasant here*, he thought. *Everything's where it should be. There are no terrible surprises lurking anywhere.*

When his uncle returned, his bald pate shining damply in the mid-afternoon light, he made himself comfortable on a chair facing Neil's.

They smiled at each other. For a minute or so, there was silence in the shop. Sounds from the street pressed against the show window: a honking horn, a pair of children's voices calling, a lonely siren blocks away, a car radio singing, "You were my first love, and you'll be my last love, I will never make you blue," and of course the tireless streetcars making their way to and from the Jane Loop.

Neil wondered how the drivers survived long, hot days like these. He remembered one heavy-set driver last summer constantly wiping his forehead with a white handkerchief, which Tony claimed was as big as a pillow case, and a younger, brasher driver, using a stiff and greasy menu card from The Big Knife Restaurant as a fan. "Food stinks in that place," was Tony's comment.

Overhead the gigantic ceiling fan whipped the air into barely cooling breezes.

Dabbing his upper lip almost daintily with a Kleenex, Uncle Herb turned to the subjects of his California sister's upcoming visit — about which he appeared to be as excited as Neil's mother — and the fact that Neil wasn't going to be attending the family reunion planned for Lake Joseph.

"My dad says I've got to work if I want spending money this fall."

Herb shook his head. "Well, it's a pity. You'll be sorely missed. Sylvia will have her work cut out to make us overlook your absence."

Neil grinned at his uncle's way with words.

"And what is your father up to these days?"

Neil hesitated then. Scrambling for something to say, he told him about the new painting, the Pollock, not hiding his dismay.

Herb sat back in his chair. "What next! First the clarinet, then the piano, then furniture. And photography — I almost forgot that damn camera of his. He's a talented man, your father. Always has been. I suspect you'll take after him. Not exactly, of course. You've got our side of the family mixed in there."

They smiled at each other again, Neil cherishing the feeling of sharing the Deekman blood. "I'm glad of that, Uncle Herb." Still smiling, he stood. "I should get going, though. I start in ten minutes." He placed his ginger ale bottle on a shoe rack next to two very daring stilettos, one bright pink, the other turquoise blue.

His uncle led him to the door, on which swirling black letters advertised *Runnymede Shoes*. "What've you got in that Sam's bag? Another musical, I'll bet."

"*The Unsinkable Molly Brown*." Neil felt instantly apologetic. "Nobody knows it here."

"She's the woman who survived the *Titanic*?" Herb closed his large grey Deekman eyes, so like Neil's mother's, and then softly began to hum the opening number of the show, a song called "I Ain't Down Yet!," breaking into words after a few bars: "I'm gonna move from place to place, and find a house with a golden stair ..."

Neil was wide-eyed. "You do know it!"

"We keep up, my boy! We keep up." Herb laughed to see his nephew's incredulity, but immediately after, taking him by the arm, he said very softly, "Your dad's one of those men who's got energy to burn. A lot was expected of him when he was young. Too much, I think. He made things to let off steam. Right now it happens to be big modern paintings. He could be doing worse, you know. A lot worse."

They stepped onto the blazing street.

"Summer in Toronto," Herb moaned, as his hand took possession of the boy's shoulder. "Look, Neil, if you ever want to talk to me about anything ... I never had a son of my own. It would be a pleasure to listen. A pleasure. Believe me. Your Aunt Violet, too, of course, she'd do anything for you."

Neil shook his uncle's hand and turned to go.

"Neil! Neil!"

He looked back.

His uncle, face suddenly very animated, was pointing along the street in the direction Neil was taking, pointing with quick jabs of the finger above Neil's head.

Neil looked up. It took him a few seconds to catch on but then he saw it, the marquee over the Runnymede Cinema: *Elvis Presley — Blue Hawaii*, it said, and underneath, the magical words, *Audrey Hepburn — Breakfast at Tiffany's.*

FOR BREAK THAT evening, Miss Fairfield's wicked sweet tooth contrived to lay on generous slices of chocolate-iced tea cake. She claimed they were meant to honour Miss Boughton's recent departure for the Alps, but the cake soon had her wandering among memories of her own Swiss travels, which Neil found not only entertaining but also mildly instructive. "When the timetable says you can expect a tram at 8:09, then at 8:09 it's there, and you had better be there, too." Miss Fairfield shook her head fussily. "8:09 and ten seconds just doesn't measure up."

Emerging from the tea room an outlandish twenty minutes

later, Miss Fairfield told him to take the circulation desk so that Mrs. Negulescu might have a chance to finish the overdue notices. Neil was only too happy to oblige. He spent the first ten minutes putting order into the titles on the book truck so that shelving them later would be a lot easier, while Miss Fairfield nodded from her desk in the centre of the floor, fondly but deferentially turning the pages of the *Times Literary Review*.

After a few minutes of tidying and organizing, Neil suddenly had the sense that someone other than Miss Fairfield was watching him. With an all-too-familiar sensation of rising alarm, he looked around, fully expecting to see Rob Neville of Durie Street. Instead his gaze met the bread-man's.

Neil was so taken aback he almost jumped. He did jump inside. The bread-man obviously knew this because he laughed. His whole face seemed to laugh and he winked before returning to his reading.

Bread-man was seated at the long table beyond the foreign language section, just out of spying reach, which meant that Neil couldn't quite make out the name of the book he was reading. It was large format. Probably an art book. Perhaps sensing his curiosity, the bread-man lifted his smiling eyes again and held the book up for Neil to inspect. *Paul Gauguin*, said the title, a sea-blue scrawl above a painting of brown women on a beach.

Miss Fairfield coughed slightly and, smiling, beckoned him over. "Do you want to go and speak with your friend?" she asked. "I can take the desk."

"It's okay, Miss Fairfield, it's not a friend. Well, I mean, it's our bread-man."

"Oh, your bread-man. I see. A bread-man with a taste for Paul Gauguin. And why not?"

All of this was said in whispers.

Neil returned to the circulation desk where, fortunately, two or three people had gathered to check out books, and he was spared the necessity of looking at Bread-man for a few minutes.

But when next he lifted his head, Bread-man was right in front of him. "How about a library card?"

Neil said, "Sure, sure."

Bread-man smiled warmly, as if to say, *You're very accommodating.*

Neil fumbled for the form. "We just need to fill this in, and then we can type you up a temporary card."

"I'm all yours. What do you want to know?" Bread-man leaned forward, smiling. He was wearing a T-shirt, pinkish-orange in colour, and very tight, narrow-legged, tan trousers. That night his hair was more golden than brown.

"Name?"

"You want me to write it? Your hand is shaking." Bread-man took the pen from him and began to fill in the blanks.

> **Name:** Jack Rookwood
> **Address:** 25 Baby Point Rd., Toronto
> **Phone:** RO-7-3224
> **Birthday:** May 13, 1941

Neil read it all upside down. Before he could stop himself he said, "I'm born on the thirteenth, too."

Bread-man handed him the form, smiling. "That's lucky for both of us. May 13?"

"No, September."

"Oh, the Virgin."

Neil's face broke out in an embarrassed grin.

"No aspersions meant. You're born in the sign of Virgo, the Virgin. I'm Taurus the Bull. That's why I put things so bluntly. I'm the bull in the china shop."

Miss Fairfield joined them at the desk. "I'll type the card, if you like."

"I didn't ask for ID, Miss Fairfield."

"That's okay. You'll vouch for him." She laughed.

Bread-man returned her laugh. Then, turning to Neil, he said in a funny library whisper, "I'll sit over there with Paul until it's ready, okay?"

Neil's only thought was, *Everything's okay now.*

But Miss Fairfield took such a long while with the card Neil began to worry that Bread-man might get impatient and just leave. He couldn't abandon the desk to assure him it wouldn't be much longer, though, because he had a stream of people wanting to take out books. Luckily, Bread-man was occupied with another book, not a big book this time, not an art book, but something looking more like a foreign language book. He didn't seem to mind the wait.

Miss Fairfield emerged from the back office, Bread-man's card in hand, just as Neil finally managed to make the shriveled Mr. Hosiak understand that his book couldn't be renewed another time because someone else was waiting for it. But at that very same moment, a voice accosted him.

"I don't suppose you've ever heard of John Osborne, have you?"

It was Rob Neville, leaning against the desk with a sneer of a smile disfiguring his face.

"In the play section. We have *Look Back in Anger* and *The Entertainer.* 822 O."

"Can you tell me what they're about?"

"*Look Back in Anger*'s about a young man who hates the system and *The Entertainer*'s about a has-been performer."

"Right out of a third-rate newspaper review. You haven't read them, have you? Of course not." Rob Neville slouched away to the 822s, which were shelved with all the literature books in a smaller room off the main part of the library, a room Neil had always found cozy and charming.

He realized Bread-man was watching him again. This time his gaze wasn't a smiling one, not even close. He wondered if Bread-man thought he was as stupid and unread as Neville did.

"What was that about?" Miss Fairfield asked, staring into the literature room.

"I don't know," said Neil honestly. "He doesn't think I know very much."

"Is that so?" Miss Fairfield made a tiny grimace. "Well, we know better, don't we?" With those words, she casually strolled towards the play section.

Neville needed no help from her, however. As she approached, he turned and looked her up and down with an expression bordering on derision that was so outlandish it was almost funny. He put two thin volumes under his arm, strode back to the circulation desk, and tossed them in front of Neil.

"Okay, bookkeeper, do your best."

"Where's your card?"

Neville tossed him the card. Pointedly looking away, he leaned once more against the desk. "I can't imagine what it's like to go through life with so little curiosity."

Neil made no answer.

Loudly enough that everyone could hear, Neville said, "You're just taking up space."

"That's enough, sir. There are others trying to read." Miss Fairfield looked suddenly six feet tall.

"Sorry, ma'am. Your employees need a little more education, I fear."

"You'll have to go now, sir." Miss Fairfield moved quickly out from behind the circulation desk, as if she would take him by the arm and escort him to the door.

"Don't worry, I'm going, ma'am. I've had enough ignorance for one night."

"My turn." It was Bread-man at the desk now, with two books, the one about Paul Gauguin and the other, a book in French, *Oeuvres completes v.1*, by Jean Genet. He was smiling again, but his eyes were not.

Neil did his duty quickly, hardly daring to look at his borrower. Bread-man was gone with a "See you soon."

Miss Fairfield stayed at his side. "My dear, you go back and get your things together. Wash your hands, take a biscuit, ask Mrs. Negulescu to come out. And then you go. All right?"

"I'm okay, Miss Fairfield."

"Indeed you are, but do as I say. It's almost closing time anyway. One of the chocolate wafers might hit the spot."

<hr />

NEIL WALKED VERY quickly along the street towards the Jane Loop, thinking he might just make the earlier bus and hoping against hope that the last half hour's embarrassment hadn't entirely disgraced him in Bread-man's eyes. He passed Parma Fruits and Vegetables, now dark. On the other side of the street, the shoe store was dark, too, but in the window above the shop glowed a warm amber light. His uncle was probably reading, his Aunt Violet mending.

As he passed Durie Street, he noticed two figures in the doorway of another darkened shop, two figures obviously engaged in some kind of dispute. He looked for an avenue of escape across the street. Streetcars were coming from both directions, leaving him no option but to stay where he was. He moved to the very edge of the sidewalk and quickened his pace.

As he passed, he heard a familiar voice speaking in a low, angry tone, "If my pupils were as dilated as yours, man, I wouldn't be making a public scene. The next time the police might be called."

"Leave me alone." The other voice was trying to sound firm, but came out pathetic instead.

"Leave you alone? Gladly. If you'll do the same for others."

"Fuck off!"

"What was that?"

"I can yell."

"Good for you. I don't mind calling the cops."

The figure with his back against the shop door suddenly broke free. His opponent made no effort to stop him, but did gracefully offer his foot as a small obstacle. Rob Neville of 255 Durie Street landed with an inglorious splat, face down on the sidewalk, accompanied by a double dose of John Osborne.

Neil hurried on, heart pounding, but the sound of someone running behind him and then a strong hand grasping his shoulder told him it wasn't finished.

"I like that," Bread-man said. "I do the gallant knight for you, my sweetie, and you run off. That's not the way it usually goes." Bread-man's hand lingered on his shoulder.

Neil felt foolish, hardly knowing how to answer his rescuer. "He scares me. I never did anything to him. I don't know why he's like that."

They stood facing each other under a street lamp. Bread-man's eyes were no longer angry. "He thinks he's a hot shot, that's all. Some guys are like that. Born to be kings — so they think. Especially when they're high on drugs. I'm not sure what he's taking. He's very edgy. Maybe coke. Cocaine."

"How can you tell?" Neil was more than surprised by Bread-man's information.

"I've seen it before. Next time get your librarian to call the cops. If there is a next time. He's scared, too. More than you probably. Where you going? The fabulous Loop?"

Neil nodded.

"I'll walk with you, Neil, if that's okay."

"How do you know my name?"

"Mrs. Gordon, of course. I happened to mention you. She went on for ten minutes almost, saying how smart and sensitive and everything you were. She told me you worked at the library and as it's kind of my local library I thought I'd pay it a visit. There's so little to do here these hot summer nights, you know, a library looks good. Now I've got something to read. As well as the chance to talk to you again."

Neil thanked him shyly.

They were quiet as they crossed at the light.

In front of the funeral home, Bread-man said, "Don't worry about what happened. I wouldn't even have known who John Osborne was."

Neil smiled, scrutinizing his companion.

Bread-man winked. "Have I got chocolate on my face?"

"Chocolate?" Uncertain where to look, Neil glanced away.

Pointing to a small dark spot on his cheek, Bread-man leaned in and whispered, "I hear it's called a beauty mark, but ask anybody who knows me and they'll say it can't be, it must be the Mark of Satan."

Neil looked momentarily shocked. "Mark of Satan?"

"But, of course, you don't know me, so you can call it a beauty mark, if you want. Though you could get in a lot of trouble discussing my beauty mark with others. It's not something boys do, you know."

Neil's face burned.

Bread-man continued, "However, if I see something I find beautiful, I talk about it, no matter what its source. A beautiful boy — or man — is as worth talking about as a beautiful woman. Get my drift?"

"Yes." Neil hesitated, uncertain whether he should call him by name.

"You know my name."

"Jack," Neil responded.

"It's short for — can you guess?"

"Jack-in-the-box?"

"Smart ass. No. John. John Henry Rookwood. Name of …?"

"I don't know."

"Cardinal Newman. The famous Cardinal Newman."

"You're Catholic?"

"To the hilt. I'm the great John Henry. My two brothers are Lawrence Augustine and Bernard Ignatius. These names give us a shortcut to Heaven, you know. No waiting time for us. Rook-wood, too, is an old Catholic name. English Catholic. The best kind of Catholic, as my dear pater keeps telling us. Larry and Bernie, or Gussie and Iggy, as I'm prone to call them, seem to think he's right. Me, I haven't been to Mass for I don't know how many years."

"We're Presbyterian," Neil said.

"That's too bad," Jack laughed.

"It's all right. I go to church with my mother sometimes. She likes it when I do. My father won't go."

"Ah," Jack said, "you're a good boy then."

"No!" Neil protested.

"It's all right if you are. Good boys are usually the wildest. At least, that's what I've found."

With a definite swallow, Neil could only stare.

"Good boys contemplate things that terrify so-called bad boys, like your buddy back there. Cowards by comparison."

Neil's stare turned into a gape.

"You, however, you play with fire. You'll have them falling at your feet."

The notion struck Neil as so preposterous, he guffawed. "Who's 'them'?"

Jack offered him a cryptic smile.

By then, they'd reached the Loop, twinkling under the trian-gular *Fresh Up with 7-Up* neon that dominated the roof of the neighbouring building.

Jack said, "You know you got me thinking about this place. There's excitement in the air here, isn't there? Expectation. Hope. That's why you like it, I bet. Me, too. A thoroughly invigorating place."

They both turned to watch a downtown streetcar filling up with passengers.

Jack said, "We're not the only ones looking for a bit of excitement, eh?"

Neil could see his bus waiting beyond.

"You're a Rayside man, are you?" Jack said, referring to the bus's destination. "Rayside sounds like California. Surfer land. Blond boys with tans." He winked.

"I'd better get it," Neil said. Though he wanted to, he couldn't bring himself to touch Jack. "Thank you so much. I really appreciate everything —"

Jack Rookwood raised his hand. His fingers just an inch or two from Neil's lips, he shook his head. "Not necessary. I did what I had to."

Then, backing up, his eyes very soft, he said, "We'll see you very soon, I hope." With these words, he began to run, a graceful loping sort of run, which his body seemed perfectly designed to execute.

ALL THE WAY home, Neil hardly knew what to feel, there were so many feelings. Excitement, of course. And pride. Someone had seen fit to fight for him. There was wonder as well. Jack Rookwood was really smart, really worldly, really "cool," as Tony or Rick would say. He thought about real things like drug-taking and the Loop. Neil admired that. It made Jack seem somehow more in touch. Without that, his looks would have put him wildly out of reach, into some kind of mythic zone. He had never met anyone so attractive, Neil was sure of that. Dr. Brazier was just a pale imitation, not even, a vague ghost of a good-looking man, next to Jack, whose eyes alone had Neil feeling almost girlish with longing. He could hear Lana Gordon saying, *Dreamboat!* and he knew just how she felt. Add to the eyes, the mouth, shoulders, hips, thighs, all perfect, and Neil began to feel helplessly excited.

So immersed was he in these feelings that, as the bus pulled into the stop, Neil realized he had once again failed to arrange for his dad to accompany him home. It was a tense moment as he stood alone at the top of Avery Street. But the words, *Think Jack*, came to him almost as if they'd been spoken. He began his descent, and at Greenland Road, noticed there were stars in the sky. This only added to his resolve. He walked on, feeling close to carefree.

But at Stanton Avenue, his luck ran out. Archie Ross appeared, walking towards him along Stanton, a baseball bat over his shoulder and a glove dangling from his hand. He must have been at the diamond in Greenland Park.

"Hey, little 'mo!"

Archie was still far enough away that Neil figured he could cross Stanton without interference, and then break into a run that might catch his tormentor by surprise. But even as the strategy was forming in Neil's head Archie had shortened the distance between them and was running himself.

Neil managed to get almost as far as the Doyles' before Archie nabbed him. Poking him in the back with the bat, Archie taunted, "Aren't you glad to see me? I know I'm glad to see you, little 'mo. I like to see little 'mos wiggle and squirm." He continued to poke, lowering the bat so it was now against Neil's buttocks and then between his legs, preventing him from moving without a tumble. Then Archie was on top of him, face-to-face. "How 'bout we take a little walk down to the railway yards. Lotsa space there. We can duke it out in peace and quiet. I'll even give you the bat. Whadd'ya say?"

Neil couldn't form an answer.

"No? You don't like that idea? You got a better one?"

Neil made a move, but Archie blocked him.

"Come on, ya little 'mo, we'll just head down Stanton and then right for the yards. You make any noise or complaint as we go, and I'll have some of my buddies take care of you. They won't be as generous as me. Or maybe I'll call the cops. 'Mos are against the law, ya know. I can tell them you propositioned me. They could lock you up. Know what I mean?"

"Archie!"

A voice, low but stern, sounded behind them.

Both Archie and Neil turned. By the side of the road lounged the Edsel, headlights off. Neither of them had heard it pull up.

"Hey, Jim ol' man, look what I found." Archie began pulling Neil towards the car.

"Get in! You! Not the kid."

Archie immediately let go of his prize. His round face took on a dazed, disbelieving expression.

"You!" the voice repeated. "I want to talk to you."

Archie looked worried now.

"You get home, kid," said the driver less sharply.

Neil slowly backed up, rubbing his arm. He could feel Edsel-man's eyes watching him with something like concern — or was he just imagining it?

Archie hadn't even closed the door before the car took off, its taillights flashing like rubies in the darkness. Neil squinted after it, a wave of dazed relief washing over him.

He could scarcely credit his luck: twice in one night, someone had stepped in to protect him. The feeling of being protected was such a strange one he almost couldn't believe it, but it was a welcome strange. His protectors were so different, too. One so gallantly romantic, the other so rough, but also kind in his way. Neil started walking again, wondering to what or to whom he owed his good fortune. He briefly considered praying or offering some kind of thanks for his deliverance.

When he was directly in front of the Doyle house, he saw the screen door was open and heard classical music trilling in the background like a nightingale. Mrs. Doyle was outside in an old apron with torn pockets, trowel in hand. Neil realized the flower boxes were back, and below them, in the shadows of the porch railings, were small green containers of flowers, probably pansies, maybe petunias. He couldn't see clearly.

"David!" she called. Her voice was high but raspy. "David! Get out here and help me!"

Davy appeared at the door. Immediately spying Neil, he bent down to pick up a small box of pansies without a word of greeting.

On the porch of his parents' house, Neil paused a second, wondering what could have made the Doyles so miserable. The break-in wasn't responsible — they were like this before. The break-in was more like the reflection in a mirror. What had happened to them? Was it recent, or long ago? Maybe it was the father, who'd always, as far as Neil remembered, been absent. But then, absent fathers weren't always a bad thing, were they?

His parents were watching TV, something loud with a laugh track and squawking voices. There was an empty glass in front of his father, who lounged as usual on the couch, feet on the coffee table. His mother's back was to him in the gold-striped armchair. Only her fair hair was visible in the dim light of the room.

He hovered.

A cat food commercial came on.

His father shifted uncomfortably, said something about "bloody reruns."

His mother answered inaudibly.

Still peevish, his father said something else, about "Julie not coming with Sylvia." Perhaps the cat had reminded him of Aunt Julie's beloved Mamie.

His mother's head turned. Though her back was to him, Neil knew her expression would be wearily impatient. He couldn't make out the first part of her response, but the last was clear enough: "At least she's happy doing what she's doing."

His father answered sulkily, "Who says I'm not happy?"

Just like the Doyles, he thought. Conversations repeating themselves over and over without the slightest variation. Ever.

As he reached for the door handle, he muttered a little prayer. "Don't let me get like this. Please." An image of a red and white Edsel, its taillights flashing, floated up to reassure him.

He opened the door.

His mother turned in her chair, smiling. "Hello, dear. There's some cheese and crackers in the fridge for you. Some green grapes, too, they're lovely. And plums. The little yellow ones. Ontario plums."

His father looked up at him over his glasses and said, "I won't be offering again. If the effort to call me is too much to manage, then you'll have to take what's coming to you."

11

JULY ONLY GOT HOTTER. BURNING days of white skies, silent trees and lawns festooned with sprinklers gave way to relentlessly still nights, heavy with heat. Neil's parents, whose bedrooms occupied opposite sides of the upstairs hall, were so uncomfortable they left their doors open, hopeful of a little cross draught. Several nights they sat till well after bedtime on the back patio with the Gordons, convinced that sleep would be impossible inside.

The Knights left for two weeks' vacation on Saturday morning, exclaiming how glad they were to escape the city. Several other families followed their lead, including the Chards, the Nearys, and the Hamiltons, who knew people with a cottage in Haliburton.

The streets gradually acquired a tomb-like atmosphere, which Neil found somewhat weird, but also fascinating. Charged with watering both the Knights' and the Hamiltons' gardens, he day-dreamed his duties away imagining an end-of-the-world scenario in which, day by day, his little corner of suburbia turned into a ghost town. As the lone survivor, he scrounged for food in the nearly empty cupboards of his former neighbours, until finally, at the very brink of starvation, a champion appeared and took him away. Mostly the champions were unknown to him, though they frequently resembled one of the free-spirited young men on his pin-up board.

At night, the daydreaming was replaced by restless, straining fantasy where the rescuing champion, now more than just a hero, showed up as Dr. Brazier (once), Jim of Edsel fame (three times) and, of course, the bread-man, Jack Rookwood (six or seven times). In the morning light, the fantasies didn't vanish. He woke each time trying to imagine how in the world he could make them real. Friday's encounters had left him with an ache, a longing, unmistakable in its direction, forcing him to admit what he had never fully admitted before: he had what they called "unnatural" feelings for men. He wanted them the way he was supposed to want girls, the passionately, indivisibly, till-death-do-us-part way. He wanted them body and soul.

Accompanying these feelings was a deep, unsettling fear for his own future. He tried to find a place for them in the world of his parents, neighbours, school friends, and over and over he failed miserably. Try as he might he couldn't see anybody accepting them, except perhaps Miss Fairfield who had seen so much of the world, and Mona Gordon, who so openly loved him, but even of them he couldn't be sure. Tony might accept them, of course, but only if they were never clearly defined, if they remained always in the realms of maybe and innuendo. There was a good chance he told himself that he could end up alone, and, worse, lonely.

The heat, the silent streets, and the nagging doubt combined to make Neil irritable, something he rarely allowed himself to be — at least in the family home, where his father tolerated nobody's moodiness but his own. His parents noticed it, but put it down to the oppressive humidity. Everybody was cranky, they said, even themselves.

His father tried rallying him at least twice a day with some variation on the theme, *Your Aunt Sylvia will be here on Thursday*, but this only further irritated Neil, to the point that on Monday night, as his father spun the tenth or eleventh variation, Neil replied, "You're making me wish she'd do us all a favour and stay home."

"You don't mean that," said his mother as she ironed her good white damask tablecloth for the special Thursday night supper.

"You deserve a cuff on the head!" His father half-rose from his chair.

"Frank, leave him be. Just get on with your slides." His father was preparing a slideshow of his photographs in honour of Sylvia's visit, photos no doubt of Val and him growing up.

"No, of course, I don't mean it," Neil griped. He continued buffing the silver plate place settings.

And he didn't mean it. He was thrilled that Aunt Sylvia was coming, in part because his mother looked happier than she had in years. In spite of the heat, she smiled a lot and even demonstrated her affection for him by stroking his hair or his cheek, and once or twice hugging him around the shoulders.

She even kissed his father a few times, a quick peck on the cheek, but still, they were appreciated, provoking a fond, if silly, response: "Ah, Momma's sweet on me! You see how Momma's sweet on me!" Such sentiment would normally produce nothing more than a slight frown or grimace from "Momma," but during these days of anticipation, she laughed and tapped him on the head as she might an adoring child.

Another part of Neil's pleasure was rooted in the hope that, because Aunt Sylvia lived in Los Angeles near Hollywood — he wasn't exactly sure how close Wilshire and Fairfax Boulevards were to Hollywood, but close enough, he imagined — she would have a more "artistic" perspective on the world and the people in it. After all, it was there that movies like *Long Beach* and *Cherry Ripe* and *Boys of the Sun* were made, and young actors with blond curls, tans and puffy lips got jobs. She might know someone with feelings like his, a friend even ...

He often remembered the afternoon when, at six, he had stood on the porch of his parents' new home bidding goodbye to Aunt

Sylvia and Aunt Julie, and Aunt Sylvia had turned to him, tears in her eyes, to say, "I'll get Hollywood ready for you, Neil."

His father had guffawed, "*Looney Tunes* could use another looney!"

Sylvia then fixed her brother-in-law with bright eyes. "I was thinking more of Paramount Pictures. You can have *Looney Tunes*, if you want."

It was with his aunt's arrival in mind that Neil put on *The Unsinkable Molly Brown* and, in the cool of his basement suite, contemplated redesigning his pin-up-board. By then, he had played the story of the wild girl who rose from incredible rags in the Colorado mountains to incredible riches in the salons of Europe so many times that his mother was now constantly humming "I Ain't Down Yet" or "Chick-a-Pen" or "Dolce Far Niente" as she scrubbed and cleaned.

His father didn't find it quite so infectious. Catching scraps of it from his workshop next door, he would barge into Neil's room every so often to offer comments like, "Sounds like circus music! Rom-tom-tom, rom-tom-tom!" or "Where did that girl learn to sing?" or "If that's the same guy who wrote *The Music Man*, he's sure in serious decline."

To each of these Neil would answer, "I don't care. I find it inspiring."

And he did find it inspiring. Just the idea that things could so dramatically change for the better calmed him during those prickly hot days — and not only calmed him. That Monday evening, as he hesitated in front of his collage with a paralyzingly critical eye, it spurred him to create.

The Colombia, Sweden and Turkey flag cards were replaced with Burma, Venezuela and Canada. He didn't actually like the Canada card because it just showed the usual Mounties on horses, but he thought it would be an appropriate welcoming gesture. Burma was very romantic with its mountains and elephants and

Venezuela had a tanned diver in a red swimsuit, which would surely remind her of California. Audrey as Holly Golightly he left in the centre, and around that he pinned pictures of her in *Roman Holiday*, *War and Peace*, *Funny Face*, and *The Children's Hour*. Bernardo disappeared, as did all the boys in their questionable movies — all except his current favourite, an Italian-looking man in sunglasses and tight jeans staring out to sea from a rocky promontory under the title, *Foam*. He looked like an adventurer, a warrior, a lookout, awaiting the arrival of enemy ships or maybe treasure boats. He was sure his aunt would find him appealing. She always liked what she called "spunky" people — at least, that was the reputation she had. To this assemblage, he added a long paper bookmark she had once given him with the flag and crest of California on it, as well as two postcards of Hawaii, which Aunt Julia had sent as a token of their trip a year ago.

He stood back and admired his handiwork. It was beautiful. He had to admit it. And yet, as he smiled to himself, he had a strong sense that something was missing. He couldn't say what it was. Something that had been there before? Bernardo? Colombia? Or, something that had never been there, never even been thought of until this past week or so? Something belonging to his real life, to himself and his longings?

Neil was suddenly unhappy. He wanted to quickly undo what he had done, but his alarm clock said ten after midnight. It was too late for another round of *Molly Brown*. He sighed, giving the board one last hard stare, and then slowly began to unbutton his shirt.

———

THAT NIGHT HE again dreamt he was in a large room, dimly lit and hung with draperies, wide draperies that billowed in response to some kind of wind. The draperies were all dark red, almost black, and as they billowed sections of wall and doorway and window came into view. Whitish in colour they were, a yellowish-white and very old. It was a grand room, he thought, maybe a ballroom. As if to confirm his impression, there were suddenly several lopsided chandeliers swaying from the ceiling — black, wrought iron chandeliers, encrusted with old white candle wax. The billowing curtains were making him dizzy and he tried several times to get to a doorway, but he kept losing his bearings and had to regroup. He awoke beating at the flapping drapes.

He was sweating. It was twenty after six. Warm light glowed on the other side of his curtains. Down the street came the shrill chatter of the Italian women who worked in the little factories next to the railway yards. One of them was laughing. He peeked out from behind the curtain and through the bushes could see them passing, most of them very small, rotund women dressed in black like mourners. They were moving very slowly, and a couple of them waved straw fans. It was going to be another hot one.

He fell back on his bed. Closing his eyes, he saw the dream room again. It was a familiar room, he knew that, but at first he couldn't place it. When he was a boy, his father had taken him to see several big empty houses the city was considering buying, houses that had once been splendid affairs staffed by many servants, but had long since fallen into sad, even tragic — his father's word — disrepair. He imagined the dream house must be one of these. The chandeliers had definitely been a feature of one of those mansions because he remembered his father telling him how many little bulbs chandeliers usually contained. He couldn't remember the exact figure but it was over fifty, way over fifty.

God, it was hot. He slipped out of his pyjamas and turned onto his side to face the wardrobe his father had made him. The bronze-coloured curtain that hid his clothes looked hot, too. He reached out with his foot to prod it, almost peevishly.

It was then that he realized where he had seen the dream room before. He turned onto his back, marvelling at the strangeness of it: two dreams in one week where big curtains disguised an old room. Why the room needed disguising — or maybe it was protecting — he couldn't figure out, nor why the curtains had changed colour. But before he could come up with any explanations, sleep claimed him and this time took him to places peopled by sweaty adventurers.

WHEN HE FINALLY made it upstairs for breakfast, his mother had a large fan blowing in the living room and another smaller one in the kitchen. She was sweating as she laboured on her hands and knees, dabbing at stains in the dining room carpet with a special potion.

"Ninety-eight today," she said rising onto her knees and smiling. "Thunderstorms tonight. I hope it cools down for Sylvia."

"Anything you want me to do?"

"Eat your breakfast, then you can dust Val's room for me. There are a couple of postcards for you."

He went into the kitchen. Three cards were sitting by his cereal bowl.

The first, a picture of Graumann's Chinese Theatre in Hollywood, came from Aunt Julia, saying how sorry she was not to be coming this year, and that she wished him well with his summer job.

The second, sent by his friend Rick, showed an island in the middle of a turquoise sea. On the back in a large navy scrawl were the words, *This is paradise. You and Tony have got to see it. Unbelievable. Nothing to do but swim and eat and talk to the girls.* Reading the tiny print, he learned that the island pictured was Mykonos.

And the third was from Val, a view of Windy Pines Lodge basking in an autumnal light. It went: *Uncle Pete is a really sweet man, so helpful and kind. Everything else is as I said it would be. Love, your sister, V. P.S. One of the chambermaids is named Lucy Colero. Any relation?*

Neil tucked the cards between the spoon jar and a little vase overflowing with fragrant white roses his mother had recently culled from the garden. Neil inhaled them deeply before reaching for his prune juice.

A staccato knock at the back door followed, accompanied by a sharp, clear, "Nora? Nora?" Mona Gordon appeared at the head of the back stairs, flushed in a loose pink shirt and powder blue pedal pushers. Catching sight of Neil, she said, "Oh, there's the boy!"

"I'm in the dining room, Mona," his mother called.

Mona seemed to hesitate before speaking, something she rarely did. "There's been another break-in. Sam Caldwell's place."

His mother rose again onto her knees, the sweat dripping from her brow.

"Like the Doyles. A regular rampage. Upstairs and down. Lydia West says it's worse than the Doyles."

"Was it the same people?" Neil asked.

"Well, nobody's been caught, but it sure looks like it. Whoever it was coated the broadloom in shellac. That's what the officer said."

"I can't believe it," Nora groaned.

"What's more, all five of his cats are gone. The vandals obviously let them out, then turned the kitty litters upside down in his bathtub and sinks, and you know what else? They gashed the upholstery on all the sofas and chairs, and the mattress, too, and tore the pillows open — the whole upstairs was floating in feathers. It's probably the first time I've ever had any sympathy for the man," Mona said.

There were plenty of stories about Mr. Caldwell. He was a widower of fifty-three who many believed had driven his quiet young wife to her early death. A stern man with an unmoving countenance, he was often seen sitting on his porch of a summer's evening wearing dark glasses and barking orders at a youngish man in overalls who came to do the gardening for him. People speculated that he lived somewhere else in the winter, as the house appeared unlit through the long cold nights, though some claimed he was there all the time, soaking up the darkness. Along with the numerous cats, of whom he was most possessive, Caldwell was also the master of a pair of large, ferocious dogs. Ask anybody and they would say that he only kept the animals to exercise his capacities for torture, as he had once done his wife.

"He has lots of enemies," Neil said. "Just like Mrs. Doyle."

"Everyone has enemies," his mother said, slowly rising to her feet.

"But Neil's right, Nora. Some have more than others."

"So the police are looking for someone who knew both Mrs. Doyle and Mr. Caldwell," he said. "They'll just have to compare lists of acquaintances, don't you think? Then they'll know."

"What a brilliant idea," Mona said. "Next thing we know you'll be working as a private eye."

Neil smiled, pleased at the idea.

Nora Bennett moved past her son into the kitchen as if she were carrying a great weight.

"Don't worry, Mom. It's all right." Neil was concerned now that her excitement over her sister's visit had evaporated.

"We could be next," she said.

"Nobody hates us, though."

"He has a point there," Mona said.

His mother's gaze, sad and tired, surveyed her kitchen as if she were seeing it in ruins. "What's happened? We used to be so safe."

JUST PAST NOON, Neil was wiping down the window sills and frames in Val's room — which was to become Aunt Sylvia's headquarters for the next three weeks — and simultaneously trying to devise a plan for getting inside Mr. Caldwell's ruined house, when he spotted Bread-man making his way up the Gordons' driveway.

He almost ran to the back door, damp cloth still in hand.

"Hey there," Bread-man smiled, holding out the brown loaf.

Neil took it awkwardly.

"Things okay at the library?"

"No sign of him at all."

"I don't think he'll bother you again."

"Do you like your books?"

"Gauguin is a real laugh! Wow, talk about the slippery slope! You know his paintings?"

"One or two, I guess. The one with the long title. My dad loves him."

"Is he into morphine, too?"

"My dad?"

"Or booze? Or sex with young girls?"

Neil looked at him, startled. "My dad thinks he's a painter."

"You don't?"

"I guess so. I mean, I don't know ..." He made a little face. "What about the French book? You read French?" he asked, more to change the subject than anything.

"*Oui, monsieur.* I studied French lit at McGill."

"In Montreal."

"*Exactement.* You ever heard of Jean Genet?"

"I know he wrote a play called *The Maids*, about two sisters who practise killing their mistress all the time, but I haven't read it."

"How come you know *The Maids*?"

"I read the magazines in the bookshop over at the mall, the British mags and stuff. *Plays and Players*, it's from London."

"Did you know that Genet wanted boys to play the maids? Boys your age, or maybe a little older?"

"Boys playing the maids?"

Bread-man laughed. "That's what he wanted. Pretty boys just like you."

Neil's eyes grew wide.

"Boy, all boy, with hair in the right places, and a bit of muscle."

"I don't have muscle. I'm so skinny."

"Lean. Long and lean. That's different."

Words wouldn't come for Neil.

Bread-man said, "It's rarely done that way. Not surprising, eh? At least in North America, home of the new barbarian." He smiled, seemingly pleased with his turn of phrase. Neil smiled back. "I guess I should get going. It's so nice talking to you, Neil."

"There's been a break-in on the street. The second in ten days."

Bread-man, who had half-turned away, looked back. "Yeah, I heard. Mr. Caldwell."

"They wrecked the place, and they took all his cats. Everybody says he —" Neil stopped, embarrassed to be saying so much, when all he really wanted was to keep Bread-man there. "He was cruel to his animals." Neil felt silly. "It may be just gossip."

"It's not gossip." Bread-man's tone was hard. "One day I saw him choking one of his cats with a piece of twine. It could have been accidental, but I don't think he's a man who ever does anything accidentally. He's the crafty bastard type, that one."

"What did you do?"

"What could I do? I told him he was hurting the cat, but he doesn't listen to what other people say. He does what he bloody well wants, and screw the rest. To be nice about it, Neil, he's a piece of horseshit. If there's anybody more deserving of a break-in, I'd like to meet him."

Neil said, "Nobody's ever really liked him."

"Glad to hear it." Bread-man's eyes softened slightly. "Don't mind me. People like Caldwell make me nuts. There are way too many of them." He knocked Neil gently in the shoulder. "I've really got to go, wild boy."

Neil backed up, bumping into the door as he did.

Bread-man didn't look back, didn't see Neil's admiration or his desire. Once in the truck, he planted his cap squarely on his head and drove off quickly, leaving Neil feeling quite lost.

12

THE DAY SEEMED TO STOP after Bread-man's visit. Neil could hardly concentrate on the tasks his mother had given him. He found his brain very slow. His movement as well. He couldn't get Bread-man's disapproval of Mr. Caldwell out of his head. To be able to see something so sharply and then draw the right conclusions — that seemed to Neil a very special gift indeed. But it was more than Bread-man's quickness, it was his comfort in his body that really captivated him. He imagined that everything Bread-man did, ordinary things like taking his cod liver oil or showering or going to the bathroom or even jerking off, would be done without awkwardness or embarrassment. These thoughts eclipsed everything that hot, but cloudy afternoon in early July. His father's pranks, his mother's sadness, even Archie Ross's menace all receded into the haze.

At three o'clock, he boarded the bus and headed for work. One of the riders was the same blond young man in short-shorts who had ridden home with him a week or so ago. It seemed like forever now. Neil had no eyes for him today except to note that the young man's legs were really muscular and that he had a pair of figure skates with him. Once he would have been unable not to stare, but Bread-man took up too much space now.

All the way to the library, riding past sights so familiar they were like family, Neil kept his eyes partially closed, wanting to hold on to the image of Bread-man's smile. He opened them fully only once, when the bus was approaching Our Lady of Sorrows Catholic Church. It was Neil's favourite church along the route, a stone neo-Gothic structure set in a nest of trees. He never let himself miss it. As the bus pulled up to the church, Neil imitated the Italian women he'd watched many, many times, and drew a little cross on his forehead. He also added a prayer for Bread-man. For Bread-man and himself, actually. "Please let us get closer," he whispered, knowing full well that Catholics would hardly approve of such a prayer. This thought saddened him, but still he prayed, muttering the words under his breath, chant-like, as they rolled past the deep green cemetery and began the most exciting part of the journey, the crossing of the Humber Bridge, which signalled the end of suburbia and the beginnings of the city proper. He always felt a tug of excitement in his chest at this point, even today with a prayer in his mouth.

At the Jane Loop he disembarked next to the skater who tossed him a quick, uncurious glance before jetting for the waiting streetcar on the adjacent tracks. Neil consoled himself with the thought that such a person wouldn't even recognize how much above him a man like Jack was. He was — what was that word his mother often used? — "tawdry" by comparison. If proof were needed, all Neil had to do was point to the obscene shorts he was wearing — his rather prissy dismissal overlooking the fact that those very shorts were currently receiving a lot of attention from a small gang of wolf-whistling Italian workmen boarding the same streetcar.

At the library, the replacement for Miss Boughton, a very brittle, grey-haired librarian named Peg Fowler, was on duty. She reminded Neil of an old-fashioned wind-up toy, the kind that made jerky movements and sour faces. She and Miss McGregor had cooked up a shelf-tidying scheme that Neil was sure would discourage even Hercules. On reflection, though, he realized the task would provide him and his thoughts of Jack with some time to themselves.

As seven o'clock arrived, he was shelf-reading the psychology section when a pair of khaki legs grabbed his attention. It was Tony, who, with his typical lopsided grin and a nervous energy that was very atypical, asked, "Can I meet you after work at the Loop?"

Neil whispered, "Sure. 8:45."

And he was gone before Neil could ask, *What's going on?*

Tony was already on the bus when Neil reached the Loop, waving from the back window to catch his friend's attention.

Neil hurried to board. It felt good to be with Tony again.

No sooner was he seated then Tony handed him a large black paper bag with fancy white lettering, like old-fashioned handwriting, saying *Zamboni Menswear*, and underneath in a smaller, crisper style, *Moda per uomini.*

Neil opened it, staring into its depths.

"Go on, take it out." Tony was laughing. "It won't bite."

Neil's hand dove to the bottom. It landed on something very feathery and fine. He grabbed hold and lifted. Out came shimmering fabric the colour of a fine old wine. It was the shirt Tony had spoken of the last time they met, but for a moment it looked like something from another world, something rare and precious, and so completely out of place on this suburban bus that Neil felt slightly overwhelmed.

"Well?" Tony asked.

"It's so beautiful." Neil turned it over in his hands. The buttons were a whitish-grey. They reminded him of pearls. "But where will I wear it?"

"Church," Tony said matter-of-factly.

"Church? I couldn't wear this to church. My mother would kill me."

Tony shook his head. "Well, special occasions then. Your

birthday. Thanksgiving. Christmas. Or when you come to visit me, ha-ha. Or you could just admire yourself in the mirror. You know." Tony wiggled his eyebrows. "Look at mine!" He reached down to a bag on the floor between his feet, a white plastic Parma Fruits and Vegetables bag, and pulled up the deep blue brother of Neil's shirt. It was actually the colour of a night sky. Against it the buttons, slightly brighter than those on Neil's shirt, gleamed like constellations.

"It's so beautiful," Neil said, "how can you carry it around in that bag?"

"It's a shirt!" Tony said.

"Yeah, but it's a special shirt."

"Yeah, but it's not diamonds."

"I guess. Thanks a million, eh?" Neil began to refold his shirt carefully. "So, does this mean you gave Bruno your drawing?"

Tony nodded, squeezing Neil's leg just above the knee joint, causing him to jump. "I need to ask you a favour," he said casually. "Can we postpone our get-together on Saturday?"

"Sure."

Tony's face turned unusually serious. "I've been hanging around with Vicki."

Neil felt his stomach drop. "Yeah?"

"Only a couple of movies. *Experiment in Terror*. Not your kind of thing." Tony tried to laugh. "She's got grandparents and uncles and cousins and everything living in their house and there's no privacy. But she can get out Saturday night and probably doesn't have to be back until late, and she suggested we get together at my place."

"I knew you liked her."

"That's all right, isn't it?" Tony snapped. "I'm allowed to like someone else."

Neil felt instantly ashamed. "I didn't say you weren't. I knew after you showed me that drawing."

"Well, you're smarter than I am, I guess."

Neil tried laughing now. "We know that already, don't we?"

Tony looked at him sideways, grinning. "I'm still prettier."

Neil thought of spilling his experience with the optometrist to shock Tony, but concern over Tony's reaction stopped him. "You owe me one," he said instead.

"I also need you to cover for me. I told my parents I'd be at your place, so they don't call home a dozen times while Vicki's there. They can't know I'm seeing her. Mom thinks she's a slut."

Neil remembered the little scene of the malfunctioning buttonhole.

Tony whispered, "It's amazing, you know ... being with her ..."

Neil felt himself pull away from Tony, extending his feet into the aisle. "What if they call and one of my parents answers?"

"They won't call. You're white folks."

"So're yours."

"But yours are whiter!"

By the time they reached Avery Street, Neil was once again reasonably content. He told Tony of the two break-ins and of his rescue by Bread-man at the library, all of which had Tony intrigued. Telling the stories also calmed him enough to recognize that, Vicki or no Vicki, his friend wasn't going anywhere.

As they stepped off the bus, Tony said, "I'll watch while you walk down the street."

"My dad's supposed to be here."

"What for?"

"I was beat up the last time you stood and watched me. A couple of guys, local creep and his jailbird buddy."

"Why didn't you tell me?" Tony took Neil by the elbow. "What's the matter with you? I'm your best friend, aren't I? I'll walk down the street with you."

"Boys!" A deep roar of a voice broke over them.

Startled, they both looked up, scanning the street.

"Boys!" It sounded again.

Tony pointed towards the Anglican Church. "Who's that?"

A figure stood on the church porch wearing a long black cape and something over its head. "Come here, boys! I'm hungry for your souls!"

The voice was still a deep roar but Neil knew the inflections.

"Dad! Quiet!" Neil marched towards the church, with Tony at his heels.

As the gap between them closed, they realized the man on the porch was wearing a devil's mask, one of the cheap Hallowe'en variety, complete with yellow skin, leering red mouth and tiny horns. He was waving his arms, calling again on infernal powers. Tony began to laugh.

Right on cue, Frank pulled off the mask and untied the cape. "The devil's what the church is all about, son. You should know that."

Tony couldn't stop laughing.

Neil's father descended the stairs. "Can you come back with us, Tony? I want your opinion about something. I'll drive you home afterwards, okay?"

Neil knew what his father wanted Tony's opinion about: the so-called Pollock in the backyard, *Windermere '62*. There was nothing he could say to stop it. The last time he complained about his father's interference with his friends, Frank had refused to speak to him for three long, chilly months. His mother had tried reasoning with her husband, something she almost never did, and for her efforts earned a place next to Neil in Siberia. He thought of it often as the worst time of his life, worse even than some of the scariest of his father's pranks. So, as they headed off down Avery Street, Tony and his father in front, Neil behind, he tried to pretend it would be all right.

At Stanton Avenue, Neil caught sight of the Edsel approaching from the other direction. The driver waved at him. Shyly, Neil waved back.

The gesture didn't escape his father's attention. He stage-whispered to Tony, "You know, Neil is making strange friends these days. That man in the car that just passed? A robber of supermarkets and drugstores. Small stuff, of course, not even banks. What kind of friend is that, would you say?"

Tony glanced over his shoulder with a wink.

On the front lawn of 31 Dominion, his father said, "You boys go round back and I'll bring out some Cokes."

"Your father's something else," Tony said, when they were alone.

In a matter of minutes Frank reappeared with a tray bearing the promised beverages. Neil expected to see a whiskey or rye on the tray, too, but it seemed that his father, for the moment at least, had no intention of joining them. He did, however, set up a lawn chair with its back to the yard and asked Tony to do him the great favour of sitting there for a moment. Then he scurried from the patio.

Alone again, Tony shrugged in Neil's direction only to be answered with a helpless shake of the head.

The wrought iron lanterns flickered into life and, in what seemed just a fraction of a second, his father was there, in his black cape, standing in front of the tarpaulin that hid the "masterpiece of modernism." How Neil wished, in that moment, for something to destroy the painting before his father could uncover it — a bolt of lightning maybe — but, of course, that would never happen. His father would, as usual, have his own way. A feeling close to hate rose to the surface, strong enough to make him turn away.

When the tarpaulin came down, Tony spontaneously stood. "Wow!" he said, "that's amazing! Is that car lacquer?"

Frank Bennett glowed.

"Wow!" Tony said again. "It's like a war zone."

"Exactly!" his father crowed. "Exactly! Tony's got it. You've got it, Tony! The modern world is a war zone. Neil didn't get it."

"I suppose that's why you called it *Windermere* then, *Windermere '62* or whatever it's called, 'cause Windermere is supposed to look like a war zone."

"Titles, titles. My son doesn't get the significance of my titles. It's ironic. Windermere is a paradise, so our neighbour says. But is it really? Is it any different from any other place today? Isn't it just a fantasy to distract us from the truth, the hideous truth? *Windermere '62* is a painting of the beginning of the end."

Tony applauded, his lopsided grin nearly falling off his face. Frank bowed repeatedly like a circus ringmaster.

"Can I take your picture in front of it, Tony?"

"Sure thing."

Frank again quickly vanished.

Overhead in a moonless, starless sky, thunder clapped.

They sat in silence till Frank returned with the camera. Like some kind of professional photographer, he positioned Tony in front of the painting, standing, crouching, facing it, and then moved him first to one side, and then the other. He snapped three, four, five, six photos. With a quick glance at his son, who had turned his attention to bats dive-bombing in the darkness, he sneaked in a seventh and then performed an elaborate bow. "Thank you, Tony, thank you for your appreciation. I rarely have such sensitive responses. I'm going to put the tarp back up. It sounds like rain. You let me know when you want to go."

His cape flapping in the wind that had risen, Frank left the patio.

For a long while, the boys sat in silence sipping their Cokes out of jewel-coloured plastic glasses while the thunder rumbled in the distance.

"Well, he's a lot more fun than my dad," Tony said.

"If you say so," Neil answered sharply.

They sat and they sipped. Conversation turned eventually to school and their plans for Grade Twelve. It wasn't a topic Neil loved.

But then, school wasn't a place Neil loved in spite of the good marks he earned. His lack of interest in the sporting life of the place left him clinging to the fringes. It was different for Tony — he was the fastest runner at school and a great soccer player on top of that. Popularity was his for the asking, if he'd wanted it.

"Mr. Dubois told me I'd better give up the English horn," Neil said, "that I couldn't ever be a good musician 'cause I'm not a good athlete, so I guess I'll take art, which I know I'm lousy at. It'll be awful taking art with my dad looking over my shoulder."

"I'll help you, if you want. You've helped me with French and English and —" Tony stopped dead. "Jesus Christ," he whispered, half-rising from his seat. "Neil! Neil!" He was pointing his finger at something over Neil's shoulder.

Floating in the hole in the hedge created by Mr. Gordon's chemical spill was a skull, a lurid yellow skull. It moaned.

With a shriek, Neil leapt to his feet. Tony grabbed on to him, frantically crossing himself as the skull floated a little higher, moaned a little louder and then was gone.

In the absence of light, Neil spied a figure creeping away.

"Dad!" Shaking Tony off, he crossed the patio just in time to see the back door close. "Goddamn him! Damn him! Dad!" he screamed. "Dad!"

The light flashed on in the Gordons' kitchen, illuminating Mrs. Gordon's startled face. Mr. Gordon appeared beside his car, his *Daily Star* in hand. "What's the matter, Neil?" he called.

The back door opened. Frank Bennett emerged, calm, collected.

"Why did you do that?" Neil shouted.

His father feigned ignorance.

"The skull!"

"What skull?" His father approached them with easy tread.

"You had a skull!"

"I still have a skull, Neil," he answered. He turned to Tony, rolling his eyes.

"I saw it, too, Mr. Bennett."

"Oh. Really? You both saw it?" He walked to the table on which sat the tray and the glasses the boys had been using. He sniffed one of the glasses. "Sure it's not the Coke?"

"I hate you for this," Neil muttered. He was aware even as he said it how wrong such a feeling sounded.

His father pulled from his pocket a flashlight. Placing the lamp under his chin, he turned it on. A lurid yellow skull floated in front of them. "You mean this?"

The boys stared. Tony laughed, not his usual light, loose laugh, but the laugh of a person who had to either laugh or cry bitterly. He laughed so helplessly, Frank Bennett couldn't help snickering. Mr. Gordon, now standing on the other side of the hedge by the hole, folded his paper slowly, tucked it under his arm, and said, "Goodnight folks."

Neil's hands, which had turned into fists at his side, unclenched. He managed to mutter a "Goodnight, Mr. Gordon," and then, with difficulty, say, "We should get Tony home."

"Of course, of course. I'll get my keys."

Alone again, Neil walked Tony from the patio to the driveway, saying as he went, "Just forget this ever happened, Tony. Think of your weekend. Think of Vicki. Forget about this."

At the edge of the driveway, they stood tensely as lightning fired the sky. Finally, the front door opened, and a frowning Frank appeared again. Neil could hear his mother's voice in the background. Not her usual quiet tone, but neither was it more than mildly displeased. *She's pathetic*, Neil thought angrily.

Tony whispered, "Your father do this often?"

"All the time."

"Fuck," Tony muttered.

Father and son spoke not a word on the way to and from the Colero house, a low, rambling bungalow with a huge Italian garden in back. Back down in the safety of his cave, Neil took a seat on the bed to wait for the tears.

Without a knock, his father entered the room. "Next time, you watch your mouth, young man. I don't want the neighbours thinking we're raising hooligans."

Neil made no answer.

"Tony's got a good eye, at least."

Again Neil said nothing.

"You could learn from him." His father left the room.

Neil took a deep breath. The threat of tears had evaporated. Replacing them was a fierce, almost desperate, longing to escape.

13

AS PREDICTED, THE RAIN COOLED everything down. So much so that the day after the storm, his mother lifted her head from ironing the pillowcases for her sister's bed to say, with a happy relief, "It feels like late spring. I hope it stays like this for Sylvia."

It did. The next day, the day of his aunt's arrival, was also coolish. This seemed to tip the scales in his mother's level of excitement. He had seen her happy before, delighted, even over-joyed once or twice, but never giddy. And she *was* giddy, giddy as a schoolgirl with a crush. He knew that she missed her two sisters terribly, but the extent of her excitement, which he likened to a burbling stream during the spring thaw, was so unlike anything he had ever seen in her, it was almost comical.

"You're going to overflow, Mom," he said.

"Yes, I'm going to overflow, darling. Watch me." And she opened her arms wide to embrace not only him, but the whole kitchen, the green lawn beyond, the Gordons' weeping willow, the sparkling clean street and its brisk traffic, the whole neigh-bourhood as far as the Jane Loop and maybe beyond, all the way to the old Edwardian semi-detached house on Crawford Street where she and Sylvia had passed their girlhoods. "I'm overflow-ing, darling," she cried, fingers fluttering like butterflies at the end of her outstretched arms.

"That's great," he said, trying not to be embarrassed by her exuberance.

"You'll see. A new me. Four o'clock this afternoon."

He left early for the library that day to check in on Tony, whom he found in his green apron dampening the vegetable stands with a fine mist from a discreet black hose. Mrs. Colero was at the till, reading the *Corriere Canadese*. Vicki was nowhere to be seen.

"You okay?" he asked as Tony tossed him his usual grin.

"Yeah, why? Oh, damn, your father really had me going." He turned off the hose and tucked it under the stand and looked at Neil closely. "I get it now, you know."

Neil looked puzzled.

"If that's typical, I mean."

He didn't mean to say it, but what came out was, "That's nothing."

Tony's dark brows met. "Do I want to know?"

"Probably not," Neil said, trying to laugh.

"Why's he do it?"

"Kicks."

"That's just sick."

"I never know when it's coming. He always catches me by surprise."

Tony looked towards his mother who was peering at them over her paper. Not unkindly, not critically, but officially, like an empress surveying her responsibilities. Her gold hoop earrings today were silver. She smiled at Neil, nodding benignly.

"I think she wishes you were my girlfriend," Tony said in low tones.

Again, Neil just blurted out a response, "That'd be okay with me."

Except for a very faint blush, Tony appeared not to have heard him. "Say hi to Miss Fairfield, okay?"

HIS EXCITEMENT WAS palpable enough that evening to provoke the usually discreet Miss Fairfield to ask why. Quite unreservedly, Neil launched into a very colourful description not only of his Aunt Sylvia, but of the whole Deekman clan, from their origins as Dutch mercenaries in Nova Scotia to their long journey westward to Ontario, with a special nod to Uncle Herb who was, after all, the library's close neighbour and sometimes patron. Miss Fairfield appeared to be very captivated by this history, even asking a question or two in the very brief pauses Neil allowed her.

When Neil blurted out that his Aunt Julie sold evening dresses to the stars, Miss McGregor, who was also listening, gasped, "Imagine!"

Miss Fairfield simply said, "You should have told me, Neil, and we could have arranged for you to have the time off. It's seven thirty. Why don't you slip away early now?"

As he climbed onto the 50-A bus that evening, no thoughts of ambush or sabotage accompanied him, no lurking fears about where his unnatural feelings might be leading him surfaced. He felt alive with anticipation. Everything he saw took on a golden hue, including pizza parlours, car lots, and Catholic schoolyards. Even the stop indicator bell, which always sounded sharply unmusical, rang silvery.

Just as he started his descent of Avery Street, however, he received an unexpected jolt. The Edsel owner was walking straight towards him.

Neil wasn't alone in his surprise, though — Jim appeared equally jolted. In a manner that felt almost embarrassed, he explained how his car was being "looked over" in the Texaco garage at the other end of the street and that until tomorrow afternoon he was operating under his own steam. This prospect seemed to agitate him. But Edsel-man didn't dwell on his loss. In a voice that sounded genuinely concerned, he asked, "You okay?"

"Fine," Neil answered nervously. The man in front of him was really tall.

"You think you can forget what happened a couple o' weeks ago?"

"I guess so," Neil answered.

"I never did that before. Honest. Archie was goading me about the homo stuff. I should've been bigger than him, like you said. Sorry about that."

Neil looked up at his former assailant, surprised to find such honest eyes looking back. This man felt so different from the one who lived behind the wheel of the Edsel. More serious, certainly. Neil smiled. "Thanks for saving me the other night, though."

Jim snorted. "Archie couldn't beat up a fly!"

"He had a bat," Neil protested.

"Yeah. But he's useless with a bat, even on a diamond. You weren't in any real trouble, man."

"How would I know that?" Neil insisted.

"I guess you wouldn't. Anyway, I'm glad I was there."

"Me, too." Neil gave him a smile.

Jim's return smile was suddenly shy. "I gotta go. I got ten blocks of walking left to do. My street's way east. And you look like you're off to a party."

"My aunt from California arrived today. I haven't seen her yet."

"California! Must be nice. I better let you go, then. See you soon, I hope."

As they parted, Neil found himself wanting to say, *I'm always around*, but he didn't quite dare. Nevertheless, everything was shining again. Warm as it was, he ran the rest of the way home.

Knowing the front screen door would be locked, he headed around the back, where he could hear voices coming from the patio. Laughter, his mother's laughter, rare species that it was, followed by his aunt's mocking tone, "Frank! Whatever are we going to do with you?"

He entered the house and climbed the back stairs to the kitchen. The dishes were piled high on the table and counter, something his mother never allowed to happen. In the dining room, the white cloth shone in the growing gloom. Crumbs sprinkled it with clues and six used serviettes made crumpled bird shapes here and there. The number puzzled him at first, until he remembered that Uncle Herb and Aunt Violet and their daughter, Sandra, would be present. Six settings, yes. In the centre a floral arrangement of freesias, pansies and roses continued to share its perfumes with the deserted room.

In the fridge, he found a plate covered in Saran wrap holding a helping each of roast chicken, green beans, mashed potatoes and parsnips. Reluctant to disturb his mother, he turned on the oven to warm it himself. After careful scrutiny of the coffee parfait in its tall, elegantly cylindrical glass, he hurried to the backyard.

Mona and Gus Gordon were leaving as he arrived. Mona exclaimed, "She looks fabulous! Just fabulous!"

"It's no Windermere, of course, but I'd say California clearly agrees with her," Gus said.

His father was beaming, sitting on the edge of his chair, a glass in hand. To one side of him was Uncle Herb, and on the other was Cousin Sandra in a flouncy blouse the colour of strawberry ice cream, her hair teased into a veritable honeycomb of blondness. She kept crossing and uncrossing her pretty legs as if taking cues from a fashion photographer.

Aunt Sylvia faced directly away from Neil, flanked on the left by his mother and on the right by his capacious, dark-haired Aunt Violet. Their profiles were turned attentively to the repartee between Herb and Sylvia. His mother showed a deep glowing pleasure, and his Aunt Violet obviously enjoyed seeing her husband mastered by his sister.

"Damn it, why didn't you make Julia come?" Uncle Herb said.

"No one has ever made Julia do anything she didn't want to do, as you well know, Herbert. I'd like to see you do anything but running around picking up after her!"

Violet roared with laughter.

"Well, well," said his father, "look who's here."

A hush fell on the terrace.

Aunt Sylvia turned slowly in her seat, peering over her wire-framed glasses. Neil's first thought was that she looked younger and blonder than she did in her photos. Prettier too, with dancing grey eyes and a sweetly mischievous smile. Quietly, calmly, never breaking her focus on him, Sylvia stood. She took a few steps towards Neil, her arms outstretched towards him. Neil closed the gap between them, somewhat self-consciously, and reached out to hug her. She said, "Just a moment," keeping him at arm's length, and after several seconds of intensely surveying him, said, "Oh, my, my," and pulled him to her.

He felt her tears on his cheek.

She let him go finally. Taking his hand, she turned to her sister. "Well, you made a handsome one, the two of you. A mighty handsome one. And so tall. The photographs don't do him justice at all. You need to get your camera checked, sir!" This last she directed at Frank.

"Oh, he runs whenever I come near him with a camera."

"Everyone runs, Frank!" Herb laughed.

"Come sit down by me, darling," Sylvia said.

Neil's father scrambled to open another chair, but his mother abandoned hers instead, saying, "I'm going to warm up his food. Would anybody like anything else?"

Everyone agreed they were all more than satisfied. Violet said, "We have to be going now, Nora. We have to make sure Miss Clark hasn't burnt the store down."

Thanks were profuse, hugs briefly but warmly exchanged, and

offers to go here and there, wherever Sylvia wanted, made with unstinting generosity. As their car pulled out of the driveway, Aunt Violet shouted from the passenger seat, "We'll see you Sunday at Marian's," and the whole neighbourhood seemed to brighten at the prospect.

"That girl!" Aunt Sylvia said, "How does she do it?"

Neil replied, "Uncle Herb always says, 'We keep up, we keep up!'" His imitation brought on laughter.

"Herb never liked others to get the better of him, did he, Nora?"

"Well certainly not his sisters!" Nora took hold of her sister's arm, wearing a softly happy smile. "You must be tired, Syl."

"Exhausted! But I'd like to watch Neil eat before I retire. I want to see his face when he gets to your scrumptious dessert."

Neil's parents washed the dishes and cleaned the kitchen, observing an unusually collaborative silence as they worked, while he ate. His aunt filled him in on the decidedly mixed pleasures of air travel, and told him a few stories about life in Los Angeles, making a particular point of emphasizing the role Hollywood played in shaping the city as a whole. These Neil couldn't get enough of. He pestered her with so many questions — "Are you near any movie studios?", "Have you seen many stars?", "Is Grauman's Theatre really as big as it seems?" — that his mother finally intervened.

"Darling, your aunt is dead tired. You can grill her in the morning."

"He's not grilling me. It's fun."

"I'll run you your bath, Sylvia."

Frank appeared at Nora's side, placing his arm gently around her waist. She normally would have shrunk a little from such an approach, but seemed to welcome it then, and covered the hand that held her hip with her own. "I'm going to get some gas for the car, so you girls have plenty for tomorrow's outings," he said.

"Don't fuss over me too much," Sylvia replied. "I'm just a Crawford Street girl, remember."

"We want to fuss," Nora said. "We need to fuss."

A loud knock shook the screen door. It was Mike Dennison, bearing a huge bouquet of red and white roses, which he presented to Sylvia with a gentlemanly flourish right out of a forties movie. "You don't know me, but my girlfriend, Val Bennett, instructed me to bring these by for you and to say that she loves you and can't wait to see you in a couple of weeks."

"Well, well, and you must be Mike Dennison. I've heard a lot about you."

He answered by glancing goofily between Frank and Nora. "Val's a terrific girl."

Neil looked into his empty parfait glass, thinking, *And she'd be a lot more terrific if she dumped you.*

Sylvia smelled her flowers. "These are so beautiful. Wasn't there once a war between the red rose and the white?"

"House of York versus House of Lancaster," Neil said, "the Wars of the Roses. Fifteenth-century England."

Sylvia threw back her head with a loud laugh. "I've always loved a facts man."

Nora and Frank laughed, too, Frank obviously pleased by Sylvia's approval. He nodded at his son as if to say, *Good for you.*

Only Mike didn't laugh. He said, rather more seriously than was merited, "Well, I hope they don't bring any wars, ma'am. They weren't meant to."

"Let me take those, Sylvia, I'll put them in a vase." His mother retreated to the kitchen, flowers in arms.

"I'm going to get gas, Mike," Frank said, heading for the door.

"Oh, I have to go, too, sir. Early to work tomorrow. I head for Windermere at four." He wished Sylvia a wonderful vacation, saying he hoped they'd meet again before she left, and with the briefest of glances in Neil's direction, also departed.

The dining room, now empty of everyone but Neil and his aunt, acquired an instant peace. For several minutes, they sat absorbing the quiet. Like a crystal ball, the coffee parfait glass gradually drew both of them into contemplation of its milky depths.

At last, Neil shifted in his chair.

Aunt Sylvia's glasses glinted in the light from the tall, thin lamp with the amber shade that dominated the buffet. As always the light reminded him of Lichee Garden Chinese restaurant, of its amber-lit mural of smoky mountains beribboned with dark streams. She turned to him, smiling the smile of a seer or sage. "Is it just my imagination, or do you not like Val's beau very much?"

Neil wanted to say, *I hate him*, but hesitated.

"I thought so," Sylvia murmured. "Well, I don't imagine you two have much to talk about. Except your sister."

"He never talks to me about Val. He never talks to me at all except to — make fun of me. He's a jerk." He immediately regretted saying this.

"You're very different from him."

He searched her face for some sign of recognition. "I'm very different from most people, Aunt Sylvia."

She reached across the table for his hand. "I expect you are, darling. That's not necessarily a bad thing, though."

"It is if there's no one similar to talk to."

Sylvia paused. "I think we'll have to have a chat, you and I."

Neil looked across at her very still countenance, praying that she knew or had guessed. He could feel his old standby tears forming, and grabbed his serviette to ward them off, should they dare start flowing.

"Sylvia!" It was his mother's voice. "Your bath will be ready in a moment."

"Coming! Coming!" She squeezed the hand she held. "Let's talk tomorrow."

"I don't work mornings," Neil said gratefully.

"Well then, morning it is." She stood, looking at him with great fondness in her eyes. So unfamiliar was he with such a direct confession of affection, he looked away, embarrassed, and as he did, her look of fondness gave way to one of worry.

NEIL WAS UP early, after a night of tossing and turning and another dream of battling draperies. This time, the draperies were very filmy, almost transparent, coloured like Sandra's blouse, a strawberry ice cream hue. The dimensions of the big room were clearer, and he was surer than ever when he awoke that it was a ballroom. He could hear a tune, but he didn't recognize it, a waltz tune, three-quarter time. The curtains seemed to be motivated by the music to sway, maddeningly denying him something he was looking for.

At eight o'clock, he was upstairs in the kitchen drinking tea while his mother and aunt sipped their percolated coffee and ate the bran muffins his mother had made the day before. His aunt questioned him closely about school, his grades, and his plans for the future. He replied, as he always did, "I'd like to write plays."

"Have you written anything?" she asked.

He shook his head.

"Why ever not?"

"I'm scared it'll be stupid, I guess."

His mother lifted her eyes with an expression of shocked disappointment. "You shouldn't let these negative thoughts get the upper hand. If you think positively, Neil, you'll see you can do anything you want. Thinking positive is the only way."

"I'm sure all writers worry about being stupid when they start, Neil," Sylvia said, "but they write anyway, and they probably find that what they write is only stupid some of the time." She stood very casually. "Why don't you show me this room of yours in the cellar?"

He had made his bed before coming upstairs. The rest of the room had been organized to perfection since Tuesday, so that when he opened his door for her, he radiated an unusual confidence.

She loved it, as he knew she would. She lifted her arms from her sides, smiling and saying, "Oh, my!" Then, walking up and down the room, she took everything in with the wide-eyed wonder of a child at Christmas. "Wonderful, wonderful," she said at last. "It's a real getaway, isn't it?"

Neil nodded.

"I wish I'd had something like this when I was your age. I had to share with Julia and your mother, you know. George and Herb shared, too. Only Marian had her own room. I used to go to the shed at the back of the garden to escape. There was a nice little space behind it where the hollyhocks grew. I used to read there." She shook her head as if it were full of cobwebs. "This seems luxurious by comparison. A place for your records and books and ..." She picked up the sleeve for *The Unsinkable Molly Brown*, which lay beside the turntable. "Your mother told me you liked musicals. I think there's going to be a touring version of this coming to LA later this year. In our subscription series. Is it good?"

"Oh, it's wonderful. The man who wrote it wrote *The Music Man*, too."

"Well, we'll have to have a listen. Any other favourites?"

"*My Fair Lady*. And *First Impressions* — it's based on *Pride and Prejudice* — and *Camelot* and *Wildcat* —"

"I don't know *Wildcat*."

"It's the one where Lucille Ball's trying to raise money from oil drilling to pay for an operation for her sister, who's crippled."

"So that's what Lucy's up to!" She regarded her nephew closely. "Why don't you write musical comedy, Neil?"

"I don't know anything about music. My music teacher says I'm hopeless. He says I should take art."

"How very encouraging! But maybe there's somebody who

could write the music. You could write the story and the lyrics."

Davy Doyle instantly came to mind, but Neil squashed the idea, certain that Davy would have nothing to do with any project of his. "I don't know anyone who would want to do that."

His aunt turned her gaze to Neil's bulletin board. She didn't say anything for a moment. Then, smiling to herself, she said, "Well, you have quite the eye for beauty, with Miss Hepburn there. You've seen *Breakfast at Tiffany's*?"

His expression was so downhearted Sylvia almost laughed.

"Why not? Surely it's played here?"

"Mom thinks it's too adult for me."

"I don't buy that. Not at all. Look at your room. You have a very cool pad, as they say. Very sophisticated. I'll take you."

"You will?" Neil scarcely dared to believe her.

"Tell me, though, how does he fit in with the overall scheme?" She nodded towards the image of the Mediterranean man on the rock in his tight jeans and dark glasses.

"Oh, I just thought he looked ... I don't know ... kind of ... I don't know."

"He's certainly nice-looking. Pity about the glasses. Eyes tell you everything you need to know about a person. But the rest is pretty nice. Do you think Audrey would approve of him?"

"I don't ... I — Yes, I think so." Neil suddenly realized who the man on the rocks reminded him of: Edsel-man. He coloured.

"I do, too. She'd be crazy not to. Of course, she'd probably want to see his eyes, but I'm sure she'd find a way to get the glasses off him. *Foam*. I didn't see the movie, but the theatre's in downtown LA. Julie and I don't go there much. It's not the safest part of town. We're old girls, Neil. Shady isn't our colour."

He laughed. "You're not old."

"I've always been old. And so, I think, have you." She surveyed his pin-up board again. "I'm not sure Mr. *Foam* would make the best sort of companion, though."

Neil turned a startled face towards her.

"I suspect he's quite full of himself. Beauty often comes with a superior attitude. Somebody a little less perfect might be better. Somebody warmer, more open, more attentive to you." She laughed. "Somebody who's not hiding his eyes!" She touched her nephew's arm very lightly. "What do you think?"

"I love you, Aunt Sylvia."

"It's a hundred per cent mutual, my dear. I really hope you find such a companion." She winked. "Now, let's go upstairs. I don't want your mother thinking we're neglecting her. We'll visit down here some more later. You can play me this musical about Molly Brown."

As they left his room, Sylvia paused at the foot of the stairs, peering into the workshop, which Frank had taken a stab or two at setting in order during the last week. Her gaze swept over the workbench crammed with tools, bottles and cans of various liquids to the magnificent steely splendour of the table saw that filled up the space next to the furnace. From there it shifted to several old wooden storage cabinets stuffed so full their doors wouldn't properly close and then up and along the rafters from which hung more tools and devices for measuring, paint brushes, lengths of rope, an old birdcage, an Indian headdress with white and yellow feathers Neil had worn as a kid, and several forms for puppet-making, which his father had also undertaken many years ago in a quest to captivate his kids. Sylvia's gaze scoured the bench again. The pale, whitish light trickling in from the window above was strangely sufficient to give anyone both a clear sense of the industry and inventiveness that defined the space, as well as its confusion and chaos.

Sylvia smiled. "Day and night, I'd say — you and your neighbour here."

Neil appreciated the suggestion and smiled.

Nora was only just getting off the phone when they returned to the kitchen. Neil could tell she'd had unwelcome news, and felt momentarily anxious that it would spoil things for her. His aunt, who was no stranger to her sister's moods, demanded an explanation.

"Oh, that was Lydia West. We've had another break-in. Over on Howard Street. The Steeles. We don't know the Steeles well at all, except they're very Catholic. They just got back from vacation and their house is in ruins."

This account did nothing to satisfy Sylvia, who very deftly set about extracting the whole gruesome history of Islington vandalism from her sister and nephew. No sooner had they completed their inventory than Mona Gordon appeared at the back door in a beet-splattered pink shirt to announce yet another break-in, involving the Chards, who lived directly opposite the Gordons.

Unlike Nora, Mona was very fulsome in her descriptions. "They carved swear words into the dining room table — mahogany, you know. And peed on the Turkish carpets. Then they plugged the bathroom sink and left the water running. The kitchen ceiling caved in apparently. Oh, and there were pictures of criminals pasted up all over the walls."

"And what was the Chards' crime?" Sylvia asked as calmly as she could.

"Irene Chard wouldn't let a black woman serve her at Morgan's. She flatly refused. And Walter Chard calls everybody he doesn't like a nigger or a kike. Lydia West claims their surname is really German and that Walter Chard served in the SS during the war. But then she said that about Sam Caldwell, too."

Nora Bennett seemed unable to stop shaking her head.

"The police can't seem to make any headway," Mona continued.

"Well," said Sylvia. "This is all very LA, I must say." She took Neil's arm. "Toronto's growing up, I guess."

BY NOON, HIS mother and aunt had left Neil for the mall. Aunt Sylvia had forgotten to pack a certain brand of skin-sensitive cosmetic in her make-up bag and wanted replacements. Neil, therefore, occupied himself tidying the patio and picking a few flowers for his own room, which he felt would only make it more appealing to his aunt. He was walking back to the house when Bread-man's truck pulled up at the foot of the Gordons' driveway, and Bread-man leapt down.

"Hey, Mr. Plays and Players, how're things?" he called as he bounced around the back of the Gordon place to make his delivery, then returned. Four of his shirt buttons were open.

Neil's eyes couldn't help straying to the patch of exposed chest, where the hair was damp from the heat. For a second he was rendered mute by a longing to see Bread-man shirtless. With a gentle smile, Bread-man adjusted his posture slightly, causing the shirt to fall more open on one side. A nipple popped into view.

Uncertain where to look, Neil thrust the bouquet of flowers towards Bread-man. "Would you like these?" he nervously asked.

"You bet I would," he said. "No one's ever given me flowers before. But they'd be kaput by the time I got them into water, so maybe I'll take a rain check. You can give me flowers when I have a jar for them."

Neil's stare had drifted upwards to Bread-man's face. It took him a second or two to realize that his idol had stopped speaking. Confused and embarrassed, he laughed an, "I'm sorry."

"Never be sorry about what you like. That's a rule I have for myself."

"I don't know what's the matter with me sometimes."

"You sure?" Bread-man's eyebrows lifted. "I bet I know what's up."

Neil looked away towards the weeping willow and the truck parked under it. "What?" he whispered.

Bread-man's hand pressed his shoulder gently. Neil automatically looked around for witnesses. The hand lingered another second, squeezing gently, warmly, then retreated into a pocket of the snug brown trousers.

"Am I right?"

Neil swallowed, his mouth dry. "Right?"

"You looking for some forbidden fun?"

Neil couldn't believe what he was hearing.

Bread-man said, "Well, if you ever want to talk about anything ..."

Neil remained frozen. All he could imagine was how dumb, how childish, how very backwards he must appear.

Bread-man laughed. "I was in the library last night, but there was no sign of you. You on vacation?" He performed his little "bim-bam" ritual — feeding the brown bread into the waiting box — and then stood back.

"I left early," Neil said, doing his best not to look as Bread-man scratched his chest. "Around seven thirty."

"I was looking forward to seeing you, too. I renewed the Genet. Man, is he ever in-ter-esting."

"I'm reading an essay on Genet."

"Never mind the essays, Neil, read the plays, or the novels."

Jack's hand found Neil's shoulder again. It felt so comforting and yet so disturbing. He took a step closer to Neil and pushed back the visor of his cap. Softly, he said, "You're looking especially good today, you know that? Lots of sleep, eh?"

"Lots of dreams."

"Dreams are good. At least, mine are." Jack's hand fell away, but he remained very close, so close Neil could catch the scent of him, sweet and salty at the same time.

"My aunt from Los Angeles is here. You'd like her, I know. She's amazing."

Jack laughed. "Well, she lives in a pretty amazing place, eh?

City of Angels. I'd love to see it. I bet it's really weird. A whole city devoted to creating illusions. Fabulous, eh? San Francisco, too, that'd be another cool place. City Lights Books, and all those beat poets."

"She's going to take me to see *Breakfast at Tiffany's* at the Runnymede."

"I want to see it, too. Holly Golightly's my kind of person."

"I love Audrey Hepburn."

"You're not alone there. When are you going?"

"My day off. Next Wednesday. Early show."

"Well, maybe we'll see you there."

"You're going?" Excitement spilled out of Neil's question. "Wow."

Smiling, Jack pulled down his peak again. "You're wow, kiddo. A big wow."

14

THE FIRST WEEKEND OF HIS aunt Sylvia's visit was one of the most exciting of Neil's life so far. On Friday, he arranged with Miss Fairfield to leave the library early again so that he could be part of a late buffet supper in the Gordons' backyard in honour of his aunt. Mona and Lana set up a long table under their maple tree and loaded it with food: every kind of salad imaginable, including the splattering beet kind and his own favourite, the Waldorf, as well as trays of baked goods "fit for the Royal Family," to borrow Gus's description.

Everybody was in a good mood. Even Neil's father, who was prone to taking several sudden leaves of absence from social gatherings, stayed in his chair, laughing along with everyone else. There were only a few moments when he stole the limelight away from Sylvia: once to announce that he was beginning a new painting called *Neil's Dream* and another time to say that he had been visited in the night by a dark presence named Vlad. The gentle ribbing seemed enough to satisfy him, and he fell back into the flow without any of his usual restlessness. Neil had to wonder what it was about his aunt's presence that produced such a remarkable effect on his father, but besides Sylvia being the smartest, coolest, most affectionate person on earth, he couldn't come up with any explanation.

Lana introduced her new boyfriend, Warren Dawlish, a slim, boyishly cute young accounting student, who was not only polite to all the adults, but also extremely friendly to Neil. Warren asked him all sorts of questions about plays and the theatre, then shyly confessed that he'd done a bit of acting in amateur theatre. "Just a few parts, a couple of dramas, you know, like *The Glass Menagerie*, you know that one? I was the Gentleman Caller. But what I really love is a good comedy."

Neil liked Warren.

That night as he got into bed, he told himself that Warren was better than cute. He was good looking. He wondered for a minute if maybe Warren harboured hidden feelings for men, the way he did — after all, he was very open and friendly in a way most men weren't. Affectionate: that was the word. The minute the word took shape in his thoughts, he remembered his conversation with Jack at the back door. Immediately warm and flustered feeling, he rolled back the sheet. Warren's blond countenance smiled at him. His lips were full and very pink. A tongue appeared, and then a nipple, a man's nipple. It was Jack's. He'd seen it earlier peeking out provocatively from the chest hair, a nickel-sized hard nipple, pointy, maybe swollen. Neil moaned very quietly. Then he saw Jack's face, and it was smiling as bright as Warren's. Even brighter. This provoked a deeper moan, and for the next twenty minutes, all else, including Aunt Sylvia, was forgotten.

The following day was an unusually busy summer Saturday for the library. There was a steady stream of people from the moment the doors opened at ten. Rob Neville was one of the first to appear. He seemed unpleasantly surprised to see Neil there and, after a curt nod of the head, avoided him, even waiting until Mrs. Negulescu was back at the circulation desk before checking out his books.

Always exciting, several people he'd never seen before came into the library. One was a boy his age, looking for a job as a page.

He was small-boned with very dark hair and a dismissive manner. Probably Polish or some other kind of Eastern European. Neil wasn't sure he wanted him as a colleague, but it didn't matter, not today, not with the warmth and good humour that had recently invaded the house. His aunt and mother would be visiting an old neighbour of theirs from Crawford Street, but that was okay; he and his father would be eating leftovers from the Gordon extravaganza, a delightful prospect, and after that he'd have his musicals to play and maybe a new pin-up board to make, before the women returned.

That afternoon, he managed to get his favourite seat on the 50-A bus, the last single seat on the driver's side, just across from the centre doors. He was happily waiting there with three more plastic-covered library books in his lap — two *Theatre World* volumes from the late fifties and a collection of short plays by Tennessee Williams — when pale-faced Davy Doyle came bolting up the steps, just as the centre doors were closing, and careened to a halt at Neil's side. Panting, he took in Neil's presence, glanced at the books in Neil's lap, and then grabbed himself the first available perch, two rows up from Neil on the other side of the aisle, next to a stocky middle-aged man in a straw hat and Hawaiian shirt. He said nothing to Neil, not even a hi, and kept his gaze focused forward the whole trip home.

Such was Neil's state of contentment that he forgot about Davy, until the bus reached the Avery stop and they both pulled the stop indicator at the same time and converged on the centre doors. They even stepped down in unison.

As the bus pulled away, Neil fully expected Davy to dash across the street so as to avoid any possibility of conversation but, surprisingly, he didn't. In fact, he seemed to have accepted the inevitable fact that they would be walking down the same street together, and he half-hovered to make sure Neil was with him.

"You been to the library?" Davy said as they reached Greenland

Road, nodding towards Neil's books.

"I work at the library."

"I wouldn't mind working in a library."

"Why don't you apply?"

"Piano," Davy mumbled. "You see *Cat on a Hot Tin Roof*?" He had obviously noticed the book of Tennessee Williams plays.

Neil spoke of his mother's disapproval in a hopeless tone.

Davy sniffed. "My mom, too, but what she doesn't know won't hurt her."

"You went on your own?"

"Yeah, when it came back last year. Downtown. It was on a double bill with *Suddenly Last Summer*. That was really weird. Some boys eat a man at the end."

"Yeah, I know, it's really creepy."

"And that old witch mother in the elevator! She was something else."

"Mrs. Venables."

Davy nodded, "Yeah, you know this play, eh?"

"'Cut that story out of her head!'" Neil quoted, without thinking, and, for the first time since he'd known him, he heard Davy laugh — a high, bright laugh that seemed almost too big for him. The effort made him red in the face and showed off his very white, even teeth. They were so white they looked unreal. Neil laughed, too, in sheer delight.

"I was just at the movies," Davy said, running his hand through his messy hair. "I was supposed to be looking for sheet music. If I'd missed that bus, I would have been supper."

"What movie you see?"

It was Davy's turn to hesitate. "*Breakfast at Tiffany's*."

"You're kidding," Neil burst out. "I'm going next Wednesday. Did you like it?"

"Yeah. The music's great. She is, too. Well, see you around." Davy took his stoop's four steps in two, without a look back.

Neil hurried home. He knew, of course, that it would be stupid to imagine any kind of regular exchange between them might be possible, but he was pleased that Davy had at least forgiven him for "snooping."

When he entered the house, he found his father sitting patiently at the dining room table with a plate of Mona's food in front of him. To his right, in the usual spot, was Neil's plate, heaped with more of the same.

Neil washed his hands, then joined him at the table.

Midway through their salads, his father asked, "Was that the Doyle boy I saw you with? You're a friend of his?"

"We were just on the same bus."

"Ah." His father applied a bit of horseradish to his cold beef. "You know his mother went to the same high school I did? Harbord."

"Was she as nasty then as she is now?"

"She was a nice girl. Corinne O'Malley. Catholics, of course. Too many kids. Corinne was the eldest. Like me. And she had to take care of the younger kids, like me. Her mother was in a wheelchair, just like your grandfather. I always felt a real sympathy for her. Not an easy life. You've no idea, of course. You're a king here."

"*I'm* a king! You're kidding me."

"Well, your mother thinks you're king."

Neil wrinkled his nose. He felt blamed for something, but he wasn't sure what it was.

After supper, his father washed the dishes and Neil dried. When they were done, Frank requested his company on the patio. Neil was surprised. His father almost never wanted his company. But, given the changed quality in his parents over the last few days, Neil optimistically accepted.

They sat silently in the golden evening light, eating Mona's hermit cookies and drinking orange pekoe tea. Eventually, his father sighed.

"You like having your aunt here?"

Neil looked at him as if he were mad.

"She's terrific, isn't she? You've got to love her spirit. Never afraid to stand her ground. She'd take on anyone." His gaze drifted into the burning clouds. "But I loved them all, the whole fam-damily. George was the one pill. Still is. Don't tell your mother I said that." He lifted his teacup, let it hover in the evening air untasted. "You should have known Mrs. Deekman. What a wonderful woman she was. You'd go over for a Sunday supper and there'd be twelve or more at the table and not a detail would be overlooked. The food was cooked to perfection and everything was so beautifully set out. There were candles and flowers and table napkins. Your mother got all that from her. Sylvia took after her dad. She could do anything with her hands. Everyone thought she'd become a carpenter like him." A small, affectionate laugh escaped him. "I loved going over there."

"Was it so bad at home?"

His father turned sharply. "Who said anything 'bout it being bad at home?"

"You just made it sound ..."

"My mother worked very, very hard, and my dad did the best he could. He was a cripple, don't forget. But they provided for us. And everybody admired them. Everybody. The Deekmans admired them. They thought I was pretty good, too. But I wasn't smart. Not like you." His voice grew stern. "My brother Cliff was as smart as you. Maybe smarter even. Got two Masters degrees. Threw it all away when he went into the bloody church. I don't understand. Living in pokey manses in one-horse towns. You tell me how that's smart."

Neil recognized this as an invitation to argue. He said nothing.

After a longish pause, his father spoke again. "The only thing I'm really good at is house-breaking."

Neil refused to look his way.

"People consult me on it. These boys who're doing the break-ins — I taught them."

Neil continued staring straight ahead.

"They're good at the hands-on part, but they need guidance. I told them not to touch Corinne's piano. I told them to go easy on the shellac at Caldwell's place. They don't get certain things. Refinements of the trade. That's why they come to me. They know I know. What they don't realize is that I've got a counsellor, too. A very special counsellor." He looked over at his son, who, besides clutching his tea cup a little more tightly, gave no indication that he'd even heard his father. "Ah well, you'll see. The police won't find the culprits. My counsellor keeps the boys very safe."

Neil began to count in his head, telling himself that when he reached five hundred he'd say goodnight.

"The light's going," his father said, after a few seconds.

Neil decided to concentrate on the long streamers of lavender and pink and apricot floating up into the burnished gold of the evening sky.

Without a word, his father got up and disappeared into the garage. He returned almost immediately, lugging a large canvas. Neil wanted to say, *Please don't start*, but without any fuss or demonstration his father leaned the canvas against the back wall of the patio next to the tarpaulin-covered *Windermere '62*, and then stood away.

It was the same size as *Windermere* but instead of a turbulent, nightmarish landscape, its subject was three large fields of pure colour overlapping one another — red, reddish purple, and reddish brown. Showing at the top and bottom of the canvas were small white shapes that looked at first like soap bubbles. On closer inspection, they turned into clouds. It was almost as if the fields of colour had been hung in front of them to keep them contained.

His father sat again. "*Neil's Dream* I'm calling it."

Neil experienced a sudden jab of alarm. "What does that mean?"

"I don't know. The title just came to me." Frank smiled boastfully. "What do you think?"

Neil shrugged, aware of possible traps. "The colours are beautiful. Especially the magenta. But I don't get the white parts. They mean something, I guess."

"Or nothing. I've just started a new book. It's by Jean-Paul Sartre. I don't suppose you've heard of him."

"*No Exit*," Neil said flatly. He'd read the play during his Christmas break.

"But I bet you haven't read *Being and Nothingness*."

Neil confessed he hadn't.

Frank Bennett smiled self-contentedly. "Perhaps what I'm painting is the 'being' part — the colours, I mean, and the white things, they're nothingness, the absurdity of human life."

"Then the title, *Neil's Dream*, doesn't make sense."

Frank's smile turned from self-satisfied to mysterious. "Doesn't it?"

"The colour parts look like curtains."

"Curtains!" His father was shocked. "They're pure Rothko."

Neil felt suddenly very shaky. "Curtains," he said again.

"No programme! No programme! Just colour. 'Being-in-itself'!"

"It's weird." Neil stood suddenly. "I better go in now."

"It's not even nine o'clock." His father's faintly flickering anxiety was back. "Wait with me till the bats come."

The pleading tone prompted Neil to sit back down. He turned away from the canvas.

For what may have been twenty minutes or even more, nothing was said. Frank lit his pipe, observed the sunset, and occasionally stole nervous glances at his son. Neil looked into the sky, too, but he didn't see much, he was so acutely aware of the painting behind him leaning against the wall. *Neil's Dream*. A dream of curtains, of draperies, hiding something, not something fluffy or bubbly, no, something solid, something very solid, he was sure of that. Still the curtains were right out of his dream. Several times, he peeked at his father who seemed caught up in happy contemplation of the fading light. How could he know? It had to be an accident, a coincidence. Try as he might, though, Neil couldn't quite shake the feeling that it was too much of a coincidence. *Neil's Dream*. He felt slightly queasy.

"If you don't like the painting, you don't have to hang it up. Of course, it's a rough sketch still. I'm not happy with the white. It's too vague." He nodded sagaciously. "Nothingness is anything but vague."

The sky was a deepening blue now with traces of hot pink and orange close to the horizon.

"Soon," his father said, "they'll be coming soon. Every night now, my bats come and with them comes a force. A dark force."

Much too loudly, Neil said, "There's no dark force."

"Oh no? Well, I tell you, I've met him. His name is Vlad."

Neil sighed, uncrossing his knees in preparation for a quick departure.

"I'm not trying to scare you. He has a very deep, rich voice. If the night could speak, it would sound like him."

"You know when people talk about hearing voices —"

"I know, I know, I'm crazy. But, I learn things. Vlad's a very interesting man. Vlad the Impaler. Ever heard of Vlad the Impaler? You would find him interesting. Maybe a bit ruthless, but colourful, very colourful. Your Mrs. What's-her-name? The Romanian?"

"Negulescu."

"Neglescu."

"No! Negulescu. 'U'."

Frank smiled. "You say it how you want. Vlad says 'Neglescu, and he should know. Ask Mrs. Neglescu about Vlad. She'll be familiar with him. Who knows, she may even be related to him."

"Look, Dad!" Neil pointed into the air above the sumach tree.

"Ah! Carmilla. At last!"

"I'm going to go in now." Neil stood quickly, anxious to escape the arrival of his father's dark allies.

"If you must," he replied without looking. "I hope Oswald comes, too. My counsellor usually shows up with Ozzie. 'Night, son." Frank Bennett stared into the growing shadows of the yard as if his son had long ago disappeared.

With one more glance at the canvas, which now appeared nearly colourless in the twilight, Neil hurried into the house. Up in the bathroom, he performed his nightly ablutions at a record speed. He wanted his room badly, wanted the safety that a locked door and his own things could bring him, but when he got there, he was uneasy, anxious.

The coincidence nagged at him. How could it be? A painting called *Neil's Dream* showing curtains blocking something from view. But they weren't curtains, they were colour fields, they were Rothko, they were not his dream. But it was called his dream.

He undressed.

His body felt damp and cool.

He pulled on a pale blue T-shirt. He would sleep in just that.

The curtains he opened slightly, eager to smell the air. It was going to get hot again, he could tell, but the air was sweet tonight. A slight breeze fanned the bushes, adding to the myriad humming sounds that made music unnecessary. Even the train whistles were low and soothing.

His father had been joking about those break-ins. All that stuff about "boys" and "counsellors" was just his typical bullshit. There was no need for worry. But the painting thing was weird. Very weird.

Turning from the window, he stared hard at his bed as if it contained a secret. He peeled back the light summer spread, a pale yellow in colour, and threw it onto the armchair in the corner.

He reminded himself then that his aunt and mother would be home soon. Soon the house would be lighter with the sound of women's voices. Everything would fall back into place and seem quite ordinary again.

It was just a freaky coincidence, that was all.

Neil pictured Jack the Bread-man's face, could see it clearly in the fading light. It made him feel warm, safe. He smiled and pulled back the top sheet.

A hand, a human hand, severed at the wrist, peeked out from under his pillow.

He jumped back with a stifled shriek, hugging the wall.

The hand was a ghastly white colour, but the wrist, where it had been severed, was blood red, jagged, a mess of gristle and bone.

His own hands fell slowly to his sides and he stared at it in fascinated horror.

Suddenly, like a new slide in his father's picture viewer, he recalled another image, this one of the room long before it was his own, before it was anything but cinder block walls and rough ceiling beams. When he was nine, he had been sent on a mission to locate his father's missing pipe tobacco in the basement. What he actually found was a figure sitting in the corner wearing a dirty beige trench coat, with a fedora pulled low on its brow and galoshes on its feet. From the sleeves of the coat protruded two arms, ghostly white, with thin, crooked hands, one of them clutching an ice pick. The tip of the ice pick was stained red. Red drops spattered the floor, marking a serpentine trail to where he stood in the doorway, too stunned even to scream. When the screams did eventually come, half the neighbourhood came with them, wondering what horror had befallen him. It had all ended with a big laugh when the figure was exposed as a fraud, nothing but a lot of newspaper-stuffed sheets dressed up in old clothes and a pair of mannequin's hands. Only Mona Gordon dared to suggest that it might have been a bit much for a nine-year-old.

Neil looked at the hand again. It was a stupid obscenity on the clean white sheet, cheap like the devil's mask, more ugly than scary in its rubbery, squishy way. It was its ugliness finally that broke the barrier, rousing his sleeping rage.

Clutching the hand as he might a wild creature that was trying to escape, he ran to the door, threw it open and, pausing in the dim light at the foot of the stairs, turned to face his father's workshop. Without any clear idea of where it would land, he lobbed the hand with as much force as he could muster into the shadowy room, listening with a kind of dull fear as it made contact with a metallic object. In the darkness something crashed to the floor, disgorging whatever it contained with a shrill clatter.

He didn't stay to inspect the damage. He went to bed and fell fast asleep.

His last conscious image was of Jack's open shirt.

Sometime later, he was awakened not by the sound of women's voices, but by his father quietly filling a metal box with nails.

15

AN HOUR BEFORE THEY WERE due to depart for Aunt Marian's afternoon "do" on Raymond Avenue, Neil went to his room to get dressed up. He settled on black pants and the wine-coloured silk shirt Tony had given him, the Zamboni shirt, not at all sure that his parents would approve. But after putting it on, Neil didn't care whether they liked it or not. He was going to wear it. Having it next to his bare skin, with no undershirt, felt so sensual, Neil could scarcely take it in. It was what being caressed must be like, he decided. He took it off and put it on several times just to savour the sensation.

Of course, the shirt reminded him of Tony, who by then had been with Vicki, had probably even made love with Vicki. He would no longer be a stranger to caresses. Then it occurred to him that Tony had never been a stranger to caresses. That huge family of his was always showering affection upon him: hugs, kisses, cheek pinching, arms casually thrown around shoulders or waists for no other reason than the physical pleasure it gave to both the giver and the receiver. He remembered one afternoon a year or so ago coming into the shop to find Tony's older cousin Claudio talking away to him with one of his hairy hands in Tony's back pocket, squeezing his bum. That was the afternoon when Neil first decided that Tony had been "born under a good star."

As he buttoned up the shirt for the fourth time, he whispered to his mirror, "I'm going to be with Jack. Soon. Very soon." The mirror made no objection, though Neil felt silly the moment he had spoken and avoided his own eyes.

Upstairs, his father sat waiting in the gold-striped armchair as his mother brushed the collar of his sports jacket. "You're not wearing that," he said the moment he saw Neil.

"Why not?"

"You need to wear a tie. It's your Aunt Marian's."

"Where did you get the shirt?" his mother asked, her eyes disbelieving.

"Tony gave it to me. It's from his brother-in-law's shop."

"You're not an Italian," his father said.

"Yes, dear, it's fine for some, but our people will find it odd."

"Who will find what odd?" Aunt Sylvia said, coming up behind him. She was adding the finishing touches to her filmy green outfit — a pair of earrings the shape and colour of marigolds.

"He's dressed for a gangland shooting."

"What are you talking about? He looks gorgeous." She rubbed the sleeve of the shirt between her thumb and forefinger. "Such a beautiful shirt. Silk, very fine silk."

His father looked like a pricked balloon. "Silk, eh?"

"But you know Marian," his mother said. "It won't be 'proper.' Nor is your hair. You should have had it cut."

"Marian's a big girl now. She can deal with a silk shirt on her nephew. And he looks so fine in it. With those smart trousers and the shiny shoes. A perfect colour for him, too. And his hair makes him look like a poet. I think I'll keep him all to myself this afternoon. Marian and Violet and Kay will have to find another nephew to dote on." She pulled Neil close to her side, her arm around his back. Her smile was full of mischief. "See if I don't."

Neil's mother continued to look mildly worried, but his father was a changed man. He stood and, putting his arms into position, smiled contentedly as his wife slipped the grey-blue jacket on them. It was an old, familiar routine Neil had seen five hundred times or more, but on this sweltering afternoon, it looked new and somehow defiant. "Like it or not, this is what we do," it seemed to say.

"Who did you say was going to look odd, Frank?" Sylvia asked. "You'll boil in that jacket."

"Can't help it. Rules are rules."

They all laughed.

Sylvia put her arm around her sister. "Don't you worry. We make a very attractive quartet."

Neil saw that it was true. In her sky blue dress, his mother had never looked prettier, and never more like Aunt Sylvia. Her fair hair and freckles, her pale skin and grey eyes seemed altered. And his father, even though he was overdressed, never looked handsomer. As for his aunt, well, there weren't words eloquent enough.

Sylvia opened her arms. "We'll take their breath away."

⁓

BASKING IN THE steamy light of Aunt Marian and Uncle Henry's rose garden, Neil couldn't have been more content. He had his Aunt Sylvia next to him, entertaining him with *sotto voce* comments and the occasional squeeze of his arm. Two large rosebushes, heavy with fragrant blossoms, were behind him. And before him was a constantly shifting scene of family folly, which, thanks to his aunt's position as guest of honour, he could observe and enjoy with the freedom of an almost invisible man.

Except for Val and Aunt Julie, they were all there. "For the first time in ten years," Aunt Violet kept saying, making ten years sound like a thousand.

Pretty, flowery Marian and her skinny beanpole of a husband, Henry, a dead-ringer for Astaire everyone said, seemed to be always in motion: Marian with bowls of cashews, chocolate-covered peanuts, and almonds with raisins, which Neil found wonderfully eccentric; Henry with glasses to be filled or glasses to be delivered. Uncle George, the somewhat portly, silver-haired eldest Deekman sibling, sat prominently in the middle of the garden, smiling benevolently like a grand poobah, occasionally pulling on his tie or belt to make sure they were behaving. His wife, the deep-voiced Kay, stood watch, an impressively towering Amazon with a shock of white accenting the raven darkness of her hair. A cluster of "the girls," cousins Sandra, Anne and Wendy, debated the relative merits of nail polishes. Wendy's husband, Gary, a somewhat forlorn little rabbit without her attention, was talking to anyone who looked his rapidly blinking way. This included Aunt Vi, in a dress covered in glittery sunbursts; blowsy cousin Doreen who lounged in the shade of an elm tree, fanning herself with one of those pretty paper fans that were a dime a dozen in Chinatown; and Neil's father, who had finally surrendered his suit jacket. His mother and Uncle Herb occupied seats to Neil's right and were kept very busy commenting on photos of cousin Ken's recent European holiday. As tall as his father Henry, but lanky rather than skinny, Ken was gregarious to a fault and a pitiless smiler. Neil couldn't help feeling the smile was a grab for attention and he hated it. Ken's very pregnant wife, Janie, who looked a lot like a lemon meringue pie in her yellowy-white maternity dress, only spoke in stage-prompting whispers when she felt it was necessary to correct Ken's geography.

George, having little to do and even less to think about, seemed to think it fell to him to get a general conversation going. Outboard motors generated little interest. Burt Lancaster as the bird man of Alcatraz, a little more. The care and maintenance of roses captured him for a while as his sister Marian tried to remember the names of the bushes that lined their fences and got hopelessly confused. But it was George's ungainly leap into the political field that got everybody riled up. Smiling at Sylvia, whom he had not stopped

gazing at since her arrival, he said, rather more loudly than necessary, "I can't believe it. You're not only a citizen of that godforsaken
country, you vote Democrat! Democrat! And he's a Mick to boot.
What would Dad have said? What would Dad have said?"

"Dad would have minded his own business," she answered,
her laugh shimmering in the garden like dappled light.

George scowled. "What do you think of it, Frank?"

"Whoever Sylvia votes for is fine with me. It doesn't affect us
anyway."

Neil knew this was a lie, because his father hated the Kennedys.
He'd told his wife he thought Sylvia was crazy supporting "those
damn Catholics."

A further political conflagration was only put out by a quiet
question from Aunt Marian: "Why are you picking fights, George?
Sylvia's come all this way to see us. Keep this up and she'll wish
she'd never come."

But it was all good, Neil figured. As the afternoon progressed,
with his aunt stroking his wine-silk sleeve on the armrest, he could
feel her affection for her family slowly seeping into him. By the
time Aunt Marian and her daughters began bringing out the trays
of food for their "high tea," as Marian called it, Neil thought he
could be happy if time just stood still and left him forever surrounded by this group of people. He couldn't recall the worry he
had experienced in the days just before Sylvia arrived. He saw
himself only as another fully-fledged member of the clan, transparent, open to all comers.

The first cloud scudded across his sky when his cousin Ken
invited him and Sylvia to take an "inexpensive tour of Greece."

Ken's pictures were beautiful, as beautiful at least as Rick's
postcard from Mykonos, and with them came a lot of interesting stories, which Ken told with the flair of a polished entertainer.
One photo, about halfway through the album, showed a stretch
of white beach curled around a luminescent aquamarine sea.

Unlike the dozens of other photos of beaches Ken had taken, this one was quite populous. There were many tanning bodies in very skimpy swimming trunks lying out under what looked like a blazing sky. Titillated by the near-nudity, it took Neil a second to clue into the obvious fact that all the sunbathers were men.

Without thinking, he gave voice to his observation. "So are beaches segregated?"

"Segregated?" Kenny said. "No. No. Men and women go to the beach together."

"But there aren't any women there."

Kenny smirked, "No. You're right." He looked around him like a detective casing a joint and, then, just loud enough for Neil and Sylvia to hear, he said, "Janie and I just stumbled onto this beach. We saw it from the rocks above, and thought, Wow, isn't it gorgeous, and she wanted to give it a try, so we went down and, lo and behold, it was a special beach. A beach for queers."

Neil kept his eyes lowered.

"It was a shock. All those men — looking for you know what."

"The sun?" Sylvia asked.

"Well, yeah, that, too."

"And the air and the sea. It looks like a lovely beach."

It was Kenny's turn to look embarrassed.

"Look how relaxed all those young men look. They have time, and they have company. How lucky. I can feel the heat, can't you? Of course, Mediterranean heat's a lot different from ours."

"It sure is. Greece's a great place, Aunt Sylvia," he said, turning the page quickly to several photos of a large port city. Piraeus, Neil assumed. Just then, the food parade began. Ken rose with his album under his arm and hurriedly went in search of his pregnant wife, who had fled inside to escape the heat.

Aunt Sylvia patted Neil's hand. "There's a moral to that story."

The second cloud in Neil's perfect sky caused more of an eclipse than the first. They were all enjoying coffee or tea and Marian's delicious little cakes iced in a fantasy of colours, when Uncle George, who had overlooked Neil after the initial handshake, suddenly zeroed in on him.

"And where did that shirt come from, Neil? Is that one of your gifts, Sylvia?"

"No, no. It isn't, though I would love to have been the giver of such a gift."

"So you have a girlfriend then who dresses you up, eh?"

"No, Uncle George."

"You bought it yourself? Good heavens, are you going to take up tango next? It looks like a dago shirt."

"It's silk, George," Sylvia said with a sigh. "Silk is not 'dago' by definition."

"Maybe not, maybe not. It's the colour I'm talking about."

"It's a beautiful colour, Neil," Aunt Marian offered. Several of the women, including his mother, echoed her sentiments.

"Well, that's what I mean," George continued. "Women, it's a woman's colour."

"George, dear, the sexes do not own colours." Kay's voice was especially deep.

"Wha'ddya mean? Blue for boys, pink for girls. That shirt's in the pink line."

Neil looked over at his father, whose face had grown very dark, almost stormy.

"You know what I think, George?" said Aunt Sylvia.

He turned towards his sister. "What's that, Sylvia?"

"I think you need a hobby. You obviously haven't got enough on your plate if you have all this energy for debating the merits of colours. I thought you were a speculative man. Why don't you take up philosophy, George? Or theology? Something to really sink your teeth into. A burgundy silk shirt is hardly worth all this mental effort, is it?"

From behind her husband, Kay gave Sylvia the okay sign. Frank's face was now brimming with smiles.

"While you think about it, George, I'm going for a walk around this lovely neighbourhood and my nephew in his wine-red silk shirt is going to accompany me. And believe me, I will feel very proud to have him on my arm." Sylvia stood, her filmy green dress shimmering, her earrings glowing like coals. She gave her hand to Neil, who rose as he took it. "Think hard, now," she said, giving her brother a light tap on the shoulder before she and Neil moseyed down the driveway in search of Raymond Avenue's pastoral pleasures.

THE HOUSES ON Raymond were mostly of the two-storey brick variety, with tiny frontages and long narrow back gardens. Solid, sturdy, unblinking, with little or no imagination, they were at most forty years old, but looked as if they had been there forever. Neil's father hated them, deemed them cramped, dark, dull, and would on every visit to the neighbourhood, remind Neil how lucky he was to live in a house with lots of yard around it and room to breathe.

Neil, however, found the street and its dwellings magical. The leaded glass windows were Old World enough to suggest English colleges full of young men in pullovers pouring over dusty tomes. The long covered verandahs spoke to Neil of long evenings of warm companionship and stimulating conversation, lubricated by exotic beverages he had no names for. The trees, older by far than the few that lined Avery and Dominion streets, he imagined as grand partners in the dance of gracious living. In the honey-coloured light of late September, when the leaves burned red and gold, he could attain a state bordering on rapture standing under their branches. The wind that shook the leaves loose and set them spinning down the sidewalks set him free, too, and the image

of hurrying down windy streets at the edge of the world, head
bent, scarf fluttering out behind him, left him almost dizzy with
excitement.

As they walked, he attempted, shyly at first, to communicate
some of his delight to his aunt. She listened very attentively, every
so often throwing out a word or two of encouragement; soon,
he lost track of where he was and began pouring out all the enthusiasm of his young heart for the street, the city, and the world at
large in a voice that belonged on a great stage.

Two brief, almost quiet, blasts of a car horn brought him back
to earth.

Startled and immediately anxious, he scanned the street to see
what wrong he had done.

Aunt Sylvia put her hand on his sleeve.

"I'm sorry for going on," he said. "I wasn't watching."

"You weren't going on. And the horn wasn't meant for you."
With her gaze she indicated a dark green car with a curved roof
idling in front of a two-and-a-half storey faux-Tudor house, one
much larger than any on Raymond Avenue. Its front door, also
dark green, occupied the centre of the façade rather than one side,
which Neil knew from his father's years of real estate news meant
a roomier centre hall plan.

He looked around him. They were at the intersection of Brumell
Avenue and Baby Point Road. The large house with its dark green
front door was number 25.

In a low, anxious voice, he told his aunt, "I know who lives
in there."

"Do you want to drop in?"

"I mean it's someone who comes into the library."

"Do you know the addresses of many of your library patrons?"

"I was working the night he applied for his card."

"Is he one of them?" His aunt nodded towards the house. Two
figures were emerging from the front door.

"Oh, let's walk, can we, Auntie? I don't want them to see us."

They picked up their pace, but the two people walking towards them were faster, and they met where the walkway to the house joined the sidewalk.

The figure in front was a young man, clearly one of Bread-man's brothers, but not the smiling, goofy one he'd seen before. This one would probably have been more beautiful than Bread-man himself if he hadn't looked so severe. Neil was disturbed by the hard line of the mouth and the chilly blue eyes. The drab but obviously expensive charcoal-coloured suit he wore over his crisp white shirt and dark tie only added to the impression of a beauty spurned. The difference between him and Bread-man couldn't have been more graphic. Bread-man was sunshine to this young man's gloominess. The only thing about him that held any hope or light at all were his highly, and probably painstakingly, polished shoes.

The other figure was a tall, gaunt man in navy blue with iron-grey hair and a once-handsome countenance that was more severe, if possible, than his companion's. The lines of suffering etched in it should have awakened sympathy, but they did nearly the opposite. These were harsh, grim lines. Neil couldn't wait to look somewhere else.

In a low, correct voice, the older man said, "Good afternoon," to them as they passed.

Aunt Sylvia replied, "And to you both as well."

The young man said nothing, allowed himself no smile. He opened the car door for the elder, then marched briskly around the car to take his place at the wheel. As he did, he glanced briefly at Neil and Sylvia. His blue, blue eyes lingered for a second on Neil's face. Something softer seemed to emerge, but it was quickly eclipsed by a frown when the older man rolled down his window, muttering, "I don't like you honking the horn on a Sunday afternoon. I've told you that before."

They could not make out the young man's response, if there was one.

"Cheery folks," his aunt said as the car passed them. "Perhaps they're going to a funeral."

Neil made no reply. An intense curiosity held him in its grip — curiosity about Jack's brother, his obvious unhappiness and his even more obvious beauty. Such amazing blue eyes he had! He wanted to ask his aunt's opinion — she would no doubt have one — but didn't dare mention his interest even to her.

He turned instead to quizzing her about life in Los Angeles. Though he had the sense she wasn't fooled by his sudden return to this subject, she gamely offered him enough anecdotes about star-sighting — Dorothy Malone, Walter Brennan, Rose Hobart, and so on — to satiate him. His favourite was a story of Aunt Julia helping Kim Novak to select an evening gown. "You know she's a very private person," his aunt told him, winking. "She keeps to herself, avoids a lot of publicity. Of course there are rumours, but she rises above them all. She was apparently very gracious towards Julia. Stars live in another world, though. They don't cook or clean for themselves. Their salaries are astronomical, and when they travel they stay in only the best places. Unlike nearly everyone else on the continent." Then, turning a pair of laughing eyes on him, she said, "You didn't tell me which one of those gentlemen was your patron."

"Neither," Neil said, nervously. "The older one must be Bread-man's father."

"Bread-man?"

"Oh, didn't I mention it?" Neil knew he hadn't, but to cover his gaffe, he said, "The patron, the library patron, is also our temporary bread-man."

"Wasn't there talk about this bread-man on Friday night at the Gordons? Didn't Lana Gordon call him dreamy?"

Neil admitted it was so. "Girls talk that way all the time. Dreamboat here, dreamboat there."

"You don't like being called a dreamboat?"

Neil gave her such an uncomfortable look, she immediately went on, "Well, that young man back there was certainly very good-looking, if not exactly a dreamboat. He's maybe a bit too bottled up to be a dreamboat."

"He must be one of the brothers, Augustine or Ignatius."

"My heavens! Poor boys."

"They've got other names, first names, but I don't remember them. They're Catholics. Jack is short for John Henry. He was named for a cardinal. The Catholic kind."

"You know a lot about your patron."

"He's very friendly. And really smart. He reads French."

Sylvia smiled. "A man who reads French is a man of the world, so they say."

They had reached Thornhill Avenue and were standing undecided at the corner, as if they had all day to choose a direction. The afternoon light sprinkling through the leaves of the big oaks and maples made the sidewalks shimmer.

"I'm sorry for blabbing," he said after they had stood a few seconds in silence. "I get carried away sometimes. It doesn't happen very often."

"That's a pity. A boy your age should get carried away on a regular basis. If you ask me, that boy back there is in desperate need of getting carried away."

"Jack's not like that."

"Good, good. Perhaps he'll give you lessons."

16

WITH NO PROMPTING FROM EITHER parent, Neil took himself to the barbershop on Wednesday morning.

A squat middle-aged man was leaving as he arrived, so that for the first time in a long while, both barbers, Ronnie and Vass, were available. There were actually three chairs in the barbershop, but Neil had only ever known two barbers to work there.

When he entered, Ronnie was sweeping up the salt-and-pepper remnants of his last customer. Vass, whose full name was Vasilis, was lounging in his chair reading a Greek newspaper.

"Oh, oh, here comes trouble," Ronnie said at first sight of Neil. He always said that.

Vass looked up and winked at Neil. "And what can we do for you today?"

"A haircut."

"Any old haircut?"

"No, a special one. I'm going out tonight."

"Ahhh, a date, is it? Is she nice?" Ronnie gestured towards his chest, with a quick, naughty squeezing gesture.

Neil laughed shyly. "It's with my aunt, who's visiting from California. We're going to see *Breakfast at Tiffany's*."

"Haven't seen it, but I know the song." He started to hum "Moon River," leaning on his broom. After a moment, he broke off. "Am I right?"

"He's Mr. Name-that-Tune, Neil," Vass said.

"Nice song." Ronnie started sweeping again, "So, you want me or Vass?"

"Do I have to choose?"

"Of course you have to choose. We both want you in our chair, but we both can't have you, so ...?"

"That's not fair." He looked from one to the other, from Vass with his olive skin and dark curly hair to red-cheeked Ronnie who looked as if his mother had just finished scrubbing him within an inch of his life, and then back again. He liked them both. They were always so nice to him, but there was something exotic about Vass that gave him a slight edge in the contest. Still, he didn't want to hurt Ronnie's feelings.

Both men laughed at his consternation. Then Vass spoke up. "I'm going to take him. You had the last one."

Ronnie made as if he were offended. "Nobody has Mr. Medland."

Neil didn't quite understand all this but he smiled, glad it was going to be Vass.

"Okay, okay. I give up. Vaseline wins."

They all laughed. Vaseline was Ronnie's nickname for Vass.

Neil climbed into the chair and Vass tied the bib around him. Then, looking at Neil in the mirror, he ran his hands through the boy's hair, checking its real length.

"So, how you want it?"

Ronnie sniggered. He was tidying up his counter, putting order into the scissors, the combs, the razor heads and the usual brightly coloured pomades and lotions.

Neil looked at him, not quite sure what was so funny.

"Don't pay any attention to him, Neil. He's just frustrated." Vass leaned down and spoke so closely into Neil's ear that it tickled. "He doesn't get any, you know. So he acts like this."

Neil knew what that meant.

"I'm getting more than you, Mr. Vaseline." Ronnie plopped himself down in his own chair. Leaning forward, he pulled open a drawer in the bank of cabinets beneath the counter and extracted what looked to Neil like a sports magazine.

"How do you know that?"

"I see that hungry look in your eye when you come in here mornings."

"You sure it's not the look of satisfaction?"

Ronnie snorted and opened his magazine. Neil could make out pictures of men wrestling.

"I make it in between, okay?" Vass said. "Good for your face."

"I always like your haircuts."

"You should see what else he can do," Ronnie said.

"Ignore him, Neil. He's bad today." Vass smiled at him in the mirror.

Neil closed his eyes, content to listen to the buzz of the razor and the metallic click of the scissors and to luxuriate in the feeling of the barber's warmth against his shoulder and arm. As Vass began to work at the front of his head, Neil lifted his hands from his lap, almost mechanically, and placed them on the armrests. Vass stepped in closer to the chair and, continuing to clip as if nothing had changed, gently pressed his groin against Neil's hand.

This always happened.

The first time, two years before, Neil had attempted to move his hand away, but Vass said, "No, it's okay. Unless I hurt you?"

"No," Neil had said.

"Then it can stay. What do you think?"

Neil had nodded his head. From that time on, it always happened just the same when Vass was his barber.

As Neil felt the pressure of the barber's groin against his hand, he smiled slightly but his eyes remained closed.

After a while, he heard Ronnie move. A drawer opened and

closed. Ronnie was standing up. He said to Vass, "You hot?"

"Very," Vass said. "Very hot."

"It's going to get hotter. You hot, Neil?"

Neil's eyelids fluttered open. "A bit. Yeah, I'm hot."

Ronnie hooted. "I hear ya. I'm so hot I need some juice. You need anything, Vass? A chicken sandwich maybe ?"

"I'd love a chicken sandwich."

It was the same conversation every time, no matter which of them was his barber.

Ronnie laughed. The bell above the door tinkled his departure.

Vass began to press on his hand now even more insistently.

Neil couldn't close his eyes again.

He knew now what hot was.

Neil looked up at Vass. "What does 'chicken sandwich' mean?"

"You know what a chicken sandwich —"

"No. Every time I come here, you say the same thing. One of you goes and then comes back and there's no chicken sandwich. What does it mean?"

Vass dropped his arms, which, up to that moment, had been hovering in classic barber mode, scissors and comb poised like birds to fly at Neil's hair. "You're chicken," he said softly.

Neil's forehead creased with puzzlement.

"It doesn't mean scared, it means young. Chicken is young. A word for a cute young guy."

Neil swallowed. He could hear Jack saying, "Forbidden fun." He swallowed again. "Chicken sandwich?"

Vass's smile was faint but there. "Ronnie and me, we're the bread. You're the filling. You see?"

Neil sat very, very still in the chair, mouth dry, heart racing, looking straight ahead at himself in the mirror. The face looking back was pale and worried. The way it stuck up above the bib made him think of a puppet's head. Like one of the puppets his father had made for him years ago, Hansel or the Frog Prince.

Maybe that's what he was after all, a puppet easy to manipulate. Is that what he was to Jack? He felt slightly sick. But then he allowed his gaze to shift to the reflection of Vass's curly dark hair and broad shoulders. The shoulders looked very strong in the mirror. Their strength reminded him of the man's penis. It probably wasn't hard anymore. For some reason that thought disappointed him. He liked the strength of the man. It would be a simple matter to have it again if he wanted, some forbidden fun.

"Sorry, Neil," Vass said.

"It's okay," he said, at last.

"We finish?"

"Yes, please."

Vass began to clip.

Ronnie came in seconds later and headed for the basement toilet. In the mirror, Neil saw Vass shake his head as if to warn Ronnie off more teasing.

Neil closed his eyes, listening to Ronnie's very light footfall on the cellar stairs. Behind him, he left a faint odour of cloves.

In a very quiet voice, Neil said, "Thanks, Vass. For explaining."

"You got to know someday, I guess."

Slowly, deliberately, Neil placed his hands back on the armrests. Vass looked down at them.

17

SYLVIA INSISTED ON TAKING THE bus to the cinema, saying, "It's been ten years since I rode on Toronto transit. It'll be fun."

Neither her sister nor her brother-in-law could imagine what fun there might be in riding a bus full of Italian factory and construction workers, but Neil thought it was very cool. Even cooler was the fact that he didn't have to point out his favourite sights; his aunt could identify them without his guidance. What was more, she added something to every beloved landmark. When they reached Our Lady of Sorrows, she commented on its quietly inviting façade, then asked him to take note of the contrast with the Kingsway movie theatre across the street where Vincent Price was starring in a bloody adaptation of Poe's *Tales of Terror*. As they passed the cemetery, she spoke of the rain that pelted down the day her mother was buried there, "beating the flowers to a pulp; it looked as if they were in mourning, too." Then, approaching the bridge that crossed the Humber, she said, "It feels like we're about to enter a new world."

The first building on the city side of the bridge was a stucco apartment block, which his father never failed to judge harshly for its sickly pink hue. Aunt Sylvia, on seeing it, merely said, "Oh, that reminds me of apartment buildings in Italy — the colour, I mean. Rosé, isn't it?"

"They have apartments that colour?"

"Oh, yes, brighter pink, too, and canary yellow, and tangerine, sky blue, rusty-red, you name it."

"I would love that."

When finally they reached the Jane Loop, Sylvia told him how she'd once dated a man who lived on Armadale across from the Loop. "He was my friend Molly's brother. I thought we had something special, but then all of a sudden he decided he had to go off and do something really useful in the world. Something in China, as I remember. He never came home. I couldn't come out to the Loop for years without remembering him and his decision." She took her nephew's hand. "But now I've got you to associate to the Loop. How about we take the streetcar to the theatre — for old times' sake?"

"It's only two stops, though."

Once they boarded, there was a wait of several minutes before the tram took off. During that time, Sylvia told her nephew about the Harbord car. "Our streetcar. We all took it to get to work. It was such a splendid route. It took you all the way from the northwest of the old city right downtown through the garment district, the Jewish market, Chinatown and the old Ward. I spent a lot of my life on that car, reading, thinking, watching people. Oh, the people." She shook her head. "In LA the buses are an afterthought. The public is an afterthought. There's no sense of a city life like here, a daily life shared with others the way we had with the Harbord car." She seemed almost tearful when she stopped talking, but she brushed aside the memories almost impatiently. "The weather in California makes up for a lot, you know."

The streetcar rolled out of the Loop. She was immediately alert, attentive. Neil pointed out Parma Fruits and Vegetables, the Polish Church and Runnymede Shoes, and, as they got off at Runnymede Road, the library two blocks further east.

"It looks like you've made this your part of town."

The cinema was nearly empty when they entered. It turned out they were more than twenty-five minutes early for the first show-ing. As they sat in the middle of the middle row, or as close to middle as Neil could calculate without actually counting the rows, they both acknowledged a twinge of excitement. Anticipation of seeing the film was high, especially on Neil's part, but that wasn't the only cause of their excitement. The slightly clammy coolness of the theatre after the heat of the street, the usher's rumpled red jacket with its tarnished gold buttons, the fresh smell of buttered popcorn mixed with the leftover scent of cigarettes floating above the smoking section at the rear, the magisterial wine-red curtain, the plush red seats — all those features added to the thrill of a night at the movies.

For a while they sat in silence, absorbing the close atmosphere, redolent, like the streetcars, of personal histories, human emotions.

Finally, Neil said, "I never thought I'd get to see it."

"Your mother didn't make much objection."

"She thinks I don't know anything. I know what kind of woman Holly is."

"We grew up in a different time, Neil."

"But you don't worry that the film will corrupt me."

"No, but your mother and I are very different people. I think it's actually quite a sweet film. But I don't want to say any more in case I give something away. How 'bout I go get some popcorn?"

"I can go."

"No," she said, a restraining hand on his arm. "Let me do it. For old times' sake."

Neil watched the people file in, in pairs mostly, or small groups. A few people showed up on their own, men mostly. Nobody really stood out, besides one woman who came in wearing a fancy black dress, black gloves and a small pillbox hat with a black net veil covering half her face. She was special, in an odd way, and so was the young blond man in evening wear who accompanied her. They should have been somewhere else, Neil thought, an opera house or something, but he enjoyed looking at them anyway. He also kept an eye out for Bread-man, for Jack, but he failed to appear.

His aunt returned with the popcorn. "Did you see the extras for the movie?" she asked.

"You mean that couple in fancy clothes?"

The lights in the theatre dimmed then. The curtain flamed a brilliant red, darkened, and parted as the snowy-capped Paramount Pictures mountain reared up on the screen. There it brooded under its thatch of clouds for a moment before fading to black.

Neil's heart was racing. He leaned forward with a handful of popcorn, scarcely breathing.

A yellow cab was rolling up a deserted Fifth Avenue in the early morning light, soft and hazy. A harmonica played the first bars of "Moon River," turning it into something plaintive, haunting. Outside a polished granite building fitted with display windows, the cab stopped. A woman in sunglasses alighted. Tall, elegantly gowned and coiffed, a tiara in her hair and diamonds around her throat, she made her graceful way across the empty pavement to the windows, clutching a white paper bag in her evening-gloved hands. The credits rolled.

Neil trembled.

The aloof yet alluring woman reached into her white paper bag, extracting a crescent roll and a take-away coffee, and peered into the glittering trays of jewels.

Neil smiled and sat back. He thought, this is *Breakfast at Tiffany's.*

From those very first moments Neil forgot where he was, forgot that his Aunt Sylvia from California was sitting next to him, forgot that he was living in Toronto, Canada and that it was July 18, 1962, forgot that he was frequently frightened, forgot that he was a 'mo, forgot everything. Not one detail escaped him, not one scrap of dialogue was missed. The world of Holly Golightly and her would-be writer boyfriend became everything to him. It wasn't like watching a film. He was there. He knew. He knew not only who and what Holly was, he knew what Paul the writer was, too, as well as the woman who kept Paul in Apartment 2-E. He knew. He even knew Sally Tomato, and the conman, and the oily Brazilian tycoon, and Doc, poor country bumpkin Doc, coming all that way to get his wild girl, Lula Mae, back. He knew them all. He knew their desire.

Later that night, waiting for sleep to come, he would make some tentative connections between this kind of knowing and his experiences of the last several weeks — with Edsel-man, with Dr. Brazier, with Vass in the barber chair and, most of all, with Jack — but in the theatre he was only aware that he knew those characters. He hugged them to him like old acquaintances.

Only once did he awaken from his enchantment. At the very moment when Paul throws open his window to listen to Holly sing "Moon River" on the fire escape, Aunt Sylvia quietly removed a tissue from her purse and dabbed at her eyes. It struck him as strange. The moment was a happy one. Paul was writing. Holly was serenading him. Neil felt hopeful for them, not sad. Then the words came: "Two drifters, off to see the world, there's such a lot of world to see." Maybe that was his aunt, too — a voyager looking for the rainbow's end.

As he caught his aunt's reaction, he glimpsed the person seated directly behind her. It was Bread-man, in a white shirt, smiling into his hand.

Neil smiled, too, but he couldn't stop to let Bread-man know he'd been seen. Time with Holly was flying by. He had to go.

The end came fast, too. Another yellow cab in the teeming rain. Late New York afternoon. Paul's challenge: stay and be loved. Holly's refusal: escape is the only option. She thrust her no-name cat out into the downpour, Paul following. Would she really do as she said? Would the airport be her destination? Holly was hovering, frightened.

Neil sat on the edge of his seat praying, praying she would get out of the cab, go after Cat, go after Paul. *Please, please* — he almost whispered it.

Soaking wet, she careened down the sidewalk into an alley lined with trashcans. "Cat!" she called, "Cat!" Paul watched her, knowing she'd chosen to stay and be loved. Cat meowed from inside an old crate. Grabbing him to her chest, she wrapped him up in her coat and moved to Paul who took both of them in his arms. "Moon River" soared above the embracing couple. It was not a lonely song now, but a joyous one.

Neil was so happy, he cried a little.

The End appeared in a flowing script.

He sat back again.

Aunt Sylvia touched his arm. "You need anything?" she asked.

"I'm okay," he said shyly.

"Did you like it?"

"It's the best movie I've ever seen." He eyed her sideways. "Did you?"

"Very much. She's such a doll."

It was then he remembered spotting Bread-man and he swung around. Bread-man was already in the aisle moving towards the exit.

"There's the man who lives at 25 Baby Point. Jack."

Bread-man saw them and waved.

"He said he was going to come."

They made their way to the aisle. Neil was surprised at how many people there were, and annoyed at how slowly they made their way out of the theatre. By the time they got to the door, Neil fully expected Bread-man to be gone, but he was wrong. Jack was standing on the edge of the curb, facing the doors. He seemed to be waiting for them — and if Neil wasn't mistaken, he even looked excited at the prospect of saying hello. If only that was true, Neil thought, if only. His grey eyes locked onto Bread-man's smile.

"How do you do? I'm Jack Rookwood." Bread-man put out his hand to the woman at Neil's side.

Sylvia shook it, with a smile. "Hello. Sylvia Deekman."

"My aunt."

Jack smiled at Neil then. "I guess you liked it a little bit ... maybe ..."

"It's the best movie he's ever seen," Sylvia said.

"Can't beat that. I liked it too," Jack said. "Maybe not as much as the book, but then I shouldn't compare them. It's something altogether different. And as something altogether different, it's pretty great."

They began walking westwards towards the Loop. Shards of colour vied for dominance of the sky, with a deep violet well ahead of the others.

Neil felt a bit tongue-tied walking between his aunt and Bread-man, but he managed to say, "I loved the opening especially, when the taxi stops outside Tiffany's."

"She sure knows how to walk," Jack said. "That's why all those directors have her walking."

"You've seen her other films?" Neil asked, as if this were an extraordinary possibility.

Jack laughingly assured him he had. "She walks all over Rome in *Roman Holiday* and all over Paris in *Funny Face* and *Love in the Afternoon*. In *The Nun's Story*, when she leaves the convent at the end, that walk is absolutely magnificent, down the alleyway to the main street, where she pauses, looks one way, then another, and then heads off into the future. And the world is at war! It's so amazing. And she does nearly the same thing in *The Children's Hour*, walking past all those people who've nearly destroyed her life, walking head high towards something new and unknown. It's stunning." He suddenly stopped and laughed. "I missed my calling, I think. I should have been a movie reviewer."

"No need to apologize. You're obviously a film buff," Sylvia said. "And an Audrey buff, too, I'm guessing."

"You're right on both counts, Miss Deekman."

"Miss Deekman will not do. If you're Jack, I'm Sylvia."

"I've only seen *Funny Face*," Neil said sadly. "I could've seen *The Children's Hour*. It was at the Odeon in the winter. I really wanted to go. But my parents nixed that."

"If you read the play, you'll know why," Jack said.

"I did read the play. The little girl accuses the two teachers of loving each other." He felt very mature saying this. "'Were we supposed to lie down and grin while you kicked us around with these lies?' Martha says that to Mrs. Tilford in that scene where she and Karen try to clear themselves."

"Maybe if Shirley MacLaine had said it the way you did, Mrs. Tilford would've capitulated," Jack said laughing.

They arrived at Runnymede Shoes. In the doorway, hands in pockets, pipe in mouth, stood Uncle Herb. "Evening to you all," he said. "I thought I'd just come down and keep an eye out. Looks like someone's had a haircut. Why are you blushing? It's a terrific haircut."

Neil was blushing because the mention of his haircut reminded him of the barbershop and the pressure against his hand, reminded him how he had turned his hand palm up on the armrest finally, offering Vass a different kind of contact. He didn't dare look at Jack.

"And we have a terrific sunset, too."

Sylvia smiled. "You look just like Dad used to. Those summer nights on Crawford, with his pipe."

"I'll take that as a compliment, Sylvia dear."

They all hovered, soaking up the sky, which was now a rosy violet.

Herb looked Jack up and down. "I've seen you somewhere before."

Jack pointed to his shoes of soft brown leather. "In May. I bought these from you."

"That's possible. I certainly carried them. You're ...?"

"This is Jack, Uncle Herb. He was at the movies. He's a regular at the library, too. And —" He looked at Jack, unsure whether to continue.

"I'm also his bread-man. Well, not just his, of course, other people's, too, though he's the only one I deliver brown bread to."

"I'm Herb Deekman. Please join us. My wife's been putting together a little post-show repast. There's more than enough food."

Jack seemed taken aback and, for some reason, a bit shy. "No, no, thank you, I should get going."

"Why?" Neil asked. "Please come in, please."

At just that moment, Aunt Violet appeared at the door in a white dress patterned in big red roses. "Well, I hope you don't think I'm going to bring everything down here. Good lord, look at that sky! This summer's been a real showcase for sunsets!"

"We have a guest, my dear, a friend of Neil's. Jack, Jack ...?"

"Rookwood."

"Rookwood?" Aunt Violet said. "You the doctor's son? Dr. Ambrose Rookwood?"

Jack acknowledged he was.

"Well, it was enough that you were Neil's friend, but now that you're my doctor's boy, you're doubly welcome. Just don't tell him about all the sweets I've made. I'm not supposed to, you know." She gestured towards her ample stomach.

"I promise."

"Caramel crunch cookies. They're Neil's favourite, eh, Neil? That's a nice haircut! And chocolate cream pie. With real chocolate, none of that syrupy American stuff that tastes like tar. Sylvia will tell you — I know my chocolate."

"How can you say no to such an invitation?" Sylvia asked.

Jack's smile took them all in.

AUNT VIOLET AND Uncle Herb's flat was almost identical to Angie and Bruno Zamboni's across the street, but where theirs always looked crowded and dark, Herb and Violet's was bright and colourful. This effect they had managed with the help of buttery yellow wall paint and window coverings that filtered rather than obscured the light. Their sitting room was crowded in the sense that it was small, but somehow, sitting on their roomy sofa bedecked with multi-coloured cushions or in one of their plush old armchairs with carved wooden arms always gave Neil a feeling of vast comfort, ease and even opulence. Everything contributed to that feeling: the old gas fire with its ornate screen, the amber-shaded deco ceiling fixtures and wall sconces, the many mirrors hung to make the rooms appear larger, as well as the scores of family photos filling the spaces between the mirrors, especially the large one of his Aunt Julia as a young woman dressed in a long violet ball-gown, pink flowers in her hair. Hand-coloured in a gilt-frame, it floated regally above the dining room credenza.

At first Neil worried that Jack felt pressured to join them and would maybe find the evening trying, but Jack actually seemed gleeful as Herb gave him an annotated tour of the family photos.

When they reached the big one of Aunt Julia, Jack said, "She looks like Ingrid Bergman!"

Uncle Herb replied, with great pleasure, "That's it, of course. Did you hear that, Sylvia? Jack here thinks Julia looks like Ingrid Bergman."

"And this young man?" Jack asked, pointing to a headshot of Neil taken when he was twelve years old. The expression was gentle, innocent, with a hint of a smile lingering on the wide mouth.

"Oh, him — that's a nephew of ours, a much-loved nephew of ours."

Jack was staring hard at the photo. "I can see why," he said.

"Yes, he was reading *Pride and Prejudice* when I snapped this photo. That's why he looks so refined, I guess."

The room laughed.

Jack took a seat opposite Neil on the sofa, beside Herb. As he did, Cousin Sandra came into the room wearing a cantaloupe-coloured dress. On seeing the handsome Jack, who stood to greet her, she instantly blushed. Violet and Herb looked at each other, smiling. Neil made introductions.

"Hi," Sandra said very shyly, "I'm glad to meet you."

"It's mutual," Jack said, shaking her hand gently.

"Sandy, help me serve, will you?" her mother called.

"I'll help," Sylvia said. "We'll let the young people talk."

"Oh, no, you won't. You're the special guest."

The food came around, a tray of cheeses and biscuits garnished with red and green grapes — probably from Parma Fruits and Vegetables, Neil thought with satisfaction — followed by Aunt Vi's incredible sweets — the chocolate cream pie was a dream — and two types of tea, jasmine and black.

Jack partook of everything with obvious pleasure. With an even more obvious pleasure — or so it seemed to Neil — he chatted with the blushing, sweet-voiced Sandra who had stolen the seat on the other side of him and insisted on hogging all his attention. Over the space of half an hour, Jack hardly looked at anyone else, except to respond to Aunt Vi's inquiries of "More?" or "Another cup?" or to laugh briefly with Aunt Sylvia in her game of one-upmanship with her brother.

It was probably the most miserable half hour of Neil's life, one for which he vowed he would never forgive his cousin. Scraps of their conversation drifted over to him, about the neighbour-hood, an acquaintance named Cathy they had both known and fallen out with, and favourite movies, especially *West Side Story*.

At one point, Jack complimented her on the dress she wore.

"It's a great colour on you," he said.

"This funny old thing?"

"Well if it's old, you've made it brand new again."

He should have known Jack would find Sandra attractive. Lots of guys did. She *was* pretty, in a teased and eye-shadowed sort of way. It wasn't her fault. He had no business assuming that, just because he imagined Jack as Someone Special, Jack would have romantic thoughts about him. Jack wasn't a 'mo.

The only good thing about it all was that Aunt Sylvia seemed to be as interested in Jack as he was. Even as she chatted with Herb and Violet, she watched him closely, proving beyond any doubt in Neil's mind how extraordinary Jack was. The thought did nothing, however, to prevent Neil sinking deeper into gloom.

Just when the weight of his reflections grew almost too much to bear, Jack turned away from Sandra and quite deliberately, daringly winked at Neil. Whether the wink meant, *You see, I've got her!* or *I haven't forgotten you!* or *Save me!*, Neil couldn't be sure. But, suddenly, he felt he could smile again.

Soon after, Uncle Herb proposed a toast. "This should be with wine or champagne or something frothy, but we'll have to make do with teacups tonight. I propose a toast to my sister, Sylvia, who's back where she belongs — in the heart of her family!"

"To Sylvia!" they all chanted.

Sylvia acknowledged the toast with a gracious bow and a smile. "Well, thank you for that, Herbert dear. I want to tell you I haven't spent a more relaxed evening in I don't know when. It will find a prominent place in my scrapbook of memories. And how special to have a new friend to share it with us."

She looked at the handsome bread-man, who said, "It's a privilege to be here, Sylvia."

"I need to remind you, though," Aunt Sylvia continued, "that it's largely our nephew's doing that we're all here like this tonight, his determination to see Miss Hepburn triumph, as well as his love of beauty, grace, and charm — we need to be grateful for that, too." She held up her teacup to Neil, who could only gawk at her, wordless.

"To Neil!"

Neil stood, crossed the room and lightly kissed his aunt's cheek. "Thank you," he said. Then, turning to the others, he opened his arms, confessing, "I love it here."

They all made reciprocal noises in his direction — all except Jack, who was simply staring at him fixedly, as he had done earlier at the photo.

⁓

UNCLE HERB INSISTED on driving them home. All of them.

Jack got out at Baby Point, thanking everybody enthusiastically. To Neil he said, "It's great to see where all that goodness comes from."

Neil's response was a deep blush, invisible in the evening shadows.

Herb then took his relatives "the back way," as he called it, along dark streets lined with fine Englishy houses on luxurious lots. The Kingsway, they called it. Neil rarely travelled such streets; his father thought the lots were tiny and the houses pretentious. *It's all just show!* he'd say. *Nothing like the old country!*

It had been late when they set out, stuffed with Aunt Vi's sweets. Close to sleep, Neil dreamed in the back seat, sometimes of his movie, sometimes of his friend who had so impressed his relatives. Every now and then a scrap of conversation from the front seat begged for his attention.

"She died a few years ago," Herb said. "I think when Vi started up with him she was already dead."

"He certainly didn't talk about them."

"The doctor probably prefers that. Nice kid, I thought."

"Too smart to be nice," Sylvia said.

"You're harder to please than me, Syl. Always have been. I liked him."

"I did, too. But 'nice' is the wrong word."

"He and Sandy seemed to hit it off."

"I think our bread-man has the ability to seem many things, depending on where he is and who he's with."

"Neil asleep back there?" Herb asked quietly.

"Seems to be. But I don't think he'd mind what we say. He probably figured out the bread-man weeks ago."

Eyes closed, Neil was now listening intently.

"You think young Jack's false?" Herb asked with some alarm.

"No, no. Not at all. It's just that he reads his audience very well. That takes great skill, great confidence. He's a very confident young man."

"A good friend for young Neil, then."

"Very likely, Herbert. Very likely."

Neil offered the dark a grateful smile. Later, cruising down Avery Street, he opened his eyes, thinking how much like little moons the street lamps seemed.

His uncle said, "That's the third police car in as many blocks."

Neil's head was out the window watching the passing police car creep slowly up the street like a sniffing beagle.

When Herb pulled into the driveway at 31 Dominion, Frank Bennett appeared almost instantly on the porch, with his wife close behind.

"Lots of excitement here, I see!" Herb called from behind the wheel. "This is supposed to be suburbia. Safe and secure and all that jazz. Isn't that what you folk always tell me? What gives, Frank?"

"They almost got their man tonight," Frank answered. His approach to the car was very slightly unsteady.

Sylvia climbed out with Neil. "Well, your son's come back positively corrupted. Haven't you?"

Nora said, "With Violet's baking, I hope you mean."

"Look, there's another one," Neil said, pointing towards a police car — perhaps the same one — going in the opposite direction.

Frank said, "I told them they won't find them. But they don't listen. My friend, the one who comes every night with Ozzie, helped them get away. They're with the bats now."

18

THE PLANS WERE COMPLICATED. FRANK and Nora would not be going straight to the Deekman reunion. They would stop in Windermere overnight to collect Val, who had been given three days off to attend the celebrations. This meant that Marian and Henry had the responsibility of driving Sylvia to George's cottage on Lake Joseph. Afterwards, Sylvia would drive back with Frank and Nora so that she could see Val in Windermere for another day or two before returning.

Neil loved complicated plans. In his basement refuge, he drew up maps for the guests, including arrival and departure time-tables, dinner seating arrangements, and bedroom assignments, as well as a programme of card games and their players. Tentative menus for lunch and supper were also composed. He wished he could be on hand to make sure that everything went according to his schedule.

He also loved Uncle George's cottage, which struck him as positively palatial, and its two Swiss-style, red-roofed bunkies. Everyone would be staying there during the celebrations, except for his parents. They'd be lodging with Aunt Marian and Uncle Henry, who had a place on the same lake, but down the road on a less sheltered bay. According to his father, theirs was the real cottage, rustic, homey, cozy — what a cottage should be. Next to it, George's was "a monster." "Why would you bother even leaving the city?" he asked anyone who would listen. Neil could think of a dozen reasons, including that rarest of rare things in cottage country, flush toilets, but he never voiced them.

As planned, Aunt Marian and Uncle Henry showed up to collect Sylvia just after lunch on Friday. Before stepping into the car, she turned to her nephew and handed him an envelope. "You take a little trip to Sam's for me. See if they have 'Moon River.'"

"Sylvia, you shouldn't," his mother said.

"Yes, I should. Remember, I'm your older sister."

Nora hugged her and Marian and they were gone.

When Neil got home from work that evening — driven in her new Renault by Mrs. Negulescu, who just happened to have a niece nearby — his father had obviously heard about the gift of twenty dollars. He said, "You don't have to buy something just because you have the money. And please, no more of that Grimes woman."

But on Sunday morning, as his mother was instructing him yet again on the care of the houseplants, his father handed Neil another envelope accompanied by the words, "Open it later."

Later was forty seconds after they drove away. Another twenty-dollar bill. His mind reeled with the possibilities, until he realized he had forgotten to tell them to say hello to Val for him. Self-castigations lasted till Mrs. Gordon called to tell him chili was served.

The meal was great, and they all laughed a lot. The cute and boyish Warren, who was also a guest, had an infectiously giddy laugh that, once started, seemed as if it would never stop.

Mr. Gordon hoped he would get to meet the fellows who were creating such a stir in the neighbourhood. "They show real inventiveness, I'd say," he said dryly.

"They're like those avenging angels," Lana said.

"I like that," Mr. Gordon said, "avenging angels."

With a sweep of her bangs, Lana declared it couldn't be Archie Ross because he didn't have an angelic bone in his body. Everyone agreed. Mr. Gordon suggested that a housebreaker of this quality had to be smart, and Archie failed miserably on that front, too.

"The police were questioning him, though," Lana said, "for over an hour the other night."

To which Mr. Gordon replied, "Well the police aren't always the brightest fellows either. They like what's obvious."

Neil scanned the table. "What about the guy who drives around all the time in his Edsel? Did the police question him?"

Lana shook her head. "Who is he?"

"Jim Barry," Warren said. "Lives a block away from my dad's. He was a gymnastics star in school. Had an amazing build. He won prizes, I think."

Mona shook her head. "What happens to these boys, eh?"

"I had a chat with your Jim Barry the other night," said Mr. Gordon.

Everyone turned to look at him. Neil was especially intrigued.

"Funny chap. Wanted to know about the willow. Says he's thinking of doing landscaping. I asked him what was it about the willow. He said it reminded him of his grandfather, who had a couple on his land in the country. He apparently liked his grandfather a lot. Memory made him chatty. Told me how he met Archie's brother in jail, as if jail were another place like Hamilton or Napanee. Told me without a stitch of shame. I told him the neighbourhood hadn't cared much for the brother. He laughed and said, 'He'll come out better.' Then he suggested that jail might help sort Archie out, too. And that was that. Nice car."

Mona Gordon said, "You didn't tell me any of this, Gus."

"You were watching *The Defenders*, my dear."

She laughed. "Can't miss *The Defenders*. That Robert Reed fellow is such a dish."

After supper that evening, Neil played several rounds of cribbage with Mr. Gordon on the front porch. In the break after the first game, he said, "Do you think Jim Barry might have done the break-ins?"

Mr. Gordon looked over his glasses across the lawn towards the willow for a long while without saying anything. Finally, he lit a cigar, puffed once or twice, then blew the smoke out into the warm night. "I don't think so. Whoever did them wasn't a single person, I'm sure of that. And I don't think it's the kind of thing he'd have any feeling for. Not practical enough. Or profitable. The people who are doing this don't care about gain. They want to make a point. And they want to show off. It's grandstanding, if you ask me. The real question is, who knows the neighbours well enough to have all the dirt on them?"

"Another neighbour," Neil said.

Gus Gordon peered at Neil. "That's the only conclusion I can come to, but who? Besides your dad, of course, who seems to want the title of housebreaker."

Neil left the Gordons around nine thirty, just after sunset. Mrs. Gordon's last words were, "If you need anything, darling, just call. Doesn't matter when."

Home again, Neil felt surprisingly calm, even relaxed. Just before going down to bed, he peered out the window in the front door. The very first thing he saw were two of his father's bats, circling over the Knights' garage across the road. The sight of them made him only slightly uneasy. So did the slow passing of the Edsel along Dominion Street. It struck him that maybe Jim Barry was just a lonely man, looking for friendship. That thought almost had him opening the door, until something else intervened: a low wailing siren. Neil shivered and retreated from his view of the street.

Perhaps the "mad marauders," as Gus Gordon had referred to them at supper, were going to be nabbed tonight.

He turned out the lights in the living room.

The siren grew louder.

He stood at the top of the basement stairs.

The siren was just outside now, red and white lights blinking.

A ridiculous idea seized him: the police were coming for him. Someone had named him as suspicious. Maybe Edsel-man. Maybe Archie. Out of spite. They were going to grill him, too.

He hurried down the stairs past the winter clothes on the landing. As he did, a coat fell off its hook and slithered down the stairs after him.

Behind his locked door, he listened, slightly breathless.

The siren was faint, but still wailing. Turning towards his bed, he flipped on the overhead. He hated the yellow light, but it would reassure him.

The siren stopped. The only sounds were of a train whistle in the railway yard, and Lana Gordon laughing as Warren honked his horn in farewell to the rhythm of "Shave and a haircut, two bits."

He replaced the overhead with the Chinese brass lamp his father had picked up in Vancouver during the war. The shade was parchment-like and the base a cylindrical column around which curled an inquisitive-looking serpent with forked tongue. It shed a warm and comfortable light onto his pillows.

Audrey smiled at him from the pin-up board.

"'It should take you exactly four seconds to cross from here to that door. I'll give you two,'" he said to her.

Outside the night grew very still from its own warmth.

He imagined the Edsel circling the block one more time. He imagined its driver scouring the streets for a companion. And then he saw himself walking down the front steps wearing just his briefs, and climbing into Jim Barry's car.

THE BREAK-IN ARTISTS weren't caught after all. There wasn't even a break-in.

The police were back Monday, though, chatting with the neighbours, but since nobody had anything interesting to say, they didn't hang around.

A grim young officer in a cruiser stopped Neil at Avery and Dominion on his way home from work. "Where're you headed?"

"Home." Neil pointed across the street to his parents' place.

The rest of the questions were equally uninspired, Neil thought, but then so were his answers. When the cop asked him what his job was, Neil wanted to say something outrageous, but nothing outrageous would come to him except, "I clean an opium den," and he knew that might get him in serious trouble, so he instead said, "I work in a library." The young officer, looking suitably unimpressed, drove off without even a thank-you.

On Tuesday, he awoke to the sound of the postman making his deliveries. Needing an excuse to get out of bed, he stumbled upstairs. He had no expectations of receiving anything, but much to his surprise, there were two pieces of mail for him. One from Rick, a postcard, this one showing a huge domed building which the small print on the back identified as Hagia Sophia. The other was a letter, written on pinkish paper with turquoise ink. It was from Val. He opened it with great curiosity. Val had never written him a letter before.

July 18, 1962

Dear Neil,

I hope you're doing well, and that Dad hasn't been bugging you too much. I guess you're all having a great time with Aunt Syl. How was the reunion at Aunt Marian's? I'm so sad I missed it.

Windy Pines is a really nice place, and the people

*are pretty nice, all except a couple from Illinois last week
who thought they knew how to do everything better than
anybody else, and spent their three days here ordering
everyone around. I hate to say this, but I think they might
have been Jewish. Anyway, I felt sorry for their daughter
who looked like she wanted the floor to swallow her up.
Her name was Leah, which is so beautiful.*

*Mike has been here every weekend, making himself
"indispensable" around the place. Uncle Pete keeps telling
him he's got people to do the chores and that Mike should
just go fishing on his weekends off, but, of course, Mike
doesn't listen to him and ends up in everybody's way.
Including mine. I'm getting really tired of having him here
all the time. I have no time to relax. He's always wanting
us to do the couple thing and it's gone too far a few times,
which scares me half to death.*

*I'm really looking forward to seeing everybody at
Uncle George's, even crazy Doreen. Hope she'll be sober
for an hour or two at least. It will be such a nice change to
be around people I really, really care about.*

*Please look after yourself. The Gordons are just next
door, remember.*

> *Love,*
> *Val.*

*P.S. Did you ask Tony if he's any relation to Lucy Colero?
I think she's a big, bad flirt.*

Neil put down the letter stunned — not because Val and Mike
had had sex, but because Val had gone and told him.

He sat for several minutes staring intently at his own name and
address, which looked so strange to him in Val's flowery turquoise
hand. Maybe she's lonely, he told himself, like Edsel-man, although

it was hard to imagine anyone less like Edsel-man than Val. Maybe she just needs someone to talk to.

He carefully folded up the letter and put it back into its virtually unharmed envelope, then checked the kitchen clock. He would have to get moving if he was going to get all his errands done before work. He didn't have to be at the library till six, but one of his errands was no insignificant matter. He was headed downtown to pick up the glasses Dr. Brazier had prescribed two weeks earlier.

After the first flush of excitement at meeting Dr. Brazier had passed, Neil wasn't sure what to think about what had happened. It didn't fit into any of his stories about passion. In fact, it was so unconnected to anything like love and living together that he found himself thinking there must be something, if not exactly wrong, at least not quite right with it, something he'd best not think about except in bed late at night or early in the morning. The same thing was true of the barbers. They, too, were hugely arousing — he fantasized about the chicken sandwich set-up every single day. But he didn't see how he could ever be special friends with them the way he could with Tony, or introduce them to his family, as he could someone like Jack.

When he showed up at the reception desk in Eaton's optical department, he was more anxious than anything else about seeing Dr. Brazier again.

It was the same receptionist with the bright red hair and lips who greeted him, smiling. "Yes, dear?"

"I'm here to see Dr. Brazier."

Her expression went neutral. "Dr. Brazier isn't with us any-more. You'll be seeing Dr. Spiegelman."

"Oh," Neil said. It was his turn to look blank. He wanted to ask what happened, but he felt it wasn't his place. What he asked instead was, "Did Dr. Brazier go somewhere else?"

"I'm sure he did. Have a seat, dear. Dr. Spiegelman will be out shortly."

Neil sat and stewed. What had happened to the doctor? The question wouldn't leave him alone. It seemed to have a life of its own. Perhaps there'd been another boy like him, or even other boys, and one of them hadn't got an erection and he'd told. Neil felt ashamed. And then very sad.

"So," a smiling voice burst in on him, "you're Frank Bennett's son. I'm Dr. Spiegelman."

Neil looked up into a shiny, red-cheeked face wearing glasses and a bushy grey moustache. He automatically stood up, putting out his hand.

Vigorously shaking it, the optometrist said, "The spitting image, the spitting image. Come on with me. I've got a nice pair of glasses for you."

They left the reception area, Neil in the good doctor's wake, noting how short and round he was. He reminded Neil of a big bowl of Jell-O. The image brought a smile back to his face.

The fitting process was, of course, nothing like Dr. Brazier's. At no point did Dr. Spiegelman even seem to be aware of Neil beyond him providing a model head for the glasses. When he'd done a minor adjustment or two, Dr. Spiegelman sat back in his seat and said, "They look mighty fine, young man."

"Dr. Brazier chose them. Said they suited me."

"Did he now?" The doctor's face revealed nothing. "Tortoise shell. Classic." Crisp instructions on wearing and cleaning them followed, after which Dr. Spiegelman walked him out to reception, told him to say hello to his parents for him, and then rolled away.

"Oh, don't you look handsome," the receptionist said.

"Dr. Brazier chose them," Neil answered.

But the receptionist was no longer listening, or even looking.

Neil headed for the escalators thinking that Dr. Brazier didn't just disappear into thin air. He had to be working somewhere. Maybe he was in the phone book. But if he had been fired, he probably wouldn't want to talk to anybody about it. Chances were, he wouldn't remember Neil anyway. What would Neil say to him? He wanted to ask if there were others like him, but that would be embarrassing for both of them. Of course there'd been others.

Neil reached the ground floor. On an impulse, he headed for the menswear department where Val had worked part-time for three years. He had to see if he could spot the so-called "fairy nice men" that Mike had made fun of three weeks before.

He wandered through sport shirts and ties and then across the wide aisle to mix with dress shirts, underwear, pyjamas, bathrobes, belts and hats. He saw no one that fit the bill. There was a lady in ties with a hairdo from a forties movie, and a very thin, gaunt woman in dress shirts with raven-black hair pulled back so severely it looked as if her face had been stretched tight by the process. A nice blond man in pyjamas smiled at him and asked if he could help. Neil couldn't see anything about the man that was fairy-like. In fact, he looked more like a young farmer, solid, capable, used to working with his hands. Neil watched him out of the corner of his eye re-packaging several pairs of shorty pyjamas with such supple skill that they became once again alluringly pristine.

Just as he turned to go, another young man, very tall, as tall as Edsel-man, with a long, horsy, but not unattractive face, showed up in the hat department, pinning on his sales badge. With a big broad leer of a smile, he said to the pyjama-man, "Well that was delicious, and I'm not talking about my egg salad sandwich!"

Neil returned to sports shirts and poked around the sales tables, hoping that someone would show up to prove to him that there were still "fairy nice men" at Eaton's. Several shirts caught his eye, a mauve one with short sleeves, and a long-sleeved sky-blue shirt with pearly buttons and another the colour of iceberg lettuce, which he especially liked — and it was even his size.

A man with an armload of shirts appeared at his side. Short, balding, with a rather prominent nose and a very contagious smile, he surveyed the sales tables with a hawk's eye.

"Daria, darling," the man said with an accent that Neil recognized as Scottish, "do me a favour and clean up this table. It's a dog's breakfast. No wonder the young man looks lost and confused."

Daria appeared on the other side of the table. A pretty, dark-haired young woman with a Star of David around her neck and a crisp white blouse enhancing the tan of her throat and arms, Daria smiled first at the man and then at Neil. "Of course, Mr. Fraser."

"I think the wintergreen would suit him. What do you think?" Mr. Fraser turned to Daria deferentially.

She narrowed her eyes as if trying to imagine the green on Neil.

Putting his pile of shirts down with an exaggerated sigh, Mr. Fraser grabbed the green shirt to hold up against Neil's face.

"Nice," Daria said.

"Of course, it's nice. $7.99 to you, young man."

"Really?"

"Really? What do you mean, 'Really?' Of course, really. Miss Rosen, take the young man's money. He needs this wintergreen shirt to restore his confidence. The heads will turn, my boy. You'll see."

Mr. Fraser picked up his pile of shirts and sashayed off, humming "Waltzing Matilda" softly as he went.

Daria laughed. "Do you want the shirt?" She was holding it now, very gently, like a sleeping child.

"Yes," he said. "Yes, I do."

He pulled the twenty dollars his father had given him from his wallet.

He felt elated.

THE NIGHT STILL hugged the day's heat close to itself as Neil descended Avery Street. The elation he had felt at Eaton's was long gone. Now he was hot, tired, and anxious, with the optometrist's disappearance weighing on him again like a bad omen. He told himself that it was the start of a wider crackdown, a witch-hunt maybe. The previous evening he'd declined Mr. Gordon's offer to meet him at the bus stop, certain that 'mo-baiting Archie was a problem of the past, that Edsel-man had taken care of him, but that night he expected Archie would be waiting for him at every turn.

The shrubs and hedges bristled with danger. If he'd had the energy, he wouldn't have taken any chances. He would have run down the centre of the road.

Neil passed Stanton without incident and was halfway to Dominion before he was stopped by a voice, a quiet voice, saying, "Hey."

He jumped, then turned to face Davy Doyle sitting on the bottom step of his dark porch.

Davy said, "You don't need to be scared. It's only me. What's in the Sam's bag?"

Neil hesitated long enough to make Davy shift restlessly. "*Breakfast at Tiffany's.*"

"You're kidding! I'd love to hear that!"

"You can come over this weekend, if you want."

"Nah, not this weekend, we're in Wasaga. Day after tomorrow, for ten days. I hate Wasaga. Stupid beaches, crowds of people. What else you get?"

"Tchaikovsky waltzes."

"Which ones?"

Neil ventured up the walk to Davy and passed him the Tchaikovsky. "I love the cover." It showed an image of dancers in ball gowns and tuxedos waltzing under glittering chandeliers.

"'Sleeping Beauty' waltz — that's my fave. I'll play it for you sometime." He hummed a bit of it in a low, melodious voice. A figure appeared at the screen door behind him. She hovered for a minute, gave Neil a shy little wave and vanished. "You got something else?"

Neil pulled *Juno*, another musical, from the bag, fully expecting Davy to give it a cursory once-over, but he peered at it in the near-darkness for a couple of minutes.

Looking down at his old chum, Neil realized for the first time that Davy was barefoot and barelegged. This struck Neil as somehow peculiar. That Davy's legs were very hairy and his hands and feet very large only added to that impression. So different from the white-faced, sad-eyed boy he had known since elementary school.

Corinne Doyle was at the screen door again. "You boys want anything to drink?"

"Sure," Davy said without turning around, "a Coke. What about you?"

"Yes please, a Coke."

Mrs. Doyle disappeared.

"This looks interesting," Davy said.

"It failed on Broadway. Only sixteen performances."

"Yeah, but some of the best musicals fail."

Neil glanced at him, surprised.

"There's *The Nervous Set*. Score's fabulous. Twenty-three performances. You know the song 'Night People'?"

"I've heard of it."

"I'll play it for you."

"*Juno*'s based on a famous play by Sean O'Casey."

"I know O'Casey." There was an "of course" attached to this information, and a roll of the eyes. "Doyle's an Irish name, you know." He glanced again at the album sleeve. "Too bad I'm going to Wasaga. You like musicals?"

"I've got a big collection."

Davy nodded. "You should have *The Nervous Set*."

"I would love to write a musical. I mean the book and the lyrics."

Davy looked at him with real interest in his eyes.

Mrs. Doyle reappeared with their drinks. When he saw that

Davy was not going to budge to take them from her, Neil reached over Davy's head for the bottles. "Thanks, Mrs. Doyle, thanks a lot."

She said, "You're very welcome," adding, "you, too, David," as she disappeared into the house.

Neil handed a Coca-Cola to Davy, who was staring straight ahead. Their hands touched briefly.

"You always so polite?"

"I don't know. I guess so. Why?"

"You're a bit too good to believe."

Neil didn't say anything, except, "Sorry."

"That's what I mean. Why are you sorry? Who cares if you're sorry?"

Neil looked at him, slightly stunned.

"Here." Davy handed him back the records abruptly, which, because of his pop, Neil could only slide under his free arm. "You see, you see, you don't even say, 'Just a second,' or 'Can you hold this for me?' You just try juggling everything and end up looking like a jackass." Davy stood, his hairy legs and big feet making him look Pan-like.

Neil started down the walkway.

"Not even going to say goodnight?" It wasn't exactly a taunt.

"I've had enough," Neil said without looking back. "I don't need anybody else treating me like shit."

There was no response.

As Neil reached the corner of Avery and Dominion feeling a mixture of numbness and grief, Mrs. Gordon hailed him from their front porch. "You must be starving."

Neil told her he'd be just a minute and nearly ran towards the house. Inside, the pent-up heat hit him hard. Sweat appeared instantly on his neck and forehead. He placed his new glasses on the writing desk. The rest of his purchases he dumped onto the dining room table.

"Damn you, Davy Doyle!" he said aloud, then swigged down the last of the cola. "I don't need you."

He turned on the large fan sitting in the archway between the dining and living rooms. At the same instant, the phone rang, making him jump.

"Hello?"

He could hear classical music in the background.

"Hello?"

It was Davy.

"I didn't deserve that," Neil said.

"I know. Sometimes it's just too much. Not you being polite. I mean everything. I won't do it again."

"Glad to hear it."

Silence.

"So maybe when I get back we can get together. You can come here. We've got a piano, sort of. A rented thing. The other one's a write-off. I'll play you the 'Sleeping Beauty' waltz. We can listen to *Breakfast at Tiffany's* and *Juno*. I'll let you hear *The Nervous Set*."

"You got a diamond needle?"

"Of course. We're musicians, eh."

"Just wanted to make sure. My albums are precious."

19

THE NEXT COUPLE OF DAYS were almost without incident.

On his day off, Neil mowed and watered the lawns, then cleaned the fish pool in the backyard and trimmed the hedge. In the garage he discovered *Neil's Dream* leaning against the wall under a layer of drop cloth. His father had blacked out all the white, bubbly bits, leaving the three panels of overlapping colour to float in darkness. It was more effective than the white, and probably closer to the idea of nothingness, whatever that was, but it was also vaguely unsettling. He quickly covered it up again. In the late afternoon, his mother called to say they were all having a wonderful time and were sorry he wasn't there with them. Aunt Sylvia sent her regrets, too.

On Thursday, he dropped by Parma Fruits and Vegetables on his way to work. He hadn't heard from Tony in two weeks. Tony wasn't there, nor was Vicki. Mrs. Colero complained, "He's out with his father. He's always out. That's why we hire Lorenzo." She nodded to the back of the store, where a young man with a thick, thick mass of curly black hair and ridiculously full red lips was mopping the floor. "He work harder than Tony."

"I don't know anyone that works harder than Tony."

Mrs. Colero made a vinegary face, but then said, "I had tea with Miss Fairfield yesterday, at Anderson's. I show her my pictures

THE JANE LOOP 199

of Parma. She is so in love with Parma. I say, how can you help it?"

For the rest of the time, he played his new records, especially *Juno*. The soundtrack and the waltzes thrilled him, too — in fact, the Tchaikovsky had him dancing around the house in various stages of undress like a Romanoff duke gone berserk — but they seemed a bit ordinary next to *Juno*. There was something about the Boyle family, with its mess of betrayal and heartbreak and despair, that completely absorbed him.

After one late-night visit to *Juno*-land, Neil found he couldn't sleep. He tried jerking off, but found his hand insufficient. What he wanted was company. More specifically Jack, a shirtless Jack, but he couldn't fully admit this to himself, because it would mean facing the unlikeliness of such a connection ever happening. So he wandered from room to room in the empty house, feeling the heat, soaking up the quiet, enjoying the absences. Not for one moment did he feel fearful. He didn't even recognize his own fear-lessness until, taking a seat on the top step of the front porch, he registered the amazing, almost eerie stillness of the hot summer night. It was past midnight. He was alone. No traffic. No birds. No pedestrians. Just the train whistle, faint, melancholy, to remind him that the world had not stopped.

He gave a little shiver, wrapped his arms around his knees, and hummed very softly the opening number from *Juno*, "'We're alive, we're alive, as the old woman said.'"

Neil must have been sitting there for twenty minutes or more when a car turned the corner of Howard Street into Dominion. It was the Edsel.

For a moment his body tensed. But he didn't move.

The Edsel pulled up to the foot of the drive. "Hey," the driver called softly.

Barely able to see him, Neil got up and walked slowly across the freshly mown lawn to the car, playing at fearless now.

"How're you doing, kid?"

"Okay. You?"

"Not bad. Could always be better, o' course." He smiled pointedly at Neil, as a police car rolled down Avery Street.

"Every night, they're around now," Neil said.

"Had my chat with them already. They don't have a clue. Whoever it is, is pretty smart." The driver looked down at his hands as if they were doubting his words. "Except at the Steeles'. Almost got caught, I hear. Someone dumped a turd right under one of their crosses. Place is full of crosses, they say."

"If they're so smart why don't they take something? The Chards aren't poor. Nor is Mr. Caldwell."

The driver shrugged lightly. "Weird, isn't it? I mean, they say it's payback or something, but it doesn't make sense to me. Like, how are the people they target any worse than a hundred other people? It wouldn't surprise me if it was a different person every time. You know, a kind o' fad. Though it's prob'ly a couple o' kids with too much time on their hands. I dunno. Why, you interested?"

"Aren't you?"

The driver smiled. "Sorta. I'm jus' glad it's not me."

"I am, too," Neil said, without thinking.

Edsel-man's smile became almost sweet. "'Course there are a couple o' people I wouldn't mind if they got broken into."

"Me, too," Neil said.

Jim was obviously not convinced by this assertion. "Yeah? Like who?"

"My sister's boyfriend."

"Mike Dennison?"

"How did you know?"

"Seen him around here a couple o' times. My mother used to work for the Dennisons. Stuck-up bastards. Dennison's the typical rich boy know-it-all. Always gets what he wants, even if it means sticking it to someone else. I'm with you. We could make it a team project." Jim winked conspiratorially. "You not sleeping tonight?"

"Just restless."

"I'm restless every night."

"You drive around a lot."

"I like empty streets at night. It calms me. Shoulda been a night watchman or something. Like in the old days, a lamplighter." He smiled again. It was a very alluring smile. "Why don't you get in and we'll drive around a bit?"

"No, I gotta get in."

"What's the point if you can't sleep?"

Neil wasn't sure what to say.

Jim frowned. "You still scared of me?"

"Yes."

"I don' wanna hurt you, Neil." His voice lowered almost to a whisper. "I want just the opposite, like."

Neil was surprised to feel himself getting aroused. He laughed nervously. "Why me?"

Jim shrugged. "You're nice. Cute, too. Real cute." The last words he said so softly Neil had to strain to catch them.

He bent over to peer into the dim of the car.

Jim's face was tanned and dark with stubble. His teeth gleamed white. His shirt was open, too, giving Neil a picture of the great gymnast's build Warren had referred to the other night. All the muscles in his flat, hard stomach were clearly defined and at the navel came the first flowering of the lower body hair. Neil stood up.

"You checkin' the goods?"

Neil laughed again, but not nervously this time. "Yeah."

"So get in."

"I can't, Jim. They'll come looking for me. Then I'll be in real trouble."

Jim's friendly face turned suddenly dark. "Jesus, you know what you are? You're a fuckin' tease!"

"Am not."

"Prove it!" The motor, which had been idling the whole time suddenly roared into life, and the Edsel disappeared down Dominion Street.

Neil looked after it, feeling strangely bereft.

That night he had his dream again. The room was very high this time and the ceiling was hung with many, many crystal chandeliers, like the cover of the Tchaikovsky waltz album. Diaphanous grey draperies fluttered with the movement of dancers weaving in and out of them, many dancers, couples, the women in long black evening dresses, diamond tiaras and sunglasses, the men, all of them, dark-haired, dark-eyed, and naked. He recognized some of the men. Vass the barber, Davy Doyle, Edsel-man. Davy Doyle's hairy legs were very clear to him as was Edsel-man's lean abdomen and Vass's olive skin. And all of them amazingly, unapologetically naked. As usual he was trying to get through the room. He managed to reach the centre, but there the circling dancers stopped him.

It was a frightening, claustrophobic moment. He started to panic — until, somehow, he knew there was only one way to get to his destination. He began slowly to undress.

20

THE GORDONS LEFT FOR THEIR holiday on Friday. The Knights were to keep an eye on Neil for the next week, but they were not arriving back until Saturday afternoon, so Mona Gordon took care that his one night alone wouldn't trouble him too much by making enough food to last a week, including as many of his favourite sweets as she had time to bake. When he arrived home Friday night from the library, the refrigerator was literally stuffed to capacity with food. On the kitchen table was a vase overflowing with pink and yellow snapdragons from the Gordons' garden and beside it was an album Lana thought he might enjoy, a collection of movie themes called *Tonight* by the piano duo Ferrante and Teicher, including his favourite, "Moon River."

His father hated Ferrante and Teicher, called them "clowns," "four-eyed goons," and "schmaltzy," and claimed that they had no business calling what they performed music. *It's mush*! he would say. So it was with a guilty pleasure that Neil put the record on his parents' hi-fi, turned the sound up very high, and sat on one of the dining room chairs eating up the lavish sentiment with as much gusto as he did Mrs. G.'s potato salad.

It had been an odd night. On his way to work he had checked in at Parma Fruit and Vegetables, where he found Lorenzo at the cash desk and Tony loading a bin with cherries. Tony was almost surly with him. "I'm real busy," he said. "I'll talk to you later, okay?" And at the library, Rob Neville of 255 Durie Street had ignored Neil altogether.

At the Jane Loop after work, he noticed the blond figure skater, again wearing his very short shorts. That evening he seemed scared or nervous or something. Neil tried all sorts of guesses as to why, but the mystery vanished immediately when a grizzled man with a paddy-wagon kind of face moved up to the skater, calling him names like "little girl," "powder puff," "fruit jelly," in a loud and threatening voice, reeking of booze.

Recognizing the sound only too well, Neil found himself unable to do anything but stare. Panic immobilized him. Several other waiting passengers stepped out of reach of the dispute, allowing the wino to move in even closer to the skater. Then, just as the bus pulled in, a rather tall and burly businessman carrying a briefcase and umbrella turned on the man. "You're a fine one to be calling people names, buster. One more name and you'll be wishing you hadn't."

"But, look at him! He's asking for it," the wino said.

"So are you." The businessman put down his briefcase and umbrella, and, like magic, the thug disappeared. Turning to the skater, the businessman scowled. "Those shorts are indecent, you know."

The skater, who was just about to thank his rescuer, turned his back abruptly and climbed on the bus.

"You should be ashamed of yourself," the man called after him.

Feeling as blamed and bullied as the skater, Neil chose a seat as far from the businessman's as he could.

The final straw came after Neil got off the bus. At the top of Avery, Jim Barry passed him silently in his red and white Edsel. Neil had decided before then that the next time Edsel-man offered to take him for a spin, he would accept, but there was no slowing down to talk, no wave, no smile, no horn, nothing. Neil waved, hoping Jim would see him in the rear-view mirror, but, if he had, he gave no indication, and the Edsel vanished at the next cross-street. Neil was more than disappointed by this lack of interest; he was scared.

He walked more quickly after that, fearing that if Jim were displeased with him, maybe Archie would be out looking for him again, primed for a payback. It didn't make a lot of sense, but he couldn't stop the fearful feelings. He was all alone in the night. Many houses sat in vacation-made darkness, the Doyle house among them. Davy was at Wasaga Beach, another favourite object of his father's angry contempt. "Pure Honky Tonk, pure midway," he would say. But even Honky Tonk would be welcome if it meant companionship.

Neil arrived home feeling very sorry for himself. Ferrante and Teicher lifted him out of it for a while, but the minute they were done, Neil knew he would have to have more music to stop himself from getting whiny. He played the *Breakfast at Tiffany's* soundtrack, he played *Juno*, but still he was blue.

Finally, he picked up the Tchaikovsky waltz album. The whirling dancers on the cover reminded him of the dream he'd had, yet another dream of an amorphous room. He didn't understand this. All the houses he knew were solid and predictable. Walls and floors, doors and windows, porches and gardens might differ cosmetically, but they were all basically where they should be. But a person couldn't really waltz, like those dancers on the album, through houses like his parents' or their neighbours'. There wasn't enough space, or enough openness. The fancy clothes, the soaring music, the chandeliers weren't designed for confinement or constriction.

A slow smile captured Neil's features as he let the disc drop onto the turntable. Tingling with excitement, he closed the curtains, locked the front door and stripped to his underwear. The lowering of the needle followed, with great ceremony. His hand shook, but the shaking felt appropriate. He would show them. Small rooms wouldn't stop him. Nor would the absence of chandeliers. Tuxedo-less, he would dance until he could dance no more.

And he did. He danced through all the ground floor rooms doing the best imitation of the waltz he could devise without ever once actually waltzing. He danced and danced until he was red in the face and the perspiration running down him in little rivers thoroughly soaked his underpants. He tossed them into a corner and kept on dancing.

In the middle of the waltz from *Swan Lake*, his favourite, the phone rang, bringing him to a careening halt against the refrigerator.

The kitchen clock showed it was nearly twenty to twelve. He had no idea who would be calling at such an hour.

He quickly lifted the needle from the record.

"Hello?"

Silence on the other end.

"Hello?"

Not just silence, but breathing. He could hear breathing.

"Hello!"

More breathing.

"Dad?"

A low laugh, maybe his father's, maybe not.

"Is that you, Dad?" He reached for his pants lying over the back of a kitchen chair.

A click. The caller had hung up.

Neil stood, phone in hand, wanting to feel angry.

He placed the receiver back in its cradle.

He waited.

Slowly, gingerly then, he walked back to the hi-fi to turn it off.

Gathering his records together into a neat pile, he placed them on the kitchen table ready for collection once his nightly bathroom ritual was completed.

Neil started up the stairs, carrying his pants. The phone rang again.

He hesitated.

It kept ringing.

He quickly slipped his pants on. "Hello."

No answer.

"Hello?"

Again no answer.

"Who are you?"

"Guess." The voice didn't sound like his father's, though it was so low as to be almost inaudible. "We know you, we know you're alone there."

Neil hung up the phone.

Quickly now, he hurried up the stairs to the bathroom.

The phone rang again. He ignored it. He finished brushing his teeth, then jumped into the shower. The sound the water made against the tub and the plastic shower curtain nearly drowned out the ringing.

By the time he was finished, the phone was silent.

Nervously, he dried himself off.

"I want my room," he said aloud to the steamy bathroom mirror.

Downstairs, he turned out the lights in the living and dining rooms and breathing more quietly, he filled a glass of water at the kitchen sink. Just as he made to reach for his records, the phone began to ring again.

He slammed down the glass, splashing water onto both his albums, and the floor.

"Dad!" he shouted into the phone. "Stop it!"

A laugh. A woman's laugh. "Oh, he thinks it's his dad," she said, "isn't that sweet?" The voice was coarse, maybe drunk. "I'm just phonin' to tell you my boyfriend's on his way over. Be nice to him, that's my advice to you." She hung up.

He stood with the receiver in his hand, trembling now.

It fell from the cradle when he tried to put it back. Twice. On the third try, the phone rang again.

Like a man condemned he put the receiver to his ear.

It was the same woman. "Forgot to tell you. My boyfriend's bringin' a buddy. He's done time but if you're nice, he'll be nice, too. Jus' give 'em whatever they want, okay?" Once again she hung up.

Neil had been terrified before, many times, but never so terrified as he was at that moment. He felt nothing except a current of terror electrifying every part of his body and mind.

He turned instinctively towards the back door. Hesitating only long enough to douse the kitchen light, he descended the back staircase and let himself out into the night.

There was only one place to go — the sumach tree. It had always given him shelter. Its mid-summer lushness would give him shelter now.

A second or two, no more, and he was on the terrace, his bare feet hurting from the gravel walk. Fearing that he would be visible over the hedge, he dropped to his knees. He heard the knee of his pants tear on the patio stone, but there was no time to worry about his mother's future displeasure: they were coming for him. He crawled across the terrace, then down the two steps to the lawn. Progress across the lawn on his knees was quicker. His waist button popped. His hands and knees were damp and probably grass-stained, but it didn't matter. Only safety mattered now.

Panting loudly, he cowered under the sumach at last, under the deepest, darkest part, his back pressed painfully against the elm hedge. It might have been five minutes, might have been ten, but his breathing eventually quieted. Around him was silence, and every once in a while, a cricket.

He peered from his refuge towards the front of the house, watching for their appearance.

Archie. It had to be Archie. And Edsel-man.

He felt sick. Edsel-man did want to hurt him.

A car passed. The hedge was too thick to see whose. Then there was the sudden blare of a radio, a song. "Runaway." He knew the driver had to be Donny Stasiuk. Only Donny would flood the neighbourhood with noise this late at night. Donny, the big "Rebel."

"Runaway" was followed by more silence.

Neil waited, feeling damp, sticky, but cool around his shoulders.

Minutes passed. Hardly a sound reached him. The train whistles were few and far between. He told himself that the hum of downtown was in the background, but he wasn't sure he wasn't inventing it. He tried filling his mind with images of downtown, of the movie theatres and record stores, of caramel sundaes at Diana Sweets, and the book department at Eaton's. He called up faces from the movies, like Bernardo's in *West Side Story*, Shirley MacLaine's in *Can Can*, Robert Preston as *The Music Man*, but they vanished as quickly as they appeared. Strangely, Audrey's Holly refused to be conjured. This left him feeling abandoned. He began to imagine that everyone in the neighbourhood had disappeared and he was utterly alone, waiting for his predators to find him.

Mrs. West. He could always go to the Wests. Even though his parents disliked Mrs. West, said she was a meddler, the Wests would probably help him. They were churchgoers. They would have to help him.

He heard voices, at first indistinguishable. Male voices, coming along Dominion, headed east towards his house.

Archie's voice.

They were coming.

Neil held his breath.

Both men were drunk, but Archie was considerably drunker. They'd obviously been to a party, one where the hostess had made her preference for Jim quite plain. Archie was put out about this and, in a shrill voice that sounded grotesque in the stillness of the night, worse even than Donny's radio, he complained about the unfairness of it all.

Jim kept saying, "You're too fuckin' loud."

But Archie didn't seem to care. "You fucked her yet?"

"That's none o' your goddamn business!"

"I'd fuck her, if she'd let me." This promise was accompanied by a burst of nearly maniacal laughter, which made Neil wonder if Archie wasn't a little crazy.

Jim was clearly fed up. "If you don't shut up, I won't get you any more invites."

And the voices moved on. They weren't stopping.

Archie and Edsel-man weren't the ones.

Neil now felt almost sick with relief.

Quiet came again.

He tried to recall the voice on the phone, the woman's voice. Had he heard it before? If he had, he couldn't place it.

Someone with a determined walk hurried along the street.

Then a car, and another car, passing each other.

More silence.

His feet hurt from his flight across the gravel, and Neil wondered if the skin was broken and bleeding. His aching feet reminded him of another evening, years before, when he'd run out of the house in the dead of night scared out of his wits. A Saturday night. Val was at a girlfriend's. His parents were getting ready to go out dancing. They were all dressed up, his mother in a peach-coloured evening dress. Before leaving, his father said, "If we don't make it back from the Royal York Ballroom, don't worry. Lots of families would love to have a little boy." At half past midnight, Neil awoke to an empty house. Recalling his father's words, he ran through the house, searching for some sign of them. Finding nothing, no one, he tore out of the house in his pyjamas and bedroom slippers. It was early winter. No snow had fallen, but it was bitterly cold. He hammered first on the Gordons' front door, getting no answer, then next door to the Wests', then back across the Gordons' lawn and onto their driveway, where the uneven gravel surface brought him down with a wail, tearing open his palms and knees. He lay down on the gravel and sobbed. It was Mr. Chard who had found him, Walter Chard, the bigot.

Neil could feel the tears forming as he remembered Walter Chard lifting him up and saying in the gentlest voice, "There, there, what is it, my boy? What's happened? There, there, don't cry. Your parents are down the street at the Hamiltons' with everyone else."

He brushed tears from his cheeks.

By now he could see quite clearly in the dark. He began to focus on the shapes in front of him, the shapes of leaves, and branches, and the fledgling buds that would soon transform into velvety crimson cones.

Neil reached out to feel a branch. Something fell into the grass. Wary, he sat back. He hated beetles, grubs, all creepy-crawlies. But nothing moved. He realized that the thing in the grass was one of his old toys, a plastic Indian, from the same set as the one his father had found a few weeks back. He peered at it. There was the headdress and a bow and arrow, ready for firing, and leggings, too, but he couldn't make out the colours in the dark.

He looked back at the branch from which the Indian had fallen. The brave had not been alone. He had a companion, a rifle-toting cowboy in the usual outfit, shirt and trousers, boots and hat. Indians usually wore a lot less. They were always bare-chested and sometimes barelegged, or even bare-assed. Perhaps that's why they creamed the cowboys in all the battles Neil set for them — they were more uninhibited, freer.

Shaking his head, he had to wonder how these enemies, many years slain, came to be sitting on a branch of the sumach.

He didn't wonder long. In the yard close at hand came a soft thud, then a rustling sound.

His hand closed around the toys as his breathing stopped.

Someone was moving quickly across the back of the yard towards the sumach.

He thought of making a dash for it, but the thought was barely formed when he felt his back encircled by a powerful arm and a hand clamped over his mouth to stifle his cry.

"Shhhh. Shhhh. Just a few seconds."

Neil squirmed in the tight grasp, trying to escape his captor.

"Just a few more seconds, Neil."

The voice was Bread-man's, Jack's.

He stopped his struggling instantly, releasing the cowboy and Indian into the soft wet grass.

The hand came down from his mouth, but the arm remained around his back, squeezing tightly.

Neil looked at Bread-man. He was breathing quickly and appeared extremely agitated.

Jack felt his gaze. He pulled Neil's head against his own. "Just a game," he whispered. "Cops and robbers."

Neil was beyond words.

A car picked its way slowly along Dominion as if looking for something.

Jack put his finger to Neil's lips. Without thinking, Neil pressed his lips against the finger — almost, but not quite, a kiss. Jack sighed and ran his finger along Neil's lips. "Shhhh."

The car stopped. A door opened, then another.

A voice said, "He could be anywhere."

"I never seen anybody move so fast."

"He could be as far as the tracks by now."

"Don' think so. We should check some o' these yards. Lotsa places to hide."

"You're the boss."

"You take 32, they're away. I'll do 34."

Neil could feel Bread-man's grip tighten around his back. As they listened to the men cross to the Knights' house, Jack whispered,

"Your back door open?"

"Yes."

"C'mon, they won't be long."

Jack let him go and proceeded to crawl across the lawn on his hands and knees as if he had been born to move that way. Neil followed him, not nearly so fluidly. Once they reached the terrace, Jack pulled Neil to his feet. They tore into the house.

On the dimly lit landing between the ground floor and the basement, Neil closed and locked both doors.

"Your room's down there?" Jack indicated the cellar.

"I can't. My feet are bleeding."

"Jesus. Sit down. There a laundry tub down there?"

"Yeah, to the right at the bottom."

The bread-man disappeared.

Neil could hear water running, then Jack calling softly, "What about bandages?"

"In the grey metal box over Dad's workbench. The light cord's in the ceiling."

The light went on. He could hear the box being opened. Immediately after, the light was extinguished.

Then Jack was on his knees examining Neil's feet. He washed them with a towel, then examined them again. "Cuts aren't deep, just scrapes really." He applied the band-aids quickly, efficiently, as a nurse might have. "There."

Neil stared at him in the soft whitish light of the landing fixture.

"What do you sleep in?" Jack asked him.

Neil looked confused. "Pyjamas sometimes. Nothing others."

"Well you can't be answering the door in nothing. You need to get out of those pants, though. You look like you've been crawling in a garden."

"My underwear's in the dining room."

"I won't ask," Jack chuckled.

Neil stood.

"Here ... Down they go." The bread-man unzipped the trousers and slid them down Neil's legs to pool at his feet. "Step up. My, my, isn't that pretty!"

Neil was sure he was red as a beet.

"Get your underpants and maybe some socks. You don't want the police seeing your cut feet."

"Why would police come here?"

"We'll talk once you're ready. Your bedroom?"

Neil pointed to the closed door at the foot of the cellar stairs.

"Now don't turn on any lights."

Neil followed his instructions closely. Underpants on, socks on, lights off.

He made his way back downstairs.

Jack was stretched out on his bed, naked.

Shyly, Neil approached him. The sight robbed him of speech.

"It's okay," Jack said. "It's okay, just leave those underpants on for now, so if the police come knocking you won't have to scramble."

No sooner had he spoken those words than there was a pounding at the front door.

Neil stiffened.

"Go on," Jack said, turning on the bedside lamp.

Neil looked down at the naked man lying on his sheets, seeing only two nipples rising out of a hard, hairy chest. Gulping, he grabbed his pyjama bottoms and hurried out of the room and up the stairs, hardly thinking about the impression he would make at the door.

The officer in front was the same one who had interviewed him several days earlier. "Sorry to bother you, son," he said trying not to stare at the semi-naked boy in front of him. "Your parents here?"

"They're away."

"You must be the only person on the whole damn block who's

not on vacation," the other officer said, a short older man.

"Just to ask you to keep your eyes open. Looks like someone's maybe been using your tree in the back to hide."

"I sit back there sometimes," Neil said defensively. "Earlier tonight I did."

The officer looked at Neil as if he were possibly a little wacky. "Well, the man we're looking for's probably long gone, and we don't think he's dangerous, but he's on the run and he may be looking for a safer place to hide."

"Why's he on the run?" Neil asked.

"Mischief," the older cop said succinctly. "Just keep your doors locked. Windows, too. I know it's hot, but better safe than sorry."

"Sorry to wake you," the younger one said without a trace of sympathy.

The two officers trundled off down the porch steps and across the lawn to their parked car.

Neil locked the door.

"Are you on the run?" was his first question to the bread-man on returning to the bedside.

Jack smiled, but his smile was tentative. He looked at the boy peering down at him. He said, "I don't like cops. That's all. I saw their car. My instinct's always to run."

Shyly stepping out of his pyjama bottoms, Neil sat on the edge of the bed with a mildly puzzled expression that was quickly eclipsed by a face of wonder and longing. He had never in his life been this close to another totally naked person, and one so perfect in every way. He tried to keep his eyes above Jack's waist, but he was finding it very difficult, especially given the distracting movement below.

"I don't want to answer any more of their idiotic questions. The police are specialists in idiocy." Sitting up, Jack reached out a hand.

"They said you were up to mischief." Suddenly unsure, Neil scrutinized him. "Are you the one?"

Jack offered him another enigmatic smile. "Well, I was beginning to think I was — at least for you."

A reddening Neil said, "No! I mean, are you the one breaking into all the houses?"

Jack looked at him with amusement. "I wish. But, I'm afraid someone's beaten me to it. I've got to hand it to whoever it is, though. They've picked some good targets. Caldwell, the Chards ..."

"You mean that?"

Jack took Neil's hand to squeeze.

Neil looked down at the hand holding his, mesmerized. Very softly, he said, "Caldwell doesn't have any friends on the street. We just tolerate the Chards."

"You, too?" Jack asked. He was shoulder-to-shoulder with Neil now.

"He was nice to me once. Mr. Chard, I mean."

"Once, eh? One nice act earns your loyalty?"

Neil smiled shyly. "He's not all bad, that's all I mean."

The bread-man lifted the hand he held and placed it on his muscular thigh.

For several seconds Neil stared at his hand lying there as if he were looking at something so foreign and mysterious that he couldn't quite make it out. To break the spell, he said, "How come you're over here tonight?"

"Visiting."

"You know people over here?"

"Sure. It's not Timbuktu."

"Almost," Neil said. He had begun to move his hand gently, in a stroking motion, over Jack's thigh. He had no awareness of this, of anything except Jack's intense gaze.

Smiling, Bread-man closed his hand over Neil's. "If you keep doing that, Neil, we're in trouble."

"What do you mean?"

"I might just have to make out with you. You know what that means?"

Neil's mouth opened and closed.

"Do you?"

"Sort of."

"Sort of?"

Neil shrugged wordlessly.

"Thought so."

Frightened and excited, Neil sought out Jack's eyes. They were bright in the light of the bedside lamp, and, more than that, playful.

"You want to?" Jack asked quietly.

Neil stared.

"Make love?"

Neil nodded his yes.

The bread-man leaned into Neil, a kiss ready on his lips. Then, all of a sudden, he pulled back, the kiss replaced by curiosity. "What were you doing as good as nude under the tree at the back of the garden? You go there to jack off at nights?"

"I was terrified," Neil said in a low voice.

"Terrified? Of what?"

"Phone calls."

"From whom?"

"I'm not sure."

"Crank calls you mean?"

"Sort of. It might have been my dad."

Jack frowned. "Your dad? Why would your dad make a crank call?"

"To scare me."

"Why does your dad want to scare you?"

"He likes to."

"He likes to? So, he's a sadist. But you're not sure it was him."

"I'm pretty sure. I mean, it probably was. I mean ..." He started to shake from an overwhelming upsurge of grief riddled with shame. "I'm so stupid, I'm so stupid."

The next second, they were both lying on the bed, the boy sobbing almost uncontrollably, the young man holding him as tight as tenderness would allow.

EVENTUALLY, NEIL TOLD Jack about Frank.

"One night my father shut me in the basement — this was before it was finished — and he told me I couldn't come up until I had killed the snake that was loose. It was supposed to be a threat to everybody in the house but me. I couldn't move I was so scared. I climbed up on his workbench and shook for an hour. Then he came down and said, 'What are you doing up there?' like I was crazy. Some nights I woke up, way after midnight, from this move-ment under the bed, like some kind of creature thrashing and moaning. That happened a lot over the years. I'd always get caught. I never learned. Val always said, 'You must like getting scared.' Dad would laugh and say I was a slow learner.

"One day when I was maybe eleven we went on a walk through Silverthorne's Bush, just me and him. He got way ahead of me, he was walking really fast, when suddenly I felt someone grab me from behind, cover my mouth, and drag me to a car. He was telling me I better stop struggling and threw me into the passenger seat. It was some guy in a black balaclava. He drove for what seemed like miles to a small shed at the back of a farmhouse and locked me in. My father showed up maybe two hours later and 'rescued' me. He said he was forced to pay a big ransom to learn where I was." The memory was painful enough to bring on a kind of moan, which Neil tried to silence with his fist. "The guy was the son of a neighbour we used to have. He always thought Dad's jokes were really funny."

"Holy fuck!" Jack's hands roamed the boy's back like the hands of a healer searching for guidance. "How were you after that?"

"I cried a lot. For hours and hours. Mrs. Gordon gave me something eventually, some kind of pill, and I slept for a day, I think. Maybe more. I've always cried a lot. Even now. It's embarrassing. I'm almost seventeen."

"I'd cry a lot, too, man, if I'd had that to deal with. Holy fuck!"

"You want me to stop?" Neil was suddenly worried he'd said too much.

"No, no, tell me everything. Just hold on."

Neil did as he was ordered. All the scare scenes he could remember, recent and not so recent, and, even some he'd forgotten. Urged on by the concern on Jack's face, they spilled out in a torrent. The bronze-eyed nocturnal visitor, the figure in the fedora with the ice pick, the staged break-in. By the time he was done, he felt quieter and safer than he had ever done in his life. Jack was so warm and his skin smelled so good, leaving him the feeling that there was probably nothing better than being naked and close with another person.

For several minutes Jack remained very still, staring alternately at the boy in his arms and the Chinese lamp over Neil's shoulder. Neil had the feeling he was trying very hard to make sense of everything. At length, he said, "Where was your mother? When all this stuff happened?"

"She was there. She just never said anything. He wouldn't listen to her anyway, even if she did."

Jack ran his hand down Neil's chest and over his belly.

"I don't think she likes it very much."

Jack snorted.

"She'll be extra nice to me after something really bad happens — like the Silverthorne thing. So will Mrs. Gordon. She'll bring me in mandarin oranges. Tinned, in the syrup. They're my favourite."

"Don't hate me, but I like your father even less than Mr. Caldwell. He only tortures animals."

"I could never hate you."

"And I don't think I like your mother very much either."

"I still don't hate you." Neil snuggled close to Jack, and kissed his neck and upper chest.

Softly, very softly, Jack said, "It amazes me, it really does, how these things go on, all this cruelty, this sickness. Your father's a sick man, Neil. And here you are —"

"They love me, too, though."

"Funny kind of love."

Neil stared at him uncertainly, not quite believing.

"My mother used to call people she liked, 'good souls.' You're one of those, Neil. I'm sure God, if he existed, would think so, too." Tilting Neil's head back, he kissed him on the mouth, using his tongue to gain entry.

Neil opened willingly, whimpering with delight. Like famished men, they gobbled up each other's kisses. The minutes disappeared as the kissing became ravenous.

It was Jack who surfaced first, breathless, gulping for air. Snapping the waistband of Neil's briefs, he whispered, "Time to lose these. You've got something important in there to share with me."

Neil laughed nervously, but the laughter soon gave way to more kissing, frantic kissing, which in turn led to nearly unbearable surrender as Jack took charge of Neil's young, untried body and made long love to him. No ridge, no fold or crease, no expansive plain, no dark lair of his body was ignored by Jack's mouth and hands. And when finally he let Neil come, the boy called out simply, "Yes!" many times.

"You liked that, I guess." Jack hovered above him in a push-up position.

As Jack's body lowered onto his, Neil wrapped his arms around him and squeezed hard, still breathing heavily. Jack took a kiss, then another. Neil could taste himself in the bread-man's mouth.

"You want to sleep now?"

"No!" Neil said, "No! I want to do what you did. I want you!"

He pushed Jack off him and onto his back. With another round of luscious kissing to set him on his way he began his long-fantasized exploration of another man's body. He lingered over every part of it as if he would never have enough of what he'd found. The taste of sweat, the tickling sensation of hair against his lips, the aching sensitivity of hard, pointy nipples, the dance of stomach muscles, thigh muscles, back muscles against his tongue, the pungent odours of groin and anus, the powerful thrusting, the nearly choking invasion of another man's hardness, and, in the end, the eruption of flavour that he swallowed greedily, intent that not a drop escape him.

He lay curled with his head on Jack's thigh after.

No sound, but Jack's breathing. No movement, but the remnants of Jack's release. And then Jack's hand in Neil's hair, pulling, stroking, clutching.

"You done a lot of that?" Jack asked after a while.

"Never."

Jack lifted his head. "I don't believe you."

"I've jerked off with my friend Tony."

"You never sucked a man before? You never made love before?" Jack sounded very doubtful.

"I told you that."

"And I told you — didn't I? — that you're a natural."

Neil sat up.

"Don't. I like your head there."

"I love you," Neil exclaimed.

"What?"

"I love you, Jack."

"Come here." He opened his arms. Neil fell in beside him. "No man's ever made me feel as wonderful as you have tonight, Neil."

"You're so beautiful. I thought so from the first time I saw you."

"I feel the same way about you."

He ruffled the hair on Jack's chest. "Was it good for you?" Neil buried his face in Jack's underarm, embarrassed by his own doubt.

"Are you nuts? Didn't you hear me? Look at this!" He lifted his lengthening cock. "It's only been five minutes."

"I'm so glad you came to visit your friend tonight, and the cops showed up."

Jack closed his eyes. "Me too."

Neil said, "You know, for a second, I thought you were going to tell me you were the housebreaker."

Jack stroked the shoulder he held. "And if I had?"

"It wouldn't have changed anything," Neil said, his face alive with desire.

"They do a lot of damage."

"It doesn't matter," Neil said. "Nothing matters but this."

Jack held the boy close. "Like I said before, I gotta hand it to whoever's doing it."

Neil hardly heard him. "Me, too," he murmured.

Silence gently surrounded them. For many minutes, neither moved.

Then Jack let out a deep sigh. "You know the Yardley family?"

Neil looked up. "Over on Pritchard?"

"Yep."

"I know Bruce, sort of." Neil lowered his head so that his mouth met Jack's nipple. His tongue played with it flirtatiously. "He's good-looking, isn't he? Blond, blue-eyed. Everybody says so. He's a champion runner, too."

"You know that his dad beats him?"

Neil abruptly lifted his head.

"You ever seen Bruce's back? Without a shirt? Well, I did, a few weeks ago. The kid was home alone, on the cellar stairs when I came for my delivery. Four or five huge, purple bruises on his upper back. He didn't see me until I did my bim-bam and then he ran for the basement. Last week I caught him again. More bruises. From a fist — or something heavier even."

Neil hid his face from the image.

"They've got an alarm now. And a dog. A German shepherd, sort of like Yardley himself, a vicious, ugly thing. They didn't have either two days ago. But I guess as they were going away for the week, they thought they'd better have some protection."

Neil lifted his head again slowly. There was a gentle questioning in the bread-man's eyes as if he were waiting for him to solve a riddle.

Quietly, so quietly he was hardly audible, Neil said, "It *is* you."

Jack took Neil's hand from his cock, placing it on his chest.

"The Doyles, the Chards, Mr. Caldwell ..." Neil said, almost chanting the names, as he sat up.

Still tightly holding Neil's hand, Jack said, "No, Neil. Not them. That was someone else, like I said, someone brilliant, a nail-on-the-head someone. I'm just the Yardleys, the failed attempt on the Yardleys. Oh, I would love to have given it to Yardley. The damage I could have done if it hadn't been for that damn dog! I would have shamed the people who broke into your other neighbours." Neil started to pull his hand away, but Jack held on to it. "Don't! You know, it makes me crazy to see what people get away with."

A long silence was Neil's initial response. Then, very faintly, he added, "I didn't know about Mr. Yardley."

"I did. So, it was up to me to do something."

"Couldn't you have told someone?"

"I did speak to someone about the boy. I called a child welfare place, as if I was a concerned neighbour, and you know what the woman said? 'We'd need more evidence to intervene.' More evidence. I could have torched her office."

Neil hardly knew what to say. "But he can't go on beating Bruce."

"Precisely. He has to be stopped. Who's going to do it? Tell me."

"I don't know. Maybe the neighbours will see."

"Maybe? Maybe? Maybe's not good enough, Neil." Jack stood.

"Where are you going?"

Jack retrieved his pants. "Fuck, I'd've wrecked the whole place if I'd gotten into Yardley's tonight. It would have been a war zone! Uninhabitable. Maybe that would have given him pause!"

Neil jumped up from the bed. "It scares me when you talk like this."

"Does it scare you more than your father's shit?"

Neil pulled back, his face wearing a look of alarm. "He's only joking."

"Joking!" Jack's voice was incredulous. "Tell me you're kidding! What your father's doing beats everything else. He should be in jail."

Neil winced.

"They should revive the pillory for him."

"Don't!" Neil clung to him.

"Look, I was scared tonight, too, Neil. But nobody else would do anything." He stepped out of the embrace to put on his pants.

"Please, don't go." Neil grabbed the pants from him. "I don't want you to go."

"I'm not going to rest till Yardley pays."

The boy clung even tighter. "Can't we go back? To where we were?"

Slowly, uncertainly, Jack allowed himself to be pulled back to the bed. Sitting next to him, Neil watched his own hand fall once more onto Jack's thigh.

The room fell very quiet. They sat like men waiting for a train to arrive, the only movement coming from Neil's gently circling hand.

Finally he asked very softly, "How were you going to get in?"

Jack scanned the boy's face. Somewhat shyly, he said, "There's a key under a flower basin by the breadbox."

"How do you know that?"

"I watched one of the other kids put it back one afternoon."

Neil said, "You think the other housebreakers get in with spare keys, too?"

"I don't know about the others," Jack said softly.

Neil swallowed loudly. He so wanted to believe in Jack's goodness. "Really? You really don't know?"

"I know as much as you do." He put a hand over Neil's caress. "Some of the people aren't even on my bread route. The Steeles, for instance."

"They're Catholics, like you."

Jack smiled. "They probably only eat panis angelicus then."

Neil wasn't sure what that was. Something to do with angels, he thought. "Couldn't you just spread gossip around?"

"Like manure?" Jack smiled again. "The neighbours know about Chard and Caldwell and Mrs. Doyle. At least Lydia West does. And your neighbour next door, Mrs. Gordon. Does anybody act?"

Neil's hand curled closed on Jack's thigh, and then opened again almost immediately.

"If you could count on the people with power to do something, like that bleeding social worker, I'd say, 'Go get 'em!' But the people with power are always afraid to act against other people who've got power. Somebody might question their right to have power, you see. So nothing gets done."

Neil was having trouble putting the pieces together. Jack's thigh was so warm and welcoming and the sense of security he experienced sitting next to him so seductive that he couldn't fully grasp Jack's argument, nor appreciate the passion behind his harsh, condemning tone. It confused him.

"The cops are out at sea in a rowboat. I promise you, if I get into Yardley's, they won't find a thing. I'll wear a hat and gloves — latex gloves. And I'll take a change of shoes. I'm too fast for them on the ground. You heard them tonight. I'll be well prepared. "

"Were you prepared tonight?"

Jack chuckled. "No, actually. I was just angrier than hell."

"I just don't want you to get caught at Yardley's, to end up in jail. I've seen the kind of men who end up in jail."

Jack's eyebrows went up.

"There's got to be another way to pay him back. Something that doesn't put you at risk." Neil turned such an earnest face towards Jack that the bread-man very nearly laughed.

"I don't mind risks, you know." Jack looked into the boy's large grey eyes, where acute anxiety battled with infatuation. "I'm sorry — I didn't mean to hurt you. Or spoil this wonderful night ..."

"You haven't, you haven't, but please don't start doing break-ins."

Quietly, Jack said, "Help me find an alternative then."

Neil stared at him wide-eyed.

"You're way smarter than me, I bet."

"What do I know?" Neil's eyes searched the room for some clue to that knowledge, but all he could make out was Audrey glowing faintly in the distance with her cigarette holder, her rhinestones and Cat.

Jack turned to face him, and with a slow, sensual smile lighting up his face, said, "You've got a lot of space in there, don't you?" He tapped Neil's chest. "Big heart."

Remembering Rob Neville's very different assessment of his heart, Neil groaned.

"I'm not sure I'm worthy of your care," Jack said.

"You are, you are. You're the most worthy." He threw himself against Jack, who immediately surrendered.

As they ground their bodies together, kissing breathlessly again, and muttering words of love and encouragement, first Neil, then Jack took the lead. They grappled, almost like wrestlers, tossing and turning until the soaking sheet and two pillows lay defeated on the tile floor and the mattress cover was a rumpled mess of damp, musky maleness. Release followed release without break, until coming down from his third and most powerful orgasm, Jack noticed a golden light teasing the curtains.

He craned his neck to check the alarm clock. "Twenty to six. I'm supposed to be long gone. They'll think I've run away to Tibet or something. My brothers, I mean."

Neil sat up guiltily. "Were they waiting up for you?"

"Always. All their lives." Jack sat up, too, and hugged him, licking his shoulder as he did. "Yum. Salt." He took another lick. "That tastes a bit like me."

Neil shivered from the feel of Jack's tongue.

"You got some clothes I could wear? I don't want to go out there dressed like last night."

Neil found a pair of khaki pants for him and a bright blue T-shirt.

"Hat?"

A cloth cap with a green plastic visor was unearthed. "Don't you want underpants?"

"Never wear them. Too confining."

Neil sat again, fighting fear and disappointment.

Jack understood. "I was thinking of coming back tonight. Say ten, or so."

Neil reached out for him. "You know, it's been the best night of my whole life."

"You sure about that? I may have criminal tendencies."

"No! You're not a criminal. You're ..." Neil hesitated, feeling silly, "Robin Hood."

Chuckling, Jack held him closer. "Well Robin needs to get his car from the cannery parking lot." Jack released him. "I'll be here to drive you to the library, okay? Ten?"

"Nine thirty!" Neil's expression was radiant.

He watched Jack cross the Gordons' lawn from the window

in the back door. In the faintly misty early morning heat, he seemed like one of those fantastic mythological creatures he'd read about in the old *Topical Encyclopedia*. But which creature? As he descended the stairs again, he remembered *Volume Twelve*, page 311: a naked youth with a helmet and winged heels.

21

NEIL DIDN'T SLEEP, HE COULDN'T sleep. Restlessness had him in its grip. He wandered from room to room. He washed and dried his bed linen. Had a sort of breakfast consisting mainly of cheese and potato salad. In between, he showered and dressed, taking special care with his clothes. He put on his tightest trousers, another pair of khakis, sandy-coloured, that drew attention to the length of his legs and his high, round behind, and with it a thin, short summer shirt of pale green and yellow stripes. Looking in the full-length mirror in his mother's closet, he thought, I know now. I know what all those others know — Vass and Ronnie, Dr. Brazier, Edsel-man. I'm another man's lover now.

The morning came on very hot and bright. Excitement obscured his fatigue, but worry nipped at the excitement like a nasty little dog. Worry about what it meant to be another man's lover. Worry about detection. Worry about the other man's feelings for him — were they genuine, would they last? But though they at first felt almost too much to bear, his nagging worries soon became a welcome distraction from another feeling that, every few moments, crawled out like a snake emerging from beneath a rock. His concern circled tirelessly around Jack's determination to get Mr. Yardley back, always terminating with an image of a handcuffed Jack climbing out of the paddy wagon at City Hall in the company of sad, sorry men. The other worries he could push away because they were too cloudy to allow for reflection, but the fear of losing Jack to the police frightened him so much he felt pain. Mixed up with this fear was something else he couldn't name, something familiar, though, a dread.

It was nearly nine thirty when an old blue Pontiac pulled up the driveway.

Neil was out of the house in a flash. As he approached the car, he could see Jack smiling, and immediately felt all worry vanish and even the fear evaporate. He was here, and safe.

Jack whistled softly. "Don't you look fine!" he greeted, as Neil settled into the passenger seat. Jack leaned over, gave his cheek a peck. "Don't worry," he said, when Neil started. "There's nobody around. And anyway, they'll just think I'm your adoring cousin."

Neil's laughter was bubbly.

"I think maybe I'll just take you down by the Humber River and have my way with you. You sure fill out those pants nicely." Jack gave Neil's thigh a squeeze, followed by a quick fondle. "You're sure good for a guy's ego, you know. I'm going to call you Mr. R. 'R' for Responsive."

Jack pulled out of the driveway, and an incredible sense of well-being flooded Neil — a sense of lightness and clarity, and open roads stretching for miles ahead.

Neither of them said anything for several blocks, but they both wore smiles.

Neil shyly put his hand on Jack's thigh. "I was expecting a dark green car." He described what he saw on his walk with Sylvia past Jack's house, the afternoon of the family reunion.

"You saw Dr. Ambrose Rookwood's car. They were probably going to Solemn Benediction or some other jolly service. That was Lawrence with him. He's my older brother."

"He's really good-looking."

"Better looking than me?"

"You're not good-looking." Neil blushed. "I didn't mean that! I mean you're beautiful."

"Very smooth, Mr. Bennett. You should see his body. Muscles upon muscles. He's got all these barbells up in his room."

"He sure doesn't look very happy."

"Miserable. He hates the pater even more than I do. But he won't do anything with his hate except let it chew him up. Sometimes I wonder if all the bodybuilding isn't about getting up enough confidence to murder the fucker." Jack frowned at the road. "He's also miserable 'cause he likes boys."

Neil looked over sharply. "He told you that?"

"No. But I've seen it in his eyes. The way he looks at men. I knew you were a man-lover by the way you looked at me the very first day."

"So both of you are then?"

"Larry likes men and only men. I like men, I like women, I like people. Larry's a man-lover, but, unlike you, he's too afraid to try. It makes me really sad for him."

Neil was confused by all this information. "You like men more than women?"

"Right now what I like is you."

The answer was perfect, as far as Neil was concerned. "Why do you both hate your father so much?" he asked.

Jack shrugged and said, "After getting to know Mr. Yardley, I'm not sure anymore, and then when you told me your stories last night, I started to think my father's a fucking saint. Well, not exactly, but he never tortured me, never beat me, never even really yelled at me. He certainly never deliberately terrified me." Jack glanced at his passenger. "But he's cold, really cold. We all think his coldness killed our mother. Heart failure at forty-six. After she died, he got even colder. Rarely smiled, rarely talked, or if he did, it was all pious shit about God's wisdom. Larry and Bernie swallowed some of the poison. I wouldn't. Larry wanted to become a priest, but they had 'doubts' about his suitability, which certainly deepened the frown in my father's forehead by several degrees. Anyway, my father's a cold-hearted, life-hating piece of work, and living in that house, especially after Mom died, has been a fucking nightmare. Like immersing yourself in a vat of ice water."

"Why are you still living there then?"

"I don't have money for a place of my own. But I won't be around for long. There's a limit to what I can take from him."

"Mrs. Knight said you were going back to university. Are you?"

"I don't know. Delivering bread seems a better use of time than sitting in French *explication de texte* seminars. All the blah-blah. The symbolism of rain in Paul Verlaine's poems. Why should I care? Why should anyone care? It all began to feel like Father. A lot of wind. Of course, he hates the fact that I deliver bread, just as he hates the fact that Larry does the books for a business run by Jews. God! I hope Bernie does something wicked, like become a busker or join a gypsy caravan. He just might, too, him and his guitars. Which of course he can only play when Father's not around. And look at you — poor Neil! Trapped in a car with a ranting lunatic! I had a girlfriend once who told me I didn't know when to shut up!"

"I don't feel that way," Neil said. "I like how you talk."

"That makes you unique."

"I like everything about you ... almost."

Jack looked over at him quickly. "Just so you know, I told the Yardleys that I won't be by this evening. That I have a prior date."

"Are you ever going to go back to there?"

"Well, if you promise to make continuous love to me for the next week, maybe I'll give the Yardleys a miss. Look, we're at the Humber." He nodded at the deep green trees along the sweltering riverbank. "It's quarter to ten, so we don't even have time for a quickie. Too bad."

Neil ran the hand that had never left Jack's thigh as far as the bulge in Jack's pants, where it paused shyly. "I'm glad you're coming over just for me."

"Selfish kid!"

They were passing the Jane Loop. He stole a quick glance. Two streetcars were waiting their turn to head downtown. Neil smiled. Parma Fruits and Vegetables came next. Tony was in front sweeping. Lorenzo was talking to a customer. Across the way sat Runnymede Shoes, its door open to whatever coolness the morning sidewalk could provide. Then they were outside the cinema where Audrey Hepburn still held court with Elvis. Neil watched it all pass as if it had belonged to another lifetime.

Jack pulled up to the sidewalk, opposite the library. Letting the car idle, he turned to Neil. "Any final words?"

Neil wanted to say, "I love you," but the words, which he had spoken so freely the night before, somehow seemed huge now, too huge for the car and the street and the hot, white sky relentlessly bearing down on them. He would save them for later. Instead he smiled and lightly stroked the palm of Jack's hand, which lay a supplicant in his lap. "Can we do more tonight?"

"'More'? 'More'?"

"You know ...?" Neil's face went very red, and he scooted out of the car.

Jack stuck his head out the window and shouted, "Wild boy!" loud enough to turn people's heads.

Neil tore across the street. At the library door, he turned to wave.

Jack was still sitting with his head out the window. "The answer's yes!" he shouted.

JUST BEFORE NOON, Tony appeared in the library in his berry-stained apron. He found Neil putting order in the Biography section.

Neil was taken aback by Tony's appearance. He was looking pale, tired and anxious, seeming both smaller and younger.

"I'll buy you lunch at Anderson's."

"One o'clock?" Neil answered.

An hour later, he took a seat in a booth at the back of the local luncheonette where Tony actually appeared to be in hiding.

Neil said, "You okay?"

"Everything's shit."

"What do you mean?"

The waitress came for their order of hamburgers and fries.

"Vicki and I are over."

Neil sat back. He was used to Tony's dramatic stories, but that afternoon he was both tired and excited, and had a much harder time following the trail of the break-up with Vicki. What eventually became clear to him was that Vicki had boasted to Mrs. Colero about her relationship with Tony and Mrs. Colero had promptly fired her. Tony's reaction was to refuse to work with his mother in the shop, which was a grave error, as it turned out, because Mrs. Colero then hired cousin Lorenzo who instantly became the new golden boy. Now that Tony was back in the shop, ordered there by his father, he was feeling horribly slighted and undervalued.

Neil made but one suggestion: "Maybe you should have told your mother you'd date who you wanted."

"You gotta be kidding," was Tony's quick response. "I don't want to go out with her anyway. She's too much trouble. Typical chick."

As Neil sprinkled vinegar on his fries and added sweet green relish to his hamburger, he was very aware that he could never talk to Tony about Jack, or any man, the way Tony was talking to him about Vicki. Nor would he ever be able to involve his family in any of his love dramas, except, perhaps, his Aunt Sylvia, and she lived thousands of miles away.

Tony tossed him a smile. "Why don't you come over tonight?

I'm upstairs looking after Gio again. Angie and Bruno are going to some party with store people. I'm designing cards and a new bag for Bruno. And ads, too. He's getting friendlier and friendlier." Tony leaned forward, lifting the hamburger to his mouth. Before taking a bite, he winked at Neil and said, "Come over and I'll fill in the details."

Neil watched him chew his hamburger noisily. Tony always chewed his food that way. "I can't. My parents have gone to this family reunion on Lake Joseph, so I'm eating with the neighbours."

"So phone and tell them you've got a better offer."

Neil almost said, "It's not a better offer," but he checked himself. "I better not. They've been so good to me."

Tony put on a hurt face that made him look like one of those tearful saints on the antique Italian prayer cards he collected.

Neil tried hard not to smile.

IT WAS SO hot he changed into a pair of shorts before heading over to the Knights. At the last minute he replaced his short striped shirt with the one he'd bought at Eaton's, the wintergreen shirt. It was so soft and cool. He could hear his mother saying, "You'll just spill food on it," but he didn't care, he wanted to look really nice.

The Knights welcomed him with the quiet generosity they had always shown. The food was excellent, a different selection of salads than Mrs. Gordon had offered at her backyard soirée, not as sweet perhaps or as rich, but delicious nonetheless, especially the cucumber, dill and yogurt dish of which he had several helpings, and the homemade scones with clotted cream.

They told him at length about their trip around the Thousand Islands, and their day in Cornwall where they attended a special commemorative barbecue for someone Mr. Knight had known all his life. "A good man, a good man. A bit too fond of the whiskey, though. And of making babies. He had eleven of them."

"Think of his poor wife," Vera Knight said. "He had the fun. She had the babies."

"Tell us, Neil, about all these break-ins. When we left it was just the Doyles. I saw in *The Advertiser-Guardian* there's been three or four more."

"It's in the paper?"

"Yeah, with pictures." Mr. Knight got up and crossed to the sideboard, where a stack of mail lay patiently waiting for Sunday opening. Above the sideboard hung an old photograph of King George and Queen Mary in an elaborately carved gilt frame. "Here. Page four. The Cope place."

Neil stared at a picture of a house on Trewell Avenue, looking very country-homey with its stone fence and towering oaks. Below it were two more pictures. One was of the dining room, showing several chairs upended and covered in something that made them shine — "shellac," the caption said. The other was of eviscerated sofas and chairs, looking like some kind of exotic animal carrion. The owner, according to the paper, was a Miss Rachel Cope. The scene reminded him of his father's attempts to create a break-in: only the shellac and furniture stuffing had been missing.

"Not a very nice woman, according to Lydia West," Mr. Knight said, buttering another scone. "A right witch apparently. She has this gate that will close on your car if you don't leave as fast as she wants." He took a bite, then smiled. "Doyle, Caldwell, those bloody Chards, the fanatical Steeles and now Miss Rachel Cope. A straightforward case of just desserts, I'd say."

Mrs. Knight shook her head disapprovingly. "There are better ways to correct badness."

"Name one, Duchess."

"I can name two: education and example."

"But, Mrs. Knight, what if a person won't be educated or won't follow an example?" Neil put out the question very carefully.

"Good point, Neil, good point!" said Mr. Knight, with a flourish of his table napkin. "Some people are just blocks of meanness."

"I don't know any such people," Mrs. Knight answered. "If people can't be corrected by education and example, what do we make of our Christian teaching? People have it in them to be good and kind and loving. Christ taught us this. All good qualities can be brought out with care."

Mr. Knight looked down at the remains of his meal somewhat chastened.

"Once in a while, of course, there is someone who defies all efforts to correct him. And then there's nothing for him but jail." She paused looking very sad. "But, if you want my opinion, these break-ins aren't the work of hardened criminals, but of kids whose parents have failed miserably in their job of raising them."

"That's what the man in the Edsel thinks, too," Neil heard himself say.

Both Knights looked at him with surprise on their faces.

Neil coloured slightly. "He apologized to me."

Mrs. Knight sat back folding her pristine white napkin. "Well, there, you see: just what I said. People have it in them to be good and kind."

Mr. Knight's mischievous grin looked to Neil very like one of Jack's. "The Duchess triumphs again. But, isn't it also true that good people have it in them to be bad?"

With a wave of her pale hand, she said, "Of course, it's true, Phil. We're nowhere near perfect, any of us."

22

JACK SHOWED UP SHIRTLESS JUST after eleven. A light, rapid knocking at the back door announced his arrival.

Neil, who had been lying on the living room carpet, jumped up so fast he almost lost his balance.

"Think I wasn't coming? O, ye of little faith."

There was a kiss, a quick one, and then another, longer, more probing.

"Yum," Jack said. "These are yours, aren't they?" He opened Neil's sweaty hand and deposited the rifle-toting cowboy and his Native enemy. "I went to check to see if these fellas were still on the branch. I found them."

"You've been there before?"

"I like it there. Very comforting. I found another warrior chief a couple of weeks ago."

Suspicion cast an instant cloud over Neil's expression. "What were you doing there?"

"Trying to catch a glimpse of you." Jack laughed at the boy's doubt. "Honest! You're very elusive, you know." He kissed Neil's nose. "Your lair gets the best of you."

"You were watching for me? Really?" Neil couldn't quite accept it.

Jack pulled him close. "Why not? You're a very interesting

guy, a strange mixture of smart and innocent, of worried and hopeful, of romantic and forward-looking. You're terribly cute, too, and, as I learned last night, very well-equipped. Yes, I'm a voyeur from way back!"

"You mean like peeping Tom?"

"Sort of, but not just anybody, only people I fancy. You're overdressed, sir," Jack said, and tossing onto the table a small cloth bag he had been carrying, he began to unbutton Neil's wintergreen shirt.

Neil held his breath.

"Why don't you take care of my shorts?"

Neil's hand shook with excitement as he undid the button and pulled down the zipper.

Jack undulated his hips and the shorts started a slow descent down his legs. At the same time, leaning into Neil, he extricated the boy from his top.

"What do you think?" Jack indicated a pair of white underpants that were so low on his hips that his pubic hair was visible and so tight that what they contained was very clearly outlined. Neil had never seen underpants like these before. "I was looking for something special for you, and I found these at the back of Larry's drawer. Don't look at me like that! I was desperate for something to please you. They're French, so the label says. Go on. I'll undo yours." He dealt deftly, swiftly, with the button and zipper of Neil's shorts. Then, as he began to ease them down over Neil's buttocks, he laughed. "Well, well, little devil."

"I wanted to surprise *you.*"

"Feels good, doesn't it?" he said, squeezing Neil's cheeks. "You should do it all the time. At the library ... give the patrons something to ponder between chapters of English history or Polish novels." He laughed again and the laugh led into a deep kiss, then a deeper one that had them moaning and pawing each other fiercely.

The phone rang.

Neil jumped.

Panting, Jack cursed it.

Neil lifted the receiver. "Hello?"

Breathing.

"Dad?"

More breathing, but raspy.

"Dad!"

Jack took the phone from him and hung it up with a crash. "Wait a second," he said.

They waited, Jack staring at the phone, Neil's gaze oscillating between it and his guest, fully tumescent in his low white underpants.

The phone rang again.

Jack picked it up. In the voice of a person just wakened from sleep, he said, "Yes? Yes? Who's this? Who's this? Hey, you realize it's almost fuckin' midnight?"

Even Neil could hear the click of the receiver on the other end.

Jack smiled, gently replacing the phone. "You'll see," he said.

It rang again immediately. Jack nodded his head to indicate that it was Neil's turn to answer.

"Hello? Yes, Dad. I'm fine ... Yes, I'm fine ... Why? ... No, I wasn't in bed ... What? ... No. I'm alone. Why? ... Was that you before? Was it? ... And last night, too? ... It's not funny ... Doreen? That was her? You can tell her, too, then ... I've had enough of the jokes. I'm hanging up now, and I'm not answering the phone again." He slammed the phone down. "It *was* him, him and my cousin Doreen. She's a lush, and he's —"

Once again the phone began its ringing.

"Don't answer it, Neil."

It rang nine times before Jack grabbed it and shouted in his irritated roused-from-sleep voice, "Who's this? What the hell do you think you're doing? I'm going to have this call, traced, you asshole!" He laughed as he replaced the receiver. "This is going to go on for a while, but we're not going to answer it again." He kissed Neil lightly, tenderly, then extracted a red toothbrush from the cloth bag and started for the stairs. The phone rang again. "Wow, he's persistent!"

The ringing continued as a happily defiant Neil followed Jack upstairs.

"I should pull the blind before we turn the light on, in case the Knights are still up," he said.

That done, Neil peed as Jack surveyed himself in the mirror. "This light sure is unflattering." He brushed vigorously. Then they traded places. A feeling came over Neil as he watched Jack's stream of urine hit the toilet bowl that he couldn't have described as anything other than safe. These shared domestic moments were as close to his fantasy of companionship as anything he'd ever experienced. Saturday evenings with Tony above the store were the only thing that came anywhere near it.

Jack stepped past him into the hallway, smacking his behind as he did.

"Who sleeps here?" Jack asked, pointing to the two bedrooms that faced each other across a shallow hallway. "Your parents?"

Neil sighed.

"Weird, eh? My parents slept apart, too. I'm in my mother's old bedroom now. My brothers won't have me in theirs for some reason. Nothing has been changed since she died. It's all there, the chintz, the heavy drapes, the Louis-Whatever chairs, the ottoman with the peony fabric, very faded. All there." Jack turned to face him in the doorway. "I kind of feel as if I'm at the scene of a crime. *Naked City*, or something. And with this heat ... it's perfect. Let me see your dad's room."

Neil quickly crossed to pull down the blind on his father's window, then turned on the overhead. Outside, there was a slight breeze stirring the maple, but it was a hot breeze, bringing no relief.

Jack looked around the pale grey room with a cool, detached expression. He examined the bookshelves and then the bedside table. "Nice."

"He made them."

"Multi-talented. Carpenter *and* terrorist. And the wardrobe and chest?"

"No, they're part of a set. My mother's got the other pieces in her room."

Jack opened the closet door, peeked in. "Everything in shades of grey. Just like my father. They have such a zest for life, eh? Maybe I should see your mother's room."

Neil led the way.

"Colour at last. Blue. Very blue and — purple, I guess. It's nice, if a bit ... I don't know — blue. That's Renoir, that poster, the lady in blue with the umbrella. My mother liked Renoir, too. Father hates him, of course, too much pink flesh." He stood at Nora Bennett's vanity, surveying her tidiness, her sense of order. Everything on the vanity table had been arranged to make the act of putting on a face extremely uncomplicated. He picked up a gold lipstick holder. "Women are funny, eh? All the paint and powder. I do like these glass perfume decanters." He returned the lipstick to its place next to the dove-grey powder box. He reconsidered the Renoir woman in blue. "You're more like your mother, I guess. You like things to be orderly, don't you? Tidy. And pretty's important, too. You're what the French call *sentimentale*. What's the matter?" He put his hand on Neil's warm shoulder.

"I don't want to be up here."

Jack flicked out the light. In the hallway, his face, which, during the investigations of the bedrooms, had looked cool and hard, softened again. A playful sensuality reasserted itself. "I'm sorry to drag you through that." He kissed Neil. "How does anyone sleep up here? C'mon — it's like a furnace."

They hurried down the stairs out of the smouldering silence.

Neil turned off the living room lights. Jack made his way over to the hi-fi, to examine the record albums lying on top.

"Ellington? Your dad's a jazz man, eh? And this?" He held up *Juno*.

Uncertain of Jack's reaction, Neil was hesitant to answer. Men usually thought Broadway musicals were corny.

"Are you a Broadway boy?"

Neil blushed.

"I've never heard of *Juno*. I like *West Side Story*. You ever heard of *Carnival*? My brother Bernie's taken to playing 'Love Makes the World Go 'Round' — that's from *Carnival*, isn't it? On his guitar, and singing. He's got more of a folky voice. But it sort of suits the song. Pretty song. And what about the Ferrante and Teicher? I bet that's yours."

"No, it's Lana Gordon's. She gave it to me 'cause it has 'Moon River' on it."

"Let's take it down, and the movie soundtrack, too. We need a bit of movie music for our bedtime."

"No, we don't." Neil wasn't enjoying Jack's joking tone anymore.

"Hey," Jack said, "show music's great. Upbeat. Upbeat's always good. But you're right. We don't need any accompaniment except 'Moon River'! It's our music. You see," — and he touched Neil's cheek with the back of his hand — "I can be *sentimentale* about some things, too."

TWO MORE SHORT delays occurred on their way to bed.

At the bottom of the basement steps, Jack stopped to examine the workshop he had entered the night before in search of bandages. "Impressive, eh? Man, that saw's a monster. It could really slice a guy up." Jack turned to Neil. "Did he do that painting in the backyard?"

Neil's silence was the perfect answer.

Jack turned out the light. "So, he can do all this, why's he need to scare you?"

"He's always saying there's no point in making anything, it's already been done by somebody else, and better."

Jack grimaced. "Love that defeatism."

They were in the bedroom now. Neil switched on the Chinese lamp. When he looked around Jack was staring at his pin-up board, the skin of his back gleaming with sweat. He wasn't sure why, because he found Jack so accepting, but he felt very exposed and vulnerable.

"Audrey, Audrey, Audrey. She really is beautiful." Jack half turned to Neil. "If you met a girl like her, would you fall for her?"

Neil shrugged uncertainly.

"I like that about you." Jack held out his hand. "You're not afraid to not know." He offered Neil a couple of little kisses. "You don't have to fall for her, you know. I might go for her, but I'm not sure, I could also just be bullshitting."

Neil planted his face in Jack's hair. The smell was like some kind of fruit.

"But you gotta tell me the story behind Mr. *Foam*, there."

Neil looked at the image of the dark-haired young man on the rocks. "I can't think about him with you in the room."

Jack placed his damp forehead against Neil's and gently took hold of his cock. "Maybe I should put up sexy boys in my mom's room, in place of the little prints and things, see if I get any comments. I can just see my father. Spontaneous combustion! Poof!" Jack's laugh was hard, brittle.

"Can we go to bed?" Grabbing his arm, Neil began pulling him across the floor.

A sweaty tug-of-war ensued, provoking peals of laughter until, without warning, Jack dropped his ferocious resistance and Neil toppled backwards onto the bed. Jack jumped on top of him, claiming a loud victory. "That'll teach you to mess with a master!"

Jack didn't cling to his victory, though. Within seconds, he was huskily urging Neil to take him wherever and however he wanted, and in this way, over the next couple of hours, they continuously swapped the roles of conqueror and conquered, master and boy, giver and taker.

At one point in their lovemaking, pulling back from release, Jack asked very softly, "You asked me a question this morning. You remember?"

"I remember."

"And I answered."

"I remember."

"Have you changed your mind?"

"No." Neil's voice was very quiet and slightly anxious, too.

Jack rose from the bed. Picking up the cloth bag he had deposited on the sofa beneath the pin-up board, he extracted first the clothes he had borrowed from Neil that morning, and then a small bottle. Neil couldn't see what it was, but when Jack returned, he stood at the foot of his bed, his erection very prominent, and took the lid off the bottle.

"Vaseline," Jack said with a smile. "You ever heard of Vaseline? Recommended for a smooth ride."

A look of sudden understanding crossed Neil's features.

"What's that look about?" Jack was slowly massaging his cock with the petroleum jelly. "Tell me about you and Vaseline."

Neil told him about the barbers, Ronnie and Vass, and how Ronnie's nickname for Vass was Vaseline, and about the chicken sandwich offer, which had finally been explained to him. As he spoke, Jack carefully, gently, entered Neil with a Vaseline-coated finger. Meeting with no resistance, he added another.

Neil was suddenly still. "I need to go upstairs."

Jack nodded. "You do that."

It was a few minutes before Neil was back downstairs, smiling. "I think I'm ready now."

Jack coated his fingers in Vaseline again. "Go on, tell me more about your two barbers."

"Now, Jack."

"Already?"

Neil said, "Yes, please."

Jack slipped into him easily.

Neil gasped, clutching the sides of his bed.

"Wait?"

"No!"

"It's not hurting?"

"It doesn't matter."

Jack looked down at the discomfort in the boy's face, waiting.

"No, don't wait. Please don't wait."

Bending over him so that they were chest to chest and face to flushed face, Jack began to fuck him in earnest, slow and steady at first, but quickly building into a powerful rocking motion, which produced its own wet, slapping sound as soaking thighs collided with slick buttocks. In only minutes, Neil was gripping Jack's back with a look of stark amazement on his face.

"I'm coming!" Neil, his grey eyes wide with wonder, reached up and took two handfuls of Jack's golden-brown hair.

"Pull it!" Jack commanded.

Neil was already pulling, straining to reach Jack's red, wet mouth. "Kiss me!"

Jack lowered his head, and Neil, hungry for his invader, attacked his mouth, with his own lips, tongue, teeth.

Very soon, Jack's cry of release filled Neil's mouth.

"Don't move. Please."

"I couldn't possibly move," Jack murmured

"Good. Forever. Let's just stay like this forever."

"I have no objection." Jack's voice had never seemed so soft.

And they lay like that until nature eventually engineered a separation. Even then, Jack simply lay out full length on top of Neil.

There was no sound for a long while, except for laboured breathing.

It was Neil who spoke first. "Was that all right?" The question was not a rhetorical one.

Jack lifted his head. "Were you in another room?"

"No, it's just I don't have any experience."

Jack lowered his head again onto the pillow next to Neil's. "I don't have a huge amount either, but, frankly, I can't imagine making love getting any better. Fucking hell, are you crazy?"

Neil clutched Jack tightly in response. "It was so wonderful. Better than anything I ever imagined. Better than any of my fantasies. Better than — than anything in the world."

"So, you've got your answer."

"I don't want to let you go." He held on even more tightly.

"You don't have to — I'm here, I'm here. Now rest."

"Jack?"

"Yes."

Neil hesitated.

"Yes?"

"Nothing. I love you."

"That's not nothing." Jack lifted his head to kiss him, and ended up staring into the deep grey eyes.

━━━

THEY LISTENED TO *Breakfast at Tiffany's*. Then, much to Neil's chagrin, Jack put on the Ferrante and Teicher version of "Moon River." When it was over, Jack said, "That's like a lot of really sweet cake. Viennese pastry, maybe. Can we hear the soundtrack again?"

The strummed opening of "Moon River" filled the room. Jack

began to sing along, and as he tumbled down next to Neil, he sang it through to the end.

Neil said, "I love the line, 'two drifters, off to see the world.' It's what I always wanted, you know, a special friend to see the world with. My friend Tony and I used to talk about traveling together."

"Why 'used to'?"

"It'll be different now." When Jack offered no comment, Neil continued, "Don't you see? Because of this."

"Yes, I see," Jack said softly.

Neil sighed deeply. "I don't know how I'm going to go back —"

"You're not going back, Neil. You're going forward. Remember you're always going forward."

"In a few weeks I'll have to go to school."

"You have to?"

"I want to go to university. I want to study English. I could go to Montreal — except that my dad won't support me to go anywhere but here." Neil looked shyly into Jack's eyes. "Would you mind if I went to Montreal?"

"Boy, you ask the nuttiest questions." Jack turned onto his back. "You know, it's funny. Lovemaking always seems to turn into discussions about the future. Why is that, I wonder?"

"Because it's so big."

"The future?"

"No. Lovemaking."

"Yeah, it's big, but it's present, it's now. We're here. Not there. Not two years away, not five years away. We're here now. I want to be here." Jack turned abruptly onto his side again. "Look, Neil, I don't know what's going to happen. I dropped out of university. I took to the road for a year — almost a year. Drove all the way to the West Coast in the Pontiac, doing odd jobs. I worked for a touring carnival, operating the ferris wheel. Got as far as Seattle, where I met someone — a girl, a really great girl named Linda, very cute, lots of fun. I stayed a few months, and then one early January morning I woke up — it was raining, I remember, a grey drizzle — and I said to her, 'It's been great but I gotta be on my way.' I got in my Pontiac and drove very, very slowly back through the Rockies, then the prairies, doing more odd jobs, until I ended up in Toronto. At my father's door. Don't ask me why. I thought I'd had enough of him to last a lifetime. I tried telling myself that I was here to check in with my brothers, who weren't particularly overjoyed to see me by the way, and then I'd be off. Talk about bad faith. Next thing I know I'm living there, on Baby Point Road, delivering bread by day and irritating the hell out of him by night. I look at myself in the mirror every morning and I say, you can do better than this, and some days I believe it. Then, I run into you, and I'm thinking, no, this is what I need to be doing. But what is this? I don't know. Loving isn't an occupation. It's not a vocation. It's a fire under you to get you going. But get you going for what? I don't know where I'm headed, Neil. But, wherever it is, you'll be welcome."

Tears filled Neil's eyes. Jack wiped them away.

"Come on. No sadness. That's what dwelling on the past and the future always brings. Know that we're going forward and now that we know each other, going forward will be a lot less lonely, a lot more fun. So, stop. Maybe you'll go to Montreal and maybe I'll be there and if so we can keep each other warm. You'd like Montreal."

"You don't like it here?"

"Well ... let me see. I love the Arcadian Court." They both laughed. "My mother used to take us there for lunch, and she used to look so beautiful in her fancy clothes and her little hats with veils. She'd let us order anything we wanted. In that fabulous room with the chandeliers overhead and the waitresses in uniform. We'd laugh a lot, something we rarely did at home, and then afterwards, she'd get us candy from the candy department. We could choose that, too. She moved so beautifully that everyone, men *and* women, used to watch her."

"You move like that, too."

"You saying I'm a fruit?" Jack play-punched him in the shoulder, but he appeared to be really moved by Neil's observation. "Thank you for that."

A long silence intervened, filled only by their breathing and the summer noises playing at the window. Soft summer noises. Even the crickets and tree toads spoke in hushed tones, and the traffic, sparse as it was, seemed to roll by reverently.

Neil found himself smiling. "I want to be a writer."

"You don't need university for that."

"I want to write plays." Neil looked down thoughtfully between their bodies, carefully tucking his upper hand between Jack's thighs just under his balls.

"You trying to heat me up again?"

Neil rolled against Jack, who held him tightly and rolled onto his back so that Neil was lying on top of him.

"Do you ever go soft?"

Neil ground his cock against Jack's.

"I guess I got my answer. So — your turn to try the Vaseline."

Neil's eyes grew very large. "You want me to do the same?"

"That's right. But, careful, I'm not as easy a lay as you!"

Neil bit his neck.

"Owww, tiger! That's what I mean. Next to you, I'm a sissy. You're a big boy, too, so you'll have to take it easy at first. I'll let you know when you can let 'er rip."

Neil sat back on his haunches, hair damp, eyes brilliant, cheeks red.

Chuckling, Jack passed him the Vaseline.

23

WHEN IT CAME TIME FOR Jack to leave on Monday morning, Neil wouldn't let him go.

"We've just spent maybe thirty hours wrapped around each other."

"I want thirty more."

"I've got to go to work."

"Couldn't I walk you to your car?"

"It's down at the end of Avery in that used car lot and I can run to it in probably less than a minute. Why don't you let me have the pleasure of imagining you curled up in our bed, stinking of sex? I'll be back tonight."

"You promise?"

"I say what I mean. I'll be back every night but Wednesday. It's the anniversary of my mother's death and Father's arranged some kind of memorial Mass in the evening. I'm going to show fraternal solidarity." Jack grinned as he slipped on his briefs. "I knew you were a crazy sex fiend."

Neil was pleased with that image of himself. It recurred over and over again during the days that followed, especially when he was alone, but it didn't always bring with it a sense of pleasure. Sometimes, as he moved through those long, sultry afternoons — he rarely got up before noon — he had a very strong sense that what he had done in embracing Jack was not only forbidden, but maybe even dangerous, bringing with it the threat of harsh punishment. This prospect terrified him and to escape it he threw himself into a nearly obsessive care and feeding of his father's lawn.

On Wednesday afternoon, the anxiety of knowing he was to face a long night without Jack was so keen he even undertook to trim his father's hedge, a job he normally loathed. He had only just finished when Mrs. Knight turned the corner of Howard Street into Dominion carrying shopping bags.

Neil dropped the clippers and ran to help her. "It's awfully hot, Mrs. K."

She surrendered one of her bags. "I'm a country girl, Neil. I can deal with weather."

To Neil, she looked anything but a country girl in her yellow sundress with its wide white belt and her white star-shaped clip-on earrings. She was the queen of composure. The heat seemed to have hardly made an impression on her.

"But you, you're perspiring, and without a hat," Vera Knight said, a delicate frown wrinkling her forehead. "You know you could get sunstroke."

In her spotless kitchen, Neil placed the bag of groceries on a gleaming arborite table.

"Would you like a soft drink, Neil? I have 7-Up."

"I'm okay, Mrs. Knight. I should finish up. I'll see you for supper."

Unlike Mona Gordon, Vera Knight was rarely demonstrative, but today, she reached out to touch Neil lightly on the cheek. "You're a good boy."

"Oh no, I'm not," he countered quickly and guiltily.

"Yes, you are. Mr. Knight and I are very impressed. You take such good care of us all. We look forward to seeing you for supper." She touched his cheek again. "One day soon, you know, your worries will be over."

Even though he had no clear idea what she meant by "your worries," Neil left, feeling strangely lighter.

By the time he'd returned the clippers to their shelf in the garage and turned on the sprinklers, however, his mood was crumbling like meringue. Nervously, he wandered the streets till suppertime, searching for some sign of hope or reassurance. Nothing was offered except the vision of a hot and bulky Marge Hamilton returning from work.

"You look lost, Neil," she said, in her abrupt, but friendly way.

"I feel lost, Mrs. H." He looked at her, surprised by the directness of his words. "Everything seems so unreal today. It's like I'm in another country."

She put her hand to his forehead. "Too much sun. Inside with you, silly boy."

But it was the same at home. Nothing there seemed to make sense either. The pin-up board, the wardrobe with its secret compartment, the turntable, the bed, the Chinese brass lamp — they were all the same as before, but somehow unrecognizable since that first flurry of lovemaking. Without Jack's presence, he wasn't sure how to inhabit his room anymore.

That was another source of anxiety. Once his parents returned, how would he manage to sleep in his bedroom alone? Frightening as the implications of his love for Jack were, even more frightening was the prospect of endless solitary nights, nights without Jack. It was almost too much to even consider. The very thought made him nauseous.

That evening he stayed at the Knights' later than usual, playing gin rummy and laughing at Mr. Knight's jokes. When it came time to leave, Mrs. Knight said, "Are you all right over there alone?"

"Of course he's all right, Duchess. Come on, Neil." Offering the need for a breath of air as his excuse, he accompanied his guest across the street, watched him unlock the front door and then waited, while Neil turned on the big living room fan. When Neil returned to the porch, he said, "Look here, son, just call us, if you get scared. We do understand, you know."

Inside, the first thing Neil did was put his Tchaikovsky waltzes on the stereo. He cranked up the sound and waited until the first waltz filled the room to overflowing. Then he closed the drapes, pushed the portable furniture into corners out of danger, and, stripping naked, began to dance. The rooms were thick with heat, and very soon his body was streaming with sweat. This only made him attempt even greater swoops, spirals, and flourishes.

When the record played itself out, he put it on again, telling himself that he would dance all night if he had to. He wanted to feel too tired even to reflect. On the return of the big *Swan Lake* waltz, Neil dove onto his mother's pale green broadloom like a surfer into a luxurious wave. Lifting his arms out and back, he raised his upper body to make what he hoped was the gracefully arching shape of the swan.

Just as his neck had stretched as far as it could go, he heard a voice behind him say, "My Swan Prince."

He jumped in terror.

Jack was immediately on the floor beside him. "I'm sorry, Neil, I'm sorry. I didn't mean to scare you. I knocked at the back door, but the music is so loud, you couldn't hear me."

"What are you doing here?"

"I didn't want to lose a night with you."

Neil felt suddenly stupid, but he couldn't stop shaking. He tried to get up. "I should turn it down. It's deafening."

"It's okay, I'll get it. Don't move." Jack turned down the music. "You make such a ravishing Swan Prince. Absolutely ravishing." He knelt again beside Neil on the carpet. "Your beauty's rescued me from one of the darkest days of my life, my lord, and I will always be grateful, so grateful to you, my Swan Prince." He spoke crooningly, his mouth pressed lightly against Neil's ear, holding him with one arm and undressing himself with the other, which, given that he wore only shorts and a sleeveless shirt, he accomplished very quickly. Then, cradling the boy in his arms, he rocked and kissed him for a while before laying him back down on the rug. "Let me show you how grateful I am, my lord, how very grateful. If you'll let me ... let your humble servant in ..."

Neil's moans were barely muffled by the waltz from *Eugen Onegin*.

ONLY THE CHINESE lamp was lit. They lay on their sides facing each other, with just enough space between them for hands to explore freely. They spoke little and kissed often. Eventually Jack described the memorial service.

"It actually had nothing whatsoever to do with my mother, and everything to do with Father and his cronies at the Cathedral. 'See our deep concern for her troubled soul.' Crap, all crap. It made me crazy. Larry, too. If Larry's eyes had been daggers ... I tell you, he would have murdered them all. Only Bernie, happy-go-lucky Bernie, seemed to think it had any merit. I almost got in my Pontiac and drove off into the sunset, but then I realized I had a better place to go than the sunset, and, man, was I right! You should do your swan dance more often." Jack let a finger skim over Neil's moist chest, pausing momentarily to gently pinch a nipple. "You know, it'd be great to pack you up and take you with me to Montreal."

"You're going then?"

Jack shrugged. Neil read it as uncertainty and moved to close the gap, small as it was, between them. "I've been thinking about you going a lot," he said.

"That's nice! Can't wait to see the back of me, eh?"

"Thing is, I feel so safe with you. I've been scared most of my life. Not just here, with my dad. Outside, too. Greasers at school. Like Archie Ross. He lives down the street. Number nine."

"Know it well."

Neil described his history with the bully, ending by saying, "In the last few years, I'm always a 'mo to him. Just before I met you, he and a buddy, a guy who's been in jail, got me one night just outside the Knights' place, and pulled my belt off and unzipped my pants."

Jack pushed Neil back. "Hold on a minute!"

"They were going to 'cornhole' me — that was the other guy's word. I don't really think they were serious, 'cause it was right there on the corner, but the other guy almost choked me and tore my shirt."

"And what did you do?"

"Shouted. That's when he choked me. But the Knights came and they took off."

"The other guy live around here?"

"He apologized."

"Apologized!" Jack was staring the same way he did the night Rob Neville made his scene in the library. An icy anger coloured his eyes.

Neil pulled himself closer to Jack, seeking the now-familiar comfort of his firm arms. "Yeah, several times, told me he didn't know what he was doing and that he was really sorry, and he's tried to be friendly when I see him."

"And Archie?"

"No apology from Archie."

Jack caressed Neil's back and ass. "Well, it sounds to me as if Archie deserves a visit from one of the break-in brigade."

Neil leaned back. "No, Jack! Don't."

"You think it's okay for him to keep on tormenting you?"

"No, but I can't fight him. He's a big guy, a sports guy."

"So, if the big sports hero came home to find everything he owns smashed, he'd have something to think about. But maybe you like being pushed around."

Shocked by Jack's harshness, Neil shut his eyes. His disappointment was so keen that, for just a second, he wished with all his heart that Jack would just get up and leave and that everything that had happened since Friday night would turn out to be a dream. He turned away.

Jack realized he had gone too far. "Forget what I just said."

"Wrecking Archie's stuff's not going to make him nicer, you know. Probably the opposite. I bet Caldwell and the Chards just get meaner."

Jack started to protest, but the sight of the boy's gentle determination, so clear in the lines of his long back, forced him to swallow whatever counter-argument was arising. He opened his arms. "You may be right about all this."

"I am right. There's probably something awful going on in every house on this block. You and your heroes could spend the rest of your lives getting even. And what's it going to prove? Education's the only thing that's going to change things. Education and example."

"You're like a dog with a bone, boy."

"No, sir, that's you. You and these stupid break-ins. You won't let it go."

"You told me I was like Robin Hood."

"Well, now you're the Sherriff of Nottingham."

Jack went for Neil's ribs, but he was unmoved.

Neil's gaze fell into Jack's lap. His hand followed, fishing. "My being right gets to you, eh?" he said.

FRIDAY NIGHT, JACK was later than usual. Neil had thought to greet him with another dance, maybe to "Waltz of the Flowers." He concocted a little pouch of a costume out of one of his sister's silk scarves; it barely covered anything but felt wonderfully cool and soft against his skin. But when eleven thirty and then eleven fifty passed and there was no Jack, Neil changed back into his shorts and stepped out onto the front porch to survey the streets.

The heat had abated slightly with the sunset. The song of the cricket serenaded a violet sky flecked with gold. There has to be a storm soon, he thought.

Two of his father's bats swooped by.

They were followed by the Edsel, slowly purring its way along Dominion towards Avery.

Shyly, Neil waved.

The Edsel slowed down, stopped.

Shirtless and shoeless, Neil approached him.

Jim was shirtless, too.

"What's up?"

"Waiting for a friend. You?"

"Cruising," Edsel-man answered. "Good friend?"

"Yeah." Neil felt proud.

"Some guys are lucky, I guess."

Neil felt bold, too. "You're really good-looking, you know."

"Fat lot o' good it does me." Jim smiled.

"I'm sorry about the last time," Neil said. "I should have come for a ride."

"Well, maybe next time we meet ... I should get going. I told my mom I'd help her move an old sofa to the sidewalk for pick-up."

"Where do you live?"

Jim's smile turned sexy. "You wanna come home with me?"

Neil laughed. "Not tonight I can't."

"Barry's the last name. 49 Lilac. We're in the phone book. If he doesn't show."

He drove off in the same slow purring way he had arrived.

Neil felt excited by him. Excited and guilty. He climbed the porch steps, opened the front door.

A smiling Jack was sitting on the sofa, nude, running his sister's scarf through his hands.

"Should I be jealous?"

"No. That's the guy I told you about."

"The one who tore your clothes off?"

Neil knelt on the floor between Jack's knees. "Where'd you come from?"

"I came up Dominion. Through an assortment of back gardens actually. You know the Nearys have a beautiful rose garden. Dozens of different kinds of roses. The perfume is indescribable. I saw you come out on the porch, looking sexy, and while you were staring at the moon or whatever, I hightailed it across the street and came in through the back door. Then your boyfriend drove up —"

"Stop." Neil leaned in until his lips could brush Jack's chest. The scent from his groin mixed with the heat to make Neil feel almost weak with desire.

Jack laughed. "Hungry, eh?"

Neil reached for Jack's cock.

"I've got something for you." Jack reached back and handed him a photo.

Neil turned it over, expecting to find a picture of Jack, but what looked back at him was the face of Archie Ross. Round, smiling a large, uneven smile that, instead of making him look friendly or jovial, only made him seem dishonest.

"Where'd you get this?"

"From his lordship's dresser."

"Jack!"

"I didn't touch a thing except the picture frame. It suffered a little damage, and he'll have to pick the glass out of his bed, but that's it. I got out just in time, too. He was coming in the front door as I was crawling out his bedroom window. It's good that Mrs. Ross has all those flowering vines. They make great cover."

"Jack!" Neil stood, holding the photo out in front of him like something potentially toxic that must not be breathed in.

"I'm sorry, Neil. I couldn't help it. I had to do something."

Neil sat in his mother's gold-striped armchair.

"But I promise you, nothing was touched but the frame."

"And you were almost caught."

"Don't rub it in. I need a lot more practice, I guess."

"You're going to end up in jail. Maybe you'll get blamed for all the break-ins."

Jack ignored him. "Looking around that room of his, I'd say Archie's not the brightest light. Lots of trophies. Bowling trophies. Some sports hero. How I wanted to rearrange things. But I didn't. The room smelled, too. He must whack off a lot." Jack attempted a small smile, like a boy sensing his sweetness will win another reprieve from his parents. "His underwear is Fruit of the Loom. That's worth scrawling on his walls, but I didn't. And he has a magazine under his mattress. You want to know what it was?"

Neil struggled not to smile.

"It was a black guy with a huge dick plowing this little blonde with perky tits. Talk about capacity. I thought, I know someone who'd like to trade places with her."

"You're bad!" Neil was up, towering over Jack on the sofa.

"I didn't mean you. I meant Archie." He pulled an innocent face, then leaned forward and unzipped Neil's shorts. "Whoa, jackpot! No underwear *and* a hard-on!"

Neil dropped to his knees again. "Jack, what am I supposed to do with this photo? I don't want it."

"I didn't think you would. Let's go into the kitchen."

Jack placed the photo face down on the kitchen table.

"If you could say anything in the world to this goon, what would you say?"

Neil stared at the white page. "I don't know."

"Anything."

"I don't know." Neil squirmed.

"Say it."

"'You'll pay.'"

"Just that?"

"'You're going to pay.'"

"Okay." Jack reached for the pen that sat on a little shelf beside the hall phone. "I'll write it. YOU'RE. GOING. TO. PAY." He inscribed the words in capital letters on the back of the photo. He stood back to admire his penmanship. "You have scissors?"

Neil fetched them.

"Okay. So cut the photo into four pieces. But look at his face while you do it."

Neil did what he was bid, cutting the photo into four almost equal rectangles. As he dropped the final quadrant onto the table, he felt an overwhelming urge to use the scissors to gouge out the eyes of his quartered nemesis. He hesitated.

"Go on," Jack whispered.

Neil took one of the pieces containing an eye and, setting it on the breadboard he had left on the table that morning, he jabbed the twin points of the scissors into the eye.

"The other?"

Neil brought the points down again with such force that he embedded the scissors' point in the wood.

"Where are your envelopes? Stamps, too."

Neil rummaged in the carved writing desk near the front door for the requisitioned items.

"I'll address them. You put the stamps on."

Neil watched Jack write, again in block letters, *Mr. Archie Ross.* Applying the stamps, he felt strangely exhilarated.

"Okay. Now you stuff the envelopes and seal them. I'll stand here and admire your neatness and precision." When he was done, Jack said, "Now you're going to cover your pretty ass and walk down to the mailbox on Orion and post one of them. Tomorrow, when I go to move the Pontiac, I'll post another and then on Monday and Tuesday we'll send the remaining two. I'll take one and mail it over at your mall there, you take the fourth and mail it at the Jane Loop."

Neil put on his shorts and looked around for his shirt.

"You don't need a shirt. Just tell your friend in the Edsel you're off limits. When you get back, you'll have to show me what you were going to do with this." Jack dangled the scarf playfully in Neil's face.

But Neil's focus was Archie's name on the envelope. "Promise me you didn't do anything else."

Jack crossed his heart. "I probably need to get some lessons before I try it again. You think those other guys might teach me?"

24

SUNDAY CAME TO FAST. NEIL knew it would. He had tried to prepare himself with reassurances that it wasn't "the end," it wasn't goodbye, it was only a "see-you-later," but with the first light of dawn pressing on the curtains for admittance, he found himself extremely unready for the day.

From the stained and rumpled sheets, Jack watched him rise and stare forlornly at the growing light, which, clearly determined to match the occasion, was turning up grey.

"You haven't forgotten I'm traveling by bus today? Come back to bed. We've got five hours yet."

Neil climbed back into bed and they intertwined their legs. He placed his head on Jack's chest. "If you go away, what will I do?"

Jack was clearly disturbed by the thought of Neil's loneliness. "It's easier liking women, you know."

"But I don't. Not that way. I like men. I like you. I love you, Jack, I love you."

Jack hugged him, whispering, "It's mutual. Okay? Mutual."

"Sometimes, I think that what I want is sinful."

"Sinful's a bullshit word dreamt up by ugly, dried up old men afraid of life." Neil watched the anger seize Jack's features and then just as suddenly let go, leaving it rather confused and hurt, almost boy-like.

"And then I think there must be something really wrong with me that I don't care," Neil said, looking into Jack's eyes for some sign of affirmation. "But I can't really make it stick. And now after being with you it will be impossible. It's been the best thing in my life. There's nothing terrible about it, except it has to stop."

"Not 'stop,' Neil. No way are we going to stop. It's called a hiatus, a little break. But as long as I'm here, we'll find a way to get together. At the very least we can see each other at the breadbox and the library. You'll still have chances to tell me how amazing I am." He chuckled.

Neil grinned. "I'm your mirror, eh?"

"If you were my mirror, I'd get really vain."

Neil ran his hand down one side of Jack's face, pausing at the lips, swollen with lovemaking. Jack sucked sensuously on his fingers.

"I'll be glad to see my aunt again. She's the one person I could probably tell."

Jack said nothing, but Neil's words made his eyes water. He looked down.

"Is that a bad idea?"

"No, no. I'd like to tell the whole world how I've spent my week making love to an extraordinary boy ... But can I? Dare I?"

"Would your mother have understood?"

"My mother?" Jack seemed taken aback by the question. "I don't know. I know her best friend was a queer guy. He was an antiques dealer. Got her a lot of the furniture we still have on Baby Point. One day when I was with my mother in his shop, I saw him look at a young blond delivery guy who came in, arms bulging with boxes. He had wanting written all over his face. I recognized it, of course, because I felt the same wanting, too, even then. There are lots of us, Neil. All over the place."

"But they're not you."

"Let's stop talking about them then. Let's be here with each other."

Very softly, Neil said, "Going forward?"

"But I want you backwards."

Laughing, Neil turned over onto his side.

JACK LEFT AT eleven. Though most of the neighbours would be at church, as a precaution he wore a white shirt and tie, with his dark slacks and a grey fedora shading his face. Neil laughed at the sight of a respectable Jack, laughed and longed for nothing more than to hold him all summer long.

He spent the next few hours cleaning, not only his room, but all the ground floor rooms and the upstairs bathroom as well. Although part of him wanted to keep the smell of Jack in his bed, he washed the sheets, the pillowslips, and the assortment of towels and articles of clothing that had been used in their lovemaking, all except his sister's scarf, which he hid in his secret compartment under the floor of his wardrobe. This he would take to the dry-cleaners near the library. He opened his windows wide to air the room, but fearing the scent of sex would still be detectable, he put on a pair of shorts and sandals and scavenged in the garden for fragrant flowers. Only the red roses at the back of the yard offered anything like a strong enough perfume. He snipped ten blooms and placed them in a pretty blue vase with gold flecks, which he found tucked away at the back of the dining room buffet, telling himself that he could pretend later they were picked in honour of his parents' homecoming.

By the time the bed was remade and the clothes were dried, and put away, the room already smelled of roses. He sat on the teak sofa below the pin-up board, the music from *Breakfast at Tiffany's* adding its soft, jazzy glamour to the space. For a moment, he was positively delighted with his fresh room. But then, in a puff of smoke, his happiness vanished. Jack was no longer present. All traces of him had been erased, all traces except for "Moon River," which he could now hardly bear to hear.

He stood up, removed the needle from the record and stared blankly down at the turntable.

"What am I going to do now?" The question tormented him. It didn't lead to tears, but it did wrap him up in a thick, dull ache that left him feeling almost breathless. He needed to do something, to occupy himself. But there was nothing left to do. His world was once again in order. Mother and Father would see it and approve. The only change resided in the roses, but these they would hardly notice. And then in a day or two the roses would droop, the petals would fall, and there'd be nothing left to remind him of the day Jack went away.

Overcome by a terrible sense of deprivation, he finally curled up on his bed and fell asleep.

A GENTLE VOICE calling his name woke him. He turned over groggily.

His aunt, in a bright pink blouse and white pants, smiled at him from the doorway. "Hello, dear. Doesn't it smell pretty in here?"

"Hi, Aunt Sylvia. The roses are for upstairs."

"But they smell so nicely here."

"I'm sorry, I'm a bit dopey." He sat up. "Did you have a good time?"

"Splendid. And you?"

"I bought a shirt with the money you gave me."

"Oh, let's see it."

He stood to take the wintergreen shirt from his wardrobe and realized he was topless and, though she wouldn't know this, he wasn't wearing underwear either. Smiling to himself, he quickly donned the shirt and then turned around to face her.

She smiled. "You do have a good sense of colour, my boy. Come on, let's go up and show the folks." She put out her hand.

"I also bought *Breakfast at Tiffany's*."

"You managed to get two things?"

"The shirt was on sale."

Upstairs, his mother was already in the kitchen, planning meals. His father was standing by the hi-fi with the Tchaikovsky waltzes in hand. "Since when are you into classical music?" he demanded, but didn't bother waiting for an answer. With great energy, he launched into high-flown praise of his son's care-taking efforts, claiming he'd never seen the place looking so fine. His mother focused on his excellent taste in shirts, as her sister had done, and then asked to see his new eyeglasses, which, he realized, he had not yet worn. These, too, were greeted with great enthusiasm.

Once upon a time Neil would have received such commendation with something close to joy, but as he modelled the glasses, he had only a pair of strange feelings: a sort of sadness for the man who had picked the tortoise shell style for him, and a sensation of being anchorless, like a balloon hovering among tall tree branches. He couldn't really make much of his mood. He did, however, find it incredible how clear everything looked.

THEY TALKED TILL ten on the back terrace. His father had brought *Neil's Dream* out of the garage for an airing, but besides looking at it from time to time through critical eyes, he made no other reference to the canvas. Mostly he was attentive to the flow of happy reminiscences that animated his wife and sister-in-law, adding every so often his own memories, most of them some variation on his admiration of the Deekman clan.

Neil's contribution to the conversation was small. It consisted principally of answering questions about the neighbourhood. His mother was relieved that there had been only one break-in while they were away, to a house several streets over owned by a woman — Rachel Cope — she'd never heard of. His father was principally gratified that the Knights and Gordons had looked after his son so well.

Neil said nothing about his conversations with the police nor anything about his adventures with Jack. He felt an urgent need to keep Jack as separate as he could from the domestic scene. This had the effect of making him restless and distracted, and sick with longing. But, mixed in with those feelings was also a strange sense of power or strength, for which he had no explanation.

Just after the first bat was sighted, his mother and aunt rose to retire, both of them yawning.

"It will be nice to have a quiet day tomorrow," his mother said. "Just us and the Knights." She took her sister's arm.

"I'm all chatted out," Sylvia said, bending down to kiss Neil on the cheek. Her lilac scent was pungent in the night air.

When they were alone, his father said, "Maybe we can have another lunch downtown before you go back to school."

Neil nodded his acceptance of the plan.

"Look! Ozzie!" His father pointed to a single bat spinning circles above the sumach. "My friend will be here soon."

Neil felt no twinge of apprehension, no fear.

"Oswald was up at the lake every night. He follows me everywhere, you know. He got me an interview with Vlad, who counselled me on your gift."

"Gift?" Neil didn't turn to enquire.

"It will be here tomorrow. It's a very wise gift. A *memento mori*." Frank scrutinized his son, perhaps perplexed by his calmness.

In a low, but firm voice, Neil said, "Why did you make those phone calls?"

"Oh, for heaven's sake! It was just fun." He pointed to another sky-diving creature. "Look, Yorgo! They're all here tonight. They're glad I'm back, I guess."

"What if I told you I didn't think it was funny?"

His father stared into the navy sky, smiling. "I'm sure I was once a bat."

His voice still low and firm, Neil said, "You don't care, do you? That I don't find it funny."

"Maybe it's time for you to get a sense of humour, son. You're a bit dry, you know, a bit stuffy."

"Dull. You called me dull last time."

"Did I? Dull?" His father's smiled broadened. "I think 'stuffy's' a better word."

"Did your father do this to you?"

"My father fell from a ladder!" Frank's answer was sharp, even snappish. "I was his crutch, for God's sake. He depended on me!"

Neil said, "So you've told me —"

"Then don't ask stupid questions."

"Maybe he tormented you from his chair."

"Don't you dare talk about my father like that!"

"Like what? If you feel it's okay to torment me, why shouldn't it be all right for your father to torment you?"

"You're very full of yourself tonight!" Frank barked.

Neil said, "I'm going to bed."

"He was a fine man!"

"As fine as you?"

Frank Bennett looked over at his son suspiciously. "Better by a long shot."

Silently, Neil rose. "I don't care that you don't care, you know. Not anymore."

Frank said, "Tomorrow you'll have your gift. You'll see then how much I care for you." He laughed again, but it wasn't very convincing.

Neil made his way along the walk towards the back door. The Gordons' weeping willow at the end of the drive seemed to be sighing in the night. He looked up at the canopy of stars, recalling the last time he'd made this journey along the back of the house in the dark, the sense of urgency then, the torn trousers and bleeding feet, and the strong hand of his rescuer — and captor. He opened the door and rushed up the back stairs into the hallway, almost colliding with his aunt, now clad in a flowing kimono covered in swallows and peonies. Her glasses glinted gold in the hall light.

Placing a hand on his arm, she said, "Tell me, did you and your friend have words?"

"No, no words." He stared at her, mouth open, then directed his gaze to the floor, to her Chinese slippers and the Turkish runner.

She lifted his chin. "Then, what is it? I wasn't born yesterday, Neil."

He looked over her shoulder into the bright light of Val's room, dreading the onslaught of tears.

"You go to bed, darling. Sleep long. It's a holiday tomorrow. We'll talk later."

LATER WAS MUCH later, as it turned out.

Neil woke to the intoxicating perfume of the roses on his bedside table. It was past ten thirty, but he didn't move for a long while, fearing that if he moved, the images of Jack he had dreamed would dissolve. Jack had been on a horse, galloping down a twisting country road in a redcoat, like a British soldier from another era. Then he was bare-chested somewhere, with ropes of pearls around his neck. Then finally, laughing and tossing flowers at him from a passing parade float that had tall trees on it. "Going forward," Neil said to himself. Then to the room, "Going forward."

He turned to stare into the heart of the roses next to his bed. A little prayer escaped him: "Please have him call. Please, please call."

At noon, the family joined the Knights for lunch in honour of Governor Simcoe, whose day it was. Neil felt more relaxed, but he was still restless. They were all restless, he realized. His own he could explain, but their restlessness was puzzling. Perhaps, as September approached, it was the call of routine they were feeling and maybe even craving. Not him. His old routine filled him with dread. Until he found a new one that anchored him the same way Jack did, he would hate routine.

On returning home, his father busied himself preparing the barbecue for steaks, and his mother, refusing all aid, disappeared into the kitchen to make homemade scalloped potatoes au gratin.

"I'd like to see your room again, Neil," Aunt Sylvia said.

As he opened his door for her, he couldn't help wondering if she could tell that the room was different. He felt it, so clearly. It was not his old room anymore, though it hadn't had time to become an entirely new room either.

She paused on the threshold, sniffing the air. "You should always have roses in here," she said, before stepping into the room.

He followed her, closing the door behind them.

"Why don't you put on the movie music?"

He lowered the needle, and "Moon River" floated up from the turntable. Like the scent of the roses, it soon filled every crack and crevice of the room.

Aunt Sylvia patted the sofa next to her. "Now," she said, when he was seated, "you don't have to answer me, if you don't want to — I won't be cross if you refuse. But, what happened with your friend? You were out of sorts last night."

Neil looked into her eyes, the same grey colour as his own. Inspired, perhaps, by their candour, he confessed to her his feelings for Jack, and with them, his great fear that Jack was likely going to move on. "I don't know what I'll do when he goes."

Her brow wrinkled. "That's the awful thing about life, Neil. People go. They come and they go. And sometimes it breaks your heart."

"I don't want that!"

She took his hand. "A smart young man like that — his gifts are probably underused as a bread-man. He's probably got other things to look into."

"If his father wasn't here he'd stay, I bet."

Sylvia squeezed his hand. "You don't know that, darling. You're as smart as he is, though. You'll find a solution. Maybe he can help you do that."

"Has it ever happened to you?" His question hung in the air, just a scrap, a tatter.

"Two or three times, in fact. Dear friends, dear, dear friends went, and they didn't return. I thought I wouldn't survive long when Molly Warner went off to New Zealand to teach. But I did." She smiled. "Your friend hasn't left yet, so perhaps you should follow your mother's advice and think positively. As long as he's still here, there's a chance he'll find a way to make the city work for him. How much did you see him when we were away?"

He hesitated only a second. "A lot."

Suddenly commotion broke out above them. They heard the front door flying open and the heavy footfall of more than one person tramping across the living room floor. There were shouted directions and loud, male laughter, followed by Nora Bennett's voice saying, "For heaven's sake, Frank!"

"Neil! Neil!" his father shouted down the stairs.

Opening the door a crack, Sylvia called up, "We'll be there in a moment, Frank." She closed the door again, facing him. "I hate to say it, but you'll have to keep your affection for Jack to yourself. There's very little understanding of what you feel out there. And sometimes there's downright hostility. Even if what you feel is entirely innocent ... You see? And for heaven's sake, not a word to your parents."

He hugged her.

"Neil! Neil!"

They climbed the stairs slowly.

"It's your present," his father called, a large grin on his face.

Sylvia stood aside to let Neil pass. His father was facing the fireplace. On his mother's gold-striped chair sat Mike Dennison, tanned and also grinning.

"Look!" Frank commanded.

Neil's gaze followed the pointing finger.

Leaning against the fire screen was a very old gravestone, greyish-white in colour.

"Vlad told me, 'You must get a gravestone, the gravestone of a child who died in infancy.' That's what he said, and Ozzie took me there. It's for you — a memento mori. Look!"

"I see," Neil said, more puzzled than anything.

"You don't see. Look!"

Mike chuckled, his face flickering with a mean delight.

The inscription was very faint, weathered by time. Neil squinted, then remembered the glasses in his shirt pocket. "Somebody Barrett. November 1, 1855– January 28, 1857."

"Just over a year!" his father exulted. "Died of the plague."

"What am I supposed to do with this?"

"Study it. Memento mori."

"No thanks." Neil turned away.

"He didn't see the initials," Mike prompted.

"Look at the initials, Neil!" his father ordered.

Neil looked back. *N.C. Barrett.*

"They're your initials! N.C.B."

Neil stared hard at the gravestone, as it sunk in.

"Just what the doctor ordered!" Mike hooted.

Trembling, not trusting his voice, Neil walked out of the living room. His aunt stood quietly in the doorway. His mother watched him anxiously from the kitchen. At the top of the stairs, he turned around and softly said, "You want me dead, is that it? You want me dead."

His father laughed. "Memento mori. Look it up. It's an ancient custom. Memento mori."

Mike's grin kept getting bigger and bigger.

Neil could stand it no longer. "Mike, you're a stupid creep to have anything to do with this crackpot!"

"Neil!" his mother called softly, as Mike stood, ready to defend his honour.

His father's face fell, grew dark. "What did you say?"

"You heard me!" Neil answered. He stormed down the stairs.

"Come back here! Come back!" his father hollered from the basement doorway, his face glowing with anger.

"That's enough, Frank!" Sylvia's voice was unusually harsh.

It was harsh enough to stop Neil on his downward descent. He looked back from the landing.

Mouth open, shoulders slumped, Frank turned towards Sylvia like a confused adolescent. "It was just a joke," he protested.

"Neil's not the only one who doesn't find it funny," Sylvia said.

"I think it's great," Mike said with a lame sort of defiance.

"What about those steaks, Frank?" Nora prompted.

NEIL SAT ON the teak sofa in the growing darkness, waiting. For a sign, a sound, something from Jack, something to revive him. He was very tired. And he ached with loneliness.

It had been a quiet supper. No one had found much to say, beyond a few comments on Val's decision to go into nursing. "She's such an upbeat girl," his aunt said, "so charming and likeable. I could imagine her on radio or TV."

To which his father, looking in Neil's direction, added, "Such a waste." It had been the only time during the meal that his father had deigned to notice him.

Neil didn't care. Not now, not tonight. Going unnoticed by his father left him free to be alone with his feelings for Jack. That's all he really wanted.

The others had gone to the terrace right after supper with tea. Neil had fled to the basement empty-handed. To wait and to hope.

His turntable played Russian waltzes. Tchaikovsky's was the only music big enough to take him where loneliness wasn't the only option. And he had it only because he'd followed a beautiful man who looked like Jack into the classical music section of Sam's. As he listened, he tried imagining what it would be like to live with Jack, to be his companion during the day and his lover every night. He tried picturing a flat, something like Uncle Herb and Aunt Vi's, but not over a store. An apartment maybe in an old brick low-rise, with streetcar tracks at the door and a sense of the city all around. There'd be a grocery store just half a block away and next to the grocery store, maybe a bookstore or, better yet, a cinema showing second run features like the Runnymede. There'd be a little park, too, full of crimson maples, where their dog could run. And from the park they could see the Imperial Bank of Commerce dominating the city skyline, and, beyond it, maybe even the lake. He couldn't imagine where he'd find a place that met all these demands, but surely they weren't all that outlandish: Toronto was big enough to provide.

An hour or two drifted by in this way, at the end of which he was quiet and smiling.

Eventually he heard the back door open and his mother climb the stairs to the kitchen. This was followed by the sound of a kettle meeting the burner. She would be making her nightly hot water and lemon drink. And one for her sister with a bit of grated ginger added.

He stood and stretched.

The phone was ringing.

Ten after ten said the clock. His mother would be angry.

"Neil?"

He dashed up the stairs, mouthing, "Sorry," as he took the phone from her hand.

"Evening, Mr. R. You celebrating the great Simcoe?"

Neil giggled. "Sort of. We had lunch with the Knights. What about you?"

"I slept in his honour. All day. Except for a trip to the mailbox. The father and one of the brothers went to Aunt Rose's barbecue. The other brother played 'Love Makes the World Go 'Round' about forty times. Nice accompaniment given my mood. I finally told him, 'By George, I think you've got it.' I should get him to learn 'Moon River.'"

The kettle whistled. His mother filled her cup.

"You making tea?" Jack asked.

"That's my mom."

"Ah, difficult to speak then."

"A bit. What are you doing?"

"I'm lying on my bed, naked, talking to you. I wish you were lying here next to me, naked, but I guess the phone will have to do for now."

"When?"

"When? Ah, when. Yes. Plans need to be made. Will I see you at the breadbox tomorrow?"

"No, I'm going downtown."

His mother made her way down the back stairs and out into the steamy night again.

"My aunt wants me to look around with her." Neil was torn.

"That'll be fun."

"Not so much fun as seeing you."

"Go to the Arcadian Court for me. Have an éclair — chocolate, with whipped cream. It was always my favourite."

"I'll try, but they talk of eating at Eaton's." Neil whispered, "I'm alone now."

"Well, let me tell you — I miss you, Neil. M-I-S-S you. The bed feels lonely."

"Can you imagine how my bed feels?"

"I have imagined. Over and over. How your bed feels. Tell you what, why don't you go downstairs after we hang up and, say, twenty to eleven, you jack off and think of me over here, doing the same. It's a poor substitute, but ... call my name when you come. I'll call yours."

"I love you," he whispered into the phone.

"Ditto."

Neil hung up, his hand trembling with anticipation. He had nine minutes before their date. Debating whether to leave his bathroom routine until afterwards, he hovered in the entrance to the living room for a few seconds. Long enough for the dull white stare of the gravestone leaning against the fire screen to bore into him.

N.C. Barrett.

Neil Cameron Bennett.

He found the implications of this gift almost too much to consider, but he knew now that he had no choice but to stare them down.

He also knew, beyond all doubting, that Jack wouldn't find it funny either.

25

HIS AUNT'S LAST FEW DAYS with them sped by. Tuesday she took Neil and his mother downtown to lunch in the fancy restaurant upstairs at Eaton's called The Georgian Room, where amid a sea of polite, mostly middle-aged women wearing summer dresses and pastel lipsticks, he enjoyed a feeling of sophisticated living, eating strange foods like vichyssoise and quiche lorraine. His aunt and mother reminisced about their downtown "careers." After lunch he was taken to the St. Regis Room, the evening dress department at Simpson's, where his Aunt Julie had worked as a shop girl. Aunt Julie's old boss, Mrs. Buchanan, was still there, an elegant, grey-haired woman in an emerald-green dress with a flared skirt that struck Neil as very bold, especially for a woman of her age. Her glittery purple jewellery and very high purple heels only added to this impression. She recognized his aunt and mother instantly, and greeted them with real warmth.

At two twenty, the ladies took refuge from the heat in Loew's movie theatre, as they watched Henry Fonda struggling for his political life in *Advise and Consent*. At four thirty, they joined his father and Mr. Hamilton for the homeward drive.

Neil headed for work. Making his way slowly up Yonge Street, he catalogued the treats of the day, which were plentiful and required ordering. More than once, he found himself dreaming up ways for his aunt to split her year between Toronto and Los Angeles. He was going to miss her when she left. She had become his one sure ally.

Inevitably, perhaps, a sense of loss began to gain the upper hand, dovetailing neatly with his fears about Jack's departure. He walked right past the record stores, Sam's and A&A's, without so much as turning to look in the windows. He walked blind to everything he normally loved: the art deco façade of Eaton's College Street, which had always reminded him of a very polished doorman, now baking in the sun; the bar called the St. Charles with its funny clock tower that looked like a big spying eye; the buff-coloured Westbury Hotel, which, rumour had it, drew gay men to its bar; and, of course, the movie houses. He ignored the sad, worn, and tired expressions of other pedestrians coping with the steaming pavement and the breathless air. His wine-red silk shirt, which he'd worn for the occasion, clung to his skin like a sucking mouth. His face was streaked with sweat.

What would he do when Sylvia and Jack went? He had no idea, picture, or plan. It was all a blank: next week, next month, next year. School felt like a chasm. His friends, all except Tony and maybe Rick, were perfect strangers. The only thing he knew for certain was that he couldn't go back to whatever he'd been before, not now, now that everything had been revealed, spoken. He couldn't pretend that his feelings were a passing thing, to be replaced in time by simpler joys and pleasures. No, they were permanently his to deal with. But what would he do? He was no anarchist, no runaway, no rebel. If Jack wanted it — and perhaps there was still time for him to see that he wanted it — they could make a life here. Beyond that, his imagination faltered. He didn't even want to think beyond that. It was too bleak, too lonely. Ever since confessing his loneliness to Jack, he had been unable to escape the feeling, growing stronger with every day, that he had always been lonely. Without Jack, he told himself, there would be no escaping his loneliness — ever.

He reached the terminal at Bloor and Yonge for his westward journey, anxious, exhausted. As he stepped up onto the waiting streetcar, he felt a hand lightly but definitely touch his backside. He thought that someone had accidentally bumped him, but when he felt it again, more definitely, in the crease between his buttocks, he turned to look. A large bleached blond woman was climbing the stairs beside him, clutching several bags full of shopping. Behind him stepped a dark-haired man, slight-of-build, with intense dark eyes and a deep five o'clock shadow.

Neil frowned, but the man's gaze was non-committal.

There were only half a dozen empty seats. Most of them were located near the back. Neil took one of these, the last double seat, which other passengers had avoided because of the scalding sunlight pouring in through the adjacent window.

The car began to move. Neil set his attention on the street. Out of the corner of his eye, though, he could see the dark-haired man scanning the aisle for an appropriate perch, seemingly without any luck. After a few seconds of this charade, his gaze fell, as if surprised, on the seat next to Neil. A little smile creased his face and he advanced, easy, cat-like, a slight sway to his walk.

Neil pretended to see only the passing sights. He leaned out the window, one elbow resting on the window ledge. A new building was going up just east of University Avenue, next to the heavy, dull Household Sciences Building. It was presently enveloping the whole street in a haze of whitish dust, but once it was done, they said it was going to be the latest thing in apartment living, with fancy shops on the second floor and even a theatre, a theatre-in-the-round. The very thought of such a theatre gave him a few seconds of keen pleasure, driving off feelings of loss and departure, until suddenly his intense admiration for the construction was broken by a tap on his thigh.

Startled, he looked at the man beside him.

Still smiling, the man pointed to the little bronze plaque attached to the window frame: *Please Keep Arm In.*

Immediately Neil drew in his forearm.

"It get cut off," the man said in a thickly accented voice. "I see once. Two fingers. Chop. Like this." The man demonstrated the disappearance of two fingers with a large hand remarkable for the fan of dark hair covering the back.

Neil grimaced.

The man smiled at him like a performer pleased with his reception. He then made a point of looking away to listen to the two Italian women in front of them chatting volubly and loudly in their Calabrian dialect.

Neil wondered if he, too, was Italian, but not wanting to appear too interested, he turned away to watch the museum, the conservatory of music, and university football stadium pass in quick succession.

In the seat behind him two pre-teen children squabbled over a bag of jujubes, while their big sister across the aisle read a glossy movie magazine, oblivious to their dispute.

Neil closed his eyes. Oppressive heat made the streetcar boil. He would have to change his shirt before work. Perhaps Uncle Herb could lend him one.

Another tap on the thigh.

Neil turned. The man beside him seemed to be saying something with his eyes, but Neil couldn't read the message and shrugged.

"Are you happy?" he whispered.

"Happy?" Neil thought the question an odd one. "I guess so."

The man sat forward on his seat, twisting so that his body was at right angles to Neil's, facing the window. "I'm happy," he said in the same low voice.

Neil started to think the man was crazy.

The man's glance dropped to his lap, where it lingered an

instant before rising to seek Neil's reaction. "Very happy."

Neil suddenly realized the man was talking about an erection pushing noticeably against the fabric of his trousers.

"You come home with me?"

"No. I'm going to work."

"Ten minutes. Fifteen. I live on Christie."

"No. I can't."

The man touched Neil's thigh again. "You make me very happy. Ten minutes."

"I can't." Neil's voice grew louder.

Withdrawing his hand as from a flame, the man looked around furtively. No one was listening. He smiled and moved in again, using his hand to smooth Neil's thigh up as far as his crotch. "You nice boy. I make you happy."

"No, no, I don't want you to, I don't want you." Neil pushed past the man, nearly knocking him to the floor, then hurried to the front of the car, not really noticing that other riders were looking at him as if *he* were a bit off. Nor did he see the dark-haired man with the hairy hands shrug his shoulders at the other passengers, then tap his temple with a crooked finger.

Neil grabbed a seat beside an old black man who dozed. Following his example, he immediately closed his eyes, telling himself he didn't want this, not this fumbling with strangers at the back of streetcars. He wanted Jack. Just Jack.

Uncle Herb wasn't in the store when he arrived. His Aunt Violet, fanning herself with a rolled-up *Globe*, sent him upstairs with instructions for his cousin Sandra to get him a shirt from her father's cupboard.

Sandra, who was freshly showered after a day of life-guarding, a towel wrapped turban-like around her head, took his measure with squinted eyes and pursed lips, looking every bit the fashion commentator. She pulled a short-sleeved black shirt with red trim from the back of her parents' closet, a look of triumph on her face.

Neil thought the shirt was weird, especially the red trim. However, the image the mirror returned to him was very flattering. The shirt actually made him look sophisticated.

His Aunt Violet thought so, too. "That girl has an eye!" She gave him a big red smack on the cheek, which she then had to remove with a white handkerchief. "You look after yourself, Neil. You're looking a little peaky. Oh, and you better take care of whatever that is sticking out of your pocket or you'll lose it."

It was the fourth and final posting to Archie Ross, 9 Dominion Street, Toronto 18.

He dropped it in the mailbox just outside the library.

THE CAR WAS in the driveway when he got home, which probably meant his father was at work in the garage on his painting.

Neil hovered for a minute. He could just go inside, but that would only delay the inevitable encounter with his father's sullenness. With delay came aggravation.

His father barely acknowledged him when he entered. He continued daubing little spots of yellowish white on the black areas below and above the three coloured panels, turning them into pieces of night sky. Or so it looked to Neil.

"I've changed the title," his father said, without looking at him. "To *Night Colours*."

"Why not *Being and Nothingness*?"

"Unavailable," Frank said. "Did you say 'hello' to Miss Fairfield for me?"

Neil suppressed a sigh. "Yes, Dad."

For the first time his father granted him a scanning glance, then turned back to his canvas. "This one will be my masterwork," he said, as if to himself.

Neil strolled into the backyard. Vera Knight, sipping a glass of sherry, was sitting with his mother and aunt.

His appearance in Uncle Herb's shirt provoked a number of positive comments, including a brief account from the two sisters of his uncle's longstanding flirtation with haute couture. "Dapper Dan — that's what we all called him," Nora said.

In the first obvious pause, Neil bent down and, thanking her for the "fabulous day," kissed his aunt's cheek.

"It was fun to see the old downtown again," she said.

The words "old downtown" stung him. "You'll be glad to get going, I bet."

She peered at him over her glasses. "No, but it will be good to see Julie. She's missing me, she says."

As he started towards the house, he heard Mrs. Knight say, "Phil's arranged for an extra couple of days off so we can take Helen down to Niagara. She so wants to see the Falls, and the weekend's no time to go."

He took his salad plate to the dining table, but before he could sit, he decided he would rather dine in splendid isolation.

At the bottom of the cellar stairs, he noticed that the gravestone was propped against one of the storage cabinets in his father's workroom, its back to the viewer. No wonder he's upset, Neil thought. He's been sent to the doghouse.

Inside his room, the curtains were open. His mother had obviously been tidying, something he had asked her repeatedly not to do. Nothing seemed out of place, however, and the bed, made up to perfection with the bronze-hued spread pulled tight and the pillows fluffed up, looked very inviting. Something lay on the spread, gleaming white and square. It was an envelope. He put down his plate.

Mr. N. Bennett, the printing said.

He knew the sender. Hand trembling, he gently unfastened the seal.

There was a card inside, an antique postcard, hand-tinted, showing two people in a huge field of long grass — two young men on closer inspection — one of them pointing out a rainbow that hung in the wide, open sky like a miracle. The tinting was delicate, the mood joyful. On the back were these words:

N.

Waiting 'round the bend?

J.

Holding the card very carefully by its edges, Neil sank to his bed. Everything else disappeared, even the long passage of mournful train whistles from the railway yards at the foot of the street. The world was there in his hands. This was all he wanted, all he was waiting for. Jack's call to go forward.

26

WEDNESDAY HIS DAY OFF, WAS his aunt's last full day. From the sidelines, he watched as she made telephone calls, packed, made more calls, and then, in the afternoon, went for a ladies' lunch over at the mall with his mother, Mona Gordon and Vera Knight. Canadian souvenirs for Aunt Julie had to be bought as well: cheese and maple syrup and some kind of over-the-counter analgesic that Aunt Julie swore by.

In their absence, he performed the usual Wednesday lawn-mowing chore. Afterwards, still restless, he wandered down to the railway yards to watch the trains from a hot, grassy embankment. He and Davy Doyle used to do this when they were in Grade Three together, but today it wasn't Davy he was imagining as his companion. He was convinced that Jack would love the yards. Even when there was no train flying past, there was always a sense of movement in the air. For many minutes he imagined Jack and himself making a life switching trains as they searched for meaningful work, just like the men in *Grapes of Wrath*. He remembered the night he and Tony played out their sex game to the sound of that film. It made him sad, knowing he could never go back to that kind of play. Even sadder that there was no likelihood of Jack and him ever riding the rails together.

After the railway yards, he wandered in the steaming sunlight over to the mall to search out a going-away present for his aunt. The whole time, as he wandered from shop to shop, a question plagued him. Should he call Jack? He had thanks to offer. That would be reason enough to pick up the phone, but try as he might, he couldn't shake the notion that his calling would be felt as an intrusion. Not by Jack, but by Jack's family, whom he had never officially met. To use a phrase his mother was fond of, the Rookwoods weren't "our sort of people."

Nevertheless, at seven that evening, just after his Aunt Violet, Uncle Herb, and Sandra took their places on the patio for an evening of fond farewells, and just before his Aunt Marian, Uncle Henry, Cousins Anne and Wendy, and Wendy's husband Gary showed up for the same purpose, Neil found the courage to make the call.

"Hello." The voice was not Jack's. It was a clipped, precise hello.

"May I speak with Jack, please?"

"Jack has just gone out. I don't know when he'll be back."

"May I leave a message?"

"You may." Neil guessed this was the brother he had seen on the street that Sunday, the older one, Lawrence Augustine. He sounded very proper.

Message delivered, Neil headed for the yard.

For the next hour he listened to the antics of the Deekman family with a free-floating attention. Apparently his Uncle George had been rushed to hospital up in Muskoka with an irregular heartbeat, but it turned out to be nothing, and Doreen had broken her ankle on the dock in the middle of the night — a piece of news that Neil secretly relished. As for Cousin Ken and his adoring spouse, Janie, their baby was soon to pop.

"Could be happening as we speak," Henry said.

"I hope it waits till September," rejoined his wife, "it's a much nicer month."

His father's good humour had returned, partly in response to the warm reception his *Night Colours*, was receiving from the gathering. It now hung in the place formerly occupied by *Winder-mere '62*. Even his wife said, "That's the best you've ever done." Wendy went further than that and asked him if he would paint her something for their terrace. Gary couldn't have seconded the request more energetically. As his father nodded his head in a let-me-think-about-it way, Neil could actually see him expanding with pleasure and pride.

At a certain point, his mother, Aunt Marian and Aunt Violet disappeared into the house to assemble platters of sweets.

Uncle Herb said to him, "I hear you look better than I do in my black shirt. My wife and daughter both told me."

"Don't listen to him, Neil." Sandra looked nothing like a life-guard tonight in her sleeveless lavender blouse and white skirt, and her hair a candy floss extravaganza.

"Herb has never welcomed competition, have you, darling?" Sylvia said.

Suddenly Aunt Marian was back. "There's a phone call for you, Neil."

"Take it upstairs," his mother instructed when he tore into the house.

Sitting on the edge of his mother's bed, he lifted the receiver. "Hello?"

"I'm an idiot. Forgot the library's closed on Wednesday. I'm outside it right now."

"I'll be there tomorrow."

"I can't tomorrow. I've got to go see a man about a placement."

"What placement?"

"One of my father's connections. Can't tell you more. Wait till we meet. I'll come by Friday night. Maybe we'll have a chance after? By the way, is that your buddy Tony with the hair and lips?"

"He's got hair and lips."

"Plump, very kissable lips?"

Neil felt a little pang of jealousy. Jack had obviously spotted Lorenzo, not Tony.

"I almost forgot my plums," Jack said.

"Stop it."

"And tell me you didn't see one kissable guy on your adventure yesterday?"

An image of the dark-haired man who had accosted him on the streetcar surfaced, but Neil instantly disqualified it. "I want to kiss you."

A brief silence was followed very gently by, "You've no idea how much I miss you. A whole week of the greatest lovemaking I've ever had — and then, desert. No wonder I'm randy. Lips has nothing on you."

"Thank you for the card."

"It shouted 'you.' Look someone's making faces at me for talking too long. I'll go and see you *vendredi*. Love you."

A click.

"I love you, too," Neil said to the emptiness on the other end of the line.

***

HE WAITED IN his room with *Plays and Players* for the inevitable goodbye from his Aunt Sylvia, which came earlier than expected. She was dressed for travelling and to his eye looked even more worldly than she had on her arrival. She already seemed distant. Her impending absence felt like some kind of curse waiting to land, and his dread made speaking without tears very difficult.

She sensed his distress and, after telling him her mascara couldn't deal with a lot of crying, assured him several times that she'd miss him, too.

As she embraced him, he asked, "You don't think I'm terrible?"

"Terrible!" She pulled back. "Of course not! We love who we love. There's nothing more to say as far as I'm concerned. But remember what I told you. This has to be your secret for now."

"It'll be lonely," he whispered.

"There are worse things than lonely, Neil. Like being sick or poor or frightened." She placed him at arm's length as she had done that first evening. "I told your mother that Julie and I would like to have you with us this Christmas. Depending on your fall, of course. You may have other places to be."

His thank you's couldn't have been more heartfelt.

She stepped free of his clinging hug, once again blaming her mascara.

"Wait," Neil said. Turning to his bedside table, he picked up a small package gift-wrapped in silver paper and crimson bow.

His aunt immediately protested, but Neil wouldn't listen. He insisted she open it. Sitting on the edge of Neil's bed, she carefully unwrapped the package, so carefully that nothing was destroyed. Under the silver and crimson was a navy blue box with a gold crest on it, and inside the box swathed in white tissue, she found a porcelain monarch butterfly. She lifted it delicately from its casing to examine it. When she looked up again, her eyes were wet.

"It's you," Neil said, realizing afterwards he was repeating Jack's words to him.

Rising, she wrapped him tightly in her embrace. "Give my best to your Jack."

27

THAT EVENING A COOLING BREEZE arrived. Most welcomed the change. Even the shops he passed on his way to the Loop seemed relieved, as if they'd just shrugged off a very heavy weight. Still, Neil couldn't help feeling the coolness was a comment on the void left by his aunt's departure, as well as a chilling return to the status quo. He was dreading his homeward journey.

Before the dread got complete hold of him, however, he encountered the blond ice-skater at the Loop. This evening he carried his skates and was dressed somewhat more modestly in what Neil termed "regular shorts." His muscular legs and bum were still eye-catching but not quite in the same Go-on-ogle-me way. The G-o-o-m way, Neil told himself and giggled.

"What are you laughing at?" asked a familiar voice.

It was Tony, who told him, "I missed my bus, thought I'd take yours. And look, here it is. It heard me."

They boarded just behind the skater. With his eyes, Tony signalled his awareness of the unusually muscular backside.

"You should see him in his usual shorts," Neil said, as they took their seats near the centre doors. "They barely cover him."

"Bet you like that, eh?" Tony squeezed his friend's thigh just above the knee, provoking the hoped-for jump. "I was thinking I might run into you. Next weekend — holy shit!"

Neil turned.

An older woman was boarding the bus, her beehive of blond hair alive with a dozen paper butterflies. Both boys snickered, but the snickering turned into outright amazement when they saw her dress, which came with two filmy panels forming wings down her back. She smiled at everybody with outrageously red lips and bright blue-shadowed eyes and seated herself near the driver with whom she obviously — at least from Neil's perspective — intended to flirt. Something about the woman's unapologetic oddness gave Neil the feeling that things would turn out all right after all. It was the strangest feeling, but he didn't question it. He silently thanked her.

Once he'd recovered from his fit of giggles, Tony informed Neil that Bruno and Angie were going out again the following Friday for a big bash and wouldn't be home till very late. They wanted him to babysit Gio, who, apparently, would hear of no other minder. He made it clear that he would only do it if Neil could stay over, too. They'd agreed, albeit reluctantly on Bruno's part. According to Tony, Bruno wanted him all to himself. This little tidbit Tony communicated in a hoarse whisper.

Neil looked at him astonished. "Bruno gets into bed with you?"

Tony shushed him.

"You let him?"

"What am I gonna do? Scream blue murder? Angie's got another baby coming. I don't wanna make her miscarry or something."

"So I'm supposed to be your bodyguard — is that why you're asking me?" Neil couldn't stifle the note of irritation in his voice.

"Sort of — but not just! We always have fun, don't we?"

They rode for a while in silence. When they next spoke it was about the store and Cousin Lorenzo, who Tony really seemed to want to hate. "My ma lets him take the cash!" Though the temptation was great, Neil resisted telling him about Jack's appreciation of Lorenzo's mouth.

At Montgomery Road, Davy Doyle, sporting a damp towel around his neck, also boarded the bus. Davy had never liked Tony, and Neil fully expected him to find another place to sit, but in what Neil recognized as Davy's typical Fuck-it-if-you-don't-like-it way, he joined them, explaining that he'd just been to the swimming pool. "I'm taking lessons."

Tony said, "Scares the hell out of me, putting my head under water."

"Swimming's unnatural," Davy agreed.

"I love to swim," Neil said.

Tony laughed. "You like unnatural, though."

"Screw you," Neil said.

"See what I mean!"

In this mood, the three teens arrived eventually at Avery Street.

"Do you want me to come down Avery Street, or is Davy enough protection?"

"Davy's more than enough."

"See you then. Don't forget next Friday."

Neil and Davy watched the headlights stream by as they waited to cross the street.

"He's so full of himself," Davy grunted.

"Yeah? And you're so rude."

"Point taken. What's that about protection?" Davy asked once they had crossed Bloor. "You been hassled?"

Neil was surprised by the question.

"By Archie Ross?"

"How did you know?"

Davy didn't turn to look at him. He stared thoughtfully at the pavement as they walked. Nothing more was said, in fact, until they passed Stanton Street. Then Davy said, "He tried to scare me. I can run, though." Davy smiled. "An' I've got a great kick."

They were in front of Davy's house now. As usual, classical music was wafting out of the screen door.

"Mozart's seventeenth piano concerto," Davy said confidently.
"You like Mozart?"

"I don't really know classical music. Except Beethoven, which my father loves, Tchaikovsky's waltzes, and Debussy."

"Debussy?" Davy wrinkled his nose. "Funny knowing Debussy and not Mozart. We better have a music night, soon. Tomorrow we're going to bloody Windsor. My mom's examining. We're back Tuesday."

"I'd like to write something with you."

"Yeah?" Davy lifted his eyes to Neil's face. They were bright with surprise.

"The words, I mean."

"Not the music, eh?"

Neil flinched.

"I'm just kidding, for God's sake." Davy poked his shoulder. "You're so sensitive! Like a bloody girl. Wha' do you wanna write? A musical?"

"Maybe after I see if I can write a song or two."

"I'll get to work."

Still smiling at the thought of collaborating with Davy, Neil reached the intersection of Avery and Dominion to find Archie Ross coming towards him from the direction of Howard Street. He carried a baseball bat, but no glove. Nor was he dressed to play ball. He wore dress pants and a white shirt and shiny black shoes. Except for the bat, he looked as if he were coming from church.

Neil hurried across the corner and looked over his shoulder anxiously, but he needn't have bothered. Archie wasn't even looking at him. He walked like a man who was unable to see anything but the ground immediately in front of him.

A slow smile spread across Neil's face. He had probably received all the envelopes now. How had he looked, when the final piece of the photo arrived? Did he show it to his mother? Did he call in the police again? Neil felt a pang of guilt, which was immediately followed by a low laugh.

The car was in the driveway and the garage light was on. He entered the house. His mother sat in her gold-striped chair with a small bowl of mixed nuts in her lap, watching *The Defenders*.

"Aunt Sylvia get off all right?"

"The plane was on time."

"You're going to miss her, I bet."

"You've no idea." His mother looked quickly back at the screen. "Your aunt really liked her present."

Neil glanced at the TV screen. The young Robert Reed was smiling. Neil smiled, too, in response. Mona Gordon was right: he *was* cute.

"By the way, what happened to your trousers?"

"Ask Dad."

She faced him again, questioningly.

Sighing, he gave her a very brief account of the crank calls.

His mother refocused on the TV screen. "I'll have a talk with George."

"George!" Neil's laugh came close to bitter. "What's that going to do for me? Doreen's not the problem anyway. She's just a drunk."

"Neil!" His mother scowled. "This isn't like you."

He moved towards the cellar stairs.

"There's another letter for you," his mother said to his back, almost as if she were offering him compensation. "Down on your bed."

Neil couldn't get down the stairs fast enough, but on the cellar landing he was forced to make an abrupt halt. At the foot of the stairs, leaning against the wall beside his door, was the gravestone. It was set on a small platform made of a thick, dark wood, probably a scrap his father had scavenged from a building site on one of his real estate tours, and was draped in a stiff plastic creeper, metallic green in hue. Around the base were strewn plastic flowers in yellow, pink, orange, and mauve. In their midst lay one of Neil's old puppets, a puppet his father had called Convict Joe in honour of his black-and-white-striped uniform.

The back door opened behind him.

"What do you think of my garden display?"

Neil walked slowly down the rest of the steps.

"It's not staying there. I'm going to put it in the garden. Vlad advises it. For the health of the neighbourhood. He's told me to pull up that old peony bush that doesn't bloom anymore and put it there. I'm trying out different designs. What do you think?"

"Goodnight, Dad."

He closed the door quietly and threw himself on his bed.

A square white envelope fluttered to the floor.

For a minute, Neil did nothing to retrieve it. Then, still prone, he reached over the edge of the bed and fished it up.

Mr. Neil Bennett, esq., proclaimed the heavy hand.

Inside, another antique card, this one sepia-toned, showing a lagoon in fog. Peeking out of the fog was the prow of a gondola containing two passengers, two young men it appeared, of Anglo-Saxon persuasion. Behind them towered a ghostly gondolier plying his long oar in the murky depths. In a curvaceous white hand, across the lower right corner, flowed the word *Venezia*. Neil had already forgotten the bad omen outside his door when he turned the card over and read,

N.

My Huckleberry friend?
(il mio amico Huckleberry?)

J.

28

MRS. NEGULESCU ADJUSTED THE COMB in her thick, dark hair. "Bucharest was called the Paris of the Balkans, you know. It was so glamorous. The women were very beautiful, the men very handsome." She laughed. "My husband was one of them. I was just a small-town girl. From Sibiu. I never thought a man like that would be interested in me, but, you see, miracles do happen."

Neil wanted to say, *But you're very beautiful.*

"I wouldn't want to see it now. Communists are no friends to beauty."

"When did you decide to leave?"

"We left in early '56 for Hungary. My husband spoke Hungarian, so it was easy for us. He taught in Budapest. You've seen pictures? Then you know it's a very beautiful place. And the neighbours were not Communist. Austria, I mean. Freedom seemed a little closer. Then the Russian tanks came. We left with thousands of others."

"To Canada?"

"Vienna — which we both hated. The Austrians are not just Italians who happen to speak German, which is what they tell you. The only thing sweet about them is their pastry and their *schlagzahne*. Then we came here. It's been good for us. Yes, please?" Mrs. Negulescu turned towards a customer at the checkout desk.

Neil turned, too, only to find himself face-to-face with a smiling Jack.

"Hey, Neil."

Neil felt himself redden.

Mrs. Negulescu stepped aside, "I let you take care of your friends."

Neil realized there was another person at Jack's elbow, a young man in a short-sleeved white shirt and light grey pants. It quickly dawned on him that this was the same young man he had seen with Jack's father on Baby Point.

"This is my brother, Lawrence. Larry, this is Neil. Larry wants a library card."

Larry stepped up to the desk. He seemed painfully shy and very awkward, as if he had not been out in public for many months. When Neil handed him the application form, his hand actually shook, but Neil also noticed how muscular his forearm was and then, as he glanced up the arm, how his bicep filled the shirtsleeve to capacity. The whole arm was very brown, which told Neil that this shy man was not averse to sunbathing.

Neil looked up at Jack, who wiggled his eyebrows.

Larry wrote with a hand that looked like Jack's: heavy, forceful, and in the same block lettering. "Is that it?" he asked in an almost feminine voice. When he lifted his head, Neil could see none of the coldness in his eyes he had noticed there that afternoon on the street with Aunt Sylvia. The eyes were deep, but more anxious than cold, and very, very blue. They were beautiful eyes.

Neil assured him it was all good, and though he could have continued staring into the elder Rookwood's eyes for many more minutes, he took the form to Mrs. Negulescu, who had been busying herself with clearing the hold shelf. She said, "Such clear writing! I'll be just a moment. You may take two books tonight."

"Anything you're looking for in particular?" Jack asked his brother. "Neil knows where everything is."

Larry, it appeared, wanted Irish poetry, Yeats in particular. Neil led him to the poetry section in the small room where Rob Neville had first challenged him about *Cat on a Hot Tin Roof*. "There. 821Y. There are a few of them. I don't know Yeats," he said conversationally.

"Nor do I, really. 'Sailing to Byzantium' is such a beautiful title, though. Conjures up another world, doesn't it?"

Neil drifted back to the desk where Jack lounged with a grin on his face. "You're not going to get anything?"

"What I want isn't reading material. It's staff."

Neil checked to see who might be listening.

"Don't give me that coy stuff. Those are the pants you were wearing the morning I drove you here, you sexpot. Someone you trying to impress? Bet Larry's noticed."

"What's your news?" Neil asked, anxious to change the subject.

"I can't tell you here."

"This is like torture."

"You'll be proud of me."

"Are you staying?"

"I'm not running off to the Greek islands — or Bucharest either for that matter."

"Are you going back to Montreal?"

"No. Stop the twenty questions. I'll tell all tomorrow."

"Tomorrow?"

"I'm stuck with his lordship tonight."

Neil's face didn't hide his disappointment.

"There's a damn good chance they're all headed to Camel Lake tomorrow for the weekend, so we'll have Baby Point to frolic in tomorrow night. It's not a hundred per cent sure, but I'm thinking ninety-five per cent. I'll let you know tomorrow, early."

Neil watched as Larry crouched down in front of the plays. The strength of his thighs was visible through the stretched fabric of his pants.

"I told you he was a stud. And as you said, handsomer than I. Tonight, he asked me where I was going. When I told him, he said, 'Take me with you.' He never wants to be with me, so I was kind of taken aback and said okay. I hope you don't mind."

"He's very ..."

"Introverted? The concept was invented for Larry."

Mrs. Negulescu approached with the temporary card. At the same moment Larry stood and, holding two books to his chest, returned to the circulation desk. Neil was fascinated to see that while his whole body exuded a kind of power, the walk was somewhat tentative and even a touch delicate.

Larry signed the temporary card and Neil checked out his books. *Selected Poems of W.B.Yeats* and *Lady Windermere's Fan*.

"Ah, Mr. Wilde," Jack said. "Irish and queer. Dad will love your choices."

Larry shook his head wearily. "John Henry's our bad boy. He lives to shock."

"Thank you, Mr. Muscles."

"It was good to meet you, Neil. I'm surprised you can tolerate him."

"He likes bad boys," Jack said. Winking at Neil, he edged his brother towards the exit door. "Tomorrow," he mouthed behind Larry's back.

Neil felt like shaking himself for some reason — as if he'd just wakened from a confusing dream — until he heard Mrs. Negulescu laughing.

"You would have found handsome men like that in the coffee shops on Strada Lipscani."

———

THE BACK TERRACE was crowded that night. Mr. and Mrs. Hamilton, Mr. and Mrs. Knight, and Mrs. Knight's sister Helen, newly arrived from Chepstow, Prince Edward Island. Helen was the country girl Mrs. Knight always claimed to be: fresh-faced, open-hearted, and plain-spoken. She was delighted to meet Neil and treated him to one of the brightest smiles he had ever seen.

"Your dad says you're a real brain," she said.

They all assured her that Neil was indeed a real brain. Marge Hamilton was convinced he'd also grown taller and Mona Gordon said he was looking very dashing, what with his new penny loafers and all. Mr. Knight suggested that he was taking comportment lessons on the side, to which Neil replied, "I'm a real brain in comportment." Laughter surrounded him as he bid them all a goodnight.

His father put out a stalling hand. "Before you disappear, you'll be pleased to know that my garden installation has everybody's approval."

"I didn't give you any such thing," Marge Hamilton barked.

"Helen liked it, didn't you, Helen?" Frank Bennett turned to her as to a sure ally.

"Liked it? I said I've never seen anything like it."

"Did he point out the initials on the stone?" Neil asked.

"Now, Neil, there's a boy," said his father, using the wheedling tone that came with slight inebriation.

"We know it was a child who died in a mysterious plague," said Phil. "Barrett by name. That was my mother's maiden name, by the way."

"Barrett. N.C. Barrett. N.C.B." Neil spelled out. "My initials."

There was silence.

Helen looked uncertainly from her sister to Neil and then back again.

Neil said another goodnight. By the time he reached the back door, he could hear the chatter struggling to revive. Chairs scraping the flagstones, ice crackling in glasses, Phil Knight's big laugh that sounded almost too big to be anything but nervous.

His mother was fretfully straightening things on the kitchen counter when he came down from the bathroom.

"Are you all right?"

He refused to answer.

"Let it go, dear."

"You let it go," Neil threw back at her.

She said, "I don't like your tone, young man."

"He's not wishing you were dead, is he?" Neil started angrily down the stairs. On the landing, he glanced back at her. She looked as she usually did: painfully remote. "I'd like to hang out with Tony tomorrow night. It's not a hundred per cent sure, but if he can, we'd like to watch a movie at his sister's."

"That's fine. Just let us know."

He continued down the stairs, refusing to look at the gravestone, which still leaned against the wall next to his door. Refusing to look, until he gripped the doorknob and his glance fell to the base, where Convict Joe had been joined by three small skulls. Two of them were white, plastic, and human-shaped. The third was an actual skull, the delicate skull of a small bird.

29

THE CALL CAME TWO MINUTES after he arrived at work the next morning.

"Well, Bernie and Father are headed to Camel Lake. They've just left. Lawrence, however, has opted to stay in town, but says he's going out with Cousin Stephanie to a late movie. We'll have some room to manoeuvre. I'll pick you up at the library, just after five, right?"

He called his parents immediately, confirming the "date with Tony," then sweated all morning until he could speak with Tony at lunchtime.

Tony was replenishing the tables outside the store with an assortment of quick-selling produce — plums, green beans, the newly ripe peaches, tomatoes, raspberries. His request for cover was instantly granted, but Neil refused to give his buddy any details.

"Mystery. I love it. Is it legal?"

"Not a chance."

"Whoa. You gotta tell me."

"Later."

AT FIVE PAST five, Neil climbed into Jack's old blue Pontiac Laurentian for the second time.

"Shall we just start driving and head for the coast?" Jack asked.

"Which coast?"

"You pick."

"East."

"Not as warm in the winter."

"But it's closer to Europe," Neil said.

"Good point. So then we'll go to France."

"Not in your Pontiac, I hope."

They sat looking at each other, delight written over both their faces.

Jack took Neil's hand and then, unsatisfied, leaned over and kissed Neil on the mouth.

Neil gasped.

"That's what bad boys do." He pulled away from the curb.

Surreptitiously Neil scanned the sidewalk for witnesses.

"We're clear," Jack said.

But Jack was wrong.

Miss Fairfield, pausing on the porch of the library to fish her sunglasses out of the deep straw bag she carried, saw it all. Muttering a "Dear, dear, dear," under her breath, she set out for Parma Fruits and Vegetables.

FROM THE MOMENT he stepped into the foyer of 25 Baby Point Road, he could tell he was in a foreign world. A world airy, quiet, and cool, where summer heat was forbidden. Everything was very dim and still, like a funeral parlour. Straight ahead was a wooden staircase, gleaming darkly. At its summit an arched window of beveled glass transformed the late afternoon light into something almost icy. On either side of it hung a stiff crucifix of tarnished bronze. The Persian runner offering a deeply coloured path up the centre of the stairs had probably long ago given up competing with the coolness for preeminence.

Neil shivered slightly. "It's so quiet."

"There's lots more like this."

Before they could move, a man appeared at the top of the stairs.

"Hello, Neil." It was Larry in shorts and a singlet.

Jack whistled.

"Idiot." Larry started down the staircase.

Neil could see now how big and muscular Larry's shoulders, arms, and calves really were, but the same impression he had had the night before in the library, of a quality almost delicate in Larry's movements, was exaggerated by the descent. The contrast was almost comical.

"I've made us supper," Larry said.

"You didn't need to do that," Jack said brusquely.

"We'll eat in the kitchen, not the mausoleum." Smiling at them both with a mocking deference, he said, "This way, please."

Neil felt Jack's hand take possession of his shoulder. Whether this was for Neil's benefit or his own, though, Neil couldn't have said.

The kitchen was large and brighter than the foyer, and very, very white. The cupboards, the appliances, the curtains on the long windows that gaped onto the garden, were all white. A round table covered with a white tablecloth and laid with plates and cutlery beckoned in one corner. The thick band of cobalt blue rimming the plates offered the only departure from the pristine monotony of the rest. Another agonized Christ, this one in gold, stared down somewhat gloomily at the spread.

"I apologize for not using the silver, but the servants haven't been up for polishing lately, so we're forced to deal with stainless steel tonight. And the china, I'm afraid to say, is not bone variety. I trust you won't mind, sir." The mocking tone continued unabated. Behind it, though, Neil sensed a genuine desire to please.

"I thought you were eating with Stephanie," Jack said grumpily.

"A snack before the movie."

"Which movie are you seeing?" Neil asked.

"He's seen *Breakfast at Tiffany's*," Jack said.

"Three times. We're not doing Hollywood tonight. We're off to Europe. Stephanie insists. *Last Year at Marienbad.*"

Neil had seen the advertisements in the paper. It looked very foreign.

Larry placed three large platters, one heaped with potato salad, one with vegetable salad, and the third with cold meat, in the centre of the table and then sat.

Instead of serving himself as Larry advised, Jack sat back in his chair. "You didn't need to go to all this trouble."

Assuring him it was "absolutely no trouble at all," Larry helped Neil and then himself to food.

"Not going to eat?" Larry asked, his first forkful poised mid-air.

"Sure." Jack lifted some beef from the meat platter.

Uncomfortable with the strange tension hovering between the brothers, Neil said, "This is an amazing spread!"

The compliment brought forth a real smile from Larry and a burst of laughter from Jack. "Such a hedonist you are!"

"Don't let him make fun of you. Eat as much as you want," said Larry. "The meat's from Cranston's on Bloor — the best butcher shop in the city. The potato salad's our mother's old recipe. Johnny used to ask for thirds of Mom's potato salad. The green salad's my concoction, but there's not much you can do to spoil fresh greens, is there? I've added pine nuts and pomegranate seeds. Something our cousin Stephanie taught me. It's all good for you."

"And it tastes wonderful!" Neil said.

Jack nodded a kind of agreement. "Neil's appetite's one of his best features."

Neil blushed. "You are bad."

An understanding dawning in his eyes, Larry Rookwood lifted a very white napkin to his lips.

UPSTAIRS, LOUNGING IN the twin armchairs that filled the bay window of Mrs. Rookwood's old bedroom, Jack and Neil listened to Larry preparing to go out and sipped Darjeeling tea, which Larry had made in a large hand-painted china pot decorated with fruits and flowers. Fruits and flowers also covered the bedspread, the curtains and even the armchairs they were in, leaving Neil with the feeling they'd strayed into some enchanted, if faded and dusty, bower.

They talked in soft voices.

"He knows," Neil said, listening to the sounds of the shower next door.

"I don't mind," Jack said, unbuttoning his shirt.

"What if he tells your father?'

"Not a chance. I told you, he hates my father."

"What better way to get back at him?"

"He couldn't. He's too much of a girl himself."

"He seems really nice."

"Oh, he is. He just needs a good husband to keep him in line."

Neil couldn't help giggling.

Jack laughed, too. "And fuck him silly."

"Stop."

"You won't be saying stop once Larry's gone, I hope."

Neil reached across the scuffed and stained marquetry table between them for Jack's hand. "What's your news?"

"Well, first, let me tell you about the Yardleys."

Neil drew back.

"Inspired by the success of the Archie caper, I had the idea that maybe Yardley should get some anonymous mail, so I sent a little letter, signed, *Concerned Neighbours*, saying, *Dear Mr. Yardley, We've seen the bruises on Bruce's back, and beg you to stop beating your boy. If you don't, we'll report you.* Then I sent letters to fifteen of his neighbours, recounting Yardley's crimes. In a summary but potent way. I got the names out of the City Directory."

Neil saw Larry, naked except for the large white towel around his waist, pass the door and take the narrow staircase to the third floor. He stared too long.

"I like 'em skinnier," Jack muttered. He paused to assure himself of Neil's attention. "Remember you said, isn't there another way? In fact, you kept harping on it. Find another way. Well I thought and thought, and finally it dawned on me. The little exposé I wrote to the inhabitants of Pritchard and Howard streets was quite punchy. I thought I could be writing for a bigger audience. Exposing evils to the world. It was your idea. So, I'm going to Ottawa to study journalism. It's rather late for applications, but that's where connections come in. It so happens that my Uncle Jazz is a muckity-muck at Carleton, head of philosophy or something, and he's 'seeing what he can do.' I've already sent in my high school transcripts, which, of course, are breathtakingly brilliant, and the transcript from Montreal, which, though I left in rather a hurry, is also fairly impressive, especially in *explication de texte*, so ... the only problem will be convincing my Uncle Jazz and Aunt Lily that they wouldn't find me a congenial tenant."

Neil felt small and insignificant in his chair. "When do you go?"

"A week Monday. To get myself set up. Next week's my last delivering bread. Your new man starts on the twentieth."

Neil was very quiet.

"I owe it to *you*." There was almost a gloating quality to his words.

"What am I going to do?"

"Go forward."

Neil brushed the words aside with an impatient hand.

"Journalism's really big at Carleton, you know. And, look, Ottawa's closer than Montreal." When Neil made no sound, no movement, Jack spoke out more impatiently than he intended, "I can't stay in this house, Neil. I'll suffocate. When I told my father, he just threw a cheque at me. Nothing else. Just a cheque."

Neil's reply came very softly. "We could find a place. I could change schools."

"And live together? Like a couple?" Shock sounded in Jack's voice.

"Why not?"

"Your parents would have me arrested. You're underage — and what we do is illegal."

Neil said, "You don't want to live with me."

Jack sighed. "Look, Neil, if I was going to live with anybody, it would be with you."

"Is that true?" Neil turned his attention to the fading light that bathed the window in gold.

Quiet intervened. Neil leaned back in his chair, his gaze scanning the shadowy room, looking for more comfort than Jack's words had provided. The walls were covered in delicate prints and small oils in gold frames. Pretty things decorated the dresser, the vanity, the night tables — vases, small lacquered cases, a very old china doll, perfume decanters.

"Isn't it hard living with your mother's stuff?"

"Not in the least. I adored her. We all did. Larry, Bernie ... my father wouldn't come in here after she died, the coward. It's all just as it was six years ago. The top drawer of the vanity table is full of powder boxes. Full. From France, England, Belgium, Switzerland. They've got names like Rachel, Peachblossom, Rose Sauvage. Face powder. I open that drawer and I can smell my mother."

"It doesn't make you sad?" Neil wondered if he'd ever felt so sad.

"Of course, but sadness is all right."

Neil disagreed. The kind of sadness he was feeling that evening was not all right. But he had no confidence that his disagreement would be heard or even allowed. Jack was the kind of person who liked knowing better. That much was clear to him now.

His gaze deserted the late Mrs. Rookwood's vanity for an old and not very good turntable, which sat uneasily on a straight-back chair with a deep green velvet back and seat.

"All that's mine," Jack said encouragingly, "and the records underneath. Why don't you have a look?"

Neil's hands opened in front of him like a blank page. "Maybe I should go."

Jack now barked at Neil, "Look, go if you want, but don't play around. Have some guts."

Shaking, Neil stood. "I do have guts. I wouldn't be here if I didn't, you asshole!" He started towards the door, surprised by his use of such an epithet.

Jack grabbed him. "Oh no, you don't." He pulled Neil to him. "What do I have to do? Get a skywriter? I love you, boy."

"But you're going!" Neil began to sob.

Jack closed the door with his heel. "There, there, Mr. Bennett. There, there. Don't, don't ... please, don't cry." He held Neil very tenderly.

After several minutes they heard Larry coming down the stairs. "Johnny?"

Jack opened the door slightly.

"I'm off."

Neil felt Larry's eyes on him. It had to be obvious he'd been crying.

"You can have my car, if you want," Jack said to his brother. "As long as you bring it back by midnight or so. I'll have to get Neil home."

The brothers descended the stairs. Neil wandered over to the turntable, wiping furiously at his tears. Bending down, he inspected the albums. Jazz. The sleepy kind of jazz his father liked. Even one or two albums his father owned. Neal Hefti. *Rare But Well Done.*

Larry's voice drifted up the staircase. "Is Neil all right?"

Neil couldn't hear what Jack answered, only the sound of the door sending Larry out into the hot city evening.

Jack was back upstairs almost instantly. He, too, had tears in his eyes.

THEY LAY IN the darkness on damp sheets, illuminated only by the light of the streetlamp that seeped in through the branches of a huge maple in the front yard. Neil was sure he could hear the streetcars down on Bloor as they negotiated their way in and out of the Jane Loop. But, of course, that was impossible. Bloor Street was many blocks south. He counted them: nine. Nine blocks. But he wouldn't let go of the impression. The Jane Loop was the turning point, the place where transfers happened, the beginning of the big city life he dreamed of.

The Jane Loop would be there once Jack had gone, but the thought brought no pleasure or comfort. He glanced at the man next to him. Jack seemed to be enthralled with the shadows on the ceiling, which changed whenever the cooling breeze rustled the window screen. Neil glanced up at the shifting shapes: there was a man with a humped back and then a patch of reeds and then a dog perhaps, or a fish, or a bat. He thought of his father. Quickly dismissing the shadows, he turned onto his side. "Is your uncle's name really Jazz?"

"For Jasper."

"Jasper. Like the stone?"

"Ambrose, Jasper, Julian and — get this — Sebastian. The four Rookwood brothers. Mother Church's finest."

Neil smiled to himself. "I like Jasper best." He paused a second. "And I like Johnny better than Jack. Except Jack's a better name for you."

"For what reason?"

"It's the name of a tricky guy, isn't it? Jack o'lantern, Jack Straw, Jack the Ripper."

"Jack Kennedy?" Jack rubbed the boy's backside and kissed him.

They heard the front door open.

Neil rose. Sweaty, semen-smeared, he padded down the hallway to the bathroom. He set the shower running and then stood with his back against the door, listening.

The brothers had obviously met.

He couldn't hear everything they said, but some words stood out.

"I had no idea about you, Johnny."

"It's Neil's doing."

"Not entirely," Larry said.

Neil climbed in the shower. As he pulled the curtain over, he could just hear Jack say, "But he made it serious."

⸻

THE CAR PURRED in front of the gloomy Bennett house like a big cat waiting to pounce. They looked at each other, hands entwined. Jack promised to call, assuring Neil they'd find a way to get together. "You can call me, too," he said.

"ROger7-3224."

"That's just weird." He smiled tenderly. "Can I kiss you?"

Neil kissed Jack by way of an answer.

"Bold thing."

Neil got out, fumbling in his pocket, then turned back. "I forgot my key."

"Don't you have a spare?"

"Yeah. I just think it's funny, forgetting my key tonight. This isn't my real home anymore." He turned away.

Jack sat watching him retrieve the spare from under the porch stairs. Then, as Neil applied the key to the lock, he waved and drove slowly away.

Neil didn't catch the wave, but the driver of a passing Edsel did. Very softly, he tooted his horn. Neil turned, expecting to find Jack still in attendance. He waved.

The Edsel seemed to hover. Neil could feel the driver's eyes on him and though he couldn't see them, they felt kind and sympathetic. Very briefly he considered jumping into the Edsel and going for a very long ride. But the Edsel wasn't waiting. It rolled off with another very gentle toot.

Inside, the house was very still and very close, almost breathlessly so. He could hear his father snoring upstairs.

The longing to be far away overwhelmed him for an instant. Let me go, he whispered. Strada Lipscani, Budapest, Mykonos, Hagia Sophia, Hollywood, anywhere as long as it was far away enough. Suddenly he remembered his aunt's offer of a Christmas in LA. Reassurance claimed him. "I'm going," he whispered to the still room.

He started down the stairs.

Once again he was brought to a stop on the cellar landing.

At the foot of the stairs, next to the door of Neil's room, his father's display seemed to have grown. It was more garish, more grisly, more menacing. Handcuffs and an old icepick had been added to the offerings at the gravestone's base, along with another small weathered skull. Not a bird's this time, something bigger. A still burning stick of cloying incense was stuck in the wooden shelf. Several others had already burnt down, leaving small trails of ash as tokens of their devotion.

Sitting down on the top step, Neil covered his face with his hands.

30

WHILE HE SLEPT THROUGH SUNDAY morning, the display was changed again. All the flowers disappeared. The creeper, too. Instead, a string of small blue Christmas lights was draped around the stone, lending it a sinister aura. The skulls, which now numbered two white plastic human skulls and three actual skulls of indeterminate origin, were arranged to serve as a guard for the pitiful crumple that was Convict Joe. Clipped to the string of lights at a level with the dead child's name was a paperback book cover with a lurid yellow title, *The Undead*. Beneath the title was the image of a not-quite sealed wooden coffin. The handcuffs sat at the very edge of the shelf, in the centre, with a tea light in the middle of each cuff. When Neil finally emerged from his room, the tea lights were flickering.

He quickly turned his back on it, thinking, *The Gordons are coming home. He's getting ready for another showing.* The Gordons did come home, but, thanks to the bumper-to-bumper traffic, not until well after sundown. By that time it was too late for a showing.

There was a phone call just before nine o'clock, as his parents were nearing the end of another *Ed Sullivan Show*. Neil was listening to his Tchaikovsky waltzes, the only record that seemed to provide some relief from his yearning for Jack and his fears for the time when Jack would no longer be there. When the phone rang, he heard his father say, "Tell them to call back," as his mother crossed the living room to answer. His father had drunk too much that afternoon and was probably stretched out on the sofa. He didn't hear anything of his mother's conversation with the caller, except for when she said, in a louder-than-usual voice, "Frank, take the phone. I'm going upstairs to use the extension." The television was turned off and his father finally climbed the stairs to the second floor.

The house fell silent then.

Neil continued to play the Tchaikovsky with Lillian Hellman's *The Little Foxes* open on his lap, unread.

When, after eleven, he went upstairs to brush his teeth, both his parents were still up. Their doors were closed, but light was trickling out below, and from his mother's room came the sound of voices.

"I knew this was going to happen," he heard his father say.

"I don't believe it." His mother's voice was angry.

"I never bought that goody-boy stuff."

"You never said so." She absolutely wasn't going to take her husband's word.

"That kind always does what it bloody well pleases."

"I don't believe it," she said again. "It's disgusting. My worst nightmare."

"You encouraged him."

"That's not true, Frank, and you know it."

"I'll make him pay for this."

Neil quickly locked himself in the bathroom, as his mother's doorknob turned.

When he started for the basement again, Frank stepped out of his room into the hallway. Neil turned to say his goodnight, but his father's stare silenced him instantly. It was the stare of a man who had witnessed an accident, or worse.

Shaking his head, his father closed his door again.

Seconds later, as Neil shut the door to his own room, a horrible thought suddenly struck him: I've been found out. His relations with Jack had been made known to them. It was he who was disgusting.

He sank back onto his sofa, feeling sick.

But surely they would have asked to speak with him. Surely.

He got up from his sofa.

Halfway up the stairs, he paused on the landing. He couldn't ask them. It was impossible.

Back in his room, he paced to the bed where he sat down briefly before rising again to pace back to the sofa.

For the rest of the long night, he performed this minimal choreography, pausing at most twenty minutes to stretch out on the bed to see if sleep would be kind and take him, and when it wouldn't, he would be up again, dancing.

He reviewed all the likely suspects, coming up with a very short list of two: Mrs. Gordon, who must have guessed, and Tony, who almost knew. But it was an unconvincing list, he knew that, and besides he couldn't really see either of them betraying him. Of course there may have been someone else who had seen Jack and him somehow, somewhere, had seen their affection and reported it, but who? Jack's brother, Larry? But, why would Larry do that? He couldn't see it.

He also reviewed his possible options, over and over, until his head hurt and his body ached. If worse came to the worst, he told himself, I'll just go away with Jack. I'll finish high school in Ottawa, then work to pay my way to college. Jack would take him, if his parents didn't want him or at least didn't want him the way he was. Jack would have to take him. Where would he go otherwise?

The answer didn't occur to him until the first morning light was nudging his curtains: Los Angeles. It was obvious. He sighed and, for the first time in many hours, relaxed. Like one of those little freaks of nature that sometimes occur to mirror the moods of humans, a breeze as light as a sigh ruffled his curtains.

He crossed to the window, and pulled back one of the curtains. The breeze was actually delicious. He closed his eyes, letting it lap at his face like a friendly cat.

It was just after six. His mother would be coming downstairs soon to make his father's breakfast.

He sat on his bed to wait. It wasn't a long wait. A few minutes later he heard her soft tread as she made her way into the kitchen. Kettle sounds were followed by the closing of the refrigerator door and the slight rattle of cutlery.

He was exhausted, but though he lay stretched out on his bed, he knew there was no chance he could sleep. Not until he found out — for that he would have to wait until his father had gone. He would not risk a showdown. His feelings for Jack were too precious. Though his mother would not, could not understand, she might not condemn him absolutely.

The time came when he heard his father's voice in the Gordons' driveway, and then Mr. Hamilton's. Mr. Gordon's voice, understated as usual, was inaudible.

As soon as the car pulled out of the drive, he climbed the cellar stairs to the kitchen. He realized with a shock that he was still wearing last night's clothes.

She looked up at his entrance. She sat at the table with her cup of steaming water, as she did every morning before breakfast. Her face was pale, her eyes dark-circled. She had not slept either.

"Are you all right?"

"I'm fine," she answered flatly.

"There's something wrong."

"Val's not well, dear."

"Not well?" The sense of relief washed over him in a huge wave. Then, almost immediately, he was worried again — about Val.

"No. We got a call last night. We'll have to go and see her.

Maybe Wednesday, if your father can get off."

"Is that all?" He hadn't meant to say it, but it tumbled out.

His mother frowned. "What do you mean?"

"I mean there are doctors up there and everything."

"Yes. Of course there are."

"Is she really sick?"

Her answer was evasive. "We don't know yet. Would you like your breakfast now?"

"Would you rather be alone?" Neil asked.

"No, I'd rather make your breakfast. How about poached eggs?"

"Sure. I don't usually get poached eggs on weekdays."

"Well, you're a good boy, aren't you?"

Neil showed a puzzled face.

"Sometimes ... I guess."

Approaching him, his mother took him by the elbows. "Be a good boy. For me." Her face looked so sad Neil thought she might cry.

31

MONDAY EVENING NEIL TELEPHONE THE Rookwood
house three times without receiving an answer. The fourth time,
the younger brother, Bernard, picked up. In a rather sleepy voice,
he assured Neil that he'd pass on the message if Jack got back
"in time." In time for what, Neil wondered, but he didn't ask. He
tried again early Tuesday morning, knowing full well that Jack
would probably be long gone.

Half an hour before bread delivery, his mother went shopping with Vera Knight and her sister Helen. Neil waited in the
kitchen until he saw the truck pull up at the end of the Gordons'
drive. Watching Jack jump down and stride up the driveway with
his loaves gave him such a pang that he had to look away. He
remembered the first time he saw Jack jumping from the bread
truck, remembered, too, his delight and excitement to realize that
men could move gracefully.

He heard Mrs. Gordon saying, "Deserting us already! You
fickle boy!"

"That's what I'm best at, Mrs. Gordon, fickleness."

"Oh, get on with you. Well, keep in touch."

"I'll be back on Friday, you know."

Neil was waiting at the door when Jack rounded the corner of
the Gordon house.

The bread-man stopped at the sight of him. For a second, he simply stared with a big grin on his face.

Neil opened the door, putting out his hand for the bread.

"Jesus Christ, why am I going?"

"You're stupid."

"You may be right. You're also very beautiful."

"Tomorrow night …" Neil saw Mrs. Gordon at her kitchen window overlooking the driveway. They exchanged waves. "Tomorrow, my parents are going away. Val's not well, and they'll be away a few days."

"Sorry about your sis, but I can't say I'm sorry about the rest. What sweet news!"

"Use the front door."

"Ah yes, the Knights will be away. You're getting pretty sneaky."

"I was never sneaky before I met you."

"Come on. Inside." Jack steered Neil onto the cellar landing. "Good. Put your hand in my pocket. There's something there for you."

Neil slipped his hand into the snug-fitting brown pants of Jack's uniform. "Nothing."

"Deeper."

Neil dug deeper. There was a pulsing against his hand. Neil turned beet red.

"You weren't embarrassed the other evening. Anything but. But there's something else. Really. Try the other pocket. Something separate from me."

Neil fished in his other pocket and pulled out a rectangular white envelope.

"Now I better get going before Mrs. Gordon starts having her doubts." Jack kissed Neil three or four times, scattered kisses with no definite target. Then he was off, running down the driveway like some kind of deer.

Neil watched him go, feeling almost certain that Jack's

impending departure was just a bad dream. They would find a way to be together — they had to.

"Such a nice fella," Mrs. Gordon called to him from her verandah. "He sure think's you're the cat's meow."

"He likes *Breakfast at Tiffany's* as much as I do," Neil said, out of some need to justify that liking. He crossed the driveway towards her.

"You and that woman!" Mrs. Gordon laughed. "I hope Val's going to be all right. I don't like these mysterious illnesses." Her blue eyes smiled on him, but they cooled as she said, "Have you heard anything from Mike?"

"Nothing, I'm glad to say."

"What's the matter with Mike?"

"We don't like each other. I wish Val would get herself someone like Warren."

"Warren's a sweetie, that's for sure. I just hope our Lana holds on to him. Well, dear, I've got dusting — oh, did you hear about the Yardleys?"

Neil played dumb.

"I ran into Lorna Ruff yesterday at the Mall. The Ruffs got a letter, an anonymous letter, claiming that Yardley beats his kids. Several people got the letter apparently, even the pastor at the Anglican Church up there where the Yardleys go. The boy's gone to live with Mrs. Yardley's brother, so there's got to be some truth in the story, I'd say. But imagine sending such a letter. Whoever did it has nerve. It was pretty graphic according to Lorna, describing bruises and cuts and things."

"That's a good thing," Neil said.

"I agree, dear, I agree. Too much of this horrible stuff happening. People doing what they bloody well like, not paying the consequences." She shook her white mane and straightened her lilac-coloured shirt. "Now that we've settled that, the feather duster calls. Tomorrow night. Chili at six."

Just inside the door, Neil paused with the news Mrs. Gordon had given him. Jack was a crusader, that's what he was. One day, he would really change things. Neil picked the white envelope up from the step where he'd set it earlier and gently broke the seal.

It was another old postcard, but not as old as the others. Two young men in World War II military uniform standing on a ship deck, staring out towards a turbulent sky, the arm of one resting easily on the shoulders of the other. On the back:

N.

Moon River and me.

J.

⟨⟨⟩⟩

MISS FIONA MCGREGOR tapped him on the shoulder very lightly. "Neil," she said, "Miss Fairfield would like to talk with you. She's in the tearoom. She said you could finish shelving later."

Puzzled and curious, he wheeled the cart back to the desk. Then, encouraged by Miss McGregor's gentle smile, he went to find Miss Fairfield. She was sitting at the tea table, a cup of something hot steaming before her, a lemon ice wafer balanced precariously on the saucer edge.

"Have a seat, Neil. But perhaps we should close the door first."

He complied with her two requests of course. Sitting down opposite her, he was suddenly overtaken by anxiety. Her face gave him no cause for it, however. She wore her accustomed calm and her eyes danced with their usual liveliness. Her beautiful, thick white hair reminded him, as usual, of Queen Mary's.

"This is none of my business, I realize that," she started. "I've known your father for many years. He's been so helpful acquiring land and space for the libraries ... when I was on that Committee with the Chief Librarian ... well, he was very charming and dedicated. Yes, dedicated is the word. So, I am interested in you, especially interested."

"Yes, Miss Fairfield." He had no idea where she was going.

"Well, this is difficult for me. The other evening when I was leaving work I saw you and a young man, your bread-man, I believe, in a car, his car, I presume, out front."

Neil blanched.

"You know what I saw, I suppose?"

Neil could barely speak. "Yes."

"As I say, it's none of my business really, but I'm concerned. You're just sixteen."

"Seventeen next month." His voice was a whisper, his mouth dry.

"I see. Do you know what you're doing, Neil? Your parents would be very shocked, and I'm sure quite hurt."

"I do. Know."

Miss Fairfield looked very doubtful.

"I know what I'm doing." His voice was louder than he meant it to be.

"He's a few years older than you, isn't he? And from what I've seen of him, he's pretty sure of himself."

"He hasn't done anything with me I haven't wanted."

Miss Fairfield picked up her ice wafer and then promptly returned it to the saucer.

"He loves me." Neil was shaking.

"Well, he says he does, I'm sure."

"He does. I feel it. And I love him. Totally."

Miss Fairfield sat back in her chair uncertainly.

"Miss Fairfield, I've known since I was a kid. I never really called it for what it was until this summer. I saw him jump down from a bread truck and, well, it was like I'd been expecting him."

Even as he spoke, Neil was aware this wasn't a very accurate picture of his discovery, but it was near enough the truth to pass.

She stared at him over her teacup, her head nodding involuntarily.

"I know they'd be shocked and hurt, but I can't help it. I just can't help it. I love him."

"And he loves you? You're very sure?"

"Yes, yes." Neil felt the tears on his cheeks.

Miss Fairfield put down her cup. "Now, now, I didn't mean ... Oh, dear, I didn't mean to upset you, my dear boy. You are very special to me." She stood and, walking around the table, she let her white, bony hand fall onto his shoulder very, very lightly like a snowflake.

"He's going away. He's going back to university, Miss Fairfield, and I won't see him for a long time. He says I did it, I got him to see he had to do something with himself. But I won't see him now for ages."

"A man needs an education, Neil. He doesn't live on love alone."

"I know, I know."

Gingerly, Miss Fairfield touched the boy's hair, smoothing it as she might a cat, a pillow or a piece of silk. Neil had the distinct feeling that she had never touched a boy's hair before. "Now, now. It's hard. I know, it's hard."

"You think I'm sick?"

"Sick? No, no. Not sick. No. This is not a new thing. The world's literature is full of it. The world is full of it. No, no, not sick. Just not very welcome. There are laws, stupid laws, but still laws. You must be very careful not to draw too much attention to yourself."

"I know, I know." He still cried.

"You'll have to be very strong, too. Stronger than men usually are. It won't be easy. Unless things change. It won't be easy."

He shifted in his chair, sat up, wiped his eyes.

"Keep him in your thoughts and your prayers. Someday, you'll meet again."

"He says I have to go forward."

"He's right. You both must go forward. We all have to go forward. The alternative is ... well, we don't need to talk about that, do we? You certainly don't." She walked behind him and fetched a box of tissues from the shelf above the sink. "You blow your nose, have a cup of tea and a couple of ice wafers — they're just right for this kind of weather. Did you smell the fall in the air tonight? I did. And your friends down there at the fruit shop tell me the Concord grapes are coming. Frankly, I love September best. The first apples, the pomegranates, then the pumpkins." Her girlish laugh bubbled up and over. Her eyes danced with such vivacity, he couldn't help smiling. "There now. You'll be fine." She crossed behind him again to open the door. "Take your time. I'll go keep Miss McGregor company till you return."

"Miss Fairfield?"

"No need to worry. I will treat all this as confidential, Neil. I don't envy you the day they find out. But, never mind, perhaps they'll surprise us. Right now, you make the most of the time you still have. Right now."

32

WEDNESDAY CHILI AT SIX WAS the usual round of good humour and gossip. Warren showed up laughing and flicking his fair hair out of his eyes. He teased everybody about something, but always in the most affectionate way. Neil was not used to this kind of teasing. It was so different from what his father offered, and it only made Neil like Warren more. When Mrs. Gordon asked Neil whether there wasn't a nice girl at the library he wouldn't enjoy asking out, Warren boyishly rushed in with the comment, "Oh, Mrs. G., men of the theatre don't have time for the dating game. That's for simple guys like me. Men of the theatre fall passionately in love and that's that!"

"Well, I never!" Mrs. Gordon replied.

"Isn't that so, Neil?" Warren turned to him for confirmation.

"Yeah, that's right," Neil laughed. "That's me." It felt funny to be telling them the truth in the guise of a joke.

"Dear me! Passionately in love! At sixteen!"

"Tsk, tsk, Mrs. G.," Warren said. "Passion comes early for artistic types. It's their inspiration."

"Are you telling me that your feelings for me are boring?" Lana wanted to know with a shake of her bangs.

"Not boring, no. They're very nice."

"Nice," Lana cried, tossing her napkin at him.

"Warren Dawlish, you are the limit!" Mona laughed.

"I may be, but I know what I'm talking about." And he flashed Neil a big grin. "He probably has three hundred pages of love poems stashed away in his room. Under his pillow."

"That would make for a rather lumpy sleep," said Mr. Gordon. After everyone had finished laughing, the conversation turned towards neighbourhood news. Yardley's crimes were revisited along with their exposure. After a lot of speculation passing as analysis, Mr. Gordon finally pushed his chair back from the table and, crossing his legs, said, "Well, if you want my opinion, and I'm not sure why you should, I don't think a concerned neighbour sent those letters. I think the chaps who did the break-ins are behind it. They've changed tactics, that's all. Safer by far. Smarter. Ultimately more effective. You gotta hand it to them. Very difficult to trace, if not impossible. Apparently, the letters were mailed from different places around the city."

"How do you know all this?" his wife asked him.

"People tell me things. In this instance, a police detective."

"Goodness, *The Defenders* has nothing on you."

"I heard from the Knights that something happened like this with Archie Ross," Neil said.

"Yes, only it was a smaller operation," Gus Gordon replied. "Maybe only one person. Glass in the bed. A stolen photo, mailed back in pieces with a threat scrawled on the back." He smiled and turning to Neil, said, "But I think the Ross break-in is something quite separate from the others. I think it's the work of different people. We know Archie's not well-liked. In fact, some people probably hate him, don't they, Neil? If it wasn't that I know you so well, I might even think you'd done it."

"Gus! You're the absolute limit!" his wife cried.

Neil took another casual spoonful of blueberries from his bowl. Mr. Gordon smiled. "But I believe I know you too well."

NEIL SAT QUIETLY on the sofa waiting for Jack. Only one lamp was lit, the desk lamp, a sinuous wrought iron lamp of pre-war vintage fitted with a shade that vaguely aspired to be a pagoda. No music played. Through the screen door came a very soft breeze, smelling of autumn and hinting at loss.

Feeling safe in the silence and the sadness, Neil waited, hands on his lap, letting his thoughts go where they wanted. They followed the train whistles, imagining he was on his way to the other side of the country, to the ocean, where there would be ships to take him across the Pacific to Hong Kong or Taipei or possibly even Bangkok, but he knew he had no real desire to go to any of those places. He had no real desire to go anywhere but downtown. His thoughts came up with potential jobs — selling pyjamas at Eaton's or Broadway musicals at Sam's — and when these jobs floated away, he thought of his upcoming university career, of the classes he'd take and the books he'd read and the room he'd rent. His thoughts did not rest for long, always returning to the hands folded in his lap, as if an important clue to happiness lay there.

He had no idea what time it was. He could have left the Gordons an hour before or three hours. It didn't matter. I could wait here forever, he told himself.

Finally, headlights glaring against the curtains broke his meditation. A car pulled into the driveway.

Neil stood up, baffled by the arrival, and fearful of the delay it might create.

The screen door opened. It was Jack.

"Yes, that's the Pontiac."

"You're going to leave it there?"

"The Knights are away. And I don't assume Mr. Gordon or anybody in that household is prone to taking midnight constitutionals."

"Mr. G. gets up at five thirty."

"I'll be gone. Good." Jack closed and locked the door. "We'll just have a nice visit then, like ordinary folk."

Neil remained standing, staring.

Jack stared back, his eyes dark, his expression expectant, slightly nervous even. He had brought a scent into the room, a faint scent of — bread? Neil wasn't sure.

Jack spoke first. "Let it be known: John Henry, alias Jack, Rookwood loves Neil Cameron Bennett."

Neil laughed, "Passionately!"

And Jack was on him.

Just before they fell to the floor, Jack pulled off the throw Neil's mother used to protect her couch, and spread it out on the carpet. "Not just to keep the spunk off the broadloom. Last time the rug-burn was brutal."

They stayed on the floor for hours, making love, eating, listening to music, laughing, talking, as if there were no tomorrow.

At one point, Jack confessed, "I never felt jealous about anyone before. For the first time, the other day I felt it and now I can't shake it."

Neil looked puzzled.

"My brother. He hasn't stopped asking me questions about you. I mean, he has never shown any kind of interest in my friends, but you he can't keep quiet about, and, believe me, it ain't because of your Broadway musicals."

"You're making this up."

"Am not. He thinks you're sexy! And I saw how *you* looked at *him* the other night."

"You told me his body —"

"I know what I told you. Doesn't mean you have to devour him in front of me."

Neil propped himself up on one elbow. "Are you serious?"

Jack smiled. "Yeah, partly. I suddenly feel jealous. I'm going away. He'll be here."

"I don't want your brother. It's you I want."

"I actually said to him, 'He's my boyfriend.'"

"Really?" Neil couldn't keep the excitement out of his voice.

"Then I apologized, 'cause even if you are, I have no right to own you."

"I wouldn't mind you owning me."

"People aren't property. If you found my brother hot, well, that's your right, and if you want to suck his cock, that's your right —-"

"But I don't, I don't."

"I believe you. But if you did, you could — as far as I'm concerned."

Neil sank back on the carpet and covered his eyes with his arm.

"You see, how this jealousy stuff messes things up," Jack said, reaching for Neil.

Neil brushed his hand away. "I hate the way you make wanting me so much into a bad thing."

"That isn't what I said." Jack kissed him. "I can't deal with feeling jealous!"

"Well, you'll be gone soon and you can forget about it."

"I deserve better than that, Neil."

"Then act like you do."

THEY HEADED FOR the basement at two. Neil let Jack go ahead.

At the second step from the bottom, Jack stopped. "What the hell's that?"

"My father's latest art piece."

"Fuck, is he morbid or what? It's a baby's gravestone."

"He's worse than morbid."

"Where'd he get the stone?"

Neil explained.

Jack looked over his shoulder at Neil. "Strange pastimes."

"It's supposed to be a memento mori for me. The best part is the initials."

Jack crouched down in front of the stone.

Carefully, he brushed Jack's shoulder with the tips of his fingers.

Jack stood immediately. His eyes were so cold with rage, Neil stepped back. "Why is it still here? Why didn't you smash it?" "He'd go out and get another one. Or something worse. Look," he gestured towards the workshop. "He has a treasure-house of toys there. He might build me a coffin next, fill it with dirt, and play Dracula."

Jack looked at Neil, face hard. "I hope your father fucking pays for this."

"He won't. He never has. It'll go on till I can get away."

Jack turned back to the stone and, with a sweep of his hand, tore the book cover from the clip holding it to the string of Christmas lights. He ripped it into dozens of pieces, scattering them like confetti over Convict Joe and his cranial posse. When he finished, he took Neil's hand roughly and pulled him into the bedroom.

"No music. No light."

Jack wound his arms around Neil. "Fucking, fucking shit-faced bastard." His hold tightened. Into Neil's hair, he muttered, "My poor boy, poor boy," over and over.

Eventually Neil could hardly breathe.

JACK WAS BACK the next night with a plan. Not for dismantling the installation, but for celebrating their last weekend together. He was excited. Neil had never seen him more so. It was excitement bordering on agitation.

"Your parents tell you when they're coming back?"

"They said Saturday afternoon or maybe Sunday. They're calling tomorrow morning."

"Okay. You're going to Tony's —"

"I was going to cancel."

"No, I'm gonna pack Friday night. Then Saturday I'm gonna pick you up at the library — and I promise I won't kiss you in front of any library staff — and we're going downtown to have supper and see the sights. I thought maybe Lichee Garden. You told me how much you liked it. Then we're getting a motel room and making love until I bring you back. I'll have my stuff in the trunk and just take off from here — or close to here. Which means I can leave Toronto with nothing between you and me but love. Is it a plan?"

Neil nodded. "Tony will cover for me if they get back Saturday."

The previous night, Jack had been too upset by the gravestone to see anything but Neil. Tonight, facing the pin-up board, he noticed that Neil had removed his flag cards and replaced them with the three postcards Jack had given him.

"So, I've been framed."

Neil laughed. "I even kept the envelopes. They're in the secret compartment."

"You keep mentioning this secret compartment."

"Under the floor of my cupboard." Neil bent down and lifted the floor. "You see?" He reached in and took out the three envelopes, which were very nearly as pristine as they were when he'd received them.

"Is that your sister's scarf in there? The posing strap? You ever going to return it? And what are those? The white things?"

Neil feigned innocence.

"Come on. Show me."

He shyly pulled out a pair of underpants, torn at the back.

"Put them on."

Childishly, Neil hid the underpants behind his back.

"Come on. You made a posing strap outta your sister's silk scarf. What's a pair of gauchies to that?"

Neil slipped them on.

"Turn around."

Red-faced Neil obeyed.

"Fuck. Did you tear these?"

"There was a little hole, I made it bigger."

"What you get up to, boy. Such a little tramp. Well, let's see if we can make that hole even bigger." He pushed Neil face down on the bed. "That's nice, now arch your back, come on, lift your ass. That's it. That's it."

When they were done, Neil said, "Just lie on top of me."

"Your wish is my command."

Neil reached around behind him and gripped Jack's thighs. "I'm better when we're close like this. I can forget you're going and everything. I can imagine that everything's going to turn out all right in the end."

"Funny, lying like this just makes me think how wrong everything else is." Jack kissed the side of Neil's face. "You know, I told my father to fuck himself this morning. Told him I didn't want any more of his and Uncle Jazz's great plans for me."

"You're still going?"

"Yeah. But I told him, I'm not going back to university to be a performing seal for the fucking Rookwoods. This is for me."

"What did he say?"

"Nothing. He always says nothing. A cold stare. A cold wrath. That's all you ever get. He doesn't need to say more. His message is clear — you're damned. He thinks he's God. And so did I, once. So did we all, Larry, Bernie, even my mother, I think, for a time. She must have. And then she took to wearing black, like that character in the Chekhov play — 'I'm in mourning for my life.' The power some people have. He must be God." He kissed the boy again. "Am I too heavy?"

"No. Never."

"I told him I'd send him back all the money but the tuition.

I'll even pay that back one day. I want to owe him nothing. I'll get cheap digs. I'll find work. Best recommendation in the world: I've been a bread-man. I know how to deliver." Chuckling, Jack humped the boy beneath him. Neil responded by arching his back. "But I tell you, Neil, if I get any more of that you-owe-the-family shit, I don't know what I'll do. Maybe head to the East Coast. Close to Europe, you know. France, Italy, Greece. I don't want to be respectable if all it means is being a good son."

"Please don't do anything dangerous."

"Life is dangerous, Neil."

"You know what I mean," Neil replied softly.

He rolled off the boy, pulling him to face him, chest to chest. "No vandalism? I'll do my best. There's one thing you've gotta do for me, though." He pointed towards the secret compartment. "You leave yourself open for constant inspection. No secret's safe from him, I bet." Realizing he had startled Neil, Jack lowered his voice to say, "You'll need a brand new secret compartment. For all the mash-notes you'll be getting from me. It's time to get inventive. To get secretive. Really secretive."

33

THERE WAS NO QUESTION THAT the nights were getting cooler. And longer. It was only twenty after eight and it was already nearly dark. The breeze that came with the dark, ruffling hair and rousing litter, brought shivers in its wake. People were walking faster along the sidewalks than they did a couple of weeks ago. Even the streetcars seemed to have picked up their pace. They were certainly plentiful that Friday night, packed with travellers heading downtown for the last revels of summer.

Leaning out Tony's window, Neil thought, *It all just goes on and on.* Tomorrow and the day after, and the day after that, everything would be going on just as it was tonight. It didn't seem fair, or right, when going on for him would mean going without.

He remembered the last time he had leaned out this window with Tony. Six weeks before, was it? Or seven? He was a kid then. What was he now?

In the years to come, Neil would remember this evening, this leaning out towards the movement and lights, more vividly than almost any other event. The memory would always come with a sense of something momentous waiting to happen, and a feeling that, no matter how hard he wished to, he had no control over how it turned out.

A hand touched his back. It had probably started out as a playful slap, but it ended up a semi-caress. For a split second, he thought it was Jack's.

"Boy, he just doesn't want to go to sleep. I had to read a story to him. Sorry."

Gio had been in a rambunctious mood that evening, demanding game after game of snakes and ladders from the boys. For a while, Neil found it all diverting, even helpful in keeping his own fears at bay. Not just the boy's squealing delight, but also Tony's obvious affection for him. But after a while, he began to feel uneasy, restless. Perhaps it was because he recognized that having kids and playing father, as Tony seemed so adept at doing, was not going to be part of his life. That recognition led him to wonder, as he had many times over the last few weeks, how a secret life could be made bearable. He thought he had found the answer — love. But love was leaving, and would not be easily replaced.

Leaning over the balcony rail, they surveyed the street side by side.

"What've you been up to?" Tony asked.

"Lots." Neil laughed.

"So tell me."

"You won't understand."

Tony looked sideways at him. "I can try."

"Maybe I need more reassurance than that."

A couple, arm-in-arm, walked by below. Her voice floated up, "You better behave now."

"You been having sex?" Tony said.

Neil glanced at Tony. Did he dare talk about it?

"Tell me," Tony said.

"You guessed it."

Tony took a deep breath. "It's a guy, right?" When Neil didn't either confirm or reject the possibility, Tony insisted, "I'm not stupid, you know!"

"I never said you were." Neil squirmed.

Suddenly Tony turned to him sharply. "It's not Bruno, is it?"

Neil laughed nervously.

"It's not, is it?" Tony's voice was almost shrill.

"'I'm not stupid, you know,'" Neil threw back at his friend. "You say he stinks of bad cologne — and cigarettes." Neil made a face. There was a long silence.

Then in as nonchalant a voice as he could muster, Tony asked, "Do I know him?"

"Nope."

"For God's sake, tell me," Tony said, almost like an order.

Frightened now, Neil said, "You can't tell anybody. He was our bread-man."

Tony glanced quickly at Neil. "*Was* your bread-man?"

Taking a deep breath, Neil told his friend the story of Jack's decision to return to university as briefly as he could, and the implications this had for their connection.

Tony shook his head uncertainly. "I sure didn't feel for Vicki the way you look right now. It was great and all, but she and I were — well, what's the phrase? Cat and dog? But maybe that's the way it's supposed to be for a guy and girl."

"I'm sure that's true, not that I know anything."

Tony took some time to consider the street below. "You never wanted a girl?"

"Occasionally. I fantasized, but the fantasies about guys are always — I don't know, more — exciting's not the word, though they are. They're deeper. If that makes any sense."

"Sure. It's just the other way 'round for me," Tony admitted.

Silence fell between them again. They listened to the rumbling of the streetcars as Neil's gaze travelled up over the roofs of the stores opposite into the indigo sky, where the stars glittered brightly.

Tony said, "You did everything?" It came out tentatively. "In bed, I mean. Did you —?"

"Fuck?" Neil's voice was louder than he had intended. "Yeah. Lots."

Tony nearly gulped. "What was that like?"

"He said I was a natural."

"No shit! What're you going to do now? This is bad, him going away."

"I guess I can get the sex. There was this optometrist — though he's disappeared actually. And there was a guy on the streetcar who wanted me to come home with him, and another guy who drives around the neighbourhood in an Edsel who's looking for fun, and he's really good-looking — but it's not just sex I want."

"Man, oh man." Tony stared hard at the store opposite, a cheese store, with a window full of signs advertising newly arrived products from Europe. "Where'd you do it?"

"In my bed. And once at his place."

"You do it every time you got together?"

"Yeah. Not just once either."

Tony turned to him wide-eyed.

Across the way, Uncle Herb and Aunt Violet's living room light came on. Neil shivered. *There* was a comfort he couldn't rely on anymore. He was just outside the range of that light now. He could appreciate its glow, but not its warmth, not now.

"It's getting cool," Neil said, feeling hopelessly sad all of a sudden.

"You wanna sit in the living room?"

"No. The night's good. So much softer than the day."

Another pair of streetcars passed, one going forward, the other — Neil didn't want to think about where the other was going.

Several minutes passed, and then Tony touched Neil's back again, gingerly at first, as if it were different from the back he touched earlier — an unknown, uncharted territory. Neil let his hand settle without comment.

"Thanks for telling me. I mean, I guessed and everything, and you're not exactly subtle. You gave lots of clues. I think I was a little bit freaked at first. A little bit." Tony held up his hand creating a small gap between his thumb and forefinger. "But then I figured that's just how things work for you, and if you're okay with it, why shouldn't I be? So, it's okay, Neil. I mean, my cousin Claudio's probably like you, and he's a great guy, too."

Neil sighed with relief. "I've always counted on you to get things, Tony. But it has to be between us."

"It's not going anywhere. Promise." He rubbed the small of Neil's back for a while before saying, "It didn't hurt or anything — having a dick up your ass?"

"Actually, not much, but that's probably because I wanted it."

Out of the corner of his eye, Neil caught Tony watching his hand making small circles. It seemed as if he were trying to make up his mind to do or say something.

Neil looked back at the street, back at the soft golden light in his aunt and uncle's window. He felt like crying, but he wouldn't let himself: no more tears.

Tony's hand slipped under his shirt, the wintergreen shirt recommended by Mr. Fraser, and gently began its circling motions against his flesh. "Is this okay?"

"What do you think?"

A few more circles and Tony's hand was sliding under the waistband of Neil's shorts.

"You know," Tony said. "You and I are best friends. So, if you want, we could do things. I mean, we already do things, but —"

"You're asking if you can fuck me?"

Tony's hand froze.

"It's okay," Neil said.

Tony started to withdraw his hand but then seemed to have a change of heart and instead delved deeper until he was massaging the top of Neil's cheeks.

Neil let him explore for a minute, enjoying the heat, the pressure, the way Tony made his flesh feel succulent. It was almost too good. He straightened, forcing Tony's hand to retreat.

"It's only if you wanted to," Tony said, embarrassed.

"Right now, I can't."

"It wouldn't be just about sex. I mean, we're close."

"You're right, but — you know, you're going to get a girl ..."

"That doesn't have to interfere."

"She might have other ideas."

"She won't have to know."

"Look, you know I love you ..." Tony leaned back, surprise written all over his face. "Yeah, that's right, I love you. Not the way I love Jack, but I love you, and maybe we can do that sometime, but right now I can't, Tony. I feel like I'm about to fall off a cliff or something. That probably sounds stupid, but it's the way it is."

Taking his hand, Tony pulled him away from the window, enfolding him in a big, warm embrace. "Yeah, sometimes I think I'm just like Bruno. A selfish horny bastard."

Neil was surprised by how much comfort he felt pressed against his old friend, and even more surprised as the comfort edged towards arousal. He told himself, *I can't let this happen, I can't let this happen*, but he didn't pull away.

"Let's sit down," Tony said, gesturing towards the plump pink velveteen sofa.

Neil was too tired to resist.

"I've got something for you." Tony turned to the shelf below the TV and pulled up one of his sketchbooks. From under the front cover he lifted a drawing. A piece of white tissue paper held in place by scraps of masking tape lay over it like a mist. "It's for you."

Neil took the drawing, staring.

Tony sat next to his chum. "What is it with you and gifts? You like this on Christmas morning?"

"I wasn't expecting it, that's all."

"Well, you gotta lift the tissue paper." Tony leaned in and with his typical Mediterranean flourish, exposed the drawing. It was a black and white portrait of two buses, one beside the other, with the Jane Loop's brick wall providing a cozily familiar background. The one bus was the 50, the other the 50-A.

"I know it's not very realistic. They're never together like that. But it feels right."

"I don't care," Neil said. Suddenly, without warning, tears were in his eyes.

Tony sat back. "Jeez," he said, "you're the best person to make things for."

"I love it. Even better than the shirt you gave me."

Tony's response to this was a shy gesture aimed at the TV. "We could watch a movie, if you want."

"No, let's go to bed."

"You that bummed out?"

"Sort of."

"You wanna sleep by yourself?" It was obvious from Tony's hangdog expression what answer he wanted. "I can sleep on the couch."

"On this? No way. Besides, you wanted to keep Bruno off you."

"I don't have pyjamas or anything."

"Nor do I. We'll figure something out."

Tony's lopsided grin slowly took shape. "I guess you know a lot more about sleeping with someone now." He turned off the frilly glass lamp of many colours.

In the street below, a couple of streetcar bells headed in opposite directions saluted each other.

34

THERE WAS SOMETHING DIFFERENT ABOUT Jack. Neil could feel it the moment he stepped into the car. He had seen him edgy, tense, angry, cold, but never like this. It was more like anxiety or even fear. It didn't fit him. Jack tried to be bright and cheerful, even did what he said he wouldn't — kiss Neil in front of the library, with tongue and all — but something lurked underneath that worried Neil.

"You look great. Is that silk?"

"Yeah, it's a gift from Tony."

"Tony earns a lot selling peaches."

Neil explained the origins of the shirt.

"Sweet. The red is gorgeous on you. How was the night?"

"With Tony? Nice."

"Nice, eh? You keep each other up?"

"No." Neil was lying. He had sucked Tony off. He was glad he had — Tony had been so excited. But he felt guilty, too. Indignation was the only cover he could find.

Jack seemed to grow quieter for a minute.

"And your night?"

"Goodbye, goodbye, goodbye. I said my goodbyes. It was very touching."

"What's the matter?" Neil touched his thigh. "You seem very upset."

"My brother Lawrence actually had tears. I think he's feeling abandoned. Funny. He couldn't wait to see the back of me two years ago."

"I guess he feels closer to you now that he knows."

"Knows what?"

"That you and I are — friends."

"Friends!" Jack seemed to be scoffing.

Neil withdrew his hand.

"Why'd you do that?" Jack asked in an irritated way.

"I don't understand what's happening."

The car headed south towards the Polish district. Neil noticed a sign for fresh pierogis in a store window, and outside the restaurant next door a placard advertising four unpronounceable Polish dishes accompanied by Kawa. Neil found himself wondering what Kawa tasted like. Jack sat grim-lipped at the wheel.

"Please speak," Neil said.

"I can't, Neil. This goodbye stuff is just too much."

"You always tell me to be here and now. Don't spoil it, you would say."

"Would I now?" Jack smiled in spite of himself.

"It's all that's keeping me going."

"So I better show up, eh?" Jack pulled over, and shifting the gear into park mode, turned to Neil with an expression of such intense anguish on his face that Neil felt momentarily frightened. "You've got to forgive me. Just forgive me."

"There's nothing to forgive."

"You don't feel it now, but you will. The resentment and the bad feelings. I'm sorry for any hurt I've caused you or will cause you."

"Stop it! Stop it! I don't care about hurt. I don't care about later. I'll deal with later. Please stop talking about forgiveness when I've got so much to be glad about."

Jack didn't seem to know what to make of the word *glad*.

"I'm glad about you. With you I got love."

Jack just stared at him for a minute, wordless, and then pulled back into traffic, turning east into College Street, where, in the late afternoon sunlight, all traces of Polish delicacies vanished and groups of dark-haired men clustered on the sidewalks, outside coffee bars and billiard halls, talking, laughing, gesticulating with an energy that Neil never saw among men of his own culture. He smiled. Two men stood with an arm around each other's waist.

"What you smiling at?" Jack asked softly.

"The men. All the beautiful men."

AT THE TOP of the stairs, Madame Wong, sparkling in her tight turquoise dress with its mandarin collar and rhinestone buttons, greeted them with regal calm.

"Rookwood. For two," Jack said.

"Please follow me, Mr. Rookwood." Brandishing two menus, she swept into the dining room. Their table was against the wall beneath the mural Neil so loved. As she seated them, she smiled at him, a very prim, careful smile that belied the crimson gash her lipstick had created. "It is nice to see you. Your parents are well?"

"Yes, thank you."

"Good, good. Enjoy." She hurried away, her inky black hair glittering like Audrey's with diamantine gems. She served as a kind of beacon of dignity to the army of servers in black and white who scurried from kitchen to table and back again laden with platters of food, the sweet-scented food that Neil had grown up believing was real Chinese fare. One of these servers was very quickly at their side, bowing, smiling ever so slightly, earnestly wondering how he could be of help to them. Neither Jack nor Neil needed any help in deciphering the menu, and the order was quickly taken.

Just as quickly, a beer appeared for Jack, and a liquid concoction made of grenadine and fizzy water was handed to Neil. A small, brightly coloured paper parasol, the handle of which speared both a maraschino cherry and a slice of orange, tilted jauntily from the side of Neil's glass. He laughed with the delight of a child.

"This is so perfect."

Jack laughed, too. "I should have had one of those."

"Not a big guy like you. This is a bit girly, isn't it?"

"I didn't want to say anything, but, now that you mention it …"

"Do you think I'm girly?" Neil was serious now.

Jack leaned forward, nodding his head in the affirmative, "Especially when you're nailing me to the bed with your dick."

Neil said, "So no one would suspect?"

"That you put out for guys?"

"I don't want to be beaten up. It's bad enough being seen as smart. If they start seeing me as queer, too …"

"Well, the only way around that is probably to get a girlfriend, but I don't imagine you want to play that game."

"It wouldn't be fair."

Jack answered. "Of course, you could do what I do. You could keep moving."

"You called it going forward."

"Yeah, I did, didn't I?" He looked down into his beer. "Though I've gotta say sometimes now it feels more like 'keep moving.'"

"What if you didn't?"

"I wouldn't know how to not move."

"Well, you'll probably get married one day and have six kids and two houses, a city house and a country house, and be unable to do anything but stay put."

"What a nice picture!" Jack's look of surprise had a bit of hurt stuck to it. "And what if I come back here and claim you as my bride, eh?"

Neil simply shook his head.

"You don't know, Neil. We can't know."

"Well, I know if you came back, I know what I would do."

"You might be head-over-heels with somebody."

"Maybe. It doesn't matter, though." Neil tilted his head to one side, scrutinizing his friend. "You're not coming back."

As he finished speaking, a bevy of waiters was suddenly upon them with trays heaped with steaming dishes.

"You think we have enough?" Jack said.

THE SIDEWALKS ON Yonge Street were teeming with pedestrians, the streets clogged with traffic. Signs above shop entrances winked seductively. Music blared from car radios. The song he'd heard the night he crouched under the sumach, "Runaway," floated by them heading north. And, a few minutes later, a fragment of "I Can't Stop Lovin' You" burst upon them.

"There!" Jack pointed to a young man in skin-tight white pants and a sleeveless top.

"He must be chilly."

Jack laughed. "You're supposed to be admiring the body, not worrying about his health."

"Is he really blond?"

"You are too much!"

"He's cute, though."

"This is the so-called strip. In there," Jack gestured with his thumb to the left, "there's apparently a bar where the boys come to meet. It's a respectable hotel with a secret. And across the street, the place with the clock tower."

They drove farther down Yonge, Neil drinking in the sights greedily. The landmarks he knew so well, the bargain shops like Half-Beat Harold's, the fleabag hotels, the sleazy movie theatres, had been magically transformed by the night lights into a glittering midway.

"There!" Jack said again. Two young men this time, one blond, one dark, in T-shirts and jeans, James Dean wannabes, hovered on the street corner, uncertain whether to go on or retrace their steps. "I bet the blond's the active one."

"No, it's the brunet," Neil said. "He looks pushy,"

"In public, but behind closed doors, he probably can't wait to give it up. That's the way it usually goes."

"That's not the way it works for us," Neil said quietly.

"But that's because what you and I have is very, very special."

They turned east again for a block and then south. The street was darker and less travelled than Yonge. In the longer shadows lurked many men, cigarette tips lighting the sidewalk like fireflies.

"There's another one. The Astronaut. Not so safe, I hear. A bit rough for a guy like you."

"What's it got to do with me?"

"You're not curious?"

"Sure, but ... I can't drink. They wouldn't let me in."

"If I were staying, I'd borrow Larry's ID and I'd take you. We'd go together."

"No one would believe I was twenty-two!"

"Sure they would, and even if they didn't, they're not going to turn a cutie like you away."

Neil took hold of Jack's thigh. "Can we go to the motel?"

"I just want to show you one more place."

It was on King Street. Jack pulled over, and they watched as men, singly, in pairs, or even larger groups, made their way along the sidewalk and disappeared under a sign that said *Letros*. Some moved with a kind of feigned nonchalance, some with obvious anticipation in their steps, others with a quick nervousness that looked a lot like escape from pursuit. Most of the men were nicely but casually dressed. A few, looking to Neil like men who worked at City Hall, wore suits and ties to complement their fastidious grooming and crisp, masculine bearing. They could have as easily been headed to a meeting as a nightclub.

"Fabulous!" Jack said upon watching two such attired men enter the bar. "What a joke!"

"Suits and ties?"

"I wonder if they put them on hangers before they screw?"

There was something in Jack's tone, a kind of scorn, which irritated Neil. He said, "So what if they do? Men in suits have the right to make out, too."

"They're queers. Why pretend they're good old boys?"

"Maybe some guys like that. If you wore a suit, I think I'd find it really sexy."

"If ever there was motivation to buy a suit, turning you on would be it." Jack took Neil's hand.

"How come you know all these places?"

"A guy I did it with a few times in the spring kept on and on about the scene, as he called it. He wanted me to go with him. I didn't want to. I told him I was only a part-time queer. That I wouldn't fit in. That didn't stop him, though. I heard about all these places. Detail after detail. He was really hooked."

"But you know where they are."

Jack looked away, embarrassed. "I drove around looking for them, just to see them. Tourist-like. Now I wish we had time to check them out together. It would have been fun. But, at least you know where they are now."

"I won't be coming to them."

"Don't say that."

"You know that's not what I want."

Jack knew he shouldn't ask, but he couldn't stop himself. "What do you want?"

"Not to be jerked around," Neil said to himself.

Jack eased the car from its berth. "I want The Willows Motel. That's what I want."

35

IT WAS VERY, VERY LATE.

The blurry sound of traffic from the expressway to the north competing with the gentle lapping of the lake to the south was strangely soothing to him as he lay against Jack. His hand dove in and out of the moonlight laving Jack's side.

"Do you think they believed we were cousins?" he asked at last.

"Does it matter?"

"No. They were nice."

"Irish."

"How do you know that?"

"The name. Finnegan."

"I didn't notice."

"There was a nameplate on the desk."

"I didn't notice any willows either."

"They're right by the water. Four or five of them. Big. Like Mr. Gordon's."

"You do see everything, don't you?"

"You miss the girlie calendar, too?"

"All I saw was you," Neil said.

"Neil?" Jack pulled him closer under the thin white sheet. "Tomorrow —"

"No, don't talk about tomorrow."

"I was going to take you to Sunnyside. The swimming pool along the lakeshore."

"My parents went there when they were kids." In his mind's eye was a photo in the family album of his father and mother, their innocently smiling faces peeking over a shared beach towel.

"My mother used to take us, too. I'd like to show it to you. It's another happy memory for me."

"Like the Arcadian Court? I'm game."

"But I'm not sure I want even Mother to come between us."

"It's up to you."

"How can you be like this? So calm?"

Neil laughed. The laugh was almost harsh. "I'm terrified. I just cover it well."

"Neil, Neil ..." He rained light kisses on Neil's shadowy face. "What's the matter with me, eh? You're so open. And I can't just say, 'That's it, buddy, I'm here, I'm here for you,' but, you know," his voice fell to the level of a whisper, "I can't, I really can't. All this scares the crap out of me."

"What's 'this'?"

"Loving you." As he spoke these words, Jack Rookwood looked pale and drawn, leaving Neil to wonder if this was the first time he'd ever confessed to failure. The wondering seemed to elicit a response. "I'm no better than my old man," Jack said, as he closed his eyes tightly. "Can't deal with too much love."

"I don't think loving scares me," Neil said after a while.

"You're fearless, that's why. Absolutely fearless."

Neil kissed Jack's chest, relishing the feeling of the hair against his cheek, trying not to cry. He didn't want to cry, absolutely didn't want to.

"You get on with things, okay?" Jack didn't know what else to give the boy now except the assurance that life doesn't stop. "Don't sit around waiting for me."

"I'm not crazy," Neil said in a very low voice.

Jack gave him a playful poke. "I may be back. Who knows?"

Neil pulled back. "Don't keep taunting me." Jack tried to pull him close again, but Neil resisted him, saying, "You break your own rules all the time. Be here, be here. I'm here. A hundred per cent. Stop playing with me!"

Shocked by his vehemence, Jack sat up.

Neil lay in the pool of dappling moonlight alone, concentrating on the sound of waves. Thoughts flickered like little flames in his mind, one thought brighter than the rest. Neither words, no matter how lovingly spoken, nor acts, no matter how full of passion, were what was important now. There was something bigger than these, a place where he and Jack actually seemed to blend together. It was the best place of all, but as he stretched out in the shadow of the expressway, straining to keep the lapping sounds clear, it was obvious to him that Jack couldn't find his way there tonight.

For what seemed like ages, neither spoke.

The traffic seemed very close, and with the hum of the expressway, there came a sense of great distances to be covered and great sadness to be endured. It was in the silence that followed a particularly busy rush of vehicles that Neil felt he could hear that sadness most clearly. He closed his eyes as a way of shutting it out.

Then, very softly, Jack said, "You know, a moment ago you felt just like my mother. She was so steady, steady in her feelings about things. She never believed that Ethel Rosenberg was guilty of spying for the Commies, said it was impossible. She kept a photo of Ethel in her wallet, like a kind of prayer card. It was there the day she died. I didn't inherit her consistency. I think maybe Larry did, but not me."

"Lie down. You're just beating up on yourself."

Jack let himself fall backwards. His head landed on Neil's thigh. He turned his face towards Neil. "What now, my friend?"

Neil didn't answer.

Jack took hold of Neil's semi-erection. "There's always this."

"I'd rather you hold me."

"Done," Jack said, crawling up the sheet to Neil's side.

———

WHEN THEY WOKE, it was after noon. The sun was watery but warm.

Neil stared into the heat.

Jack said, "You okay?"

"I had a dream."

Jack turned onto his side to face the boy.

"But it could have been a memory." Neil's voice floated in the thick, damp air, a summer leaf unexpectedly torn from its branch.

"Memory of what?"

"My father ..."

"Oh, God! Not him." Jack raised himself up on one elbow.

Neil still hadn't looked at Jack. "Just him. He was standing with a suitcase in the doorway of my bedroom wearing a coat and hat, and maybe boots. It was winter, I guess. That was the dream part. It reminded me of a time years ago. My mother was in LA visiting her sisters. Uncle Herb and Aunt Violet had taken Val and my cousin Sandra to some weekend skating thing. Dressed just like in the dream, Dad said, 'It's better I go. I'm no good. You'll be happier. All of you. If you need anything, I'm sure the Gordons will be happy to take you in until your mother gets back.' I started to cry. Imagine that, eh? I cried and cried. I heard him go out by the front door. And then I really cried. Screamed even. Ten minutes later he knocked on the door. He just smiled when I answered, and said, 'How about some cocoa?'"

With a gentle groan, Jack lay back on the bed, closing his eyes.

"It was a dream and a memory together. Funny, eh?"

Faint sounds of expressway traffic buzzed fly-like in the room.

"We've got to eat." Jack rubbed his belly, smiling faintly. "I'm so hungry I'd even go for a couple of those fortune cookies." He had turned them down at Lichee Garden because he didn't want to see the fortunes.

Neil sat up. "I don't want to, Jack."

"What do you mean?"

"I want to go now." He looked at Jack for the first time.

"But we still have time, don't we? Tell me we've still got time!"

"No. No more time." Jack sat up, too, and pulled Neil against him. But Neil would not allow himself to collapse, to surrender. *It has to stop*, he told himself. He stood. His wine red shirt beckoned to him from the lone armchair. He rolled it into a ball before burying it in the white plastic bag brought along for the purpose. "I want you to take me to the Loop. The Jane Loop. I'll get the bus. It's just right."

"You sure?" Jack stared hard at the boy as he began to dress, hoping his gaze would be enough to stop him. "I need to be with you as long as we —"

"There's not much point anymore. Your stuff's in the trunk, right?"

Jack looked down at the dark green linoleum.

"You can go right up Jane to the highway. There'll be a coffee bar or a doughnut joint on the way. I couldn't eat anything. Not even a fortune cookie."

"Oh, Jesus, Neil ... We can't just let everything go ..."

Neil shrugged helplessly. "Looks like we have to."

THEY STOPPED OUTSIDE a men's shop, Cecil Ward, just opposite the Loop. Neil looked across the road, remembering that only a week before, in Jack's mother's bed, he'd thought of the terminus as rock solid, unchanging. But now, in the white heat of mid-afternoon, it looked as if it were going to float away. Or dissolve. He had a feeling that the next time he arrived from the suburbs in his 50-A bus, there'd be nothing there but a bus stop. The streetcars would be long gone and even the street, busy Bloor, would disappear, leaving him no access to his beloved downtown. What he was looking at, he told himself, was the death of the Jane Loop.

He shifted in his seat.

Jack was very still.

Not a word had been spoken from the time they got in the car.

Neil looked at Jack, with a faint smile. "I know you'll make a great journalist."

"We'll see." Jack's face had never looked less like smiling.

"You have my address."

"You bet. I'll send you mine when I get one."

"If you ever head for Europe ... Let me know. I want to see Europe."

"I won't forget."

They looked at each other.

"Bye," Neil said.

"You don't want to wait till your bus comes?" The pleading tone was there again, but softer than earlier.

"Nope. I'm gone." He quickly opened the door onto a deserted sidewalk.

His first glance took in the Odeon Humber cinema along the road. It was a place he'd always loved coming to; it had such a hushed atmosphere, like a church, and its seats were so soft and roomy. Today, though, its marquee seemed to mock him: Cary Grant and Doris Day were starring in *That Touch of Mink*. Placing his hands over his eyes, like a visor, Neil peered at an approaching bus. It was the 50. He didn't need to hurry. But what was the point in stalling? His hands lifted from his sides. They were empty. He had forgotten the white plastic bag containing his silk shirt.

He bent down and looked through the open window.

Jack stared back at him, a stunned look on his face.

"I must have left my red shirt in the motel room."

Jack's eyelids fluttered.

"It had a good ending anyway." Neil pulled his wallet from his pocket. "This is for you." Out of one of the slots normally used for cards and ID, he slid a photograph of himself taken that spring outside the library by Tony. It showed him smiling in front of a flowering forsythia. Neil dropped it gently onto the passenger seat. "It's light and portable. I don't know what else to give you. You probably don't want things."

In the merciless heat, he crossed the street without once looking back. "Coward," he said to the sun-blanched sky. "He's a coward!"

Long after the 50-A passed on its way back to the suburbs, the blue Pontiac remained marooned outside the menswear shop, its driver unable to make out anything but the emptiness next to him.

36

HAD NEIL BEEN LOOKING, HE would have seen Jack's two brothers walking over the Humber Bridge, heading towards the Jane-Bloor intersection, but his eyes were tightly closed, refusing to contemplate the return to what was once called suburbia. They only opened as the 50-A pulled into the Prince Edward stop at the edge of the Kingsway, just in time to see the blond skater board the bus. Neil almost didn't recognize him. He was wearing a white shirt and pale blue tie tucked into beige suit pants. In one hand he carried the suit jacket and in the other either a Bible or a hymnal. With a somewhat superior air, he chose a seat close to the front. Neil glanced at the church next to the stop, another stone House of God called All Saints Anglican. Perhaps the skater was a parishioner, but, Neil reasoned, church was over long ago. What's taken him all this time to get to the bus stop? Without warning, he shivered. Why wasn't the skater wearing his shorts today? It was too hot for those clothes. Too hot, too wrong. The whole picture was like a bad omen.

His mind closed down after that, declining to think about anything except the blinding effects of the afternoon sun on the shop windows that lined a nearly empty Bloor Street, and the intense depth of the shadows, which the sun had no power to exclude. It was only as the bus was passing St. Andrew's, his mother's church, that a sense of long, tedious days filled with many things not said, not done, barely imagined, finally broke the barrier he'd erected. It being a Sunday, there were only three other people on the bus in addition to the skater, all sitting near the front. Neil was at the back, alone and undetected, as the tears came in a flood. He knew he'd have to get off early and walk the rest of the way home.

With any luck, he thought, he would not have to share his reddened eyes with his parents. Even though it would mean having his father in a foul mood, he hoped they were still battling the vacationland traffic.

The suburban streets were as still as the city streets. More so even, because the houses that lined them made a great pretense of being unoccupied by real people.

He walked slowly along Wilmot Street, crying unashamedly. It was stupid, he knew. Anyone might appear at any moment. Someone who knew him, someone who would ask questions, show concern, phone his parents later. But no one did. He walked unnoticed, his wintergreen shirt growing stickier and stickier under the unkind sun.

Turning into Dominion Street, his tears abated somewhat. He passed the Ross house, which turned a blank face to the street. And the Nearys', whose rose garden had so impressed Jack, was no more expressive. He passed the McIntyres and the Wellingtons. None of them were looking. They were all probably buried in their back-yards, sprawled on lawn chairs, sipping beer, adjusting sprinklers, reading magazines. Invisible alien, he passed them, seeing everything and nothing.

As he reached the Marsh house, which his mother often referred to as "that cute little bungalow," smothered under a thick blanket of Boston ivy, he saw that there were cars in his parents' driveway.

He pulled his glasses from his pocket.

Not just cars. Police cars. One sat in the drive, one was parked on the side of the road in front of the house.

The first thing that occurred to him was that someone had been injured — his mother, his father, perhaps his sister. Or that there had been an accident.

His stomach sinking, he picked up his pace. As he reached the corner of Avery and Dominion, he was almost running.

Everyone looked up at him as he burst in the door. His mother was in her chair, his father opposite her on the sofa. A policeman sat next to his father.

A second officer sat on one of the dining room chairs, Mona Gordon on another. Gus Gordon leaned against the doorjamb separating the hallway from the living room. Nothing seemed disturbed, except the expressions on their faces.

Nobody said hello to him except Mona.

The policeman was saying, "I'm guessing they thought they were in some danger and got out before they finished."

"Did you lock both the doors?" his father barked at him, with a dark scowl on his face.

"Of course I did," Neil said. He knew then what had happened.

"You said there's a spare key, sir," the second officer said. "They've used a spare key before. The Caldwell place."

"How would they find it?" his mother wanted to know.

"Watching the house. They know things, these guys. They watch, they listen, they know."

Neil remembered unearthing the spare key a week ago while Jack watched from the roadside.

"It's your friend in the Edsel," his father said to Neil.

"Who? What are you talking about? What's happened?"

"So you'll get fingerprints?" Gus asked.

"We'll do our best, but they've no doubt taken precautions."

"What's happened?" Neil felt slightly sick.

Gus Gordon moved out of the doorway, gesturing towards the stairs.

Two garish red arrows, one painted impasto-style on either wall of the staircase, pointed luridly upstairs.

Slowly, Neil made his way towards them.

"Don't touch anything, son," one of the policemen said. "The paint's not dry."

Neil started to climb. The painted arrows looked like suppurating wounds on the wall. Red paint flecked the banister and broadloom as well. Neil was reminded of the stained shirt his father wore the night he fell out of the closet, claiming he'd been stabbed.

He reached the landing and turned to face the next bank of stairs. The same matching scarlet arrows gashed the walls here, too.

He climbed very slowly.

At the top, he looked right into his father's room and groaned. The bookcases were smashed and all the books they'd held rendered spineless. The mattress had been gutted, its stuffing replaced with battered skulls, plastic creeper, handcuffs, and Jean-Paul Sartre's *Being and Nothingness*, its grey paper bookmark clinging to pages 20–21. Around the headboard twinkled a tiara of blue Christmas lights. The room smelled strongly of urine, and something else — was it liquor? On the walls, in the same thick red paint were messages, a different one for every wall. *GOD IS A CRIMINAL* read one. *GOD IS A DEVIL* read the second. *GOD LIVES HERE* and *GOD IS DEAD* proclaimed the third and fourth. And there in their midst, hanging by his neck from the ceiling light, was Convict Joe, limp and pathetic.

He stared for many minutes at the wreckage, before turning and, like a man in a trance, crossing the short distance that separated his father's room from his mother's.

In the doorway of his mother's room, not even a groan or a

gasp escaped him. It reeked so intensely of perfume, of several perfumes, clashing, he scarcely dared to breathe. Everything was covered in a pinkish-white film. The air seemed thick with it. It took him moments to realize it was face powder. But so much face powder. Where had his mother kept all this powder? As he scanned the vanity table, empty of all its contents, he took in for the first time that the dusting that coated everything was only partly powder. Feathers, hundreds of small white feathers lay beneath the powder. These were clearly the stuffing from his mother's pillows, which now lay limply on the bed.

He took a small step into the room. Something crunched under-foot. Amidst the powder and feathers, he could make out beads, many coloured beads. His mother's necklaces and bracelets had been broken and beads flickered in the carpet like some kind of treasure left behind by retreating tides. It was all so eerie.

He was about to turn away when he noticed the Renoir lady, the lady in blue with umbrella, which had adorned his mother's wall for years. Her glass protection had been shattered. Over her eyes, a black blindfold had been crudely drawn. The reflection from what remained of the glass pulled his attention back to the vanity table, to the mirror above it. Partly obscured by the powder were the words, *SHAME ON COWARDS*. They had been scrawled in the same red paint, or perhaps lipstick, bright red lipstick, the kind his mother rarely wore. Bright red, but now faded, scar-like, under the face powder.

He went down the stairs. Everyone in the living room was standing now.

"They must have heard something, that's all I can think," the senior policeman was saying again, as if trying to convince himself of something.

"Gus said there was a noise," Mona insisted. "He actually got up and looked out the window to check."

"It must have been that tombstone you heard. It's the only

thing that would make a loud enough sound. All the windows
were shut."

"And there was no light," Mona said.

"Nah, these guys are masters of the dark. Masters. I've never
seen anything like it. You can thank your lucky stars they didn't
get to the ground floor. They didn't get to your room either, young
man. Someone will be by later to dust for fingerprints."

His father escorted the police to the door.

"Oh, Nora," Mona said, "I'm so sorry."

His mother, looking terribly wan, gave a weak little smile. "I
had a feeling when all this started that we wouldn't escape. I don't
know why. It's not how I usually think."

His father returned to the living room. For a second, it looked
as if he would head for the kitchen and the liquor cabinet. Instead,
he turned to Neil. "Where were you this weekend?"

"With Tony. I told Mom, when she called."

"You and Tony did this, didn't you?"

"Frank." Nora let go of a weary sigh.

"Are you crazy?" Neil demanded.

His father's expression, already dark, now turned black. "What
did you say?"

"I said, are you crazy?" Neil's voice was loud with anger. So
unfamiliar was he with angry outbursts, he couldn't have stopped
himself if he'd wanted.

In a flash, his father had pushed him hard into the wall and
was banging his head against the plaster, shouting, "What did you
say? What did you say, Mr. Know-it-all?"

"Frank, Frank," Gus said, stepping forward. "That's enough!
Leave the boy alone." He tried grabbing Frank's arm, but Frank
kept elbowing him back.

Neil fought, but only his arms were free enough to use. They
flailed wildly, knocking lamps and pictures and an ornamental
plant. Only a few blows actually hit his father.

Mona yelled, "For God's sake, Frank, have you lost your mind?"

Then, rising above it all came his mother's voice, unrecognizable in its shrill fury, "LET HIM ALONE."

His father immediately dropped his hands and backed up, surprise and fear written all over his face. Neil slumped against the wall, coughing, red-faced, the top button of his shirt torn off. His father's face was very clear to him, though. He'd seen it like this the day Aunt Sylvia challenged him about the gravestone. A strange thought took shape: he's afraid of women's anger. But the thought was swept away by the rising tide of his own rage.

"Why are all my things ruined?" his father asked in a pathetic little voice.

"They weren't all yours, Frank," his wife answered sharply.

His father's moustache trembled.

Neil stood very straight. His voice raspy from his father's choking, he said, "Your things are ruined because you don't know when to shut up! You want the world to know just what a funny guy you are, how really wild and wicked and dark and — macabre — isn't that the word you like? — how macabre your jokes are. You go on and on about them. They're your favourite subject! If you only knew how stupid you sounded, how truly ignorant you are!"

Nora stepped forward, a pleading hand outstretched. "Neil, darling, please ..."

"Well, it's true! He's always showing off! Can't help himself. He's the big bogey man! Everyone knows how much effort he puts into scaring me to death. The whole damn neighbourhood knows. Ask anyone, they'll tell you. Ask them who they've told. His so-called humour is famous!" Neil turned back to his father. His voice lower and suddenly very mature, he said, "One of them's on a mission — to stop people like you and Yardley — people who get away with bloody murder! It's payback time, Dad. You can thank yourself for this."

Frank Bennett's eyes bugged.

Neil looked at Mona, whose eyes were wet, then at Gus, who nodded gently at him, and finally at his mother. "Mom?"

White-faced, Nora didn't know where to look. Her face showed both defeat and shame. She turned to Mr. Gordon anxiously. "When did the police say they were coming back?"

"Later," Mona said impatiently, "later."

At the bottom of the cellar steps, he wanted to avoid looking into his father's workshop, because he knew Jack would have been at his most ruthless there, but he couldn't.

The gravestone lay shattered in the middle of the workshop floor, sad little pieces of relic, nothing more. The rest of the room was a nightmare, a scene from a scary movie, or a house of horrors. Automobile lacquers had been dumped, thrown, sprayed over everything, so the room glowed garishly. Even that magnificent machine, the saw, wore competing coats of colour, and maybe something else besides. Was it shellac? He remembered the description of the damage done to Miss Cope's furnishings. Shellac. The smell was overpowering.

He closed his door on it.

Throwing himself on the teak sofa, he fell asleep almost immediately.

He was dimly aware later of some people arriving on official business. A large man poked his head into the room, looked around, grunted and left again without another sound. Another man, smaller, slighter than the first, with a wispy blond moustache and grinning for no apparent reason, opened the door a few minutes later, and took note of Neil on his sofa. He, too, disappeared without a word.

Neil slept.

He didn't know what time it was when his mother knocked to

tell him they were going to the Gordons' for supper.

"I'm not coming. I'm not hungry."

"You've got to come."

"No. I don't."

"What will I say to her?"

"She'll understand that I don't want to be with him."

His mother closed the door.

LATER, HE WENT up and scrounged an apple, a peach, some brown bread and peanut butter. Back in his room, the Tchaikovsky waltzes danced very softly.

As he ate, anger stirred in him again, but this time not against his father.

Jack had tricked him.

Friday night. He'd done it when he said he would be packing. And all day yesterday — all night, too, as they made love — he had known. A terrible trick, and then to leave him to face it alone — trick within a trick. Jack's sense of outrage was obviously more important to him than anything else. *GOD LIVES HERE. GOD IS DEAD.* What kind of payback was that? Jack was as big a show-off as his father. Who knew? Maybe they were in cahoots. Maybe they'd dreamed up the neighbourhood break-ins together — all of them but the last one, of course. He could see their bent heads together over a hand-drawn map, chuckling as they plotted.

"It's not fucking funny," he swore, over and over.

But anger wasn't Neil's strong suit. It left him feeling empty. Sadness was better. Great numbing sadness. Better by far. Jack was gone. There was nothing to be done now anyway. Or said.

Donny Stasiuk roared by — it had to be Donny. The song was loud, a girl group. It was the one about the postman — "Do you have a letter for me?"

The tears welled up again, but he was almost too tired to cry. He had to stop crying. He was nearly seventeen.

He climbed the stairs again, to the bathroom. There, having decided against any further examination of his parents' rooms, he peed, then washed and brushed quickly. He could hear Mona Gordon's voice. They must all be on the Gordons' front porch.

He ran down the stairs, only just managing to get into his room, when his parents opened the back door.

He heard them pause on the landing, talking in low voices. Then, the sound of their footfall descending the stairs.

A gentle knock.

"Come in."

They stood just inside the door.

"Son," his father said, "I'm sorry for earlier. Things got out of hand."

Neil let his gaze drift to the pin-up board where Audrey seemed to be laughing at them all, or maybe trying to reassure him that one day he'd be laughing, too. He had an image of himself wearing a rhinestone necklace and he almost smiled.

"We were very upset, darling," his mother said.

"It's a bad mess," Neil conceded.

His father nodded. "That's only half the story."

Neil sat on the edge of his bed.

"Your sister's pregnant."

Of course she is, Neil thought. "Mike?" he asked.

"Who else?" his mother said.

Though Neil didn't know this, the story was an all too common one. Mike had offered to pay for an abortion apparently, and Val had flatly refused. She'd also refused to marry him. Fortunately for her, Mike's uncle and aunt were willing to keep her at their place in Windermere until the baby was born. When Neil asked why she didn't come home to have the baby, he was met, in unison, by, "We don't want her to! Think of the figure she'll make!"

"She'll give the baby up for adoption. Then she can come home." Nora Bennett made it sound very that's-that.

"You see, everything's ruined," his father said. "Not just my things. My daughter, too. Ruined."

His mother looked especially grim. "We told the Gordons. I didn't want Mona guessing. We're going to tell the Knights. That's it. You must keep this very quiet. It's nobody's business but ours anyway."

"Poor Val," Neil said.

"Poor!" His mother's voice was sharp and incredulous. "That's one word for it. Silly little tramp."

Neil squinted at them standing in the doorway, where they looked very small and dark and mean.

"The rooms upstairs," his father added. "Nobody in the family needs to know about that. Do you understand?"

"Goodnight," his mother said, disappearing out the door.

His father hovered an instant longer, searching for something, a sign, a clue, or perhaps a miracle. "Do you understand?" he repeated.

Neil said, "I'm going to go see Val. Before I go back to school."

"Suit yourself." His father turned and left as well.

Neil sat, listening. Eventually, he heard the liquor cabinet opening. It didn't matter now, nothing mattered. Jack was a liar, and a traitor, too.

"What am I going to do?" He said it very softly, collapsing onto his pillow ready for another storm of tears. As his head landed, there was a small crunching noise.

His hand snaked under the pillow.

An envelope, white, crisp as a starched collar, emerged. *Neil Cameron Bennett, Forever*, decreed the familiar heavy print.

He sat up again and opened the envelope. It was a photograph of a bridge at night in the rain, illuminated by beautiful globes of lamplight. Paris, Pont Neuf, said the small print on the back.

And the message:

> N.
>
> *In honour of our connection.*
>
> *Love,*
> *J. xxx*
>
> *Aug. 19, 1962*

The card fell to the floor as the storm broke.

He cried and cried, until, sore with grief, he curled up on his bed seeking forgetfulness in sleep.

37

THERE WAS A DREAM.

A room, a high-ceilinged room, old, plaster cracking, mouldings worn, a room bathed in the gentle warmth of afternoon light streaming in at tall windows, many windows, with fluttering white curtains and a view of rolling golden fields, up and down, in haying season, before the harvest. He stood watching from the windows, golden fields, soaring birds and a lone figure, still a black speck in the distance, crossing the field directly opposite, moving slowly, slowly across the golden field waiting patiently for harvest, moving towards him, something shiny, golden in his hand.

He awoke with a start. The room. Again, the room and, with it, curtains. More curtains. White curtains. But these were where they should be. By the windows.

He sat up, unaware that he smiled. It was half past nine.

Voices, women's voices. His mother's and — he wasn't sure whose. He crossed to the door, listened. They were by the back door.

"When the Wests told us we were positively shocked."

His mother said something.

"We have never been liked, Walter and I. We don't know why. We're not the only ones who don't care for coloured people."

Irene Chard.

His mother said something.

"But you and Frank have always been a model for the neigh-bours. I can tell you that. They all think the world of you. So it was very shocking to hear the news. Blasphemy on the walls."

"Thank you for your concern, Irene."

"Oh, Nora. Life is hard enough without going through these things alone. Walter and I are very much with you."

"Thank you, Irene."

"Of course, it's also good for people to see that even the best aren't immune."

His mother said nothing.

"But I don't want to keep you. If it's anything like what we went through, there will be a horrible mess to clean."

"Yes, Irene, thank you."

"We'll see you soon, Nora. If I can be of any help ..."

The door closed.

Neil took a step or two back and waited.

Nothing, then a soft, stifled sound. Mother crying.

Neil sat down on his sofa. Elbows on his knees, he waited. Should he go up? Yesterday was the first time his mother had ever really come to his rescue. Should he go to hers now? He slipped into his jeans, threw on a T-shirt. At the foot of the stairs, he paused, still uncertain. He stared into the house of horrors to his right. The paint-splattered walls crouching in the shadows of the morning seemed even more violent. But the gravestone was gone. All that remained of it were powdery traces.

She was at the table, unapologetically crying.

He touched her lightly on the shoulder. "Don't listen to her."

"I'll have to listen to her. And all the others. It's what I deserve."

"Don't."

"Don't tell me don't. Let me pay." She sat up, drying her eyes on the table napkin. "You want your breakfast?"

"Just sit." He had never seen her looking so wretched. "Dad sleep on the couch?"

She answered by covering her mouth with a napkin, stuffing back sobs.

"I didn't hear him snoring. I didn't hear anything. He must have cleaned away the gravestone." He paused uncertainly. "I can help you clean upstairs."

"No!" Her hand slapped the oilcloth. "I'll do it. A professional is coming tomorrow for the bad stuff, all the beads, the powder, the feathers. Mona called them this morning."

"I didn't know you had so much powder."

"Only a bit of it was mine."

Neil sat back. He knew whose powder it was. For a split second, he felt a huge urge to tell her how it all happened. For a split second it was on the tip of his tongue. But the second passed. Sighing, he crossed to the refrigerator.

His mother remained very still, watching him pour milk onto cereal. "If it weren't for you," she said, "I would have been out of here ages ago."

His hand shook. "No, Mom, don't say that."

"It's true. You should know."

"I don't want to know," he said.

She stood. "Mona's taking me shopping. I'll just wash. Are you all right?"

Wait till you find out about me, he very nearly said. A little shiver escaped him, but it was quickly replaced by a strange smile, part excited, part devious.

When, several minutes later, Mona Gordon opened the back door and trilled, "Nora," he was spreading raspberry jam on his last piece of toast.

"She's upstairs getting ready, Mrs. G."

Mona took his mother's seat. "Is she all right?" she whispered. "I saw Irene Chard at the door."

"The neighbours are talking, are they?"

"Lydia West asked us for details. We gave her very little. The police gave her more, I think. But they'll all want to know. And if they're not told, they'll make things up."

"Mrs. Chard was horrible."

"Isn't she always? Lydia thinks it's the young chap in the Edsel."

"It's not him. He's not a bad guy. It's more likely Archie Ross." He knew even as he said it that he was accusing Archie falsely.

"I shouldn't say this, but one of our neighbours said it sounds like the sort of stunt your dad might pull."

"Who said that?"

"I'm not telling. I told him that was impossible — your parents were away."

Neil shrugged. "It's true though, it does look like Dad ..."

Mrs. Gordon placed her bag on the table, smoothed out her bright pink pedal pushers, then, very, very quietly said, "I'm sorry about all this, Neil, Gus and me, we're both sorry."

Neil said, "It's not as bad as what they did to the other places."

"I'm not talking about the — break-in."

Uncertain, he looked into her eyes. He was surprised to find shame there.

"Too many people standing around not saying anything. Lana's sorry, too."

"It's okay, Mrs. G. You were always on my side."

Mona shook her head. "You're way too nice, Neil."

"Not anymore," he answered. "Everything's different now." And it was, he thought, completely different: *I'm a good boy no longer.* From now on, he would have to hide and pretend, lie and sneak — that is, until he could get downtown to real life.

Mona looked at him sadly.

They heard a tentative footfall coming down the stairs.

"Oh, Mona, I've got powder all over the soles of my feet. I couldn't get into the closet without stepping in it. It's all over. And the beads. They hurt when you step on them."

"Well, tomorrow it will be back to normal. Don't worry."

Mona pushed herself up off the chair. She gave Neil a kiss on the head and took his mother's arm. "Let's have a treat at Kresge's," she said. "Something fattening — like butter tarts."

SEPTEMBER WAS ONLY ten days away. September and school. He loved September and the changing colours — it was his birthday month, after all. But he hated the thought of returning to school. He dreaded the jeering and taunting, the terrible cost of hating sports or the struggles with science, the stuff guys were supposed to be good at. The languages he loved, and history and geography, and he might even like art, if he could keep his father out of it, but the prospect of two more years of everything else left him daunted this morning. He sat on his bed, facing the window for the longest time, occasionally allowing himself to wonder where Jack was, but mostly wishing he could close his eyes and wake up at university somewhere far away.

After a while, not wanting to lose himself in the old world of make-believe, he got up and walked over to his turntable. He didn't want music or musicals, but he crouched down anyway and opened the doors of the record cabinet.

Get your own secret compartment.

It was as if Jack were there, the words were so clear. He wanted to reject them, but he couldn't.

Get your own secret compartment.

He slowly straightened. Behind the records, there was space. Several inches.

Crouching again, he pulled up the floor of his cupboard. There wasn't much there. Torn underwear, a bottle of Vaseline, the envelopes Jack's cards came in, and an article from the newspaper about a nightclub downtown — one upstairs, dimly lit, through beaded curtains, where queers hung out. Tucked away at the back, beneath a 1956 calendar with pictures of a different Indian tribe for each month, were two special pictures from the LA papers. A muscular blond man, naked but for a small towel held coyly in front of his genitals, and two shirtless, dark-haired young men staring into each other's eyes.

He quickly emptied the old compartment. Then, kneeling in front of the new, he pulled his record albums forward to make more space at the back and dropped the underwear and Vaseline behind them. He was about to do the same with the rest, when it occurred to him he could use the albums themselves for the paper matter. They would provide better protection. Albums he rarely listened to, like *House of Flowers* (into which he slid the newspaper article) and *Can-Can* (the special pictures) and *Destry Rides Again* (Jack's envelopes). When he was done, he sat back on the floor, pleased, and at the same time strangely sad. The old order had ended.

He turned to his pin-up board. It would all have to go, too.

In a matter of minutes he had cleared it, had filed the pictures, cards and souvenirs, relics of Aunt Sylvia's visit, in their appropriate boxes, drawers and record sleeves.

It took him much longer to decide what to do with the empty space. In the end, one face shot of Audrey as Holly, staring through the Tiffany's display window, breakfast in hand, and one of his old flag cards, No. 80, the United Nations. That was all. Until he could find something else that spoke of real promise.

He wrote a card to his Aunt Sylvia after, a few lines: *It was so wonderful seeing you and I miss you a lot. Jack has gone to Ottawa for journalism. Gone for good, I think. Love to Aunt Julia and, of course, to you, N.*

He wrote one to Val, too, just three sentences on a pretty card of a rose bush: *I'm going to come up and see you very soon. I'll come by bus. Thinking about you. Love always, N.*

He put both in envelopes, addressed them, and took them to the mailbox on Orion, where he couldn't help recalling the last time he'd posted something there: a quarter of bully Archie's face. The memory was encouraging.

Mother came home, much later, in a cheerier mood.

He mowed the back lawn, a gift to his father, as she ironed Uncle Herb's shirt, the black one with the red trim.

After an hour's nap, from which he woke despondent, he set off for work, with the shirt on a hanger, swathed in white tissue paper. The street was emptier than usual, and the lawns were sere from lack of rain. A couple of lawn sprinklers spun unattended.

It was just four o'clock.

There would be time to visit with Uncle Herb and Aunt Violet.

At the bus stop, he closed his eyes against the sun, which, though hot, was not scorching. Every so often, a whiff of autumn floated past.

He was roused by the toot of a car horn.

Edsel-man smiled at him from behind his steering wheel. "Where you going?"

"To work," Neil replied.

"What's the matter? You all right? You look far away."

"I've never been more here."

"I heard your place was ransacked."

"Who told you?"

"The police. I had the perfect alibi though. I was in emergency most of the night with food poisoning. Never eat at the Lotus Blossom, by the way. Food's nearly lethal."

"Are you all right?"

"Don't I look all right?" He opened his arms. The two sides of his shirt parted to reveal the lean but muscular torso. "Where do you work?"

"Runnymede Library," Neil replied, without the smallest hesitation.

"I could take you, but my mom's expecting a lift down on the Queensway. I can pick you up, though. What time you finished?"

"Eight thirty."

"How 'bout it?"

Neil approached the door, bent down.

Edsel-man scratched his belly, a smile teasing his stubbly face.

"Sure," Neil said, and straightened before he could change his mind. "That'd be great."

"Cool," Edsel-man said. "Very cool. Eight thirty?"

"Bloor Street, a couple of blocks east of Runnymede Road."

"Got it." Edsel-man waved and, grinning, drove off with a squeal of his tires.

HIS AUNT AND uncle had no time to talk. Kids with their parents were trying on back-to-school shoes. Many parents, many kids.

Uncle Herb said, "If you're looking for extra work, my boy, you've come to the right place."

All Aunt Violet managed to communicate, as she took Uncle Herb's shirt, was "Another Audrey's coming to the Runnymede. Thursday. *War and Peace.* I saw it six years ago. You'll love it. Say hi to your folks for us."

On the street again, he stared across to Parma Fruits and Vegetables. Lorenzo of the full red lips was sweeping the walk.

Lorenzo was pretty. He looked nice, too. Sweet — was that the word?

Maybe Tony was also working this afternoon. Tony wasn't nice, not in the sweet way — or pretty. Tony was real. Edsel-man was also real, maybe too real.

What had he done, saying yes like that?

Maybe nothing would happen. Maybe Edsel-man would drive him home.

That was crazy. He didn't want Edsel-man to drive him home. Not really.

Edsel-man knew what was what. That's what Neil wanted.

Someone who knew enough to shake him up, make him see it all differently. He wanted another viewpoint. One that didn't involve magic or miracles. There was no point waiting around for miracles.

He crossed the street.

Mrs. Colero was at the till, chattering in Italian to a man who might have been an elder brother to Tony. It was Cousin Giacomo, Mr. Colero's brother's son, on a visit from Bari. He laughed a lot and said, "No Engleesh, no Engleesh."

Mrs. Colero said, "Tony helping his dad."

So early, too early for the library, but where else to go?

Lorenzo smiled as he passed him on the sidewalk. A sexy mouth. "It's good?"

"Bene, grazie," Neil replied.

Lorenzo opened his eyes comically, "Parl'italiano?"

"Poco, poco."

"Bene, bene."

The last time he walked from the fruit store to the library, two days ago, he was on the way to his last date with Jack.

Giacomo. Jack. He supposed Jack would always be somewhere, ready to jump out at him.

Audrey's name loomed large on the cinema marquee. *War and Peace.* Ball gowns, soldiers marching, and lots and lots of snow — the prospect filled him with impatience. Still, there was Audrey ...

He was forty-five minutes early to be exact. Miss Fairfield was at the circulation desk with the new page, the elfin boy named Robert Michalak, who had first appeared a month ago. Then, the boy was a promising new connection. Now, with his swoop of dark hair and delicate features, he was only another innocent, living in a world Neil had left behind.

Neil smiled at Miss Fairfield, who nodded. Robert Michalak didn't even look up.

Neil took a seat in the smaller room with the fine arts, the poetry, the plays. This was his room now. The old oak table down the centre was his, too. No one else was there.

He picked the first book from the small stack left on the table. A picture book of European architecture. Churches, castles, chateaux, opera houses. Slowly, he turned the pages. It was all so far away. But he continued turning.

At twenty to six, the elf passed him heading for the tearoom, carrying old magazines from the periodical rack. He didn't seem the curious type.

Miss Fairfield approached. "I have something for you. Mrs. Negulescu was going to make sure you got them, but it's better this way."

She beckoned him into the back room. The tearoom door was closed. He supposed Miss Boughton and Mrs. Negulescu were in there having supper.

"These are for you." She pulled three books out of a library bag. The first, a small black book, its spine reinforced with thick black library tape, was called *The Epic of Gilgamesh*. The second, in slightly better condition, was a thick green Modern Library book by Walt Whitman, *Leaves of Grass*. Miss Fairfield had put a bookmark with a purple tassel at a place a third of the way through.

"The thingy marks the 'Calamus' poems."

"I've never read much poetry."

"It's time you did."

And the third was a brand new library book with a Mylar cover. James Baldwin. *Another Country*.

He looked at her, puzzled.

"You can keep the first two, Neil. You see their condition. We'll have to replace them. The third you must bring back. Sometime. I ordered a second copy."

"Thank you," he said.

"They're no random gift, Neil. After our conversation, I went looking, remembering. They may help you."

He looked down at the books, realizing what she had done.

"Is your young man still here?"

"Gone." He mustn't cry. She would be so upset.

"Read the Whitman."

"Yes, ma'am."

"Courage now."

His lip quivered.

"Step outside and take a breath of air. I'll see you tomorrow night."

When he returned, at a minute to six, it turned out that the entire 600s and 700s needed straightening and shelf-reading. "They're a bloody mess," said Miss Boughton, sizing him up through her Coke-bottle lenses. "You've got the touch, I know."

He hated the 600s. Applied science. Plumbing. Car mechanics. The 700s were better, art books, including the one about the painter Paul Gauguin, which Jack had borrowed, but they were all shapes and sizes — very difficult to keep upright let alone straight.

Still, it kept his mind on something other than either Jack or the future without Jack.

He'd made his way through the 600s, and had just finished with the 730s, the sculpture books, when a voice said, "Evening, Neil."

He jumped.

Lawrence Augustine Rookwood, himself a striking sculpture, smiled shyly, tentatively. "I came for my card," he said almost apologetically.

Neil, who had been on his knees, stood awkwardly. He, too, felt shy. "Hi, Larry."

"I'm going to keep the Yeats, though. I love Yeats."

Neil nodded, a smile frozen on his face.

"Am I disturbing you?"

"No, no. You just startled me."

"I'll let you be."

"No!" It was too urgent. He actually felt like clinging to Larry.
Larry himself looked startled. He said, "I hope you're all right."
Neil's lip started to tremble again. Again he warned himself
not to cry.

Larry's expression, however, was nothing if not sympathetic.
"Look, I'm sorry, Neil, really, really sorry." He reached out a hand
and gently squeezed Neil's upper arm. Gentle though it was, Neil
could feel the power of the man's grip. "It can't be easy."

Neil could have said, I don't want to be here anymore. But
what came out was, "Do you think he'll ever come back?"

"It's impossible to tell. Johnny does what he wants. Period.
Always has. If I were you, I wouldn't hold my breath."

Neil received this information as another blow.

"He writes a good letter, though I'm sure that's not much
consolation. You never know. Bernie, our other brother, says he
won't last a term at college. He doesn't tend to stick at things. If
he doesn't, he may head back."

"Or go to France."

"France?" Larry shook his head. "Maybe France, maybe
Greece. Or Vancouver or Japan or the South Seas. Johnny always
has somewhere else to go." Larry's voice shook with more than
impatience.

"It doesn't matter." Neil was angry at himself for caring.

"You know, Cousin Stephanie and I are going to a movie
Saturday night. It's going to be either *A Taste of Honey* at the
International or *The Birdman of Alcatraz* downtown. Why don't
you come with us?"

"Oh, you don't have to ..."

"I know I don't have to. It'd be fun. Stephanie's a ball. She
likes cute guys, too."

Blushing, Neil said, "I'm not sure ..."

"Come on."

Neil couldn't resist Larry's brilliant blue eyes.

"You'll be working here, I suppose. I'll pick you up. We'll go to an early show, then head to Vesuvio's for a pizza. How about that? We'll drive you home, of course."

Neil smiled for the first time.

Larry smiled, too. "Which film would you like to see?"

"Oh, I shouldn't decide."

"No, it'll be a majority vote."

"*Taste of Honey*, I guess." He had read about *Taste of Honey*. It contained a queer character.

"That's the one I wanted to see, too. Poor Stephanie. She's positively crazy about Burt!" He passed around to the other side of the bookshelves to scan the play section.

"Can you recommend any plays?"

"Sure. What are you looking for?"

"I was thinking I should get to know Tennessee Williams."

38

THE HEAVY LIBRARY DOOR CLOSED behind him with its usual thud, followed by the sound of sliding bolts.

A deep blue twilight. No stars yet.

Uncertain, he lingered on the porch until the familiar toot-toot informed him that Edsel-man was very prompt.

Neil deliberately smiled as he climbed into the car, hoping to disguise his nervousness.

Edsel-man smiled big, too, offering him his hand to shake.

Neil took it a little awkwardly. It was a strong grip, which did nothing to alleviate Neil's agitation. But then he noticed the most extraordinary thing — Edsel-man had shaved. Not only that, his hair gleamed with brilliantine, and the tight deep-green shirt with white buttons that he wore looked brand-new.

"You look nice," Neil said.

"Thanks." Edsel-man smiled through his embarrassment. Neil had the sense he wasn't used to compliments, maybe even feared them.

"Really nice," Neil said again. "And your car," he added, anxious not to alarm him, "your car's fabulous."

"You've had lots of invites."

"It's so big."

"Yeah, I like it." Edsel-man started the car.

Two young men walking past admired it, too.

Edsel-man beamed. "It's a special car." He pulled out into the traffic heading west towards the suburbs. "Where you wanna go? How much time do you have?"

"I don't know. Say ten thirty or so."

"You ever stay out later?"

"Weekends."

"Right — I saw your boyfriend drop you off last weekend."

"He's not my boyfriend."

"Yeah, well, I'm no judge of character, but the guy sitting behind the wheel o' that Pontiac looked pretty gone on you."

Neil didn't want to talk about Jack. "He's left."

Edsel-man looked sideways at Neil. "The city?"

Neil nodded.

"Hope he's got a good reason."

They drove past the fruit store and his aunt and uncle's shoe emporium. Both were dark. Their darkness gave Neil no pause, and he had to wonder why. What he was doing could potentially put him in trouble. It didn't matter.

The Jane Loop was all of a sudden next to them. Neither bus nor streetcar was loading tonight and the platforms seemed to have no more than half a dozen waiting passengers. But all it said to Neil was, *Change comes sooner than you think.* He glanced at his driver who looked to him almost, but not quite, like a regular guy instead of an ex-con.

Neil said, "This is my favourite place in the city." He wanted Jim to know that.

Jim gave him a baffled look.

"The Jane Loop. It's where everything begins."

Jim's bafflement only increased.

"The city. Life."

Now Jim nodded, recognizing the gist of Neil's preference. He grinned. "Yeah, even in a car, once you cross that bridge, Jane's the borderland."

The light changed.

On impulse, Neil put his hand on Jim's thigh. Was this a confession of loneliness or a craving for comfort? Neil wasn't sure.

Jim glanced at Neil, then at Neil's hand. The car sped up. Jim said, "You sure about that?"

"What do you mean?"

"I was just gonna drive us around a bit."

Neil started to take his hand away.

"You don' have to do that. I'm jus' wond'rin', you know what you're doing?"

"Yeah," Neil said, "I know."

"It feels good, man, real good."

Neil began to stroke his thigh.

"But I've gotta drive, too, an' that's gonna get me too excited. Jus' go easy."

Neil let his hand rest. Staring out the windshield at the red taillights in front of them and the white headlights whizzing past, Neil said, "You've been teasing me."

"Me? Teasing *you*? You crazy?"

"Flashing your body."

Jim might have blushed, but it was too dark to really tell. "So, where are we gonna go? This wasn' my plan, you know. I was just gonna drive us around."

Neil believed him. "I don't mind," he said. Very gently, he let his hand curve around the inside of Jim's thigh. Its hardness felt almost comforting. For the first time in days, Neil experienced something like joy, a high, skittish, possibly dangerous joy, but still joy.

Jim whistled, "Man, oh man."

Neil kneaded the thigh moving closer and closer to the obvious excitement in Jim's chinos.

Jim took a sharp left at the street bordering the western side of the cemetery. "There's a new subdivision going up down here.

Lots of empty streets, half-built houses, machines, dumpsters an' stuff. We'll find a place."

Neil's face registered concern.

"Don' worry, I'm not stupid. Not about this kinda thing."

They said nothing more until Jim pulled into the site. Under a navy sky, dotted with stars, it looked more ghostly and abandoned than something in the first flush of life. To Neil's eye, it bore a startling resemblance to the cemetery they'd just passed. His joy flickered and went out. His hand left the pulsing warmth of Jim's lap for his own cool one.

The car stopped. They were behind a tractor, between two unfinished garages.

"Whatsa matter?"

"It's so ... I don't know — remote ... or something."

"Look, Neil, I'm not gonna hurt you."

He looked at Jim, at the shiny hair, the clean-shaven, angular face, the crisp green shirt, and was convinced. "It's just I've never done this."

"Never done what?"

"This. In a car."

Jim laughed. "You said it yourself. It's a big car. Come on. Let's get in the back."

Neil followed him into the back of the Edsel.

It was awkward for them both at first. They were all elbows and knees, uncertain of where and how to turn, and what to do with shirts and pants and shoes, but finally Neil just laughed and, yanking Jim's chinos down over his knees, dived head first into his lap. He sucked him vigorously, amplifying Jim's little whimpers until they reached full-scale moans, and when he had him really, really wet, he pulled off his own underpants, and in a swift movement that had Jim goggle-eyed with amazement, planted himself on Jim's hardness.

The only indication of the intense discomfort this act cost Neil was a loud groan that could have easily passed for pleasure. They were face-to-face, chest-to-chest. Jim grabbed his hips, as if to assist Neil in the ride, but there was no need. Neil knew what he was doing. In fact, over and over, Neil kept telling him, "I know, I know." This knowing let him quickly ride out the pain.

Jim's focus was on the meeting of Neil's thighs with his own, on Neil's leaking cock pressed between them.

"Look at me," Neil said.

Either too intent on his genital pleasure or too bashful to comply, Jim maintained his lowered gaze.

"Look at me!" Neil ordered, lifting Jim's face by the chin.

Jim almost batted his hand away, but caught in the intensity of Neil's expression, he let his hand press Neil's chest instead and then pinch a nipple, once, twice, many times, increasingly tighter. Neil winced in agony — or else an extremity of pleasure — and ejaculated copiously between them, saying, as he had done the first time with Jack, "Yes! Yes!"

The flash of hostility that had met Neil's command to lift his head was long gone and the look of pleasure that had replaced it now contorted into incredulous surprise as Neil rode Jim to the finish.

"Oh, fuck me, baby! Fuck me!" Jim cried, "Fuck!"

THEY SAT IN the front seat again, staring into the darkness, their hearts still racing.

The night had cooled and there were many, many stars now.

"I've never done that before," Jim said in a low, nervous voice. "Fuck a guy, I mean."

Neil didn't need to ask, *Was it all right?* He knew.

"Jesus Christ! Fuckin' amazing."

"You have a girlfriend?"

"Whadd'ya asking me that for? I jus' finished fucking you! What does it matter?"

"It doesn't. I just figured you'd have girlfriends, that's all."

"Nah. No girlfriend. Not right now." There was something in his tone that suggested, *Maybe never.*

"Well, I don't either," Neil laughed.

Jim started to laugh. He said, "Goddamn it, you're so fucking cute."

Neil watched him, puzzled for a moment. Then, in a quiet, satisfied, almost sleepy voice, he asked for the time.

Jim turned the key. The dashboard lit up. "Five after ten. You okay?"

"I could stay here all night."

Jim shook his head unbelievingly.

"I won't say anything."

"What's that mean?" Jim looked at him, eyes bright.

"I don't want any trouble."

"What trouble?" The fear in his question turned his voice sharp.

"If anyone found out I'm queer, I'd be dead. I've got two more years of school to survive."

"Who's gonna find out? I'm sure as hell not gonna say anything. It's between us, man, between us."

Neil was suddenly very unsure, even frightened.

Jim put out his hand.

Neil stared at it.

"Gimme your hand."

Neil obeyed.

Clasping it, Jim said, "I promise, Neil — between us."

Their hands remained clasped for many seconds, Jim looking as if he'd never done anything so final before.

Neil said, "It's strange, eh? That I'm sitting here with your hand in mine. When you think how we met."

"You don' need to remind me, okay?" Gently releasing Neil's hand, Jim started the car and backed out.

"It's just a long way from there, that's all." In fact, it seemed like a lifetime before. He looked up. The sky, a carpet of flickering stars, was more brilliant than he ever remembered seeing it.

When Jim next glanced at the boy beside him, Neil was smiling. "What's so funny?"

"Nothing. I just feel better than I have in days."

"Yeah." Jim squeezed Neil's thigh. "You really like to have a good time, eh?"

They took the Queensway home. Jim pointed out the street where his mother did factory work, then talked about his own prospects for employment, which, in the last week apparently, had finally amounted to something tangible. On Monday he would start learning the landscaping trade at the side of a pro. In November, when the pro turned his skills to house renovation, Jim would have the opportunity to follow him in that, too, if he chose.

"Mr. Holt's a good guy. A lot of experience. An' I get evenings off, an' weekends. At last, things are changing."

"I hope so," Neil said fervently.

Jim eyed him curiously. "Why'n't you come build planters with me?"

"Me? Mr. Muscles? Not a chance." Neil smiled. "You'll look even better once you've been hauling stones and dirt and sod around."

Jim squeezed his thigh again, even brushed Neil's balls with the back of his hand. "You're pretty well-packed, aren't you, kid?"

"How old are you?"

"Twenty-two. As of last month. Why?"

"I don't like being called a kid."

"Yeah, okay." Jim sniggered. "You sure don't act like a kid."

"Somebody once told me I've always been old."

They didn't speak again until they rolled past St. Andrew's Church.

"Do you want to let me out at the top of Avery?"

"Why?" Jim's frown darkened. "You ashamed to be seen with me?"

"I didn't think you'd want to be seen with me. What if Archie sees you?"

"Screw Archie! Man, that guy's got more to think about than what you're doin' in my car. He's pissed somebody off, real bad. Somebody's threatened him, he didn' say how. He even took a night job to keep outta the way. Down at the cannery."

Smiling, Neil studied Jim's profile. He looked like that conspirator in *Julius Caesar*, the one called lean and hungry. Cassius. Lean, hungry, so different from Jack. But handsome, too, really, really handsome.

Without warning, Jim pulled into the parking lot of the Anglican church next to the bus stop. The car dove into the deep shadows provided by a pair of old maples.

He's changed his mind, Neil thought. A pang of disappointment was replaced by a strange feeling of relief.

Jim said, "I just wanna sit for a few minutes. That okay?"

"Sure. It's nice here with the trees."

They sat quietly. Every few seconds, one of them would steal a glance at the other. In the dark behind them, a tabby cat watched for careless prey.

It was Jim who broke the silence. "You sure you're queer?"

Neil took a deep breath. "Sure."

"Since when?"

"Since ... forever. I didn't know I knew till this summer."

Jim frowned. "The guy in the Pontiac?"

"I guess it was him. He was just a ... trigger." The words were patently untrue, but Neil didn't care. Jack deserved everything he got.

Silence filled the car again.

Finally, Jim said in a very low voice, "I might be, too."

Neil stared into the shadows at the handsome profile. "What?"

"You know ..."

Neil's stare didn't waver.

Suddenly, Jim turned towards him, and grabbing him first by the back of the neck, pulled him in for a deep, wet kiss. The kiss lasted many seconds. As Jim pulled back, he swore, "Shit! Another first, man, another fucking first!"

"I wasn't expecting that," Neil said, quietly.

"You hard?"

"After a kiss like that? Are you kidding?"

"I'm like a fuckin' rock. Jesus! What are we gonna do? There's no time. An' anyway it's too dangerous here."

"You're amazing, you know."

Jim leaned in and kissed him again, a wetter, sloppier kiss than before. "Fuck, I could come jus' doin' that."

Neil stroked Jim's erection through his jeans.

"My mom works evenings next week. If you're free, we should get together at my place. I can pick you up at work again. Any night you want." He started the car.

"How 'bout Monday?"

"You got it." Jim was grinning now.

As they passed the Doyle house, Neil noticed that all the lights were on. A shimmer of music floated off the porch.

Then they were at Avery and Dominion.

"Nice drivin' you, Neil," Jim said, putting out his hand.

"Nice riding with you, Jim."

They both laughed and shook hands.

"49 Lilac. Number's in the book. Barry. Don' forget, sexy."

Neil crossed the lawn as the Edsel's taillights grew smaller.

Mr. Gordon waved at him from his porch. Beside Mr. Gordon, a dark figure, which was neither his daughter nor his wife, waved, too.

Neil opened the screen.

Two very strong smells greeted him. Booze and paint.

On the couch, his father lay snoring. To Neil he looked curiously empty, purposeless, sad, like a once-loved rag doll. A small amount of pity infused his scrutiny. He felt as if he were seeing something he was never meant to see, a kind of confused and rumpled despair.

He turned his attention to the staircase. It had already been stripped of its broadloom and its walls were covered with a white primer, which, thick and chalky though it was, did not entirely obliterate the red arrows of accusation.

He looked back and forth between his father and the clean-up. All trace of Jack's handiwork would soon be gone. And then, would it all start up again — the tricks, the so-called fun?

Neil shifted his bag of library books from one arm to the other. The three books Miss Fairfield had given him and three others, two play collections and Truman Capote's *Breakfast at Tiffany's and Other Stories.*

He never really understood what made him do it. He watched his father for another forty seconds or so and then, slowly, deliberately, pulled the Capote and the play collections from his bag and let them fall.

His father woke with a jerk and a loud groan. Barely managing to pull himself into a sitting position, he shook for several seconds, squinting into the alcoholic haze enveloping him and sloppily rubbing his face. He appeared to be wrestling with some terror or other, which he couldn't quite locate in the room. He sat forward, belching loudly. Neil wondered if he was going to be sick. Another groan escaped him, louder than the first. He put his hands up in front of his face as if warding off some awful vision.

Neil was actually surprised that his mother hadn't awakened. She was sleeping on the other side of the wall, after all. But maybe she didn't want to hear. Maybe she'd decided, *I don't hear you anymore! I'm deaf to you.* Whether that would mean more protection for her children or an even greater retreat into positive thinking, Neil was at a loss to say. He sensed that from that moment on, the future was entirely uncertain. It was a strange, even frightening prospect, and he took a deep breath.

Frank Bennett turned his bleary gaze in the direction of the figure in the doorway. "Who?" he started to say.

"Sorry, I dropped some books."

His father stared at him as if he were a stranger. Then, rising unsteadily, he wobbled towards the staircase. "I'm going to bed," he slurred.

"You are in bed," Neil said.

"Teeth," his father said.

With a grim gaze, Neil watched his father ricochet from one wall to the other as he stumbled up the stairs. Once he reached the landing, he paused and said, "Phone."

Very calmly, Neil collected the three library books. As he bent down, he could feel a lot of dampness in his underpants, which brought on a smile.

On the kitchen table lay a postcard from Rick in Luxembourg. *Low in the Low Countries. Pretty girls are scarce, so's the sun. Looking forward to seeing you again.* Beside it sat two notes in his mother's hand: *Tony called 9:15 p.m., Davy Doyle, 9:45 p.m.*

He shivered with a dark pleasure. He was in Jim's Edsel at nine fifteen and nine forty-five. He would go to Jim's next week for sure.

His father made it downstairs again with only one near-fall.

"I'm going to get my toothbrush, Dad. Then I'm going out again. I'll use the backdoor."

"Late. Don' be late."

"We'll see."

He ran upstairs. Peed. Fetched his toothbrush from the holder and a clean facecloth and hand towel from the linen closet. With a defiant smile, he thought, I only need to come up here now for the bath and the toilet.

He left the upper hall without looking either left or right. *That was then*, he told himself. *It's over.*

On his way past the living room, which was very dark now, his father called out.

"Don' get pain' on yourself."

"Don't worry about me!"

"It's gonna all come out," his father answered through a big yawn.

Neil ran down to his room with his books and his toiletries. Dumping them onto the very empty bed, he lit the Chinese lamp and went out again through the back door.

"You're a busy man tonight, Neil," Mr. Gordon called, as the boy hurried past.

Neil stopped, turned. The dark figure next to Mr. Gordon was a grinning Warren Dawlish. "I am, Mr. G. Lots happening."

"Good to keep busy, I always say. How's our pal in the Edsel?"

"He's starting landscaping."

"So he wasn't just talking through his hat? How extraordinary." Warren's grin grew whiter.

"And what about our bread-man? My wife is quite downhearted."

"I don't know."

"Is this the dreamboat Lana's always talking about?" Warren wanted to know, his eyes never leaving Neil's face.

"The very one," Gus chuckled. "Mona said you two were great friends, Neil."

"He's in Ottawa."

"In the political line? I hope not. They're all scoundrels."

"Journalism, I think he said."

"More scoundrels." Mr. G. puffed on his cigar.

"Where's Lana tonight?" Neil asked Warren, hoping to distract both him and Mr. Gordon from their subject.

"Lana's borrowed my car to take Mrs. G. to the late show.

Cary Grant and Doris Day."

"*That Touch of Mink.*" Neil's smile was forced. "See you, Mr. G."

"Indeed you will, Neil. We'll have ourselves a game of crib real soon."

"See you, Warren."

"You know, if I were a girl, I think I'd take an athlete in an Edsel over a drop-out in a bread truck." Warren shrugged playfully. "But then I'm not a girl, am I?" Warren's blond smile continued twinkling in the night as Gus Gordon guffawed.

Uneasy with the teasing, Neil turned and hurried up Avery.

The Doyle house was still brightly lit. Music poured out of the screen door. Piano music, solo piano music.

Neil walked slowly up the porch steps.

The music was ravishing. Quiet, thoughtful, and full of yearning, it made Neil think of "Moon River." He didn't want to break its spell as it drifted up like a silken balloon into the night air. For just a second, he imagined that Jack could hear it, that Jack would like it. But it didn't really matter now. *He* liked it.

Too soon, it ended.

He raised his hand to knock.

"That was very fine, Davy, very fine. Even on that lousy thing, it was fine."

"I'm glad, Ma."

Neil knocked.

"Who's that?"

Davy appeared in the hallway in tiny shorts, which made his hairy legs look especially long and Pan-like, and a very boyish striped jersey. "It's Neil Bennett, Ma."

Mrs. Doyle stepped into the hallway wearing a floral housecoat over her skinniness. "Come in, Neil, come in."

"No, Mrs. Doyle, I need to get back. I just wanted to tell Davy I got his message. I didn't want to call in case you were asleep."

"That's very thoughtful. I'm very, very sorry to hear about your break-in, Neil. Your mother called me when it happened to us. I'm going to call her, just give her a day or so to settle down. It's a terrible, terrible business. I wonder how many more we'll have."

"Whoever it is will get tired one of these days."

"They don't take anything. That's what I don't get. It's pure vandalism."

"Some people probably find that exciting."

"What a terrible thing ..."

Neil looked into her worn, lined face and said, "Some people find picking fights exciting and calling people names exciting and hurting the ones they love ..."

With a guilty sigh, Mrs. Doyle retreated to the living room.

Davy stepped out onto the porch, closing the door behind him. "Hey," he said. "They wreck your stuff?"

"Not a thing."

"My clothes still stink of shaving lotion. That's why I'm wearing these kids' clothes."

"That was such beautiful music, Davy. Where's it from?"

Davy pointed to his chest.

"You? You wrote it?"

"Well, it wasn't abracadabra."

"You're such a jerk ... But, it was beautiful, really, really beautiful."

"I wrote it for us. For our project. It just needs words."

"It doesn't need words."

"Sure it does. If it's gonna be our project."

"I can't imagine writing words to that ..."

"That's probably what Johnny Mercer said to Henry Mancini." Davy smiled mischievously. "Or maybe not."

"Do you really think I can?"

"What do you think?"

"It's so beautiful, Davy."

Davy couldn't help but smile.

"Okay. You're on. But I need to hear it again. A lot."

"No problem. Just tell me when you're free. How 'bout tomorrow?"

Neil laughed. "Yes, yes, I'm free tomorrow."

The words floated up into the trees, a different kind of music.

ACKNOWLEDGEMENTS

Great thanks go to Marc Côté for his encouragement and editing, to Bryan Ibeas for his very sensitive final edit, as well as to Barry Jowett for seeing the whole project through to completion. I'm grateful to Betsy Warland for first putting me in touch with Cormorant Books and to Claudia Casper for her thoughtful feedback to an earlier version of the novel, which gave me hopes that it might have a future.

Several friends, including the dedicatees of this book, read and responded to the ups-and-downs of Neil and Jack — and me — with great dedication. They include: Andrew Benedetto, Caroline Duetz, John Elmslie, Joan Grundy, Sarah Hunter, William Kimber, Arlene Moscovitch, Elisabeth Pomès, David Pressault, Jean Connon Unda, and Tracy Westell. In their different ways, they all helped me to bring my characters more vividly to life.

A final thank you to two teachers, Dorothy MacDonald and Jay Macpherson, who many years ago fostered in me a great love of the novel.